A bit of a Nomad herself, **K.A. Finn** has wandered around Ireland and the UK for decades before settling back in Ireland with her husband and kids (two and four legged).

Visit K.A. Finn online:

www.kafinn.com
(trailers, excerpts, artwork, playlists etc)

Facebook: kafinnauthor

Instagram: kafinnauthor

Twitter @K_A_Finn

Also by K.A. Finn

Nomad Series (Space Opera)

Ares

Nemesis

Perses

Chaos

Mania

Cronus

Talos (TBA)

Blackjacks Series (Paranormal Romance)

Breaking Phoenix

Reviving Davyn (2022)

Defying Shep (2023)

Unraveling Fallon (TBA)

Broken Chords (Rockstar Romance)

Broken Rock (Tate)

Fractured Rock (Gregg)

Split Rock (Tate – 2023)

Crushed Rock (Luke – TBA)

Shattered Rock (Dillon – TBA)

BREAKING PHOENIX

K.A.FINN

Cover design by Deranged Doctor Design
www.derangeddoctordesign.com

Published by Cooper Publishing
www.cooperbookservices.com

Edited by Desert Mystic Literary Editing
www.desertmysticliteraryediting.com

ISBN: 978-1-914177-37-8

Coming next

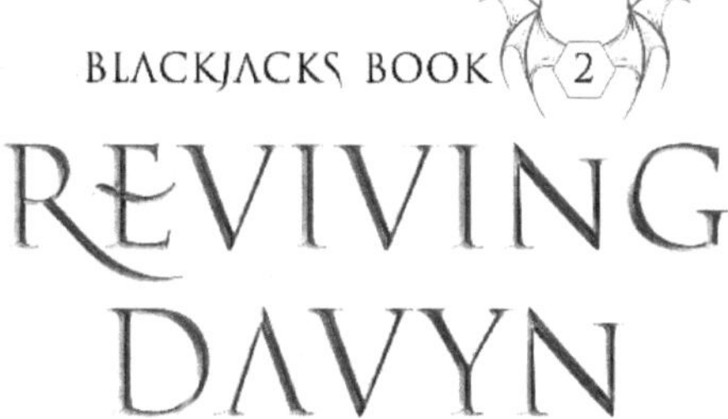

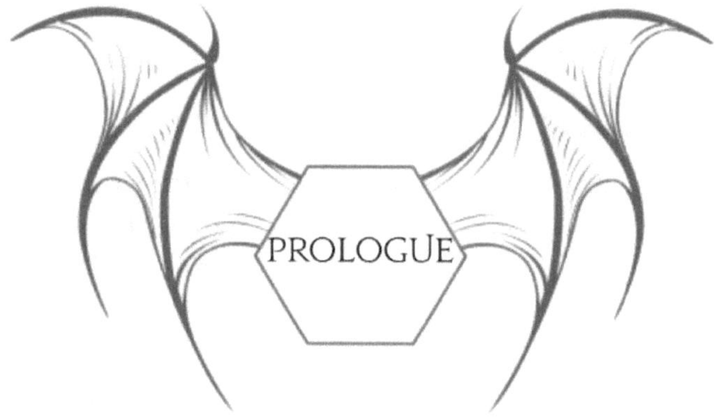

Court stands in the shadows, watching her apartment. He checks the time on his cheap watch and grimaces to himself. Two in the morning. He's been standing in the freezing rain for three hours. The hunger is refusing to leave him too. He'd helped himself to some food from a street vendor about four hours ago. Luckily the man was a little too overweight to give chase for too long. Even after the burger and chips, the cramps kept pulling at his gut, making thinking difficult. All he desperately wants to do is crawl into bed and bury himself under the duvet. Just a shame he doesn't have a bed let alone a duvet.

He straightens up as a group of girls approaches the building. They laugh and talk loudly amongst themselves as they huddle under three enormous umbrellas. A few of them are being helped along the path by their friends. Explains why he was waiting in the rain for so long. They must have been out for the evening. Right in the middle of the group he spots her. He can't let her to go inside the building. There's no way he'd get through the security on the door.

Court pulls down his hood and hurries across the street. He's got one shot at this. There's a strong chance they'll scream bloody murder and he'll be chased off by every security guard in the area.

Two of the girls notice him approach, their alarm displayed on their faces. Here goes nothing.

'Excuse me?'

The group stops and she looks over at him. Nothing registers on her face for a few seconds then her eyes open wide. 'Court?'

'Hi, Thea.'

'Oh my god! What are you doing here?'

'Can I talk to you for a minute?'

'Thea, who's this guy?' one of the other girls asks as she eyes him suspiciously.

'Don't worry. He's my brother. You go ahead.'

The group lingers a little longer, clearly not thrilled about leaving her alone with him, then make their way inside the building.

'I can't tell you how glad I am that you remember me.'

Thea frowns as she examines him. 'What do you mean remember you? Are you okay? You look terrible. Where the hell have you been? It's been two years without even a text. What happened?'

'Two years? You haven't seen me for two years?'

'No. What's going on, Court?'

'I don't know. I've been looking for you for weeks.'

She gestures for him to follow her around the side of the building to the garden. Thea leads him under the covered patio area around the back and shakes her umbrella out before closing it. 'Okay, talk. Where were you?'

'I wish I knew. I woke up in a forest about a month ago and the only thing I remember is you.'

She frowns at him for a long time before she speaks. 'This isn't a joke, is it? You're being serious.'

'No, it's not a joke.' He groans and doubles over as a wave of cramps hits.

'Okay, okay. One thing at a time. You need to feed.'

'I just had a burger. Don't think it agreed with me. I feel like shit.'

Thea directs him towards one of the metal chairs against the wall. 'Sit down.' She pulls up another chair in front of him. 'Okay. Let's take this one step at a time. You must be starving. We better find you someone. The burger isn't going to keep you going. Feed, then we can talk.'

'After that dodgy burger I don't want to risk anything else.' Thea sits back and stares over at him. 'Why are you looking at me like that?'

'When you say you don't remember anything, do you mean you don't remember anything at all? I mean like... anything.'

He shakes his head no. 'Just you.'

'So you don't know what you are?'

'What I am? What the hell are you talking about?'

Thea takes a deep breath. 'Okay. This is going to be a fun one to explain. I guess there's no easy way to put this. You've got cramps because you need food, and I don't mean a burger. Well, you need regular food too, but you need something else to stay strong and stop the cramps.' She frowns and looks away from him. 'I'm not sure how often though. I think you said it depends on whether it's human or your own kind.' She curses and looks back at him again. 'I'm sorry. I was still trying to get my head around it when you disappeared.'

'Thea, what the hell are you taking about? What do you mean my own kind?'

'You need blood.'

'I'm sorry, I need what?'

'Blood. You're a vampire, Court.'

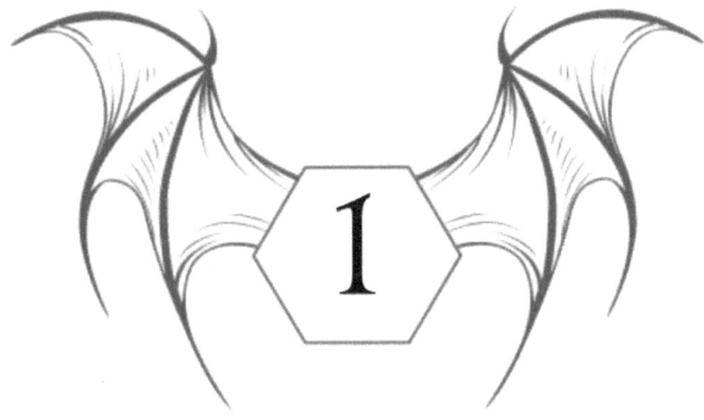

1

One year later...

Phoenix ducks as a round strikes the wall just over her head. She peers over the edge of the balcony to the floor below and returns fire. She looks at the mezzanine level about thirty feet below and a good sixty feet opposite. The crates and building supplies will offer more shelter, but she'll have to get there first. Stepping back into the shadows she arches her back, releasing her wings. The cool air hits the sensitive membranes, sending chills of anticipation through her body. She fires down at her attackers then launches herself off the railing.

Despite the situation she smiles as she glides across to the other side. She lands, using her wings to keep her balance as she spins quickly tucking herself and her eight-foot-tall wings behind the nearest pillar. Cement dust flies in her face as her attacker gets a little too close for comfort. Phoenix bares her fangs and growls as she waits for a break in the gunfire then dives out from behind her cover.

This guy is seriously getting on her nerves. It's time to end this. With her gun in her hand she extends her wings and leaps off the ledge. She beats her wings and rises through the air over the courtyard. She twists to the left as she glides around the side of the building and spots her target behind the remains of a SUV. Phoenix fires and smiles when she hears a loud, 'Fuck!'

A siren sounds from overhead signalling the end of the training session. Phoenix stops in mid-air, beating her wings to keep her off the ground as she holsters her weapon. Her attacker steps out from behind the car, holding his arm. Dust powders his short dark hair and black t-shirt. He mutters to himself in Spanish as he stalks towards her. She doesn't speak the language, but she recognises a few of his choice words.

'Did you really have to shoot me, Nix?'

Phoenix drops to the ground and walks over to him. 'Sorry, Bastian. Let me see.' He lifts his hand off the wound. Blood trails down his arm, tracing a path over the heavy black tattoos covering his skin. The tattoos cover both his arms from his shoulders to the backs of his hands. The marks are symbolic, each one detailing his past - well, his past crimes. And Phoenix has no intention of asking him to give her the sordid details.

She touches the underside of his arm. 'What are you complaining about? It's gone straight through. You'll be fine in a few hours.'

'That's not the point. You shot me.'

They both turn as a loud, slightly maniacal laugh echoes around them. Bastian groans as another female steps out from behind a building. Her waist-length auburn hair is twisted in a braid which sways as she approaches. Her tall, powerful body is pure, lean muscle. She may be laughing, but her dark blue eyes are serious, as always. Fallon isn't known for being light-hearted.

'What the hell are you laughing at, Fallon? She got you too.'

Fallon glances down at her leg and shrugs. 'I lasted three minutes longer than you.'

'You've got fucking wings,' he complains.

Fallon sits on the bonnet of a car and crosses her arms. 'Have a bit of wing envy, Bas?'

'Nix, is it all right if I shoot Fallon?'

Phoenix laughs as she pulls her wings back inside her body, rolling her shoulders as they settle inside her. 'Do what you want. Just clean up after yourselves.'

She leaves Fallon and Bastian to their squabble as her phone rings. She pulls it out of her pocket and swipes her thumb across the screen. 'What is it, Willow?'

'I just heard from the team you sent out. They were attacked by the Order. We've got some wounded coming in. Nothing serious. They're on their way back for treatment and they're bringing a civilian with them.'

Nix closes her eyes and curses under her breath. She squeezes the phone and tries to get her anger in check. 'Okay. I'm on my way.'

She slips her phone back in her pocket and calls out, 'We've got injuries coming in. The doc will probably need your help, Fallon. They're bringing back a civilian too. Bas, can you deal with him?'

'Sure thing.'

'And contact Ethan. Tell him we'll need a safe house for the civilian.'

Fallon and Bas hurry off leaving her alone with her anger. Tension between the Blackjacks and the True Order have ramped up over the last few years and she seriously doubts the situation will improve any time soon.

Like the other Blackjacks, Phoenix - or Nix - is from mixed parentage. Her vampire father fell in love with a human woman and have the sort of relationship it's difficult not to be envious of. They are a large part of the reason Nix started the Blackjacks. If the Order had their way, Nix wouldn't exist and that didn't sit well with her. So, twenty-four years ago, with close friend Ethan's help, she formed the Blackjacks and has had barely two minutes to herself since.

Some days they win, other days they lose... and lose hard.

Every single time she sends her team out, she is putting their lives at risk. The True Order would show no hesitation in wiping each and every one of them from existence. It was her job to make sure that didn't happen.

She hurries out of the training room and enters the main compound next door. Standing five stories tall, the purpose-built training room is complete with houses, sheds, roads, streetlights, gardens, and cars. No expense had been spared in its construction. It was a vital part of their training and was constantly in use. The height gave the female vampires the space they needed to freely fly while they trained with the males.

The smaller, but no less impressive compound next to the training centre has been her home for over two decades. Hidden in the remote Vale of Ewyas near Abergavenny, the compound offers them somewhere safe to live and train. Somewhere to be themselves away from prying eyes.

She walks along the corridor leading from the training room and enters the garage, smiling to herself when she hears two very loud voices. She stops in front of the two men – one human and one vampire, and rests her hands on her hips. 'Okay boys. Can we both take a breath?' They continue their argument, completely ignoring her. 'Hey! Shut up!' That does the trick. They both stop and glare at each other. 'Thank you. Fletch, how about you go first. What's wrong?'

Their human doctor crosses his arms and looks over at Nix. His long, dirty-blond hair is tied up in a messy bun, but the front is sticking up as if he's been dragging his fingers through it.

'Perfect timing, Boss,' he says in his thick Scottish accent. See if you can make this irritating, stubborn, arsehole see sense.'

'What's the problem?'

Fletch scrubs his hand through his hair again, dislodging more strands from the bun. 'The problem? Have a wild guess. Refusing treatment. Again.'

Nix holds up her hand to stop Fletch. She turns away from him to face the source of his irritation. Davyn doesn't seem to be able to support his own weight and is leaning heavily on his car. More importantly, the impressive hole in his leathers is oozing blood which is pooling on the ground around his boot.

'Davyn. I don't think I need to ask what's wrong with you. So, why are you refusing treatment?'

'I don't need him to look at my leg. It's fine.' His green eyes glow as he glares over at Fletch.

'You've got a fucking hole in your leg, Dav. A hole.' Fletch gestures towards Davyn's leg and the ever-growing pool of blood.

'I said it's fine.' This time he snarls at Fletch, showing his impressive canines.

'Oh you really think that's going to work? You can bare your gnashers at me all you want. I will be treating that leg.'

'And I said it's fine.'

Fletch crosses his arms and glares up at the tall vampire. 'Is it now? Care to tell me where you got your medical degree, Dav?' Davyn narrows his eyes but doesn't respond. 'Exactly. One of the first things I was taught in medical school is that when there's a hole in someone's leg, it generally means they need medical attention - stubborn vampire or not.'

'I'll feed.'

Nix points a finger at Fletch, stopping him before he responds. 'Even I can tell that wound is going to take more than a feed to repair itself. It needs stitches.'

'At the very least!' Fletch shouts over Nix's shoulder.

'Yes, thanks, Fletch. Please Davyn, let Fletch do his job. He'll clean it and patch you up. It'll only take a few minutes.'

Davyn's green eyes target her, and she knows she'd have better luck convincing a wall to cooperate. Davyn does what he wants, when he wants, and she always felt like she was walking a fine line when she tried to get in his way. She's glad he's on their side. He is cold and cruel and without a doubt, the best damn fighter she has ever seen.

He may be an invaluable member of the Blackjacks, but that doesn't mean he's a fan of the whole team player thing. He'll do what he's told... most of the time. But she's never sure how he'll react when she pulls rank. Just like she's about to.

'Let Fletch see to your leg. That's an order, Davyn. I need you fit and well. Having you laid up with an injury isn't an option. You're going to let him stitch it and then you're going to feed. Do you hear me?'

The silence hangs in the air as his glowing eyes refuse to leave hers. She doesn't back down though and eventually, he nods. Nix discreetly releases the breath she was holding and smiles. 'Great. Okay, Fletch. I'll leave him in your capable hands.'

'Oh joy. Thanks!'

Fletch offers his arm to Davyn to help him walk to the med bay, but all he gets is another snarl. 'I can walk.'

Fletch holds up his hands and gestures for Davyn to go ahead of him. Fletch looks back at Nix and gives her an exaggerated double thumbs up before following Davyn from the garage.

The wind whips Court's hair back from his forehead as he crouches on the rooftop. His pale blue eyes search the surrounding streets, looking for any sign of life. A little after three a.m. on a cold Sunday night means the pickings are going to be slim. Anyone with half a brain is going to be tucked up in their cosy home, not wandering the streets.

He squeezes his eyes shut as an invisible hand pulls and twists at his gut. Breathing through the pain, he forces himself to his feet. He's running out of time. Again. He has to stop doing this to himself. Sooner or later he'll push himself too far. Putting off feeding is just delaying the inevitable. Whether he likes it or not, it's something he must do. There's no escaping that fact.

Ignoring what's going on with his body, Court vaults over the side of the roof and slides down the emergency ladder. He drops the final twelve-feet and scans the dark alleyway. Then he hears something.

The sounds of the city disappear as he focuses on the footsteps approaching the mouth of the alley. The heavy, stumbling steps can only belong to someone who's been drinking. It'll make for an easier target. The basic need to feed instantly overtakes any doubt or hesitation he may have felt about what he's going to do.

Court silently moves towards his approaching prey, keeping to the shadows as his heightened vision searches for any unwanted company. In his current state, he'll only be able to handle one person.

He reaches the end of the alley and takes a deep breath. Stale beer, cheap aftershave, and cannabis. He grimaces to himself. Just for once he'd like someone clean. As if his body is telling him not to be so damn picky, the pain hits, doubling him over as it pulls at his gut.

The man reaches the corner and Court grabs him roughly by the neck of his shirt, dragging him around the building. He slams the man against the wall, muffling his shocked protests under his palm. Before he changes his mind about what he's about to do, Court holds the man's head to the side. His canines are way ahead of him as usual. He sinks his teeth in the man's neck, and gags as the blood hits his tongue.

As soon as he's taken enough, he lowers the man to the ground, and walks away. Court makes it down the street before he crouches in the doorway of the nearest building and takes slow steady breaths. If he throws up he'll be back to square one again. He pulls a packet of gum from his jacket and stuffs two pieces in his mouth to mask the leftover taste.

At least the blood helped ease the cramps a little, but as usual, he'd gone too long between feedings. It'll take a few hours for his full strength to return. What he needs right now is to get home and collapse on his bed until that happens.

He pushes to his feet and heads home. It takes longer than it should, but he finally reaches the old apartment block where he lives. He skirts the chain-link fence surrounding the building, slowly making his way towards the gate at the far end. He trips on a rock, landing hard on his ass. Not quite the graceful entrance he was planning on. He sits on the ground and curses himself. He wouldn't be in the dirt if he'd fed yesterday. Fuck it. Might as well take the easy way in while he's down.

Ignoring the heavy lock on the gate, he pulls himself under the fence and somehow gets to his feet barely managing to stay upright. Fucking pathetic. It's his own fault. He needed to feed regularly and ideally not target people who'd just spent the evening in a drunken stupor.

If he did those two relatively simple things, he'd be walking home in full control of his legs. Instead, he waited until the last fucking minute when he has no choice. Again. Fuck, he downright hates feeding, but it's what he has to do. His body needs the blood, craves the taste of it, the strength it gives him, but his brain has a permanent block up. It hasn't got on board with whatever he is. It's been a year. It's about time his brain and body got on the same page.

He targets the front door and concentrates on putting one uncooperative foot in front of the other. The large FOR SALE sign attached to the door is chipped and peeling after too many years waiting for someone to buy the building. The last tenant left the block of flats around five years ago and the premises was put on the market. Unfortunately for the owner, there are at least six other premises for sale in the same area, each one in serious need of refurbishment. When he approached the owner a year ago enquiring whether he'd be willing to rent one of the top floor apartments on a month-to-month basis the owner had asked no questions and happily took the money.

He gets to the bottom of the stairwell and groans to himself. The elevator sits next to the stairs but as it isn't actually connected to anything it's not going to do him any good. Feeling worn out and slightly drunk, he slowly climbs the metal steps to the third floor.

At times like this he seriously regrets not taking one of the ground floor apartments. Paranoia had guided him to the top floor though.

At least from the windows in the living room he could see both ends of the street below.

He's got no reason to assume anyone will be coming after him, but this whole vampire thing is new to him. He'd prefer to play it safe – especially as it's not just his life on the line.

The pain continues to ease, but the foul taste is refusing to go anywhere. The few pieces of gum he chewed just added a minty flavour to everything else that was in the blood.

The lone strip light fixed to the ceiling of the staircase puts in a valiant effort to light the space but is clearly coming to the end of its life. He makes a mental note to replace the bulb tomorrow. Just like he did the day before, and the day before that.

Court puts a hand on the wall to keep himself upright as he stumbles down the corridor. Dismissing the first three doors he stops at the fourth and leans heavily on the frame. It takes three attempts to convince his key and the lock to cooperate and another two to re-lock the door once he's inside. He stumbles over to the peeling leather couch and flops over the arm, landing with a whoosh of expelled air.

He wants nothing more than to clean his teeth a few dozen times, but he can't find the energy to move. A touch on his shoulder makes him shout in surprise. A light switches on to his left and he blinks as his sensitive eyes take a hit.

'What's wrong?'

He rubs his eyes and forces a smile on his face. 'Nothing, Thea. I'm good.'

His sister wraps her cardigan around herself as she lowers to the floor in front of him. 'No, you're not. You left it too long again, didn't you?'

'I just forgot.'

'Like hell you did. You did your usual ignore it and hope it'll go away thing. You're a vampire. It's not going to go away, you idiot. You really have to get that through your thick skull.' She gives him her best stern glare and it nearly works. She may only be twenty-eight, ten years his junior, but she's more than capable of being a responsible mother figure when it comes to him.

He knows she's right. Life would be far easier if he could accept what he is and what he has to do, but it's not that easy. Unlike him, she's human which still sounds weird when he thinks about it. He's not human and she is. They have the same hair colour, they both have blue eyes although his are a few shades lighter than hers, and they even look alike, but they're a whole different species. How the hell that happened he has no idea.

Since the day he showed up on her doorstep a year ago, nothing else substantial has come back to him. The little he knows about what he is came from Thea, and her knowledge is nearly as limited as his.

They had been raised separately and Thea only found out she had a brother when Court showed up four years ago with paperwork proving they were related. No fool, Thea had checked out his story and found it to be true.

Court had told Thea about being a vampire a few weeks before he disappeared for two years. Irritatingly he hadn't left a 'How to be a Vampire' manual behind. What he does know is that he needs blood to survive and ideally human blood. Animal blood took the edge off the hunger, but as much as he shied away from hunting for humans, he eventually had no choice.

'My body knows it's a vampire, but my brain still thinks it's human. Feeding is getting a bit easier though.'

'You just have to force yourself to do it. Delaying it will only make you sick. Set a reminder on your phone. Stick it in the calendar on the wall. Do something so you're not leaving it to the last second.'

He rolls onto his side and closes his eyes as Thea's face swims in front of him. 'I know, okay. You can lay off the lecture, Thea. Now, get to bed. It's nearly one and you've got work tomorrow.'

She brushes her dark brown hair off her shoulder and chews the inside of her cheek.

'What?'

'I was thinking about that. I don't have to go.'

He sits up and rubs his forehead as his head spins. 'We're not having this conversation again. I don't need you to watch me. You're going.'

'I know you don't need someone to watch you, but I can't help worry about you. Especially when you do pig-headed things like starving yourself. It's not on. Promise me you won't do it again.'

'Thea—'

'Promise me, Court.'

He holds up his hands. 'Fine! I promise. Now, go to bed and leave me alone. Please.'

'Are you sure you're okay?' she asks as she hands him a bottle of water.

He drinks half of it, then smiles at her. 'Sure,' he lies. 'Never better.'

Nix gets to her bedroom and locks the door behind her. She checks her watch and groans. Half an hour to herself before the debrief with Davyn and Shep. Just enough time for a very hot shower.

As with the rest of the compound, no expense had been spared with the living space. Each room had a large seating area, an equally big bedroom, and a bathroom. There is a total of thirty-two rooms of equal size and design in the compound. Six were occupied by her team with five more by support staff and two housekeepers.

Compared to the Order, their numbers are pitiful. Even if she includes the staff working with Ethan, they still fall short. What they desperately need is more Blackjacks. A lot more. But that will take time. What they do isn't for everyone and there isn't exactly a queue of vampires waiting to join them and put their lives in jeopardy.

More's the pity. She'd happily open the doors and welcome as many new recruits as possible. Her co-founder, Ethan, was doing his best, but so far, the response had been less than enthusiastic.

She stifles a yawn and looks longingly at her bed. She's exhausted. Her team is exhausted. They're pushing themselves to the limit and it's only a matter of time before mistakes creep in and her vampires get hurt.

First things first, find out what the True Order were playing at when they attacked Davyn and Shep.

She throws her clothes in the hamper and pads across the deep pile rug to the bathroom. She showers quickly then dresses in faded jeans, a white t-shirt and Converses, then runs a brush through her long dark hair. With a few minutes to spare she decides to head to the meeting early. Being in this room for too long, being alone for too long leaves time for thinking and reminiscing and that's the last thing she needs to do.

She takes the lift to the lower level and walks along the polished concrete floor. Doors line each side of the corridor leading to various offices, workspaces and a smaller but impressive additional gym fitted with exercise equipment instead of buildings. The last door on the right houses the med bay run by their resident doctor, Fletcher or Fletch Marsh.

He was a fairly new addition to the team but when Fallon suggested her human half-brother, Nix had immediately agreed. The doctor instantly fit with the team and she honestly doesn't know what they did without him.

She pushes open the set of steel doors to the briefing room at the end of the corridor. Inside, the air is cool and clean with a faint trace of citrus furniture polish. A large screen takes up the far wall at the head of the rectangular table surrounded by twelve leather chairs - half of which she's yet to find occupants for.

Nix takes a bottle of water from the mini fridge beside the door then settles in her chair at the head of the table. Over the years, the worn leather had moulded to her body, hugging her close as she leans back and waits for the others to get here.

Before she can stop herself, her mind drifts to the previous occupant of the chair to her right. Her second in command had responded to a True Order attack on a young mixed-blood vampire. He hadn't been seen since. That was three years, two months, two weeks, five days and... she shakes her head. The pain of his loss still tears at her gut and time is doing nothing to heal the open wound he left behind - both in the group and in her heart.

They had naturally assumed the Order was behind his disappearance, but all their searching came back with nothing. If they captured or killed a Blackjack, she has no doubts the Order would have advertised the fact. It would have been a massive feather in their caps. There's no way they would have keep something like that to themselves.

'Boss? You okay?'

She blinks and looks up at Shep. 'Sorry?'

'You look a little spaced out.'

'I'm fine.' She nods towards the door. 'You alone?'

'Yep. First to the party.' Shep drops down on his chair, leaving the one to her right empty. He yawns loudly then leans back, pushing the chair to its limits. He scrubs a hand over his messy dark blond hair then crosses his arms over his wide chest.

'Are you okay?'

He smirks and wiggles his eyebrows. 'Of course. Just glad Dav is a slightly bigger target than me. You can partner me up with him again. Apart from the total lack of conversation, he's a laugh.'

'Davyn? A laugh.'

'Yep. Well, by laugh I mean he's fun to wind up. I reckon he took that bullet just to get away from me.'

'You know you don't have to piss off everyone you work with.'

'Yeah, but it's fun.'

He closes his eyes and rests his head on the back of the chair. Shep continuously drives her to the brink of wanting to strangle him, before doing something that changes her mind. While he follows orders, his tendency to follow parts of his anatomy other than his brain pisses her off. His cocky attitude and 'I-don't-give-a-damn' outlook on life regularly rubs members of the team the wrong way.

He is dependable in a fight and unquestionably loyal, but she just wishes he could tone down his horny teenager side. It didn't help that it was never difficult for him to find a willing partner. She had hoped having his baby sister, Willow, join the group would calm him down, but three months in and she's yet to see much of a change.

Bastian, Fallon, and Willow arrive at the same time and take their seats opposite Shep. Shep glances up at his sister and winks. 'You good?'

Willow smiles at him and nods. Not for the first time, Nix is amazed at how alike they look. With her waist length, blonde wavy hair and deep brown eyes, Willow is striking. Nix wasn't overly convinced about her place on the team initially, but with their pathetic numbers compared to those of the Order, she couldn't really afford to turn away a willing member. She had put Fallon in charge of her training, and within a month, Willow was transformed. Still quiet and a little reserved, give her a gun and someone to fight and she came out of her shell. All they need now is a few more like Willow and they might have a chance of surviving the next year.

Ethan is the last one to arrive to the meeting and takes a seat opposite Nix. Ethan Croft had been with Nix since day one, collating information from vampires working in various sectors across the country. It was the job of Ethan and his team to sift through all the data from hospitals, law enforcement, etc. to see if there was something the Blackjacks should be looking at.

Even though a vampire himself, Ethan's bloodline was so diluted with human blood he was more human than vampire. He transitioned before he hit his thirties as all vampires do, but instead of getting the full list of fun vampire traits, his human DNA won out. While he did have fangs, he didn't need blood to survive and was able to stay out in daylight as long as he wanted without any issues.

Their paths had crossed when Nix had come across a couple killed by the Order. They were Ethan's parents. It didn't take long for their friendship to develop and for Ethan to become the financial backing for the group. As the sole beneficiary of a substantial inheritance, Ethan had built the compound and funds their work.

As usual, he's wearing his signature blue shirt with blood red tie. His brown hair is cut tight to his head and his blue eyes are serious. 'Hi Nix, guys. How's Davyn?'

'His usually cheery self,' Nix says. 'Fletch is keeping him in the med bay for a few hours, but his leg is already healing.'

'That's good news for Davyn, not so much for Fletch. So, I had a chat with the civilian Shep and Davyn rescued. He has no idea why the Order targeted him. He works in a law firm. He has no family, no ties to the local community, which in itself could be a reason. He doesn't draw attention to himself. The attempted abduction makes no sense whatsoever. Did you notice anything, Shep?'

He shrugs. 'We were just hanging out being all stealthy like on the top of a building and Dav heard the guy shouting for help. We took a peek and saw five Primes chasing this guy down. We got in between them, and they didn't appreciate it. There was a bit of a scrap, and I grabbed the civilian. Dav told me to get him out of there. I got him out of the way and Dav dealt with the Order. He was hit but still managed to take down them down. The last one bugged out, so I left the civilian with Dav, tracked him down and made sure he wouldn't be coming after us again.'

'Brief and to the point as usual,' Nix says. 'Fletch had a quick chat with Davyn. He doesn't have anything else to add.'

'Shocking.'

Nix glares at Shep. 'Yes, thank you for that. So, we're no closer to figuring out what the Order was playing at.'

Ethan shakes his head. 'Appears not. I'll go back to my office and see if I can find anything else that might help us. I'll drop the civilian at one of my safe houses. Can you spare someone to go with me to his house and get some supplies?'

'Bastian, you good to help out?'

'Sure.'

'Great,' Ethan replies, smiling at Bastian.

'We probably should get the word out,' Nix says. 'Tell people to watch their backs for a bit. This could be an isolated incident, but we shouldn't take any chances. If the Order has decided to try their hand at kidnapping, it will put everyone at risk.'

Ethan nods. 'Absolutely. I'll see if this is an isolated event or part of something larger. I'll let you know if I find anything.'

Nix looks at the file of the vampire Davyn and Shep saved. Ethan is right. There's nothing off about him. Nothing to say why he was being targeted. She'd prefer if there was. If this is a random attack, it could very well be the first of many. With six of them, there's no way they can cover the area needed to keep mixed-blood vampires safe.

'Okay, everyone get some rest. We may need to head out if Ethan finds something.'

She waits until it's just herself and Ethan in the room before she speaks again. 'What's your gut feeling on this?'

He sits back and loosens his tie. 'Honestly, I've got a really bad feeling, Nix. They kill us – not kidnap us. I'm not saying one is preferable to the other but taking us alive... it worries me.'

She couldn't agree more.

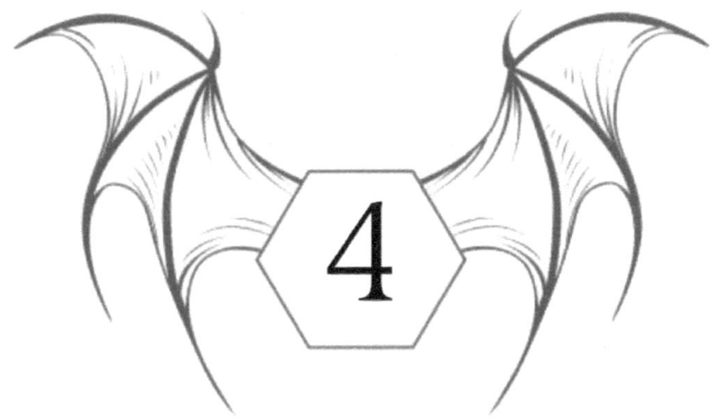

'You should ask her out.'

Court glances up from the portable cooker. They are dining in style tonight - beans on toast, just like last night and probably tomorrow too. 'I should what?'

Thea places two plates on the table at the side of the kitchenette, each one with a slice of toast on it. 'Don't give me that innocent look. You know what I mean.'

Court dishes out the beans and hands a plate and some cutlery to Thea. He sits down and shovels a forkful of beans in his mouth. He takes longer than necessary to chew them, hoping Thea will drop the subject. One look at her tells him that's not going to happen. She's staring at him, the plate of food untouched in front of her as she gives him one of her trademark looks. 'What?'

'The woman at the till in the supermarket. You should ask her out.'

'Change the fucking record, Thea. Eat before it goes cold.'

She takes a mouthful, chews then pushes the plate away. 'I mean seriously - all the eyelash fluttering and hair curling. I thought she was going to faint on the loaf of bread. You must have noticed that.' She fans herself with her hand as she flutters her eyelashes. 'Do you need me to help you pack your bags?'

Court glares at her. 'You finished?'

'Are you going to ask her out?'

'Thea, leave it.'

'No, I will not leave it. You're becoming a hermit. What am I saying? You are a hermit. You spend most of your time locked up in here. The only time you go out is to feed and I practically have to twist your arm to do that. You need a life, Court. Go to the shop tomorrow and ask her out.'

He slides half his dinner onto her plate, his appetite suddenly gone. 'You seem to have forgotten one tiny detail.'

She finally goes back to her dinner, chewing thoughtfully as he rinses his plate. 'You don't have to bring her here. You could take her to a fancy restaurant.'

He throws the dishtowel at her. 'Nice try but you know that's not what I mean.'

'Oh, the vampire thing,' she says as she smirks at him.

Court can't help but laugh. 'Yeah, the vampire thing.' He sits down opposite her and pulls on his boots. 'Not exactly something you can just bring up in conversation. Anyway, things are fine the way they are. I'm fine, okay. Stop worrying.' He gets up and pulls on his jacket.

She stands up and brushes off her pyjamas. 'Where are you going?'

'I just need to pop out for a bit. Keep the doors locked and your phone with you.' He leans down and kisses her on the forehead. 'Do you need anything?'

She shakes her head and sits back down. 'Glad you're going out to feed without me having to twist your arm.'

'Yeah, well maybe I didn't fancy another lecture.'

'Whatever the reason, it's good.' She smiles at him, but it's not her usual cheery one.

'You okay?'

'Yeah. I don't mean to lecture you about it, Court. I really don't. I just…' She lowers her head and closes her eyes. He sits beside her and wraps his arm around her shoulder.

'I was joking, Thea. I know you're watching out for me.'

She lies against his chest and blows out a long breath. 'I'm sorry. I just hate seeing you like that.'

'Like what?'

'Don't do the whole innocent look thing, Court. We don't live in a mansion with dozens of rooms. I hear you moaning in pain when the cramps hit. I've seen you barely able to move because you're too weak.'

'Shit. Sorry, Thea.'

'I'm not looking for an apology, you idiot. I know you hate feeding and I know I'm a pain in the ass by going on about it, but I'm terrified if you keep starving yourself you'll take it too far.'

'Hey, nothing is going to happen to me. I'm being a stubborn fucker, I know. I'm done with the cramps too. Why do you think I'm trying to get a head start on it tonight?'

She wipes her eyes and sniffs. He hugs her close, hating that she's crying because of him. Again. He's failing miserably at this big brother thing. All he seems to do is worry her or make her cry.

'I'm so sorry, Thea.'

'You've nothing to apologise for.' She pushes away from his embrace and wipes her face. 'Now go before you're left with drunken louts again.'

'I love you.'

'I know. Love you too.'

He manages to force a small on his face before he leaves her in a shitty apartment to spend the next few hours worrying about him. Yeah, what a great brother he is.

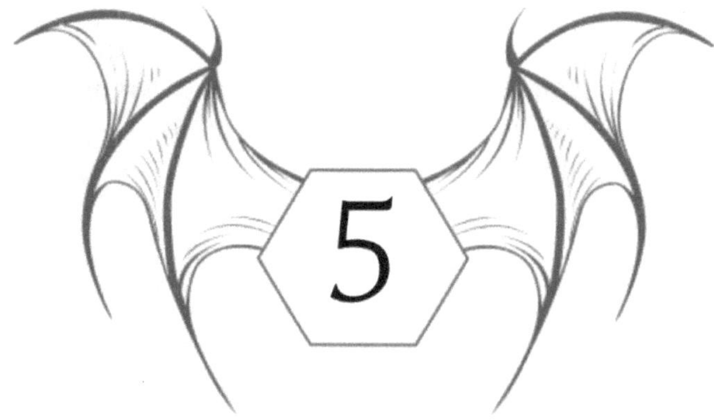

5

Ten minutes later Court's in the worst part of town wandering the streets. This late on a weekday means the streets are practically empty – just a few staggering drunks and him. He should have taken more from the guy last night but couldn't stomach the taste of his blood. He needs to find someone, but feeding is the last thing on his mind.

He knows Thea is trying to make him feel better by showing she accepts what he is, but in truth it's making him feel worse. She's twenty-eight years old – she shouldn't be dealing with this sort of shit. At her age she should be in her own place, with a good job and someone to share her life with, not living in a run-down building with her vampire brother.

The only thing he can do for her right now is to feed before the hunger takes hold. Facing up to the inevitable he targets the first person he sees. He wants to get it over and done with so he can get back to Thea. It didn't feel right leaving her alone like that.

Homing in on a lone man staggering towards him, he picks up his pace. He waits until the man has just passed him before turning and dragging him down the alley. The twenty-something year old reeks of beer and cigarette smoke which makes Court's stomach lurch. He focuses on breathing through his mouth which is helped by the two large canines that push out of his gum.

The man struggles against him, but Court holds him firmly against the wall. In his drunken state the man wouldn't be putting up much of a fight against him anyway – even without his superior strength.

Wanting to get the whole thing over with Court pulls down the man's shirt collar and pushes his head to the side. Without allowing his body to touch his prey, he leans over him and bites the man's neck. Court's stomach instantly objects to the alcohol and nicotine-laced blood. He ignores his stomach and concentrates on getting what he needs as quickly as possible.

Feeling dirtier and more disgusted at himself than ever, he pushes off the unconscious man and leans back against the opposite wall. For a brief moment he wishes he could trade places with the man. At least when he woke up he'd have no memory of what happened – just a bit of a headache and a bite mark on his neck. He'd probably assume he'd just gotten lucky. He'd never guess he'd been the main course for a vampire.

Court stops in the alley that leads back home. Maybe Thea was on to something with this feeding early idea. Instead of cramps and jelly legs, Court feels strong and a hell of a lot better than he's felt for a long time. She's right. By starving himself of blood, he's been denying his body what it needs. As much as he hates being a vampire, he can't deny being a fed vampire is preferable to being a starving one.

He's about to continue back home when he hears something above him. He jumps to the side as someone drops down from the building beside him, landing where he was a second ago. Another four guys appear out of thin air and surround him.

'You need to come with us.'

Court doesn't know how, but he knows he's facing vampires.

Whatever shock he has at discovering more like him instantly disappears as the first one steps closer to him. 'Did you hear me? You're coming with us.'

'I'm good, thanks.' Court savagely kicks the nearest vampire in the side of his leg, crippling him. As the others approach, Court sees how he's going to take down each one. Like a film playing in his head, he plans every single move he's going to make, the order the vampires will fall and if they'll get up again or not. He has no idea where it comes from, but a quiet calm takes over him. Five against one isn't the best odds for walking away from a fight, but he's not worried.

The four vampires still on their feet come towards him at the same time. Court pulls the knife from the fallen vampire's belt and braces himself for the attack. Just like it played out in his head, the next goes down when Court swipes the knife across his neck. He spins and plants his boot in a chest, driving back his attacker as the knife finds its way into the heart of the next.

Once they're all on the ground, he stabs each one in the heart to make sure they're not getting up again, then slips the blade back in the belt of the first guy he dropped.

Court stares down at the men he's killed, not believing what just happened. He fought five men... five vampires. And he won. He fought them and didn't even get a scratch. How the hell did he do that? How did he know what to do? He's never fought anyone before. At least, not that he can remember. He holds his bloody hand out in front of him. No trembling. No twitching. He's calm even though it's far from how he should feel.

Whatever is going on, he knows one thing. He needs to get away from here before the police arrive. But he can't just leave five bodies lying on the street. One by one he drags them over to the overflowing skip behind the neighbouring take away. Court quickly pulls half the bags out of the bin before lifting each of the bodies in. He covers them with the rubbish, closing the lid once he's done.

It's hardly a fool-proof hiding place, but it will have to do. His priority is getting out of here. With one last look at the bodies, he walks away, picking up the pace when he turns the corner.

Thea wakes up to a loud crash followed by the sound of glass breaking. She quietly reaches under her bed for the metal pipe she keeps hidden before creeping out of her bedroom. The rough wooden floor scratches at her bare feet as she tiptoes down the corridor towards Court's room. The door is open, and his bed is untouched. She curses quietly to herself and continues to the living room.

Making her way to the alcove housing their small kitchen, she moves as quietly as she can. She pauses when she hears glass crunching under someone's feet. She calms her breathing and takes a firmer grip of the cool steel pipe, then lifts it over her head and charges. She swings the bar down hard narrowly missing her brother's head, his lightening quick reflexes saving him from a serious concussion.

He growls and shields his eyes when she turns the light on. 'Court! You scared the hell out of me.' Her eyes open wide when she sees the blood on his hands. 'What happened?'

He clenches his fists and paces the small kitchen area. 'I was attacked.'

Thea stares down at his blood covered hands. 'Attacked? By who?'

'I don't know.'

'What happened? Are you okay?'

He nods as he continues to pace back and forth in the kitchen. He's seriously worked up and that worries her. 'It's their blood.'

That does nothing to put her at ease. 'Where are they? Do we need to call the police?'

'And say what exactly? I killed five men like me. That's not going to be easy to explain.'

'Killed? You killed them?'

'They weren't going to walk away. Thea, they were like me.'

'How can you be so sure?'

'I just know, okay!' He pretty much growls at her then goes back to his pacing. She hasn't seen him this agitated before. And that's not a good sign.

'You need to calm down, Court.'

He launches at the counter, slamming both hands against the surface. 'Calm down? I've just been attacked by five... vampires and I killed them all.' He raps his fist against the side of his head. 'Something clicked in here. I saw every single move before I made it.'

'What do you mean?'

'I mean I planned out the whole fucking attack before I took them down. I was facing five vampires and I didn't give a damn. I knew I'd be able to take them. What the hell does that say about me?'

'I don't know, Court. All I know is that you're getting worked up. Just close your eyes and take a few deep breaths. You don't look so good.'

'I don't feel so good.' He holds his head before wobbling and crashing to the ground startling Thea.

'Court, you're freaking me out. What's wrong?' She crouches down in front of him holding on to his leather jacket to keep him upright.

'Court?'

He holds his head in his hands. 'My head is fucking killing me.'

'Can you open your eyes?' Thea winces as his glowing eyes leave spots in her vision. 'Okay, that's not right. Maybe keep your eyes closed.'

He arches his back and cracks his head against the cupboard door. Thea tries to pull his hands from his hair, but he won't let go. He growls at her and pushes her away. 'Get off me!' He slumps forward and clenches his fists on the wooden floorboards as he roars in pain.

Thea scurries away from him. He's had episodes like this before when his memories tried to break through, but never this bad. She's never been scared before. He lifts his head, but she doesn't turn away in time. His glowing eyes lock on to her and she feels him in her head, in her thoughts. She tries to close her eyes, tries to move away, but she's paralysed in his gaze and he isn't letting go.

Memories she had moved on from come back to her like they'd just happened. Court digs deep, pulling the painful memories back from where she had buried them. She feels tears on her face as he continues to invade her thoughts, forcing her to relive them again.

Memories of waiting for the phone to ring after Court disappeared. Of standing alone at the window hoping he'd walk down her street, alive and well. Memories of having to accept that he was gone from her life again without a word or an explanation. Of worrying that something had happened to him or, worse still, he was dead. The tears are flowing freely now as the pressure in her head builds to an unbearable level.

Then she's at the graveyard standing over her parents' graves. Well-wishers pass on their condolences as she numbly stares at the open graves.

Then he breaks eye contact and drops his head. 'I'm sorry.'

Thea wipes her faces on her sleeve and slowly approaches him. 'It's okay.'

He buries his head under his arms. His body trembles as he pulls at his hair again. She cautiously takes one of his hands in hers. He squeezes it gently then hisses in pain again. 'I'm sorry.'

'C'mon. I need to get you off the floor.' He pulls himself upright and leans heavily on the counter, keeping his eyes firmly closed. She takes his hand again and guides him to his bedroom. The twenty or so steps take a ridiculous amount of time to cross thanks to Court barely being able to hold himself upright. He crashes onto his bed and with his head turned away from her, opens his eyes. His eyes are still glowing, but he's getting it under control. 'Did I hurt you?'

Thea attempts a genuine smile. 'Of course not.'

'I'm the wrong person to lie to. How bad?'

She shrugs, trying not to make a big deal out of what happened. 'Not too bad.' His mind trick scares the hell out of her. For some reason it didn't always work. Most of the time he didn't get inside her head. It's only when he's having one of these moments that he can force his way in. It's impossible to pull away from his eyes when they lock on hers. It's like they take a physical hold and nothing can break the link except Court himself.

'I'm so sorry you had to deal with me disappearing like I did.'

'I know you would have been there if you could. Don't beat yourself up over it.' He smiles weakly but she knows he blames himself for not being there for her. Not knowing where he was or why he left like he did isn't just driving him crazy. It's not doing her any favours either. What if he left because he realised finding his sister was a mistake? That they had nothing in common and he didn't want to see her again. They're both assuming he couldn't get back to her. But what if he didn't want to? 'Hey, I don't suppose you remembered anything else about where you were?'

He shakes his head. 'Nothing I could hang on to. I honestly didn't mean to hurt you. You have to believe me. I dropped my guard. What happened with the other vampires... it threw me. And the blood I had was fucking rotten. Again.' He laughs to himself. 'Think the alcohol is getting to me. I feel like I've been on the beer for a few hours.'

'You should get some sleep. No offence but you look terrible.'

'That's a lot better than I feel. Are you sure you're okay?'

'Yes. Now shut up and get some rest.'

He squeezes her hand, then closes his eyes. Thea stays with him until he falls asleep less than five minutes later. With no choice but to leave him fully dressed, she pulls his duvet over him and goes back to the kitchen. Once she's cleared away all signs of the event, she takes a couple of pain killers, not that they'll touch the pain. Her head aches intensely. It always did after he'd been digging around in there.

Thea checks the doors and windows are locked then goes back to Court's room. His colour has improved slightly turning from grey to just pale. Even in a deep sleep he's frowning and his breathing hitches like he's in pain. There's no way she's going to be able to sleep while he's still like this. Resigned to another long night watching over him, she snuggles in beside him, throwing his blanket over the two of them.

She runs her hand over his hair, listening to him breathe as she lies awake in the dark. The contact seems to calm him. After a few minutes his breathing steadies and some of the tension in his body eases.

They can't keep going like this. The thought of spending even one more week in this place, let alone a few years terrifies her. She's putting on an award-winning performance, pretending everything is fine, but it's far from it.

She had bigger plans for her life. Working in a local legal firm was helping to pay for this place and her night classes. Studying to be a lawyer seems unrealistic right now, but Court wouldn't let her walk away from it. He wants her to make something of herself.

But then what? She could hardly have a social life. How could she explain Court? 'Hi. This is my big brother and there's a strong chance he'll try to feed from you or tear your memories apart.' Every way she thinks about their situation, she keeps coming full circle. There is nothing else they can do.

He can't hold down a job because he's too scared he'll be discovered or worse. He'd tried so many times to get her to leave. Find her own place and live her life, but she can't leave him. He's the only family she has left. If she deserts him and something happens, she'd never forgive herself. All she can do is work her ass off and get them somewhere better to live.

Then what? He'll still be... what he is. He'll still have no memory of anything from before he woke up in the middle of the woods last year. They'll still be no closer to figuring out what happened to him. And now there's whoever came after him tonight. If he felt killing them was a better option than talking to them, what exactly is he a part of? She closes her eyes and buries her face in his back and cries herself to sleep... again.

7

Nix waits until everyone is sitting before she turns on the screen at the end of the table. Davyn is out of the med bay and back in his usual seat in the corner of the room. He looks a hell of a lot better than he did when she saw him in the med bay. 'How's your leg, Davyn?'

'Fine.'

'Are you cleared?'

'Yes.'

She gives up. That's as much as she's going to get from him. 'Okay, so Ethan just sent through some footage. It appears the attack on our civilian friend wasn't a once off. They tried to take someone else from the streets a few hours ago. Unfortunately for them, Ethan says this vampire was a little more than they could handle and he was able to get away.'

Bastian shakes his head. 'How is that possible? One vampire couldn't fight a True Order team alone. One of us would struggle.'

'Speak for yourself,' Shep says, grinning at Bastian.

'Okay. Why don't we just have a look at what he sent us.' Nix turns on the footage and sits back as the image appears on the screen. The picture is from a security camera and the resolution is far from perfect. A lone figure walks into the picture. He's got the hood of his jacket up, hiding his face and his hands are stuffed in his pockets. The five Prime males appear from above, landing on the ground in front and behind him. Nix sits forward as the lone vampire looks at the team then attacks.

The Order puts up a fight, but one by one, the vampire takes them out. In less than a few minutes, the five Order soldiers are on the ground. The vampire they intended to capture spends the next few minutes hiding the bodies in the skip before walking away, disappearing off the screen.

No one in the room says anything. Nix glances at them and sees the same confusion on their faces. She plays the footage again. Perhaps it's exhaustion or her mind playing tricks on her but something about that vampire seems familiar. As the video plays again, she leans forward, concentrating on every single move. As the last Order fighter falls, she realises exactly what she's looking at... or who she's looking at.

She risks a quick look at the others. 'Am I seeing things?'

As one, Bas, Shep, Fallon, and even Davyn shake their heads.

'What is it?' Willow asks.

'Well, Sis. Either that vampire has somehow taught himself to fight exactly like Court, or that is Court,' Shep explains.

'What? Are you sure?'

Bastian nods at Willow. 'He had a certain style. He taught most of us to fight. No mistaking that.'

'It's his style all right,' Fallon adds. 'I got up close and personal with that kick of his more than once in training. What's going on, Nix?'

'Hey, Boss? Nix!'

She looks at Shep. 'Sorry, what?'

'Fallon asked what the fuck is going on.'

Fallon sighs and throws Shep a withering look. 'Not quite like that, but yeah. What's the deal, Nix?'

'Em, I...' She clears her throat and starts again. 'I haven't got a clue. I need to talk to Ethan. See if he has any more footage of him.'

'It can't be Court though, right?'

She looks back at the screen. Apart from the fighting style there's nothing about the figure to hint at his identity. The angle of the camera doesn't even tell them a rough height. There's nothing except for the way he took down the fighters. But that's enough. It makes no sense, but the person on the screen was either trained by Court or is the second in command of the Blackjacks himself. Nix gets a hold of her excitement before it can escape. It's too soon to let her mind... and her heart run away on her.

She shrugs at Shep trying to appear less affected by this revelation than she actually is. 'I'm in the same position you are. I agree it's absolutely his style. I noticed that as soon as I saw it. We can't get carried away though. It's been over three years. There could be another explanation.'

Davyn speaks up which is highly unusual. 'We're going to check it out.'

It's not a question. It doesn't have to be. If there's even the smallest chance that is Court, they have to go.

Nix jumps when the phone rings. She picks it up off her bed and answers it. 'Hey, Ethan.'

'Hey, Ethan? Is that it?'

'Sorry?'

'You think Court might still be alive. How are you so calm?'

'It's too soon to jump to conclusions. He fought like Court did, but that isn't definitive. We really need to go there and check it out for ourselves.'

'I fully agree. I've checked our information. It seems there have been a few instances reported to the local police in the same area this mysterious attack took place. People are waking up with strange puncture wounds to their necks. Nothing taken from them, so mugging is out.'

'So no human deaths?' Nix asks.

'Thankfully, no. But, as you can imagine, the police are investigating this attack and the others. We're intercepting as much as we can but if these attacks keep up, we're going to be in the spotlight. I'm presuming whoever this person is, they're new to the way things are done.'

'Or are trying to keep hidden,' Nix says.

'True. If they knew about the locations where vampires can feed safely, I'm sure they'd go there instead. Feeding from humans won't keep them going for long.'

'Ethan?'

'Yes?'

'Do you think it could be him?'

The line goes quiet for a minute. 'You know his fighting style more than I would. What do you think?'

'Without seeing for myself I don't want to go down that path. The others think it's him though.'

'The whole team thinks it's him. Sounds like you might have found him.'

'Yeah, but I don't know what to do if it is him. I mean, if it is Court, why hasn't he come home before now?'

'I guess you just have to play it by ear. I'm giving the go ahead for the Blackjacks to head to Bristol and see what's going on. All you can do is find this person and see what the story is. Phoenix, are you okay?'

'Me? I'm fine.'

'Stop being hard-faced for one minute. It's me you're talking to. Are you okay?'

She closes her eyes and tries to hold back the tears that want to come out. 'I'm fine, really. I need to be fine, Ethan. I need to be the leader of the Blackjacks for now. I just have to stay level-headed while we're there. Get us all back in one piece then deal with whatever else is going on.'

'Of course. I'll send over locations of the attacks I've found so far. Stay safe.'

He ends the call and Nix wipes her face as she heads to the meeting room. She can't think about it being Court – not yet.

Everyone is already there when she arrives, so she gets straight to the point. 'We're good to go. It'll take us about ninety minutes to get there so we should have a few hours to find him before the sun comes up.'

'What's the weather like in Bristol this time of year?' Shep asks. 'Want to make sure I pack the right accessories.'

Nix rolls her eyes at him, then decides to counter with something she knows will wipe the smile off his face. 'I want Willow to come too.'

He pulls his feet off the table and sits up straight. 'No way, Boss. She's not ready.'

'She kicked my butt in the training room yesterday,' Bastian says.

'That's not hard,' Shep replies, glaring at his teammate.

'I am here, Shep,' Willow protests.

'No offence, Wills, but this has nothing to do with you. Mind your own.'

'I don't believe this,' Willow mutters as she glares at her brother. 'I am a member of the team. Stop being an ass.'

'She wants to be out there with us.' Fallon leans back in her chair and crosses her arms. 'Girl's got serious skills, Shep. I'm happy to go out there with her. She'll be fine.'

'She needs to be more than fine. She's my kid sister.'

'Is she a Blackjack or not?' Davyn asks.

Shep glares at the fighter, not disguising the anger from his face. 'You know damn well she's a Blackjack.'

'Then she fights,' he says.

Nix holds up her hands before Shep decides to lay in to Davyn or Willow launches herself across the table at her brother. 'He's got a point, Shep. Willow is coming too. No arguments,' she adds as his mouth opens to protest again. 'You good with that, Willow?'

'Of course,' she replies, smiling smugly at Shep.

'Good. Bastian, have the bus ready to leave in twenty minutes.'

'Will do.'

'Ethan's people have picked up an increased level of Order presence in the area. It may be they've got wind of this too. If that's the case, this vampire is running out of time. Fallon, can you tell Fletch to pack some tranqs? Our friend may not want to come with us voluntarily. I'd prefer not to even go there but we better be prepared.'

'Got it,'

'Dismissed.'

One-by-one they file out of the briefing, leaving Nix alone with her thoughts. With one last glance at the empty chair beside her, she makes her way through the compound to her room, grabs the pre-packed bag from her wardrobe, and closes the door behind her.

Bastian is already in the underground garage when she arrives. She opens the door on the side of the bus and lowers the steps. As she climbs inside the lights turn on. The vampires-on-tour bus, as Shep christened it, is their mobile command centre. While flying is her preference when it comes to going anywhere, the wingless guys would always have to take other means of transport. The bus offered the perfect solution. Bastian and Shep had converted a standard rigid sider to an impressive vehicle which had bays for several motorbikes, enough weapons to arm a small army, a med bay, bunks and living quarters for them all and, of course, a fully equipped kitchen. God forbid Shep went anywhere without his food.

Davyn arrives next carrying a heavy black holdall.

'I'll meet you there, Nix.'

Nix isn't going to waste time arguing with him. He rarely accompanied them in the bus. They'd all stopped taking it personally years ago.

'Do not engage with anyone until we get there. Do you hear me, Dav?'

He nods and throws his bag in the back of his black Range Rover then climbs in and slams the driver's door behind him. She watches as he starts the car and revs the engine loudly as he drives up the ramp and disappears from view.

'Davyn going solo?' Shep asks, as he dumps his bag at his feet.

'Won't hurt having an extra vehicle I suppose.'

Willow practically skips across the garage, pushing past Shep as she steps inside the bus. She stows her bag in an overhead compartment and sits down, a smug smile on her face. Shep grimaces at her but manages to keep his opinions to himself. He points two fingers at his eyes then flips his hand around to point a finger at her.

Bastian kicks Shep's foot as he passes down the bus. 'Best you watch yourself, Shep. I vaguely remember kicking your ass when we trained together.'

'That was a fluke, and you know it. Anyway, this is family business. You mind your own, got it?'

Bastian snorts and sits at the far side of the aisle. 'Oh I got it.' He leans across to speak to Willow. 'Sore loser.'

Shep glares at the two of them as they laugh loudly. Fallon joins the others and closes the door behind her.

'All set, Boss.'

'Let's go then.' She opens the door between the cab and the back of the bus and takes the seat next to Fletch. 'Dav set off ahead of us.'

'I saw that. My driving is not that bad,' Fletch grumbles as he starts the engine. 'If he keeps heading off alone, I'm going to start to take it personally. Grumpy git.'

'If we all took his attitude towards us personally, we'd never leave our rooms. It's no harm having another car with us, especially the way he drives. Keep an eye on his locater and get as close to it as you can.'

'Got it.'

'Let's find this vampire.'

The silver Range Rover comes to a stop outside the gates to the disused quarry. Rhain slips his mobile back in his pocket as his driver gets out, keys in the code then pushes the gates open. He gets back in the car and drives through, waiting to make sure the automatic gates close after them again before he continues down the track.

The car winds down the curved road snaking around the side of the quarry. Its heavy tires dislodge a thick cloud of dust in its wake which follows them along the track. At the bottom of the track, the driver slips the car inside the tunnel, stopping just past the entrance. He opens the back door and Rhain steps out.

'Wait here,' he orders the driver as he moves deeper into the tunnel. Rhain places his palm against a hidden panel to the side of an unimpressive steel door and steps inside. Once he pulls the door closed behind him and hears the reassuring clunk of the locks slipping home, he allows himself to relax.

In his three hundred and fifteen years of life, Rhain could easily count on one hand the number of places he's felt he could be himself. This facility is top of that list. Born to an ancient line of pure-blood or Prime vampires, his parents had expected him to conform. Appearances were everything after all. As their only child, they had placed a lot of pressure on his shoulders to act according to his position in society. In other words, like a pompous well-bred bore. Which he did for quite some time and still does in certain circles.

He was the envy of many Prime males and the interest of many females. His short, thick, blond hair took little effort to look stylishly tousled and, together with his unusual gunmetal grey eyes, brought him to the attention of many an onlooker. Under his expensive suits, Rhain's body was that of a fighter. Hours of training over the last few years had turned the puppy fat of his pampered upbringing to firm muscle. Looking in from the outside, you would assume he had never wanted for anything. Expensive clothes, prestigious houses, high class cars, it was all at his fingertips, but it was far from what he truly sought.

He doesn't care about the money or the status or the endless, suffocatingly boring social events his position in society demands he attends. He seriously doubts he'd be invited if they knew what he was truly like. He clenches his fist as the tremor takes hold. He'd give up his fortune if he meant he could be free of the sickness that's slowing eating away at him.

He gets to the end of the corridor and opens the door to the main control centre. The leader of his private militia strides over to him. Maddox stands an impressive six-foot-six, topping Rhain by a few inches. Like him, Maddox is Prime as are the five men in his group. Maddox and his men had been training with Rhain for the last few years and had proven themselves competent fighters.

He looks at the eight containment cells, seven of which are occupied. His fangs descend as he glares at the cell to the far right. He could find another to fill the space, but he doesn't want to. Not yet anyway. That cell is reserved and he's going to do everything he can to make sure the bastard is returned to his cage and rots there.

Thanks to a power fluctuation on the containment cell, the donor had somehow managed to break out and fight his way out of the facility. Not that it would have been too difficult at the time. A year ago, he had been lax. With only a team of scientists protected by two security personnel, there was little resistance. Now, there are six personnel handpicked by Maddox at the facility at all times. No one would be making a fool of him again.

All their hard work has been leading up to this point. Prime numbers are in steady decline and the curse that is Blood Fever, or The Fever as it's affectionately known, is doing nothing to help rectify that. Primes need Prime blood to survive. It took centuries to realise that the very thing they needed to survive was also driving them to the brink of insanity.

It took centuries for The Fever to take hold, but once it had you, there was little to be done about it. Much like humans and their drugs of choice, blood could have the same addictive properties for a Prime.

The laws had been changed to allow cross breeding with humans, but, while that diluted the bloodlines of some of the smaller Prime clans and helped them grow in numbers, it did nothing to ease the addiction. Primes still couldn't survive long-term on anything other than Prime blood. The only way Primes and the vampire race would survive is if something drastic was done. And that's exactly what he's doing. Or trying to do.

'What have you found?'

Maddox passes him a tablet with a map of an area of Bristol on it. 'A True Order team was eliminated last night when they tried to pick up a civilian. Got more than they could handle though. He took the five of them out.'

'One civilian couldn't possible take out five Primes.'

'Unless he was trained. I saw the feed from the camera. He could fight. There have also been reports of peculiar attacks late at night. Seems the victims are always alone and wake up with no memory of their attacker. Apart from a puncture wound on their neck, they're uninjured and nothing is taken.'

Rhain opens the report and scans the information. It certainly screams of a vampire attack. 'What makes you think this is our friend? There's bound to be dozens of vampires in Bristol. The last thing I want is to draw attention to ourselves by going after every vampire that gets a little too greedy.'

'His fighting skills were impressive. He was highly trained. No way he learnt to fight like that in a gym with his mates. We've tracked him down to this location,' he says, pointing at the large building to the north of the city. 'He appeared out of nowhere a few months ago and doesn't seem to have joined any of the usual social circles. The apartment is rented on a month-to-month basis. Can't find any details on the tenant. He's a loner... well, apart from the woman he's living with.'

'A woman?'

'I don't have any intel on her. He's off the grid though. I think it's worth taking a look.'

Rhain hands the tablet back and walks over to the nearest containment cell. 'I presume the Blackjacks know about this too?'

'They're usually on the ball. The problem is, they're a few hours nearer than we are. Even flying they'll have the lead on us.'

'If it is him, we need to get him back. Even if it means going up against the Blackjacks to get him. Do you understand?'

Maddox smirks. 'I understand. About time we took them down a peg or two.'

Fletch brings the bus to a stop behind Davyn's Range Rover and kills the engine. Nix looks out the one-way window running the length of the vehicle. Something feels off about this whole thing, but she can't figure out what it is.

'Fletch, you stay with the bus, everyone else, up top. Let's see if we can find our mystery vampire.'

After checking for any unwanted spectators, Nix releases her wings, followed by Fallon and Willow. Willow takes off first, taking hold of her brother's arm, pulling him off the ground. Fallon grabs Bastian before she can, leaving her with Davyn. Without a word they grab each other's arms, and she lifts him up to the roof with the others.

Fallon, Bastian, and Davyn take up positions along the edge of the roof, while Nix and Willow stand to either side of Shep as he closes his eyes and concentrates on their surroundings. Nix patiently waits as he does his thing. Instead of having wings, each of the guys have a talent unique to them and Shep's is tracking. He can pick up a scent and, together with his other enhanced senses, picture what happened. Almost like he's seeing a past moment in time. Nix doesn't understand it, but it's scarily accurate.

Fallon's wings twitch as she paces the rooftop. Patience has never been her strong point. Shep frowns and tilts his head to the side. 'Your pacing is ruining my calm, Fallon.'

She sneers at him, but instead of stopping, her feet seem to hit the gravel roof a little harder than before.

After a few minutes he opens his eyes and points down the road. 'South-west, Boss. There's a scent but it's—' he pauses and looks over at her. 'It's familiar in a way, but different.'

Bastian twirls his twin blades in his gloved hands. 'Familiar how?'

Shep closes his eyes again, pauses then shakes his head. 'It's... muddled.'

'Muddled how?' Fallon asks, clearly eager to get moving.

'If I knew how, I would have explained using a better word than muddled.'

'Is it Court?' Nix asks.

'Like I said - it's familiar but different. It's not saying Court to me, but it's not saying it's not - if you get me.'

'Rarely,' Fallon mutters as she glares at him.

'Whoever killed those guys is a male vampire. He's tall, well-built, but not as much as Court was. He... suppose I'd describe it as freaked out. What he did, he wasn't expecting it. Kinda like it was a surprise.' Shep shrugs and stands up. 'He's running scared, Boss.'

Nix crouches at the edge, focusing on the direction Shep indicated. Whoever this vampire is, he's trying to survive without drawing attention to himself. Unfortunately, he's not being successful. The True Order didn't appreciate anyone flaunting the vampire side of themselves in public. No doubt they'll have heard about this situation too. They could even have a team on the way. If they find this lone vampire before the Blackjacks do, they'll kill him - no questions.

She stands up and spreads her wings. 'Let's go catch ourselves a vampire. Catch. Not kill, Fallon. You hear me?'

Shep snorts. 'Busted, Fallon. Think you can be on your best behaviour?'

Fallon swipes at Shep with her wings, sending him diving to the rooftop to avoid being decapitated. 'Just remember who's giving you a lift. She said nothing about not killing you.'

Shep wipes the dust from his leathers, the smile gone from his face. 'You know you can go off people, Fallon. Keep going like this and you may find yourself removed from my Christmas card list.'

Nix lifts off the rooftop, cutting off whatever reply Fallon was going to shoot back at Shep. 'Willow, you stick with me. Everyone else, let's go. When you find him call it in. I don't want to lose this one.'

Court freezes at the corner of the garage and slows his breathing as he listens to his surroundings. Someone is coming. He frowns and turns his head. More coming from that direction too. Whoever it is, they're coming in fast. He frowns and looks at the rooftops on the far side of the road. He's still getting to grips with his acute senses, but it sounds like they're coming from above too, and that can't be a good thing.

Moving as quietly as he can, he pulls the knife from his boot, gripping the blade firmly in his hand. He has no intention of meeting whoever is headed his way, but he's sure as hell going to defend himself if they get too close. Feeding will just have to wait. After losing control of himself last night with Thea, he feels like shit. One of the few times he actually needs and wants to feed, and this happens.

Court hurries along the road and ducks down the first side street he comes across. He needs to get back to Thea, but not if he's going to be dragging his mystery guests back with him.

His fangs pulse in his gums as adrenaline races through his body.

He tries to keep them at bay with little success. The large canines descend as he hides in the shadows. He zips up his jacket, pulling the hood down to keep his glowing eyes and fangs to himself.

Even though all his instincts are drawing him back to his sister, common sense takes him the long way home. He keeps to the shadows, skirting around the edge of the group of apartment blocks.

Court skids to a stop as a large man drops out of thin air, landing effortlessly in front of him. Another set of heavy boots joins the first, right behind Court. He grips the blade in his hand as he examines the two newcomers. Both are tall, well-built, and dressed exactly the same way in head-to-toe black. Whoever they are, they're not out for an innocent evening stroll.

'This our guy?' the one behind him asks.

The blond-haired one nods to the man behind Court. He seems to inhale deeply before nodding. 'That it is.' He looks at Court again and holds his gloved hands out in front of him. 'It's okay, mate. We're here to have a chat with you - that's all. We're the good guys.'

Court is no more interested in having a chat with these two than he is in going for a month without feeding. 'Get the fuck out of my way... mate.'

The two men freeze, like a switch has been flicked. The man behind Court steps around to the front and the two of them stare at him.

'I don't fucking believe it. Pull down your hood.'

'I said, get the fuck out of my way.'

The dark-haired one that was behind him steps forward and reaches out to do it for him. Without giving him a chance, Court grabs the man's arm, twisting as he pulls it down to the ground. Court slams him against the concrete, taking advantage of his momentary confusion. He steps forward and plunges his knife deep in the blond man's side as he reaches out to grab him. He pulls the man against his blade. Court pauses as the man's mouth opens, showing a large set of fangs glinting in the streetlight above them. Court shoves the man aside and uses the brief moment of distraction to slip away from his attackers.

~

Rhain locks his office door and lowers into the chair behind his desk. He places his hands on the highly polished wooden desk. As soon as his left hand hits the desk the trembling begins. As the days wear on, it is becoming harder to hide it from his men. Any show of weakness could prove fatal to his position.

He pulls a syringe from the inside pocket of his suit jacket and rolls up his sleeve. He pauses as a particularly severe tremor works its way through his body, then plunges the needle in his arm. As the medication works through his system he leans back in his chair and closes his eyes.

Of all the things that could have ended his life over the years, The Fever was his least favourable option. His father was lost to the cruel disease at a young age. As the years went by, he thought he had been spared, but it seems he's been cursed with the same susceptible genes.

He noticed the change in himself five years ago. It began gradually at first, barely more than a twinge if he didn't feed regularly, but over time the urges increased. He'd wake with excruciating cramps, the addiction pulling and twisting his insides in a vice-like grip.

A physical enemy you can fight. You can pick up a blade or a gun and end the threat. This enemy he's powerless to do anything about. It's not a fight he can win and he can't accept that. He won't accept that. He clenches the syringe in his fist. The drug he created is a breakthrough treatment for the worst of the side effects of the addiction, but it can't cure it. Nothing will do that.

But for the first time in years, he saw a semi normal existence ahead of him. As long as he took the drug, as well as easing some of the more severe side-effects of the Fever, he could feed from a Hybrid or mixed-blood vampire. The combination of the two elements gave him everything he needed to survive without having to risk his sanity by going anywhere near Prime blood.

Now that his donor decided to take leave of the facility, he has a serious problem. That particular donor was the only one whose blood made any difference to his condition. The other males added variety to the blood, but that one... his blood was the key to everything. Without it, The Fever was nipping at his heels and catching up far too fast.

He's not ready to lose himself to it. Not yet. Not when he's so close.

But unless he finds that male again, he's going to be in trouble. A year on and still nothing. With no memory he should have stuck out, but somehow, he managed to vanish. That was part of the reason they took the donor's memories from them. It made them more compliant. More noticeable if they did manage to escape.

His phone vibrates across the desk before he picks it up. The vampire the True Order assigned to deal with him is looking for an update. Barton is going to have to wait. The Order and their ridiculous ploy to ensure the rise of the Primes and the extinction of the Hybrid vampires comes in a very distant second place for him. Even if this drug could be mass produced and given to all Primes, it would take centuries to build the Prime numbers again. He's only got years left - not centuries.

He shoves the phone to the side as it vibrates again. Damn bastard is persistent and beginning to get on Rhain's already strained nerves. That's not somewhere he'd advise anyone to venture if they wanted to live.

Nix carefully lowers Fletch onto the roof and lands beside him, closely followed by Willow. She gestures for Fletch to stand back as she approaches the edge and peers down to the alley below. She trains her weapon on the two people in the darkness four stories beneath her. She narrows her eyes, allowing her heightened senses to see what others wouldn't be able to make out. Shep is on the ground, blood darkening the ground beneath him. Bastian is crouched down beside him keeping watch until the others arrive.

She hears Willow fidgeting behind her, but the newest addition to the Blackjacks has the good sense to stay put until Nix gives the all-clear. Even from here they can hear Shep's cursing, but she's sure Willow will want to talk to her brother to make sure he's okay. Nix contacts Davyn on the radio. 'We're heading down to Shep. You find anything?'

'Faint trail. We're still on it.'

'Stay in touch. We'll bring Shep back to the bus as soon as Fletch gives us the go ahead.'

After listening for another minute she finally nods to Willow and Fletch. 'We're good to go.' Nix spreads her wings and lifts off the roof. She reaches down and grabs Fletch's outstretched arm, then glides to the ground. As soon as his feet hit the dirt, Fletch hurries over to Shep. Willow crouches down beside her brother and touches the side of his head. 'Are you all right?'

'No I'm not all right! I was stabbed and it fucking hurts!'

Willow blows out a long breath. 'Sounds like you're all right.'

'I was stabbed, Sis. Stabbed.' Shep curses as Fletch pulls his jacket open. 'Hey! Watch it.'

'Quit your whining and let me do my damn job.' Fletch cuts open Shep's t-shirt and peels the material from the wound.

As he works, Nix crouches beside her fallen fighter. 'What the hell happened?' Nix demands.

'Court.'

Nix blinks a few times then looks down at Shep. 'What did you say?'

'You heard me, Boss. I don't believe it myself, but it was him and the bastard stabbed me. He came back from the dead, stabbed me, and waltzed away without batting a fucking eyelid.'

Nix pats him on the shoulder then stands up and walks over to Bastian. 'Are you telling me it was definitely Court?'

Bastian nods as he wipes his bloody palms on his leathers. 'It was definitely him, Nix. He looked different. Not as big, but as soon as he spoke...' Bastian smiles as he shakes his head. 'No mistaking that voice. I don't know how but he's still alive and just kicked Shep's butt.'

Shep lifts his head off the ground. 'He did not kick my butt. I was momentarily distracted by the fact I was facing a damn ghost. He got the upper hand on you too or did you just trip and land on your prissy ass?'

Fletch pushes his shoulder back down. 'Will you stay still. You're bleeding all over the place.'

'I thought you were here to make sure I don't.'

Fletch mutters a string of choice words under his breath as he continues to bandage Shep's wound.

Nix's head feels like it's been plunged in a bucket of water. Her team's voices echo in her ears but she can't make sense of anything they're saying. It can't be Court. There's no way it was Court. How could he still be alive and not come back to them?

Fletch waves his hand in front of Nix's face startling her. 'You okay, Nix?'

'What? Sorry, yeah. Shep okay to go?'

'He'll hold up until I can stitch him up on the bus. I'll get Fallon to bring it in. I don't want to move him too far.'

'Good.' Nix forces herself to get her head back in the game. 'Okay, good. Right. Bastian, you okay to head out with Davyn? Scope out the area. See if this vampire left any trails.'

'Will do. It was Court, Nix. I promise it wasn't Shep having a moment.'

Nix brushes her dark hair off her shoulder. 'After all this time I just want to see him with my own eyes. I'm not saying I don't believe you. Besides, there's no way anyone but a Blackjack could have gotten the upper hand on you two.' She wants to believe it's Court. Every fibre of her being wants to believe it's him. But until she sees for herself, she's reserving judgement.

~

Court looks up at his reflection in the mirror over the sink. His fangs are refusing to retract and the throbbing in his gums is driving him fucking crazy. He shakes his head angrily, squeezing the rim of the sink in his hands. A whole year and no contact with others like him, then two clashes in the space of as many days.

He should be happy he's not the only one, but he's far from happy.

The others were clearly fighters or soldiers. Their wardrobe and accessories were a dead giveaway. But why were they coming for him? He's kept to himself since he found out what he is. Why would these vampires, or whatever they were, be targeting him? What rules did he break?

He splashes cold water on his face, grimaces at his reflection, still with visible fangs and glowing eyes, then turns off the light. They're going to have to move. No choice. If those guys managed to get that close to their home, it's only a matter of time before he's found.

He stands in the doorway to Thea's bedroom and watches his sister as she sleeps. The presence of a potential army of vampires isn't good news for her either. He doesn't care what happens to him, but if they come after him, Thea could easily get caught in the crossfire. He's damned if that's going to happen. If it means killing those men, he won't hesitate.

He double checks all the locks are in place before sitting down on the couch and trying to get himself under control. They need to leave, but he doesn't want to wake Thea while he's like this. He closes his eyes and focuses on breathing in and out, but it doesn't work. He can't get those guys out of his head. He grabs a bottle of water from the fridge and wanders over to the boarded-up window. The street outside is empty. Even the usual joyriders aren't about tonight. Court breaks the seal on the bottle and lifts it to his lips... then freezes. He lowers the bottle and peers through the slats. Movement on the far side of the street. And again.

There's someone watching his building.

Court races back to Thea's room and pulls an overnight bag from the corner. He drops it on the end of her bed and shakes her. 'Wake up. Thea, wake up!'

She pushes him away and tucks her head under the duvet. 'Leave me alone.'

'Thea! We have to go. You've got five minutes to pack.'

She looks out from under her duvet. 'Excuse me?'

'You heard me. We need to leave.' When she doesn't move as fast as he'd like her to, he opens one of her drawers and shoves clothes in the bag.

'Hey!'

'I'm not kidding, Thea. I just had a meeting with at least one if not two bloody big vampires. I don't know how they found me, but they did. It's not safe here anymore.'

That gets her attention. She grabs a pair of jeans and hoodie, slipping them on over her pyjamas. 'What sort of meeting?' Before he gets the chance to answer, her eyes travel to the fangs still refusing to retreat. 'What the hell happened? Are you okay? Did you recognise them?'

Court shakes his head. 'I'm fine. They came at me and I defended myself. Never seen them before, but they're not here to make friends.' He peers out the window as Thea finishes packing her limited wardrobe. A tall, dark figure is lurking in the shadows between the buildings across the street. Adrenaline courses through his body, preparing him to face off whoever is waiting for them.

'We have to move. Now, Thea.'

Nix crouches on the rooftop beside Fallon and examines the building across the car park. At first glance it appears derelict. Most of the windows had been broken over the years and boarded up to stop squatters from moving in. Any windows lucky enough to still be intact have a heavy layer of grime covering the glass. The only sign of life is the faint glow of light from the far corner of the building. The window is blacked out somehow, but her acute vision can see the hint of life inside.

Nix closes her eyes and takes a couple of deep breaths. She's nowhere as adept at picking up scents as Shep is, but her heightened senses should be able to tell her exactly who is inside the building. Once she masks out the various aftershaves, deodorants and other products her team are wearing she picks up a hint of a scent she never thought she'd experience again. Court is in there. Now that she's closer to the scent she understands what Shep was talking about. It's Court, but also not. There's something different about his scent.

Nix tries to reign in her excitement but is failing miserably. She wants nothing more than to rush over to the building, break down the door, and throw her arms around him. There's a lot to get through before she can even consider what they once were to each other. Starting with where he's been for the last three years.

She touches her finger to the earpiece as her phone vibrates. 'What is it?'

'It's Bas. He's made me. Not sure if he's clocked Davyn yet.'

'Damn it. Okay, both of you head up. We're on the way.'

She turns to Fallon and Willow. 'Guess it's time to say hi.'

Fallon stands beside Nix on the roof ledge. 'Never thought I'd be seeing his ugly mug again.'

Nix looks over her shoulder at Fallon and nods. 'You're not the only one. I just hope he's as happy to see us.'

'Why wouldn't he be?'

Nix stands up and stretches her wings, relishing the feel of the cool breeze against them. 'Nearly three years with no word. If he wanted to find us before now, he could have. So does that mean he doesn't want to be found?'

Fallon frowns as she looks over at the building. 'There's only one way to find out. If that asshole has been avoiding us all this time, he'd better have a damn good explanation. If not, I'm going to kill him myself.'

Fallon opens her wings and lifts off the roof before Nix can reply. She looks over her shoulder at Willow and smiles. 'We better go after her before she does actually kill him.' Willow takes off, swooping low and circling the building to enter from the alley on the side. Nix follows close behind and lands next to the other two women.

Nix takes a deep breath as she looks at the door. Her heart has dropped to her stomach and her throat feels like it's being squeezed in a vice. 'Let's go.'

Rhain wakes as the first spasm works through his body. He rears back in the bed, knocking his phone and watch from the bedside table. The scream sticks in his throat as every nerve ending erupts in flames. He looks over at his desk and the case holding the vials of the drug. It's only a few steps away but it might as well be the other side of the fucking planet right now. He's trapped in this pain. There's nothing to do now but ride it out.

Time crawls by - each second filled with torturous cramps that paralyse him. He closes his eyes and begins counting. The simple task gives him something else to concentrate on until his body gives him a break. He gets to three hundred and sixty-eight before he's able to roll onto his side and curl in a ball. The pain has eased, leaving his body weak and aching. The layer of sweat on his skin has cooled in the air-conditioned room, sending chills though his abused body.

He wants a drink, a shower, and a good feed. The first and third will have to wait until he gets himself sorted. Rhain picks up his phone from the floor and calls his trusted butler. Geraint had attended to his parents while they lived and runs Rhain's house with an iron fist. Nothing happened in the mansion that Geraint didn't know about - including Rhain's addiction. He's the only one who knows how firm a hold The Fever has on him and Rhain is adamant it will stay that way. If any of his business contacts knew he was falling apart, his authority would be worthless. Any sign of weakness and someone would attack. He couldn't blame them. It's exactly what he would do.

'Geraint?'

'You've had another episode.'

'I need to feed.'

'I will have someone here in fifteen minutes.'

Geraint can always tell from his voice when he's been hit with the cramps. He pushes himself off his bed and shuffles across his room to the en-suite. Rhain frowns at his reflection in the mirror over the wide sink. His eyes are bloodshot, the irises more glowing silver than grey. His skin is pasty and there's blood on his lip where his fangs bit mid spasm. A feed will help the wounds.

He strips off his boxers and steps in the shower, bracing himself against the wall as the hot water eases his stiff muscles. His bottom lip stings like hell when the water hits.

He looks up when he hears a knock on the door. 'Yes?'

Geraint opens the door, but doesn't come in. 'Sir, she's here.'

Rhain pushes back from the wall and forces his legs to support his weight. He desperately needs the strength her blood will give him, but there's no way she could know how weak he is. She may be a regular donor for him but that doesn't mean he trusts her.

He takes a deep breath, picking up her scent from the bedroom. That alone is enough to bring a little life back to his weak body. His gums pulse at the promise of a feed, but he restrains himself. 'I'm ready. Send her in.'

The female is one he's fed from before. Her long blonde hair is lose around her shoulders, the black dress hugs curves he's explored in detail more than once. She smiles as she unzips her dress, letting the silky material slide to the ground. No underwear. Less layers to get through.

He opens the shower door and she steps in. They don't talk. They never do. She knows what he wants and she's more than happy to give it to him. He moves towards her until she's pressed against the marble tiled wall. Rhain lifts her up so she can wrap her legs around his waist.

Need takes over. There's no foreplay. She's more than ready for him. He presses against her entrance, giving her time to adjust to him. It doesn't take long. She lets him in, her head rolling back as he fills her. The water drips from his blond hair onto her breasts as she moves on him. Her long fingernails run down his chest, leaving red tracks on his skin.

As she uses him to pleasure herself, he stays still, one arm around her waist and the other braced against the wall as she screams. He feels her orgasm, feels her body squeezing him as the waves hit. Still he doesn't react. He knows other males who use their feeding companion in ways they shouldn't. Someone to feed from, someone to force themselves on then discard when they were finished. Rhain had never been like that. Without someone to feed from, he'd die. It is that simple.

There are four females he feeds from and each is treated exceptionally well. As well as being paid handsomely for their service, he never took what others did. Sometimes feeding could get out of control. It was a basic function that could go too far. He's done questionable things in his long life, but he would never do that. Sex was part of feeding for him, but it was always consensual.

No matter how desperate he was, he would always let his donor take what they wanted from him first. The control required to stop himself from taking things too far was part of the thrill for him. Resisting the urges, resisting the call of her blood, it added a level of intensity he relished. When she finally gave him permission to take what he needed... well, it was worth the wait.

The female digs her fingers in his hair and draws him closer. She writhes on him again as she latches onto his neck, her fangs puncturing his skin. Rhain closes his eyes as she bounces up and down on him. The intensity builds when his blood hits her system as she feeds, taking what she wants from him. She releases his neck briefly then bites him hard as she orgasms again. The pain from her fangs threatens to bring on his own release, but he holds it back, his body trembling with the effort to restrain himself. It's not time yet.

She moves away from his neck and licks her lips, her green eyes glowing brightly as she looks at him. Instead of giving him permission to feed, she runs her fingers down his chest to the base of his shaft. Rhain sucks in a breath as she moves on him again, her pace slow and torturous. Her fingers and her body work him, the array of sensations fighting against his control.

He knows what she's doing, and she jumps to the top of his favourite list for it. She's pushing him, testing the grip he has on himself, increasing the pleasure for him when she eventually releases his leash.

She leans closer to his ear. 'Your turn.'

The growl comes from deep within. His fangs lower and his wings slide out of his back. She liked him to have his wings out when he fed. Feeding a Prime is an honour for some fucking reason he can't understand. The water beats off his silver wings as they fill the large cubicle. Rhain releases the control he'd been keeping a firm hold on.

With the first thrust, his need takes over. It doesn't take long for his first orgasm to hit, but he's far from finished. Without pausing, he drives into her again. His deep breaths in perfect timing with her moans. She wraps her arms around his neck as his pace increases.

Her fingernails dig into the thick muscles on his wings which doesn't do anything to calm the situation. Rhain growls again then nudges her head to the side. The smell of her blood hits his nostrils even before he's sunk his teeth in. The second her blood touches his tongue he feels his strength returning.

It's moments like this all his hard work comes in to its own. She's not a Prime. Without the drug he developed, feeding from her wouldn't sustain him. Now... now she can give him what he wants in so many ways. That alone is worth the lives he's sacrificing.

He buries his fangs deeper in her flesh as the pressure builds inside him. He braces his wings against the shower stall, supporting them as he thrusts harder. The thick talons on the tips of his wings embed themselves in the wall and Rhain growls against her neck as he comes.

When the last shudder works through his body, Rhain carefully pulls out of her neck. He turns the wound towards the spray washing the blood off her skin. The female smiles lazily up at him, but he has no interest in making pleasantries. He lifts her off him and holds her until he's sure she's not going to fall on her face.

Rhain turns off the water then passes her a robe which she wraps around her body. He pulls a towel from the rack and wraps it around his waist. Still wet from the extended shower, he leaves his wings out to dry. She follows him back to his bedroom and waves at him as she saunters towards the door, her black dress and heels in her hands.

She'll stay the rest of the day in his mansion in case he needed to feed again in a few hours. The damn attacks sometimes require him to feed a few times before he is fully recovered. But unless he needs her services again, they won't see each other before she leaves. This isn't a deep and meaningful romance. It's a business arrangement and nothing more.

Geraint knocks on the door and Rhain calls for him to come in. The imposing man enters, a tray in his hand. He pours Rhain a drink and hands it to him. 'You look much improved.'

'Thank you for getting her here so fast.'

Geraint nods once. 'Are the attacks worsening?'

'Unfortunately.' He takes a sip of the single malt, the drink helping to put the last of the attack behind him... until the next time.

Geraint takes the case with the medication from the desk and pulls a chair in front of the bed. He fills the syringe with the correct dose and holds his hand out. 'Your arm, sir.'

'I can do it myself.'

'Your arm.'

Rhain sighs and raises his arm. Geraint places the tourniquet around his arm and locates a suitable vein. He injects the medication and packs the vials away. 'I have had an update from Maddox. There is still no progress.'

Rhain nods then takes another sip of his drink. He's on borrowed time. They need to find the vampire before his supplies run out. Or before the memory block wears off and he can point a finger at every single one of them. 'There's still time.'

Geraint raises an eyebrow. 'I never knew you to sugar-coat things, especially to yourself.'

Rhain smirks. 'Trust you to slap me back to reality. What else did Maddox say?'

'Another subject died today. He will search for a suitable replacement, but it may take time to test the reserve stock.'

'Keep the pressure on him.'

'Of course, sir. They have also ordered more of the by-product. It is proving to be quite lucrative.'

Rhain doesn't reply. That wasn't part of his plan. When he began the project, he had tested both Prime and Hybrid blood before the latter proved to be the correct variant. The Order had taken the drug made from the Prime blood and, unknown to him, tested it on some Hybrids they had in custody. The effects were not dissimilar to heroin for humans. Rhain had no interest in creating this Prime derivative, but he had little choice now. He needs to keep them on side.

'Sir, are you sure it is wise to associate yourself with the True Order?'

Rhain stretches his wings out, shaking the last of the water from them, then pulls them back inside his body. He rolls his shoulders as they settle inside him. 'I know what I'm doing.'

'I don't doubt that.'

'We're using them as much as they're using us. We need each other... for now. Things will change and I'm prepared for that. Timing is crucial. We need to be the ones to decide when the partnership has run its course. If we happen to take out the Order at the same time, so be it.'

Court picks up the metal bat from under the couch as the door bursts open to reveal one of the most intimidating looking men he's ever seen. His large, leather clad body fills the doorway, blocking their main escape route. Cold, dead green eyes lock on to him before moving to Thea. The man frowns slightly as his eyes linger on Thea a little too long. Court nudges her behind him as another man appears at the door. It takes him a few seconds to realise the second man is the one from the alley earlier.

A deep growl builds in his chest. The odds of getting Thea out in one piece are getting slimmer by the minute. The tall man with the dead green eyes lifts his lip slightly showing his fangs.

Court adjusts his grip on the bat, holding it out in front of him as he faces the two intruders, fully prepared to do whatever he has to do in order to protect Thea. The first man reacts by doing the opposite of what Court thought he would. He leans against the wall and stares silently at them - or specifically, Thea, oblivious to the weapon in

Court's hand. Not exactly a reaction that puts him at ease. If this guy isn't worried about the weapon, they're more screwed than he thought.

The other unwelcome guest holds his hands up in a placating fashion. He nods at the bat in Court's hand. 'You don't need that. We've just come to talk to you. You can leave that where it was.'

His voice has faint traces of an accent, maybe Spanish or South American. 'Not happening. What do you want?'

The man gestures over his shoulder and Court hears footsteps coming up the stairs. Three women join the two men, moving to the front of the group before stopping a few feet from Court.

A tall, well-built woman steps away from the group. Like the others, she is dressed in black leather with flashes of purple in her ankle length coat. Something in the back of his mind tells him he's seen her before, but he can't pull the memory back, if it even existed at all. He's pretty sure if he had met her before he'd remember - amnesia or not.

She is stunning, but that just increases her threat level. He can't let his guard drop because he's irrationally attracted to her. If the two at the door and the one from earlier are all vampires, does that mean the women are too?

The woman smiles and holds her gloved hands out in front of her. 'It really is you. I can't believe it. Where the hell have you been all this time?'

Court frowns at her as his grip tightens on his weapon. 'Who are you and what do you want?'

She drops her arms slightly as she looks at him. 'It's us, Court.'

The hair on the back of his neck stands to attention when she says his name. 'How do you know my name? Who are you?'

The woman's face drops as she lowers her arms to her side. 'You don't know who we are?'

'I wouldn't have asked who you are if I did.'

She looks over her shoulder at the others in the group. Court can see what looks like disappointment on their faces. 'My name is Phoenix, but people call me Nix. This is Fallon, Bastian, Davyn, and Willow. You met Shep earlier.'

'So, this is payback? Your friend came after me. I was just defending myself.'

'Payback? Of course not. Court, we're friends.'

He laughs, but it comes out more like a cough mixed with a growl. 'Friends? I don't know you. I don't know any of you. Are you some sort of vigilante group?'

She smiles and shakes her head. 'Not quite. We call ourselves the Blackjacks. You are one of us - a Blackjack. Second in command actually. You were on a mission a little over three years ago and vanished. We looked but... we couldn't find you, Court. Up until you attacked Shep, we thought you were dead. We've come here to take you home.'

Court stares in disbelief at the strange group of intimidating vampires. If it wasn't for the arsenal they're wearing, he'd laugh in their faces. The first vampire that burst in his room; the damn scary looking guy with tattoos, piercings, and dead looking green eyes, takes a step closer to the woman. 'We've got company.'

'Thanks, Davyn. Listen, Court. I know you probably don't believe a word we're saying, and I can't blame you. As much as I'd love to sit down and go through everything slowly, we can't. We don't have that luxury. But if you come with us, I can explain everything.'

'Who's heading our way?' he asks.

'The True Order,' the green-eyed man replies as if that will answer his question.

'They're a group of vampires who don't think we should exist,' Nix explains. 'We really don't want to be here when they arrive.'

Court jumps when Thea touches his arm. In all the confusion he'd forgotten she was there. He keeps his bat directed at the group. Not that it will do any real damage, but it makes him feel a little more in control. 'I really think we should go with them.'

He looks down at her, trying to keep these Blackjack vampires in his sight. 'We don't know anything about them, Thea.'

Thea looks over at Nix, then back at Court and shrugs. 'What have we got to lose? If these True Order vampires are on the way, I'd prefer not to meet them.'

'That's not a solid reason. We can leave. Just the two of us.'

'Two minutes out,' the scary guy says.

'Please, Court,' Nix pleads. 'Come with us. I promise we'll explain everything, but we need to get you to safety now. The Order means business. They'll most likely kill the both of you. We have to leave. Now.'

15

Nix holds her breath as she waits for Court to come to a decision. In all the scenarios that had played through her mind, amnesia - or whatever is wrong with his memory - wasn't one of them. It certainly explains why he vanished. If he had no memory of them, he wouldn't come looking for them. Come looking for her.

The thought hits her like a blow to her stomach. He doesn't remember them. He doesn't remember her, or what they were to each other. She forces the tears back as she fights to keep the smile on her face. The only objective in the next minute or so is to convince him to come back to the compound with them. They can figure everything else out once he's safe. She puts a bit more effort in her smile as she looks at him.

The once fierce warrior is a little lighter than she remembers him. Much of the muscle he'd built up through constant training with the Blackjacks has wasted away. His dark brown hair is cut short with the sides shaved and the top a little longer with a lighter shade at the tips.

She's never been a fan of facial hair, but his close-trimmed beard really suits him and, irritatingly, turns her on. He is still absolutely stunning.

She mentally kicks herself back to reality. Letting her sex drive loose isn't going to help anyone. They're a long way from getting Court to even come with them let alone rekindling anything that was between them.

'Please, Court. We've got transport near here. Come with us. Maybe seeing where you used to live will help stir up some memories?'

For the first time since she started talking, Court looks at her - really looks at her. His ice blue eyes lock on to hers and her head begins to spin. He may not remember them, but he remembers how to use his special skills. It was hard to be deceitful once he targeted you with those haunting eyes of his. Although a little rusty, Nix focuses on controlling her breathing, letting him in without a fight. If this shows him that everything she's said to him is the truth, it's worth the intrusion.

'You can trust us.'

Court refuses to release her from his stare for another few seconds. She's vaguely aware of her fighters' uneasiness behind her. Nix lifts her hand to tell them she's okay.

'You're telling the truth. You know me.'

She nods. 'We all do, Court. Will you come with us?'

'Fine, but my sister is coming too.'

Nix smiles and blinks a few times. Having Court in her head feels like being in a free fall. 'Your sister?'

Thea steps out from behind Court, a piece of pipe in her hands. 'Hi. I'm Thea.'

Nix holds her fist up, silencing the murmurs of confusion from the group. 'Of course she can come. We really have to go now. You ready?'

After getting a nod from them both, she spreads her wings and

Court and Thea back away in surprise. 'Sorry. I didn't mean to startle you. Fallon, Willow, and I will cover you from the air. You and Thea go with Davyn and Bastian in the car.'

'You can fly?'

Nix and the others look at each other. Dammit. How much of the old Court is still in there - if any? 'Davyn and Bastian will look after you.' The way Court and Thea look at Davyn would have been funny if there wasn't a group of True Order fighters heading their way. 'Davyn, keep our guests in one piece.'

'Got it.' He looks over at Court and Thea. 'I won't bite,' Davyn mumbles, not exactly helping the situation.

Nix turns to her fighters. 'Let's make sure Davyn's car gets away without a scratch.' Fallon moves to the window and kicks the frame, knocking it out. She steps out onto the sill and looks around before jumping out. Nix climbs onto the sill and looks up at the roof as she waits for Fallon to check the area out. 'Anything?'

'I'm on the roof. The Order is moving in from the West. They're coming by road and air. Dammit, they're placing blockades up around the site.'

'Time to go,' Nix says. She looks over her shoulder at Court. 'I'll talk to you properly as soon as we're out of this mess, okay?' She jumps out, her large wings lifting her towards the roof.

Davyn stands by the window. 'My car's down there. You'll need to jump.'

'I can't jump that far, not with Thea.'

'Let Davyn take her,' Bastian says. 'He's stronger than you, no offence.'

Before he can argue, Davyn scoops Thea in his arms and drops out of the window. Court rushes over, relieved to see Thea and Davyn on the ground and in one piece. Bastian nudges him to the window. 'Better get down there. Wouldn't put it past him to leave without us.'

Thea squeezes the door handle in both hands as the Range Rover speeds around the corner, accelerating between the rows of buildings. The vampire called Bastian curses as he is slammed against the door, but their driver doesn't pay him any attention. Over the roar of the powerful engine and the squeal of the tires on the tarmac, they can hear gunfire. Bastian shouts in his mic as the vehicle swings to the left and something hits the ground where they were seconds ago.

'Why are they firing on us?' Court shouts from beside her.

Bastian simultaneously opens his window and pulls a gun out of his jacket. 'They're not fans of ours.' Bastian slides his upper body out of the car and returns fire, hanging on to the handle over the door so he doesn't fall out. Thea screams as a large, winged vampire falls from the sky, landing on a stack of pallets beside them with a crash of splintering wood.

'Is he dead?' she asks.

Bastian shrugs. 'We're alive. That's the important bit.' He ducks inside just as Davyn sends the car in a controlled skid around the corner and accelerates again. Bastian curses and looks across at Davyn. 'Can't this heap go any faster?'

Davyn glares at him then looks back at the road. 'Don't insult the car.' He sticks his free hand out the window and fires behind them, his eyes never leaving the road. 'You think you could do better?'

'I can drive your baby? Really?'

Davyn glances at him again. 'No.'

'How many are there?' Court asks.

Bastian reloads as Davyn throws the car around another corner. 'There's six more heading our way. Nix and the girls are trying to stop another eight from coming after us. Hence the need to pick up the pace.'

'Give me a gun,' Court demands.

Davyn pulls his eyes from the road long enough to glance across at Bastian. He raises his pierced eyebrow then focuses on not ploughing them through a wall.

'This is our neck on the line too. I know how to fire a gun.'

'Done it a lot lately?' Bastian asks.

'I point that end at the bad guys and pull the trigger.'

Bastian shrugs. 'That'll work.' He reaches in his jacket and pulls an identical weapon out of the other side pocket. He passes it back to Court and leans out the window again. Court takes the safety off and hits the button to open the window as he takes off his seatbelt.

'Hold my feet,' he says to Thea before he disappears outside. She checks her seatbelt is firmly fastened then grabs Court's legs around the ankles. He leans out the window, pauses then fires once. A shadowy shape drops behind a building.

'Impressive,' Bastian says before he gets slammed against the door again. 'Now you're doing it on purpose,' he grumbles at Davyn.

Davyn pulls his car to a stop at the side of the road and turns off the engine. They sit in silence, listening for anything out of the ordinary. Thea jumps as Bastian's phone rings. He listens for a few seconds before hanging up. 'We're good. Everyone's either dead or bugged out. Fallon was hit in the side, so they're taking her back with Fletch in the bus. Nix wants us to head back to the compound. They'll follow in the bus or by air.' Davyn nods and gets out to check the damage. Thea barely makes it out of the car before her stomach decides to protest against recent events. Court rushes to her side.

'Hey, you okay?'

She nods, then retches again. 'Now you know why I hate roller coasters. My stomach doesn't appreciate being thrown around my body.' Her constitution was no match for Davyn's driving. The thought of getting back in the car and driving for longer than a minute doesn't appeal to her in the slightest.

Court looks up as a loud growl sounds from the other side of the car, followed a few seconds later by a powerful thump. 'What the hell was that?'

Bastian nods over at Davyn. 'I'm guessing his baby took a hit. He's probably a little upset.' He leans closer and lowers his voice. 'You want to piss off Dav? Hurt his car. Shoot him and he won't blink. Shoot the car and he'll go nuts.' Bastian takes a bottle of water from the car and hands it to Thea. 'It's just the adrenaline mixed with a bit of old-fashioned travel sickness. The rest of the drive should be less volatile. Take small sips. You'll feel better soon.'

She takes the bottle and smiles gratefully. 'Thanks.'

Davyn prowls around the back of the car. Fresh blood drips from a deep gash on his hand. Bastian nods at the injury. 'The tree didn't shoot your car. You feel better now?'

'We should go.' He disappears around the other side of the car and gets back in the driver's seat.

'He always like that?' Court asks.

Bastian nods. 'Davyn is the strong silent type. Frustrating as hell to be stuck in a car with.' The engine roars to life as Davyn presses heavily on the accelerator, revving the engine. 'Relax. We're coming!' Bastian opens the back door and gestures for Court and Thea to get in.

Court wraps his arm around her shoulders and leads her back to the car. 'You feel any better?'

'As long as he takes it easy the rest of the way I'll be okay.'

'Hear that, Davyn?' Bastian says as he slides in beside Davyn. 'Take it easy or she's going to redecorate your car.'

Davyn glares over his shoulder at Thea who smiles as she fastens her seatbelt. 'You've been warned.'

Bastian laughs but cuts it short when Davyn bares his teeth at him. 'You done?'

'Yep. All done. Shutting up now.' Bastian glances over his shoulder and winks at Thea as Davyn accelerates down the road.

Thea takes another sip of water and looks across at her brother.

They may not have physically been in each other's lives for long, but one thing hit her about Court from the start. He never visibly worried about anything. Even with no memory and his vampire side to deal with, Court had always seemed to be in control of every situation. He was her rock. Someone she could depend on no matter what. Meeting these vampires should have been a good thing. They're a link to his past – a past he didn't think he'd ever find out about. That should be giving him comfort, but he seems to have been thrown off balance by the encounter. She's not used to seeing him like this.

He must have hundreds of questions to ask their new vampire friends. Instead he's staring out the window, frowning at the landscape going past. He looks so lost.

She reaches out and takes his hand, squeezing it in hers. He looks down at her hand then up at her, smiling briefly, but it does nothing to placate her or her worries. Leaving Court to his thoughts, Thea's eyes move to their driver.

There's something about him that intrigues her. It's probably her imagination but she could swear she's caught him looking at her more than once in the rear view mirror. His green eyes are glowing slightly in the dark interior of the car so it's easy to tell where he's looking. And right now it's at her. He frowns when their eyes meet then focuses on the road again.

He's not attractive in the conventional way. His dark hair is short, shaved close to his head at the bottom with the top section longer and brushed back. His strongly angled face is partly hidden behind dark stubble. The ring he wears in his left eyebrow and the studs running up each ear do nothing to soften his appearance. Nothing about him is inviting... except for his eyes.

Her stomach tightens as their eyes meet again in the mirror. This time he holds her gaze a few seconds longer before he bares his teeth at her. She's sure it was done to convince her to stop looking at him, but if anything, seeing him like that has done the opposite. The glowing eyes and impressive fangs should have had her cowering in the backseat, not trying to make eye contact with him.

She turns in her seat and stares out the window instead of at him. What the hell is wrong with her? They've just been in a car chase with flying vampires. She should be dwelling on that. Not getting turned on by a rather large, incredibly hostile vampire snarling at her. It's exhaustion. It has to be. She just needs a few hours sleep and... He's looking at her again. It's probably her imagination but she swears he takes a deep breath before he frowns and focuses on the road again.

Needing a serious Davyn distraction, she decides to let her nosey side out for a bit. She knows full well there's no point trying to have a conversation with their driver, although the thought of having some time alone with him does appeal to her. 'So, Bastian, do you mind me asking where you're from?'

'I presume you picked up on the accent. I'm half Spanish. American human mother and a Spanish vampire father. It's not the easiest accent to shake off.'

'How did you end up here?'

He turns slightly in his seat to face her. 'Inquisitive, aren't you?'

'Sorry, just tell me to mind my own business if I'm asking too many questions.'

'Sounds like a good idea,' Davyn mutters just loud enough to be heard over the engine.

Bastian throws a look at his comrade before smiling back at Thea. 'After I left Spain I travelled around for a bit. Ended up here and heard about the Blackjacks. I passed the selection process and here I am.'

'Selection process?'

Bastian smiles again and even in the darkened interior of the car his striking face lights up. Never mind hanging out of cars and shooting vampires, he belongs on the front of magazines with looks like that. 'I think it's best we let Nix explain things to you. I'm not being evasive, there's just a lot to explain and she's the best one to do it.'

'Can I just ask you one more thing?'

'Of course.'

'Can you not fly? I mean, Nix and the other two women did, but you two...' Thea's sentence trails away as a low growl sounds from the driver. Bastian turns in his seat to face her. 'Ignore my friend here. He isn't a fan of things like conversations or politeness. All females have wings, but only males from parents who are both pure vampires, also known as Primes, will have the ability to fly. Davyn, Shep, and I are from mixed parentage, hence no wings.'

Thea glances at the rear view mirror just in time to see Davyn's green eyes glow intensely. His hands squeeze the wheel as he turns the car sharply, throwing them to the side.

'Hey, take it easy. I'm sure Nix would like our guests brought back in one piece.'

'Let Nix do the backstory stuff,' Davyn barks at him. 'You need to keep watch for any unwanted company.'

Bastian smiles apologetically at Thea before glaring at Davyn briefly then focusing on the side mirror.

Thea is eager to know more about their rescuers, at least she hopes they are rescuing them, but in the back of the car, lying against the warm leather seats, her eyes drift close.

She wakes when Court gently shakes her shoulder. She blinks as she straightens in the seat, looking around trying to figure out where they are. The Range Rover appears to have stopped in the middle of nowhere. 'How long was I asleep?'

Court glances at his watch. 'Just over an hour. We're here.'

'Where exactly is here?'

Court shakes his head. 'No idea. What is this place?' he asks their chauffeurs.

As per the rest of the journey to wherever they are, Davyn doesn't bother acknowledging him. Bastian turns in the passenger seat to face them. 'This is our home. We call it the Compound. Not the best name I know, but it's safe and that's the priority at the moment.' Bastian smiles and looks out the windscreen. 'Turn on the lights.'

Davyn flicks on the headlights for a few seconds then turns them off again. The brief glimpse showed they're not actually in the middle of nowhere. They've stopped in front of an enormous pair of steel gates. Thea couldn't think of anything less homely than the massive gates facing them. 'You live here?'

'Hey, don't knock it until you see it. The decor is a little cosier on the inside.'

The gates slowly separate, disappearing into the greenery to either side. Davyn glances at them in the rear view mirror as he rests his arm on the steering wheel. Without looking ahead of him, he puts the car in gear and pulls forward. Thea shuffles to the centre of the car, sure they are going to hit the still opening gates as the car passes through, but Davyn clearly knows what he's doing. With barely a centimetre to spare on each side, the car clears the gap and moves down a tunnel which ends in a large garage.

Davyn aims his car towards a parking area at the back of the garage, reverses his car in the last spot and turns off the engine. Without a word, both vampires get out of the car and Bastian waits by Court's door while Davyn leans against the bonnet.

Thea looks across at Court. 'You okay?'

'Still waiting to wake up from whatever this is.'

She squeezes his hand and smiles at him. 'So far, these Blackjacks have kept us safe. One of the women was hit protecting us. If they really meant us harm, they wouldn't have gone through all that.'

Court wipes a hand over his face as he stares out the window. Thea squeezes his hand, and he looks back at her. 'I'll protect you,' she says, winking at him.

He laughs and kisses her on the forehead.

'Hey, you may even learn about your past. Maybe they know what happened to you. Surely it's worth taking the chance to find that out.'

'We might as well get out. I don't think we're going to get any answers from him,' Court says, gesturing towards Davyn. 'We need to talk to Nix.'

They get out of the car and turn around as they look at the vast space. While Davyn's car is easily the biggest, the other cars are impressive. As well as a highly polished black Ducati motorbike, there's a Harley, an Aston Martin, a Mustang, two Land Rovers, and a Jeep. Her attention is pulled from the vehicles as a skylight opens in the roof. Davyn pushes off his car and walks towards the circle of light with Bastian. They stop at the edge of the light and look up as Nix and Willow drop down through the gap. Thea stares open mouthed at the two women as their wings disappear inside their bodies without a trace.

Nix turns to face them and smiles. 'Davyn got you here in one piece?'

'Yeah. Where's here, exactly?'

Her response is cut off as a large Mercedes bus drives in, coming to a stop just past the other cars. The door of the cab opens and a tall man with a thick beard and dirty blond hair tied in a ponytail climbs out, stopping when he sees Court. A huge smile spreads on his face and he hurries over to Court before he stops a few feet from him. 'Sorry, I guess you don't remember me either.'

Court shakes his head. 'I'm guessing I should?'

'Well, I can't say what you should and shouldn't remember until I check you out.' He laughs at the look that crosses Court's face. 'Sorry, I'm the resident doctor, surgeon and general go-to guy for patching up vampires, and humans of course. My name is Fletcher Marsh but please call me Fletch.' He holds out his hand and Court shakes it.

'This is my sister, Thea.'

Fletch pauses, glances at Nix then turns back to Thea. 'Is that so?

Nice to meet you, Thea.'

'Are you a vampire too, Fletch?' she asks.

Fletch laughs and shakes his head. 'I'm a full-blooded human. Now if you'll excuse me, Shep and Fallon, my delightful half-sister, need my attention. I'll see you both later.' He opens a door on the side of the bus and disappears inside.

Bastian, Davyn, and Willow walk towards a set of double doors embedded in the wall at the far side of the garage leaving them alone with Nix. She smiles as she turns to face them. 'I know you've both been through a lot in the last few hours and that you're probably eager for answers. I need to have a chat with Fletch about Fallon and Shep so I'll be tied up here for a bit. How about I show you to your rooms? You can get cleaned up and get some rest. We'll talk properly once I'm done.'

Court has never felt more out of his depth in his life. As they follow Nix through the facility, the sheer size of the premises hits him. Whoever is behind the Blackjacks has deep pockets and that worries him. After five minutes of wandering through what appears like an office block, Nix opens a door and they both come to a stop.

'This is where we live. The rest of the compound is built for function, but no one would want to live there, so we gave the old dormitories a bit of a facelift.'

Court smiles as he looks around the space. If he didn't know where they were, he would have thought he was in a regular house. A worn wooden floor stretches out through the hallway to a large kitchen beyond. A living area complete with a wide fireplace, enormous flat screen TV, and several leather couches and armchairs sits beside the kitchen. A wooden staircase leads from the centre of the hallway to the upper floor.

'Feel free to make yourselves at home. The kitchen is always stocked. Shep and his insatiable appetite see to that.'

'How is all this here?' Court asks as he looks around. 'How has it not been discovered?'

'Most of the facility is underground. The bedrooms and the training centre are the only visible structures and, as far as anyone is concerned, they are an old factory and a house. Nothing suspicious. This area is well off the beaten track and equally well protected.'

She brings them upstairs and takes the second corridor to the right. 'Some of the support staff have rooms here too, but it's mainly us living here.' She stops halfway down the corridor and opens the door. 'This is your room, Thea. Court, yours is next door.' Thea wanders around the room and turns in a circle as she takes it all in. A king size bed takes up most of the far wall, with an en-suite, and a living area opposite. 'This is bigger than our whole flat.'

Nix walks over to the en-suite and opens the cupboard. 'Oh good. They stocked it. There's towels and toiletries in here.' She checks the wardrobe. 'Spare clothes in here. We couldn't get anything new sorted for you with short notice so our housekeeper, Gwen - lovely lady, you'll like her, she took clothes from Fallon, Willow, and I.' She turns to face Thea and smiles. 'Anything else you need for now?'

Thea shakes her head. 'No. You've thought of everything. To be honest, all I'd like right now is a hot shower.'

'We'll leave you to it. Court will be next door. If you need anything dial 10 on the panel beside your bed. It's always manned so whoever answers will be able to help you.'

Nix steps outside and waits for Court to join her.

'You sure you'll be okay?' Court asks, a little nervous about leaving Thea alone like this.

Thea reaches up and kisses him on the cheek. 'I'm fine. Now go so I can have a very long, very hot shower then get some sleep.'

Nix opens the next door, turns on the light and gestures for Court to enter the room. He steps inside and looks around the enormous room. He thought Thea's room was big, but it pales in comparison.

The vast walls are painted in a light grey which compliments the thick dark grey carpet covering the floor. The giant bed against the far wall is draped in black sheets.

He runs his hand over the rails of unfamiliar clothes in the wardrobe. Jeans, shirts, and a few pairs of leather trousers, similar to the ones Bastian and Shep were wearing when he first met them. He closes the door and walks around the corner to the bathroom. The room is only slightly smaller than the bedroom. He frowns at the bottles of cologne neatly lined up beside the sink. 'Is this all my stuff?'

Nix nods. 'We couldn't bear to change anything. It's been kept clean. The staff have seen to that, but other than being cleaned, your room is untouched.'

He picks up the nearest bottle, inhaling the unfamiliar fragrance. He had hoped it would trigger something, but it brings nothing back. 'I don't remember any of this.' He looks over his shoulder at her. 'I thought something...' He shakes his head and turns away, focusing on the bottles by the sink again. 'I've wanted to know what happened, who I really am for as long as I can remember.' He grimaces at his statement. 'You know what I mean. I never thought I'd find anyone like me. It's what I always wanted...'

She leans against the door jamb and crosses her arms. 'But now you're not so sure, right?'

He smiles at her as he sits on the foot of the bed. 'It's a lot to take in.'

Nix sits on the chair opposite him and clasps her hands on her knees. 'You've had a lot of information thrown at you over the last few hours. It's going to take time for you to process everything. Thea is safe next door. The compound is secure. Get some rest. I'll arrange for food to be brought up.'

'Thanks.'

Nix gets up and walks to the door. 'Fletch has been dealing with vampires for years. If you're willing, I'd like him to take a look at you.

He may be able to figure out what happened.'

Court shrugs. 'Can't hurt, I guess. If all this was my life, I want to remember it.'

'Okay. I'll come back in a few hours.'

Nix hurries down to the meeting room while Court has a shower and gets his head around things. Leaving him alone in his room was harder than she thought it would be. He's confused and unsure about this new world he's been introduced to. All she wants to do is take him in her arms and hold him close. Feel those arms around her again, feel his hands brushing through her hair.

Nix closes her eyes and shakes her head, angry at her wayward thoughts.

She closes the door behind her, relieved to see everyone already here. She hits the control on the screen and Shep and Fallon appear at the head of the table. Both are wearing scrubs and sitting in beds with pristine white sheets. Thankfully, they will both make a full recovery and will be released soon.

'Right, so I'm sure we all know why we're here.'

'Who the fuck is Thea?'

She grimaces at Davyn's blunt statement, but as usual, he's hit the nail on the head without delaying with idle chit-chat. 'Probably could have put it better myself, but yes. I realise each of us had a life before the Blackjacks, but was anyone aware of Court having a sister?'

One by one they shake their heads. 'Shep? Fallon?'

'No Boss,' Shep replies.

'Not a word,' Fallon follows.

'Perfect.' She looks at Fletch. 'She's human, right?'

Fletch nods. 'I think so. Until I do some tests, or she tells me otherwise of course. Neither of them mentioned any vampire stuff in relation to her.'

'Doesn't mean she isn't,' Bastian says. 'She's what... mid-twenties? Maybe older? Might not have changed yet.'

'Whatever she is, the priority is figuring out who she is.' Nix sighs and resists massaging her temples. This entire situation is making her brain hurt. 'First things first. Fletch, you need to check them both out. Full blood work on Thea too. Once we have all the information, we'll decide what we're doing. Any idea why he can't remember any of us?'

'Without checking him out I can't say for sure. I need to know the extent of his memory loss. There's too many variables right now.'

'Okay, let him rest for a few hours then give him a full examination. We need to know what's going on with both of them.'

~

Nix stares out the window watching the sun rising over the wall of the compound garden. This winter is throwing a shedload of snow at them. It makes leaving the compound a challenge, but she loves it. Growing up, the rare times it snowed still stuck in her memory. There's something about it that calms her. It didn't matter what the landscape was like. After the snow fell, everything looked so pure, so beautiful. How could you not love that?

Shame it's not having its usual calming effect on her now. Her world has been thrown on its head and spun around. It was her job to stay level headed. The team depended on her. What good is she to any of them if her personal feelings are interfering with her job.

She glances over her shoulder at the door to Fletch's room. It's a long shot, but a part of her hopes he can figure out why Court can't remember anything and somehow fix him. She shakes her head as she paces the tiled floor. She has to stop making this about her. Having Court's memories restored will tell them vital information they need to know. Was the True Order behind his disappearance? If so, were they able to extract any sensitive information from him about the Blackjacks?

She seriously doubts that, but it is a concern. Apart from the fact Court was one tough SOB, if they had extracted anything of use, they would have used it to make a move by now. Ridding the world of the Blackjacks is top of their list. She's sure of that. Having an armed group of 'mongrels' standing up to them is seriously putting a dent in their plans and their image.

Nix forces herself to stop pacing and looks out the window again. It's either that or she's going to punch something or someone. Even though she had been told Court was the one to attack Shep, deep down she hadn't believed it. Why would she? He was dead. Gone from their lives forever. That's what she had told herself again and again after he disappeared.

He had to be dead. If he was alive, surely he would have come back to the Blackjacks. She had convinced herself that death was the only logical conclusion. If she even thought for one second that he was alive and well, but in hiding from them, she would have driven herself crazy wondering why.

In all her discussions with herself, she had never considered amnesia. She doesn't know whether the reality is better or worse than what she had convinced herself to believe. Somehow, having the Court she knows and loves alive and well, but unable or unwilling to remember anything about what they had is like a cruel twist of fate. He's a few feet away, being examined by Fletch. He's alive, breathing, and from what she saw, uninjured and well able to speak and fight. So what happened to make him forget?

He's here, yet he's not here. And that's nearly worse than thinking he was dead.

Fletch opens the door and pops his head out. 'I'm all done. He's given permission to discuss my findings with you in the room.'

She follows the doctor inside and leans against the wall, her arms crossed over her chest. It's either that or one of her hands might reach out to touch Court's bare skin. As soon as she sees the enormous wings tattooed across his chest, her mind takes her back to the many long hours spent in bed together when she'd trace the feathers etched on his skin.

'Nix? You good?'

'What? Yes, Fletch, absolutely.' Nothing like falling at the first hurdle. If she can't be in the room with him for a few seconds without letting her mind drift, she's going to drive herself crazy.

Fletch rests one hip against the edge of his desk and clasps his hands together. 'Okay, well overall you're in good shape, Court. I've taken scans and x-rays, and I'm afraid, I can't find any reason for your amnesia. I'm still waiting for the results from your bloodwork so there may be something there to give us a clue.

'I've compared your results with those taken from before you disappeared. You have three new fractures; two ribs and your left leg, both of which have healed beautifully. Because you haven't been drinking vampire blood you've also lost some body weight, but that should rectify itself once you start on the full fat blood instead of the skimmed variety. The guys donate regularly so we have a supply in the fridge at all times. Now, I've had the tattoo on your back translated.'

'Translated?' Court asks. 'What are you talking about?'

Fletch pulls up a photo of the tattoo on Court's back. The swirling image is instantly recognisable to Nix. 'That's Prime script.'

'That it is,' Fletch confirms.

'Hang on,' Court interrupts. 'Is it a new tattoo?'

Fletch nods as Nix examines the tattoo on his back. 'Just another piece to this puzzle my friend. You didn't have it when you left here. Correction, you didn't have it when I last examined you.'

'Great,' Court replies sarcastically. 'Do I want to know what it means?'

'Probably not but I'll tell you anyway. It means Level One Donor.'

Court grimaces and looks at the tattoo in the mirror on the wall. 'Yeah. I could have done without knowing that. Donor for what?'

Fletch shrugs. 'Wish I knew, buddy. Like I said, it's another piece in your complex puzzle.'

He runs a hand over his beard as he looks at the floor. Nix knows the look well. 'What's wrong?' she asks.

Court turns to Fletch. 'There's something wrong?'

Fletch makes a face as he takes a deep breath. 'No easy way of saying this, but I reckon your memory's been tampered with.'

'Tampered? You mean like intentionally? How?'

Fletch shrugs. 'No clue yet, but this is far from natural. Why do you remember your name? Why did you remember Thea? I'm presuming those two pieces of information came to you fairly early after waking up.'

Court nods. 'Yeah. Thea was the first thing that came to mind. My name wasn't a conscious thing. I just knew my name was Court.'

'Yet the Blackjacks and your life here are gone along with whatever happened to you while you were missing. From what I saw on the security footage you're clearly able to fight. None of your Blackjack skills seem to be affected. Now, I don't know about you two but I'm not buying that's just a coincidence.'

'You think I've been brainwashed?'

'No clue, buddy. What I do know is that I'm on the case. It may mean you and I get to spend some quality time together while we figure it out.'

'Do you have any idea who might have taken me?'

Nix shakes her head, wishing more than he'll ever know that she had the answer to that. 'We don't have the answers right now, Court, but we will figure it out. I promise. You're one of us and we will not stop until we know what the hell happened to you.'

He turns his heart-stopping eyes towards her and she has to remind herself this isn't her Court anymore. Not yet anyway. 'So what's the plan?'

'How about we start at the beginning. What do you remember?' she asks.

Court shrugs. 'Not much. I woke up about a year ago in the back end of nowhere. It was a forest, but I honestly can't remember where. I have no idea how I'd ended up there. I...'

'What?' Fletch asks.

'I only had on a pair of boxers. I had... like a graze or abrasions around each wrist and there were marks on my arms.'

'What sort of marks?'

He shakes his head at Nix's question. 'I don't know. Small cuts—no, more like holes. From needles maybe?'

Fletch glances at Nix, his eyebrows raised. 'Did you know what you were when you woke up?' he asks.

Court shakes his head. 'I found an empty farmhouse. I think the owner had recently died. There were clothes and some food. Place hadn't been touched for weeks. I hid out there for a few days then went to find Thea. She told me I was a vampire and explained the little she knew about what I was, which wasn't much. It was enough to keep me out of trouble. We got somewhere together away from people. I didn't want to risk being too close in case... well, I didn't understand myself enough to risk that.'

He rests his head against the wall and focuses on his clasped hands. Nix leaves him alone with his thoughts. She can't imagine what it would have been like to wake up, alone, in the middle of nowhere and then to discover you had fangs and a thirst for blood. He must have been terrified.

'What happened when I went missing?'

'You were on patrol with Davyn and Shep,' Nix says. 'You came across a young vampire being chased by the Order. They're the vampires trying to wipe out anything with a hint of human in them. You got ahead of the group and ambushed them. The young vampire managed to break away but one of the Order went after him while the others split up. You ordered Davyn and Shep to get the others while you went after the young and the last Order fighter.'

She stops talking and looks away from his face. 'Davyn took care of his targets first then came back to help you. He found the young unconscious in an alley with the male dead beside him but there was no sign of you. Shep and Davyn called it in, and we all went out searching. We searched for hours but you had just vanished.'

'So there must have been more fighters there than we initially thought. If we took them all out who got to me?'

Nix is strangely comforted by the fact he said 'we'. Does that mean he's accepting this was his life? 'Unless our intel was wrong. Maybe additional support was called in when they realised there were three Blackjacks in their way. Anyway, that was the last we saw or heard of you. We targeted the True Order of course. We assumed they had you, but every lead turned to a dead end. Usually they'd gloat when they purify the race, but no one was owning up to taking you.

'It's like you had vanished off the face of the planet. One month went by, then six, then a year. We kept looking, always hoping we'd find some clue or hint at what happened to you but... nothing. Until you appear out of nowhere and stab Shep.'

He presses a fist to his forehead as if trying to push the memories out. 'Nothing sounds familiar. It's like you're talking about a stranger. Shouldn't some of these things be triggering a memory? Shouldn't something make sense?'

'There's no rhyme or reason when it comes to the brain, buddy,' Fletch says. 'I hoped something would trigger a memory too. Don't be too hard on yourself. It may just take time.' Fletch gets up and stops in front of Court. 'Listen, I'll do my best to help you, Court, but as of right now, I haven't got the first clue why your memory is gone.'

'There is something you can answer for me.'

'Of course,' Nix replies, suddenly feeling a little uneasy.

'Who's Thea?'

Fletch and Nix glance at each other then back at him. 'I'm not following you,' Fletch says.

'Stop fucking with me. I know there's a hell of a lot going on here I don't understand, but I know one thing. You all recognised me. No one recognised her. If I was one of the Blackjacks, I'm guessing you'd have met my sister at some stage. From what she tells me I saw her regularly before I vanished. So, like I said, who's Thea?'

Nix sighs as she lowers onto the edge of the desk. 'We're not a close-knit bunch on a personal level, but you never mentioned a sister to any of us.'

'She's said I can take a blood sample,' Fletch says. 'I'll run it and see if anything shows up.'

Court rubs his hand over his beard. 'This is fucking unreal.' He shakes his head and curses loudly. 'She must believe she's my sister. I've been in her head. I'd know if she was lying or hiding something.'

'Did she introduce herself to you or was it the other way around?' Nix asks.

Court rubs a hand over his face again. 'Fuck. It was me. She told me I showed up out of the blue and had paperwork to prove I'm her brother. '

Nix takes his arms in her hands and squeezes. 'Hey. Look at me.'

He slowly lifts his head and hits her with his hypnotic eyes. Her throat instantly dries, and she has to swallow before she speaks. 'We will figure this out. I promise. Whoever Thea is, she's safe and has no access to anything sensitive. We're keeping an eye on her.'

'How do I know you're not part of what happened? How do I know this isn't some elaborate act you're putting on to trap me?'

'You were in my mind too. You know you can trust us.'

'I don't know what I'm reading when I do that. Do you not get it? I can't trust anything. Since I woke up in the forest, everything I've discovered has been like a blow to the gut. It's all so incredible. Am I supposed to just nod, smile and go along with whatever I'm told?'

'Of course not. I—'

He takes his t-shirt from the end of the bed. 'Can you run the test on Thea and let me know who the hell she is?'

'It's next on my list,' Fletch says as Court leaves, slamming the door behind him.

Fletch grimaces at Nix. 'Well, that was fun.'

Nix smiles weakly and looks at the closed door. This is getting further and further from anything resembling a happy reunion.

Nix lifts her head towards the spray and closes her eyes. The hot water relaxes her stiff muscles as she rolls her shoulders. She tries to tell herself the water running down her face is from the shower and not tears. She'd believe the story if the tears hadn't started as soon as she got back to her room. She curses herself and turns off the water.

Nix wraps a thick towel around herself and takes the hairbrush from the sink. She roughly pulls the brush through her thick hair then stops when she catches her reflection in the mirror. Black rings surround two bloodshot eyes - eyes which are still releasing tears faster than she can stop them. She splashes cold water on her face and takes a deep breath as she faces herself again. Yeah, that did fuck all.

Nix throws the brush in the sink and pads back to her room. Before she can stop herself, she opens the top drawer of her bedside table and pulls out a small wooden box. Buried at the bottom is a photo. She slowly takes it out of the box and stares at the happy couple as she lowers on to the edge of her bed.

Referring to them as being in a relationship was pushing it - she knows that, but, as much as she wants to deny it, there was something between them. She had fought the attraction to Court for years. Since Ethan first brought him to meet her as a possible new recruit, he hadn't left her thoughts. He'd always been stunning. The first smile he directed at her had won her over in every possible way.

She should have listened to her own keep the hell away from him order - instead she had kissed him. It was a foolish, stupid thing to do, but it had happened. She never thought he'd return the kiss or that they'd end up in bed together... more than once.

The fierce fighter demanded attention when out in the field. He was lethal, his fighting style cool-headed, meticulous, and controlled. That applied to their time alone too. He took control, driving her over the edge on his terms and she couldn't get enough. She was in charge of the Blackjacks, but was more than happy to relinquish all control when it came to Court.

Two short weeks and, as irrational as it sounds, she fell for him. And he felt the same. An hour before she sent him out on patrol for the last time, he told her he loved her. He had kissed her and said those three words - then vanished, taking her heart with him. With their relationship still a secret, she had no one to talk to. No one to help her deal with the overpowering, all-consuming loss that was with her every single minute of the day since he'd gone missing. So she had thrown herself in to her work. If not in the training room, she was helping Ethan search through data or searching their databases, hoping to find more suitable recruits. Being alone in her bed, in her room, brought back memories of the hours she spent here with Court.

She groans to herself when her phone rings. It's going to be bad news. She just knows it. 'Yeah?'

'Hey, Boss. It's Fletch. I got the blood work back from Thea and Court. You should come down here.'

'Give me ten minutes.'

She lowers her phone to the bed and stares at the ceiling. Fletch wouldn't have called her to his lab unless it was bad news. She places the photo back in its hiding place and closes the drawer.

~

Thea settles on the leather couch in the large sitting room. The rest of the Blackjacks are relaxing. Some are watching *Die Hard* on TV while others drink, eat, and imitate the action scenes on the screen. She didn't think she'd feel comfortable in the middle of a group of warriors like this, but she does. Somehow, knowing that they are all like Court, makes her feel at home. Maybe it's that fact that there are others out there for Court to talk to and that he's no longer alone and thinking he's a freak.

She takes another spoonful of her ice cream and closes her eyes as the smooth, strawberry sorbet glides down her throat. The chicken salad had been devoured along with a crusty roll and a cold beer. It might as well have been a three course meal in a gourmet restaurant. To save on money, Court and Thea had stuck to tinned food for the last few months. Beans on toast was getting a little boring.

She digs her spoon in the large bowl of strawberry ice cream and smiles when Bastian and Willow get up to show everyone how they would have performed that last fight scene. Their tumbles are interrupted when Shep and Fallon arrive.

Bastian sits on the arm of the couch, offering the seat to the two injured comrades. 'Fletch know you two have escaped?'

Shep lowers onto the cushion, his hand pressed to his side. 'Ha, ha. We got out early on good behaviour.'

Willow sits beside her brother and rests her head on his shoulder. 'You okay?'

He kisses the top of her head. 'I'm good, Wills. Takes more than a knife to slow me down.'

Thea quietly watches the interaction. She may have only been here for a few hours, but so far she really likes these vampires. They may look seriously intimidating, but they're just like herself and Court.

She licks her spoon clean, and her eyes travel from Shep to Davyn, sitting alone in the corner. While the rest of the group chatted and argued about different aspects of the programme, Davyn didn't say a word. For over an hour he had just stared at the screen with no emotion on his face. He didn't look angry, hostile, or sad. He was just there - in body at least. It was clear from the lack of reaction that his mind was somewhere else entirely.

Without a word, he suddenly gets to his feet and leaves the room. She watches as his large body disappears from sight around the corner.

'You should steer clear.'

She jumps as Fallon's voice suddenly comes from right beside her. 'Sorry?'

Fallon nods towards the door. 'I mean it.'

Thea attempts an innocent look, but it falls short. 'I wasn't—'

Fallon laughs. 'Yes, you were. Davyn isn't someone you should be looking at like that.'

'Fallon's right,' Shep says. 'Guys got some serious issues.'

'More than you?' Willow asks.

Shep grins at his sister before looking back at Thea. 'He may have the bad boy vibe about him, but it goes right to his core. Like Fallon said, best steer clear.'

'Is he always so...'

'Chatty?' Shep finishes. 'Yep. Don't think he's a people person. He's been a moody git as long as I've known him.'

'How long is that?'

Shep scratches his jaw for a minute. 'I reckon it must be about twenty years or so. Think he joined just after Court. Barely said a thing to anyone since then. Scary good fighter. We were put through serious training every day to bring us up to a certain level, but he arrived ready to go. Dread to think what he got up to before he came here. He's got a reputation for killing anyone he feeds from.'

'Seriously?'

Shep nods. 'Who knows. I've heard some interesting things about Nix too. When you head into your second century of life, you pick up a rumour or two. Who the fuck knows what's fact?'

'Well, just for the record,' Fallon says as she gets to her feet and stretches. 'Dav has never put a foot wrong with any of us. Rumours need to be ignored until they become fact. I'm beat. Night all.'

Bastian sits beside Willow, then moves when Shep growls at him. 'Seriously, Shep. He was just sitting.'

'Yeah, and I know what he's like.'

Bastian snorts. 'Pot and kettle situation, buddy.'

'Don't you buddy me when you're sliding up to my sister.'

Willow gets up and flings a cushion at Shep's face. 'You and I are going to have a serious scrap one day, Shepherd. I'm not a kid and I certainly don't need you looking after me. He was just sitting.'

'For now. And don't call me that.'

'Lay off and I'll think about it, Shepherd.' Willow glares at her brother before saying goodnight to Thea and storming up the stairs.

'Good one,' Bastian mutters as he glowers at the TV.

'I'm not going to apologise for being protective. It's my job.'

Thea shuffles forward in her seat wondering why she is even considering getting involved. 'Speaking from experience, you can still look out for her while keeping your distance.' She raises her hands in surrender. 'I'm just saying.'

'Like I said, it's my job.' Shep smirks, easing the tension. 'Sorry. Great first impression I'm making.' He scratches his ruffled hair and gestures to the door. 'She's all I got. Well, apart from these numskulls.' Bastian smiles sarcastically at him before looking back at the TV. 'I go a little crazy when I think about all that can go wrong out in the field. Guess I need to ease off a little.'

'I'm sure she'd appreciate it. Believe me, it's great having someone watching your back, but we grow up.'

Shep nods and takes a swig of his beer. 'That's the problem. Didn't see her joining this fight though. We heal fast, but I don't want her to get a fucking scratch.'

'You can't control that,' Bastian says.

'I can lock her in her room.'

Bastian snorts. 'Yeah. I'd like to see you try. She's training every single day. She's pretty damn good, Shep. You know she is. You've just got to let her prove herself with us.'

'Whatever you say.' He gets up and stretches. 'I'm heading out. Don't wait up.' He smirks and winks at Thea then heads down the corridor towards the garage.

'Sorry about him. Shep... he's...' Bastian frowns then shrugs. 'Who knows. So, how are you doing with all this?' he asks, looking around the impressive room.

Thea tucks her legs under her. 'Okay, I guess. I don't think it's fully registered that I'm in a house full of vampires. It was hard enough accepting what Court is. This is... wow.'

Bastian laughs. 'I get that. I know there are more questions than answers right now, but we are all family here, Thea. We'll help you and Court as much as we can. You can trust us.'

'Thank you. I mean that. It's Court I'm worried about more than me. This thing with his memory is making everything so much harder for everyone.'

'Day by day, I guess. Hopefully being here will trigger something.'

He looks back to the TV and shuffles down the chair to rest his feet on the coffee table. Thea tries not to stare at him, but he's not someone easily ignored. It's his eyes that capture her the most. There doesn't seem to be such a thing as single-coloured eyes in the vampire world. Bastian's light brown eyes have changed colour countless times since she met him, moving from gold to chocolate.

There is something about him that confuses her greatly. Both of his arms are covered with heavy black tattoos. She can barely see any skin left uncovered. The marks extend from under the sleeves of his t-shirt to the back of both hands. While the overall appearance didn't detract from him, when she looked at the marks closely, there's something sinister about them. Skulls, knives, and horned demons are scattered through the design. There are other images too, but she can't make them out.

She focuses on the TV again before he notices her staring at him. His appearance and the dark, slightly unsettling images on his arms don't match. She has no intention asking him about them. Whatever his backstory is, she's not so sure she wants to hear it.

Court opens the door to his room and steps aside to let Nix and Fletch in. He's barely slept the last few hours. He'd replayed every single moment since Thea entered his thoughts for the first time. He remembers waking up in the forest and her name coming to him. He knew without a doubt he needed to find her. As soon as he got himself sorted, he spent hours in libraries searching the web for Thea Adams. Why would he search for her unless she meant something to him? Why would she play along with the whole brother and sister thing if it wasn't true? He needs to know what the hell is going on with Thea. All the possibilities are driving him crazy.

'Well?' he asks before either of them can say anything.

'Have a seat,' Fletch says.

'I don't want to have a fucking seat. Did you get the results?'

Fletch and Nix look at each other, deciding who was going to draw the short straw.

'Just tell me!

'She's your daughter.'

Nix's words barely register with him. Time stopped when the word 'daughter' came out of her mouth. Thea. His daughter? He walks to the window and leans on the sill. He focuses on the fountain in the centre of the large grass courtyard in the middle of the compound. It can't be true. He'd know if he had a daughter. Wouldn't he? He squeezes his eyes shut and rests his forehead against the glass.

When he woke up in the forest, he clearly remembers thinking of her. He wanted to find his sister. He beats his head against the window and clenches his fists. Could he have remembered wrong? No. He can't have. His first memory - his first thought - had been of Thea. But why did he think she was his sister?

'We should leave you alone for a few minutes,' Nix mutters from behind him.

'No.' He spins to face her. 'You can't just drop that on me and walk away. You said you've known me for years. You must have known I had a daughter.'

'No. You never mentioned a daughter to us.'

'Why not?'

'We have no idea. Maybe you were keeping her a secret to protect her. What we do is not without risk. Shep is unbelievably protective over his sister, Willow. It puts a strain on him when she goes out with us. I know he'd prefer she was safe and far from this life.'

'Why the hell did I think she was my sister?'

Fletch stands up and leaves the room without a word. Nix blows out a long breath as she settles in the chair against the far wall. 'I'm no expert, but I can only assume that memory must have been distorted because that's what you told Thea. It might just have stuck out as the truth when you remembered her. Like I said, I'm no expert. We're all just guessing at the moment. '

Court clenches his fists again, cursing whatever had taken his memory. 'Is she human or a vampire?'

'From what we can tell she's human. The fact her father is a vampire means she could change, but there's no set rules. Without knowing if her mother was human or vampire we can't say for sure if she'll transition. It's kind of like puberty. It hits different people at different stages. If she is going to change it would probably be before she's thirty. Then again, there is a chance she won't change at all.'

He slumps back onto the seat and drapes his arms over his knees. He never even thought about who Thea's mother could be. If the Blackjacks don't know anything about Thea or her mother, he's at a dead end. Why did he not raise her himself? Why had he decided to reunite with her? Why had he told her he's her brother? Where the hell had he got the paperwork from? He may not remember any of it, but he knows he must have done what he did for a reason. Doesn't help him in the slightest. Until his memory comes back, he won't have the answers.

'Are you okay?'

He looks over at her and smiles. 'I've got a daughter. I'd prefer if I remembered that small fact without the help of a blood test, but yeah, I'm okay, I guess. I mean it's a good thing, right?' Court closes his eyes and rubs a hand against his forehead. 'She has no idea about any of this. She would have said something to me if she did. What the hell do I tell her?'

'You don't need to make any rash decisions. Take time to get used to it yourself first. You have a lot to get your head around.'

'You think?' He taps his fingers against the side of his head, as if trying to knock some of the memories out. 'It's all fucked up in here. I can't explain it. Every now and again I feel like something is familiar, but as soon as I try to focus on it, it's gone. It's so frustrating. What else have they taken from me, Nix? Thea, the Blackjacks, what I am... they took it all and I need to know why.'

Nix takes his hands in hers and looks in his eyes. He looks down at her hands and something tries to break through the barrier between him and his memories. Talk about another familiar thing to add to his list. She looks up at him and the familiar feeling jumps up a level.

'I better let you get some rest.' She squeezes his hands and stands up. 'Thea is safe. The compound is secure. She can't go anywhere, and I give you my word, no one will talk to her about this until you've had a chance to speak to her yourself.'

'Thanks.' He breathes a sigh of relief when he hears the door closing behind Nix. He wanders to the bathroom and stares at his reflection. 'You've got a daughter.' He hears the words again, but they still don't sink in. 'Damn it, Court. Remember!'

He shouts and slams his forehead against the mirror, shattering the glass and making a mess of his head at the same time. He ignores the blood working its way down his forehead, ignores the glass sticking out of his skin, and closes his eyes. Even though he's learnt more about himself in the last few hours than he has over the last year, he feels lost. How the hell is he going to tell Thea about this?

Nix sits at the head of the table and looks at each fighter in turn. She manages to hide her surprise when she sees Davyn in his seat. He's never turned up for a meeting on time. Court's return to the fold has clearly hit each member of the group.

'Fletch, you're up first.'

'Cheers. Well, I've given our buddy a thorough going over. He's given me permission to discuss the details I found. To cut a long story short - I haven't got the first clue why he can't remember us. He knows who he is, but not what he is. He remembers how to fight, but nothing about being a Blackjack. It doesn't seem natural. Now I know he could have blocked out whatever happened to him. If it was a traumatic experience, which all this evidence is strongly pointing towards, Court's brain may just have gone into coping mode and locked the memories away.'

'But...' Nix prompts.

'But I'm leaning towards an artificial reason for his memory loss.'

'But why would someone take his memory, or even want to take it?' Bastian asks.

'I dunno to be honest. Maybe they didn't want him to remember what they were doing. Or maybe they didn't want him to recognise them or be able to point them out. Maybe it was just about keeping him docile and confused. I really can't say, but I'm not liking where my own brain is going with this.'

'How the fuck do you take someone's memory?' Shep asks.

'Still working on that part. Physically, apart from a few new fractures to his ribs and leg, I can't find any reason for his amnesia. This isn't going to be a quick fix I'm afraid.'

Fallon leans forward, resting her arms on the table. 'Being here hasn't jogged his memory?'

Nix shakes her head. 'Nothing is coming back. The compound, his room, all of us... it's like he's seeing it all for the first time.' She slides a photograph onto the table and transfers the image to the screen behind her. 'This tattoo is on his back.'

'That's Prime writing,' Bastian says, looking as confused as the rest of them.

'It translates to Level One Donor.'

'Oh that sounds like all kinds of bad,' Shep says.

'Blood donor?' Fallon suggests.

Nix shrugs. 'I dread to think.'

Willow puts up her hand and Shep groans. 'You're not at school, Wills. You can just ask.'

She smiles shyly and drops her hand. 'Sorry. I remember father mentioning something about underground blood banks a few years ago. Could it have something to do with that?'

Shep snorts. 'Don't put much stock in what our dear father says. You can tell he's lying when his fucking mouth moves.'

'Shep!'

'Don't look at me that way. Besides, those blood banks were selling

Prime blood at top prices. Court is a Hybrid.'

Nix clears her throat, trying to break up the impressive staring match Shep and Willow are having. 'At this stage anything is possible.' She leans back in her chair and prepares for the next piece of news. 'Okay, so Fletch checked out Thea. From the blood tests he ran it appears she's his daughter, not his sister.'

A stunned silence falls on the room until Fallon eventually speaks. 'Court's a dad? How did we not know?'

Nix shrugs. 'Unfortunately the only one who has the answer to that is Court. Seeing as he didn't remember who she was, I'm afraid we're all at a loss. Knowing Court I can only assume it was done to protect her.'

'So he remembers his sister— sorry, daughter, but not us?' Fallon slumps back in her chair. 'Hell of a way to offend a girl.'

'Don't take it personally, sis.' Fletch says. 'Memory is a funny thing. And considering his amnesia is more than likely a deliberate thing who the hell knows which memories were taken and which ones were left alone. We just have to go slow with him. One day at a time and move at his pace. The poor bloke has a lot to get his head around.'

'There's really nothing you can do to unlock the memories?' Bastian asks.

'I'm still running tests, but as of now, I've told you all I know. We've got one confused vampire and one confused doctor. Wish I could clear things up for both of us.'

'Hate to be negative about this,' Fallon says, 'but is there a chance he was put here intentionally?'

'You mean like a mole?' Bastian asks.

'Not too far-fetched for the Order to pull a stunt like that. Using one of our own to get in the door.'

'Another possibility,' Nix says. 'If that is the case, they won't learn much. He doesn't have access to anything that'll give us issues. Access is restricted to the living quarters and gym unless supervised. That goes for Thea too.'

Shep shakes his head. 'Nah. I'm not buying that one anyway. We've all known Court for decades - well apart from the mysterious daughter that none of us knew about. Fine, so scrap that part. Maybe we didn't know him as well as we thought, but messed up brain or not, he's not going to betray us. Out of every one of us sitting around this table, he was the most level.'

Nix smiles. 'I'm with you on that, but that doesn't mean we should rule anything out. Until we know what happened to him, anything's possible. He's eager to have answers as much as we are. The Court I just spoke to is really struggling with this whole situation. He woke up in the middle of the woods with a picture of Thea in his head and no idea what he is. I can't imagine what that would be like.'

She rubs her forehead, wanting nothing more than to have a long soak in the bath and a few glasses of wine. The whirlwind of emotions she's experiencing are slowly beating her down. She should have known that Court coming back would never be as easy as she had wished for over and over again. It's like someone is playing a cruel trick on her, teasing her with glimpses of what she had for a brief moment in time, but not letting her close enough to experience it again.

'In the meantime, we need to go through everything we already know. Shep, I want you on the system if you're up to it. See if you can find any mention of a level one donor and this tattoo.'

Shep nods. 'Sure, Boss.'

'Fallon, can you help your brother on the medical side? I want all Court's scans and x-rays checked again in case we missed anything. I know you're thorough, Fletch, but I want to be sure. Send the files to Ethan too. Davyn, you and I will go back to where they were staying. See if we can find anything that can help. A map with a great big X marking the spot where he woke up would be perfect. Willow and Bas, have a chat with some of our contacts. Someone might have heard something that will help.'

'Got it,' Bastian replies while Davyn merely nods.

'Anything else?' she asks the group. One by one they shake their heads. 'Dismissed.'

Shep doesn't make a move to leave, waiting until everyone else is gone before he speaks. 'We've got a problem, Boss. Didn't want to flag it with the others until I checked with you.'

'What is it?'

'While I was putting my feet up recovering from my near-death experience, I did a little digging. From what I can make out, I wasn't the only one curious about our returned comrade.'

'How far does the digging go?'

Shep shrugs. 'Hard to say. I've passed what I found to Ethan to check. It looks like finances, rental agreement, local cameras for a start.'

'That's not unusual. The Order has done that before.'

'Yeah, but not by searching a name.'

'What do you mean?'

Shep leans back in the chair and crosses his arms. 'They targeted Court. There were feelers out for him specifically. Our boy was smart though. Don't know if he had no choice or it was a conscious move, but he hasn't left a paperwork trail.'

'So how did they find him?'

'Same way we did. Guy jumps five vampires in an alley it's going to attract attention. I've checked out his mysterious sister slash daughter slash whoever the fuck she is - I can't keep track. Everything was in her name, but from what I can make out, they don't know about her.'

'They will now. When we took her out of the apartment with Court, they'll have her on the radar too.'

'Doesn't make a difference now with them both being here, but the signs are all there, Boss. Someone wants our boy back.'

'Or they don't want him to talk. Okay. I'll have a chat with Ethan about this. Thanks, Shep. Are you okay? Your side, I mean.'

He grins widely. 'That scratch? Nah, I'm fine.'

'Really? Cause you were making enough damn noise about it at the time.'

'I'll put that down to the whole Court being back from the dead thing.' He smirks again and salutes. 'I'll leave you to it. Shout if you need anything else.' He heads down the corridor and around the corner.

She'll never fully understand him. He's like two sides to an incredibly complex puzzle. Since Court disappeared, Shep had stepped up to help Nix lead the team. He'd been a rock over the months... well, most of the time. There was something she couldn't quite put her finger on when it came to Shep though. He regularly uses jokes and light-heartedness to diffuse situations, but she knows without a doubt it's a defence mechanism.

He may joke and take the piss at the worst possible times, but it very rarely reaches his eyes. He grins and smirks and laughs, but his eyes don't. She only noticed it recently as she worked closer with him. She had broached the subject with his sister, but Willow and Shep had been raised away from each other. He completely adored his sister, but like the others, she knew little about him. Apart from a historically heated argument with Shep and his father, Willow knew nothing else.

Whatever happened between them was so much more than an argument. God knows she's had enough of them with Shep over the years. No, whatever had happened took a little of Shep with it. Perhaps it was also the reason for the line of burn marks up each of his sides that he desperately tries to hide.

She'll just add it to the list of issues she'll have to deal with sooner or later. First she needed to find out what exactly is going on with Court.

Nix leans against the bonnet of Davyn's car and stares up at the ruined building. The Order didn't hold back. Not content with coming after Court, they made sure he had nowhere to go back to. The fire had engulfed the top floor of the apartment. Whether the Order had controlled the blaze, or the human firefighters took care of it, Nix doesn't know. There's no cordon around the premises so she can only assume the Order set the blaze then extinguished it once they were sure everything Court and Thea owned was destroyed.

Coming back here had been a long shot at best, but at least it got her out of the house and away from him. She could have sent any of the other members of the team but insisted she make the journey personally. Assigning Davyn to accompany her had been a strategic move too. He wouldn't be interested in small talk and that suited her just fine.

The journey had been made in complete silence, which seemed like the perfect plan initially. After half an hour, she realised the silence gave her nothing to distract her mind from Court. Impressive backfire on her part. Instead of escaping to blissful silence, she wallowed in miserable regret, self-pity, and a helpful dose of reliving memories of being in bed with Court. Yeah, that one was especially welcome.

Thankfully, her companion either didn't notice the fact she was having a serious internal battle, or he didn't care. Knowing Dav it was probably the latter.

Even now her head is back in the compound with Court instead of here. Time to do her job and stop acting like a new recruit on her first day. She tears off her jacket and dumps it on the bonnet. 'I'm going up to have a look. You want a lift?'

He shakes his head. 'I'll take the stairs.'

Dav gracefully enters the building by kicking the door open. The place is a mess anyway. What's one more broken door on top of the smoking ruin above them? Nix releases her wings and lifts off the ground. She lands on the thick stone windowsill and crouches to look inside. She raises her gun as the door opens but lowers it when Dav steps inside. She drops onto the charred floor and examines what used to be Court and Thea's home. The landlord won't be renting out the flat again. The fire had done an effective job wiping any trace of the previous residents.

Davyn circles the crisped remains of the couch and takes the corridor to the bedrooms while Nix checks for anything that hasn't been burnt beyond recognition. Cupboards are hanging off the walls, whatever was inside no longer recognisable. The small fridge is a blackened lump in the corner, the doors also hanging open to show its ruined interior. The Order had searched the place before they torched it.

She hears crashing and banging from the bedroom and wanders in to see what Davyn's destroying. He has forced the door open to the furthest bedroom. 'Problem?'

'They left this way. Blocked the door and took off out the window.'

He tears the broken door from the wardrobe and pulls out a blackened mass. 'Nothing left to salvage. Fuckers destroyed everything.'

'Yeah. It's the same in the kitchen. Are you picking up anything?'

He shakes his head. 'Masked their scents with the fire. Don't get why they torched the place.'

'They probably did it to send us a message. Or just to be bastards.' She runs her gloved hand over what's left of the low desk against the far wall. 'I guess they weren't content enough to destroy his life. They had to make sure they did a thorough job.'

'They didn't destroy his life.'

Nix turns to look up at Davyn. His green eyes are looking straight at her. He doesn't usually look anyone in the eye and it's a little unsettling. 'Sorry?'

'He's alive. He still looks and acts like Court. He can still fight. It's just his memory that's fucked up.'

Trust Davyn to point out the obvious. 'Do you trust him?'

'If the Order wanted to infiltrate the Blackjacks, they'd send fresh blood, not someone we'd be watching like a hawk.'

He's right, and that gives her a little comfort. But only a little. 'There's nothing else here.' She pulls out her phone as Davyn leaves to check for anything she missed. 'Hi Ethan. We're at Court's place. It's been torched.'

'Thorough. Trust there's nothing that'll help?'

'Everything's gone. We're about to head back.'

'We? Should I ask?'

'I brought Davyn with me.'

Ethan laughs and that irritates her more than it should. 'Of course you did. Who else would you bring when you don't want to talk?'

'That's not the reason.'

'Of course not.'

'Goodbye, Ethan.'

Nix slips the phone back in her pocket and has one last look around the room. It's the only home Court can remember, and this has been taken from him too.

Court stops outside Thea's room and stares at the door. Standing outside the room isn't going to help get this conversation over with any sooner. He knocks and attempts his best smile when she opens the door 'Hey. Can I come in?'

Thea smiles at Court and steps aside. 'Everything okay? You look like shit. What happened to your head?'

'I slipped in the bathroom. It's fine.' Court smiles, knowing full well it hasn't convinced her of anything. The last three hours had been spent sitting on the edge of his bed in the room he doesn't remember wondering how the hell he was going to tell Thea she's actually his daughter. A daughter he doesn't remember instead of a sister he doesn't remember.

Before meeting the Blackjacks, he thought his life was as fucked up as it could get. Seems fate wasn't done with him yet. What else is buried in his past waiting to pull the rug out from under his feet again and again? It's ridiculous so much shit can land on one person in such a short space of time. He must have really pissed someone off in a past life. If vampires even have past lives.

He crosses the vast bedroom and sits on the overstuffed couch under the window. Night has settled in, the moon casting its glow over the gardens between the house and the imposing wall surrounding it. Thea lowers onto the seat beside him, hugging a cushion to her chest. 'Okay. You're freaking me out now. What's happened?'

He licks his lips and looks at the landscape artwork hanging on the wall opposite him, hoping a script will appear. Some well planned, perfectly articulated speech that will answer all her questions without messing her up more than he already has. No such luck. Whatever happens in the next few minutes, their relationship will change forever. Whether she takes the news well or not, their brother-sister bond will disintegrate, an unfamiliar father-daughter manifestation taking its place.

He'd only just become accustomed to what they had between them. Thea being his sister is the only true memory he had when he woke up. That lie has damaged him more than losing his memory had. It's like someone has removed true north from his internal compass. Without that one truth to ground him, he feels lost and more alone than ever.

He looks down as her delicate hand grasps his, squeezing it. 'Whatever it is, we'll deal with it. Talk to me, Court.'

'Fletch got the results back from your blood test.'

Her hand goes rigid on his. 'I'm a vampire?'

He smiles and shakes his head. That would probably have been a better result. 'You're human. Your blood does have some vampire traits, but he doesn't think you're going to change.' He takes a deep breath. She's given him an opening he has to take. 'It's like that because your father... your father...'

'Who's our father?'

'No, Thea. I'm... It's me. According to the test I'm your father.'

His eyes stay on her hand, still resting on his. It's cowardly and weak but he can't bring himself to look at her face. He doesn't want to watch as she pulls away from him.

The painful silence drags on, each torturous second adding more distance between him and the one person he would give his life for. Then it happens. Along with any chance of getting through this without losing her, her hand disappears from his field of vision.

Her breath hitches and she swallows a couple of times before speaking. 'How? How is that possible? You're my brother.'

Still keeping his eyes from her face he clasps his hands together. 'I don't know why we thought we were brother and sister.'

'I thought that because that's what you told me.'

'Yeah. I know. I'm presuming I knew the truth, but I honestly don't know for sure. Nix and the others... they didn't know I had— have a daughter. I can only guess I kept you a secret for a reason, but I don't remember why, Thea.'

The couch moves as she gets up, putting more distance between them. 'How can you not remember? You found me and showed me your file. Was that all fabricated?'

'I don't know. I...' He scrubs his hands over his face and curses. 'I don't know.'

'You could have told me the truth from the start. I would have been fine with that. Why did you lie?'

He looks up at her and his skin turns cold. Tears are pouring from her eyes, but they're not tears of sorrow. She's furious and confused and it's one hundred percent directed at him. 'I wish I knew, but I'm as confused as you are. I wish I could tell you what happened. I wish I could tell you why I told you I'm your brother. But more than anything I wish I could make this right. I don't want to lose you, Thea. I don't give a damn about any of the Blackjack stuff. I couldn't care less if I never find out what happened to my memory. I just want you and me to—'

'To what? Can you please go now?'

'Thea, please. I can't leave you like this.'

'I just need to be by myself for a bit, okay.' She backs into the bathroom, locking the door firmly behind her, killing any chance of fixing this before the damage takes hold. He may have found a part of his old life with the Blackjacks, but he has a horrible feeling it might just have cost him Thea.

Nix glances up from her screen as someone knocks on her office door. 'Come in.'

Ethan shuts the door behind him and sits on the chair opposite Nix. 'Fletch told me about Thea. This puzzle is getting more complicated by the minute.'

'At least we have an answer to that part of the puzzle. I know it will take them time to get used to the idea, but the True Order aren't involved with her. That's one thing I guess.'

'Very true.' Ethan sits down and crosses his legs. 'So…'

'So?'

'How are you?'

'I'm up to my neck in reports. I don't really have time for a catch up.'

'Okay, so what's going on, Nix?'

She sits back and crosses her arms. 'Ethan, I mean it. Say your piece and let me get on with my work.'

'He's been back two days, right?'

'Who?'

Ethan laughs at that and she can't really blame him. 'Seriously, Nix?'

'Yes. Court's been back for two days. And?'

'So why haven't you told him about the two of you?'

She stares at Ethan in stunned silence for a few seconds too long. 'How exactly would you suggest I bring that up? He's just found out he has an adult daughter. Do you not think he's got enough to get his head around without adding a relationship with his boss to the mix?'

'I understand all that, but he needs the facts, Nix. He's been told about Thea. He knows about the Blackjacks. Why not about you two?'

Nix lowers her gaze to her desk and sighs. 'To be honest, Ethan, I'm not sure that's such a good idea. He doesn't know and maybe it's best it stays that way.'

'Best for who?'

'Someone took Court. They're still out there. They're still trying to abduct vampires. Now isn't the time to rekindle whatever we had. All it will do is complicate an already painfully complicated situation. I need to stay focused so I don't lose another member of my team to these bastards. That's the priority.'

'Do you still have feelings for him?'

'Please drop the subject.'

'No. Do you still have feelings for Court?'

'Why does that matter?'

'Because we're friends, Nix.'

She sighs and slumps back in her chair. 'I love him, Ethan. I thought I was dealing with it, but seeing him again... I still love him.'

'Then stop being the leader of the Blackjacks for one minute and just be Nix. Tell Court that you love him. Loving him isn't going to put a target on the team. There's already one of those on each of us. Has been for years. You really should tell him.'

She laughs harshly and rubs her forehead. 'It's not that simple. He has no memory, Ethan. Nothing. The Court that came back… that's not our Court. But he is.' She scrunches her fists in her hair, resisting the urge to scream in frustration. 'This is the most infuriating situation I could have imagined. I thought I was handling this better. I guess I failed.'

'No, you didn't. You're coping brilliantly in a situation that must be a nightmare. Whatever is going on in his head, that's still Court. He's still in there.'

'You read Fletch's report. He may never get his memory back. We still don't know what they did to him. You know, I used to lie in bed and stare at the ceiling for hours. I'd play the entire situation out in my head. Court comes back, we'd lock ourselves away and make up for lost time. I had planned every single detail out, Ethan. Every. Single. Detail.' Her smile fades as the reality sinks in. 'But then this happens. Don't get me wrong, I can't tell you how happy I am to see him again, but…' She laughs to herself. 'It's a fucking cruel joke, Ethan. I desperately want him to remember me. I keep thinking that maybe tomorrow he'll wake up and suddenly remember what we had. What if he never remembers us?'

'Then you're back to my initial tell him advice.'

'Surely you can see how seriously fucked up the timing is. I can't do that to him. Not yet. I need my head to be focused on the group and fighting the True Order. I can't afford to let Court's miraculous second coming get in the way of that.'

'Wow, I almost believe you. Did you rehearse that?'

'I don't need you to believe me. I just need you to drop the matter and let me do my job. Which right now involves finding out exactly what the True Order is up to and if they were behind all this.'

Ethan chews his bottom lip as he stares at her. Hidden by the desk, Nix digs her fingers in her legs, hoping he buys her 'everything is fine' routine. It's not a lie. Just a work in progress at the moment. More like a work needing serious progress.

If Ethan has any doubts about her ability to do her job, he could request she back away from this. She tries to keep the tears of panic from her eyes. If he forces her to stand down, she'll have nothing.

'I'm not suggesting you head off with Court on a romantic getaway. All I'm saying is that you both deserve the truth. Being in love with him doesn't make you less of a leader. You've given the Blackjacks everything you are since we started. You are allowed to have a life as well. The rest of the team do too... well, some of them. Don't think Fallon and Davyn are ones for socialising. Anyway, what I'm trying to say is that you and Court did nothing wrong. You fell in love. End of story. It's not the disaster you seem to think it is.'

'But it is. When one half of the couple doesn't remember what they had, it's a huge disaster. If I tell him I risk influencing his feelings. The last thing I want is for Court to be with me because he feels obliged. I'd rather we kept it to business than have something false. Now isn't the time to bring any of this up. Please leave it alone. I'm asking you as my friend to leave it alone.'

He grimaces but doesn't argue. 'Fine. But just for now.'

'So enough about me. How is your love life? Do your grandparents still think you're a respectable male?'

His face drops and Nix instantly regrets her words. She's angry at herself and the situation, not Ethan. 'I'm so sorry, Ethan. I shouldn't have said it like that. I'm frustrated and you got the brunt of it.'

He smiles sadly. 'It's the truth.' Ethan slumps back in the chair. 'I guess we're both lost causes on that front.'

'It doesn't have to be that way for you.'

He scoffs. 'Not so sure about that. If I tell my grandparents their only grandchild and heir to their name prefers males to females I'd be disowned. You know what vampire high society is like. Same sex couples are a no-no. My grandparents are so embedded in the hierarchy they can't see beyond it. If they knew I was gay and involved in setting up a rogue group of fighters I'd be ticking so many unacceptable boxes they might just implode.' He pauses and a smile grows on his face. 'That could be an option.'

Nix laughs at the suggestion. 'It's a little drastic.'

'Yeah, well so is dictating who people can and can't fall in love with. They're expecting me to settle down and marry an upstanding female and continue their very long and distinguished line. If I bring home a male, upstanding or not, I'd be disowned. Then I'd be broke and there'd be no Blackjacks.'

'Ethan—'

'I know what you're going to say. We just need a few more years, okay. Once I build up a buffer to keep us running, I can tell them to stuff their pomp and circumstance. I may even bring home a guy for them to meet. Test out my implosion theory.'

Nix doesn't push the topic. She's had this conversation with him before and he's adamant the Blackjacks are the priority. His family are at the top of the social ladder and that means so is he. Ethan is already on their wrong side by inheriting most of his mother's human genes. Which is something he has to hide in front of his overbearing grandmother.

She detests anything human and the fact her son bred with one never went down well. She loves Ethan... well, in her own way, but maturely decided to ignore the human side of him. Maybe she thought it would disappear if she didn't acknowledge it. If they ever manage to get the True Order under control Nix fully intends on dealing with the rigid aristocracy. Their time was coming to an end too. 'It's a conversation you're going to have to have sooner or later.'

'I'll go with later for now, thank you.'

'So I guess we'll both die old and alone.'

'Don't worry, we can keep each other company. Anyway, the reason for my visit wasn't just to stick my nose in your personal life. Since Court reappeared, we've run a few checks on missing vampires in the country.' He digs in the case at his feet and hands the file across the desk to Nix. She reads the number, frowns, then reads again. 'Is this right?'

Ethan nods slowly. 'Afraid so.'

'How did we miss forty-seven vampires going missing?'

'That number covers the whole of the UK. Not that it's an excuse. We've been tracking reported True Order removals... but these are different. The vampires I'm talking about have just vanished. Their family, friends... they assumed they moved or lost contact, or are hiding to avoid the Order.'

'Are you sure that's not what's happened? It's a bit of a stretch to think they were taken like Court.'

'I'd love to say I wasn't sure, but the numbers don't lie, Nix. These vampires, all of them male, are missing.'

'Have any of them shown up again?'

'We're looking but so far he's the only one we can find. There's nothing to say more haven't resurfaced. They could be lying low to avoid being taken again. I'll keep going and send over any more information I find.'

She doesn't look up as he leaves the room, closing the door behind him. Nix stares at the number on the file in her hands. Forty-seven is a terrifying number. Ethan is probably right. She can be with Court and run the Blackjacks, but not now. Not with this many Hybrid vampires missing. Finding out what's going on will have to take priority over her feelings for Court.

Court stares across the table at Fletch. 'They tried to what?'

Fletch makes a face and clears his throat. 'From what I can make out, someone tried to alter your DNA. There's something in Prime blood which makes it pretty damn lethal to Primes in large doses. It's like Russian Roulette for Primes. Too much and they get addicted, not enough and they could starve. It's part of the reason the old families decided to allow mixed mating. Anyway, you're not Prime, but your blood has some of the properties.'

'I'm assuming it didn't before I disappeared.'

'Nope. I may not know a lot about what happened to you, but I do know you were taken for your blood. There's no other reason. Your blood has been modified, but I don't know why. The problem is until we figure it out, might be best you don't feed any Hybrids. It's too strong for Hybrids, but not quite strong enough to sustain a Prime.'

'So what good am I to them?'

'I'm guessing they have some way to extract the parts they need and use this to feed a Prime without bringing on Blood Fever. To be honest, I'm making this up as I go.'

'Are you sure he's off limits to Hybrids?' Nix asks.

Fletch nods. 'As sure as I can be without trying it out on any volunteers, and no Shep, I am not looking for volunteers.'

Shep grunts as he lowers his hand.

'It would also explain the tattoo on your back.' Fletch pulls his chair closer to Court's. 'Listen, I know this is probably scary as hell.'

'You think? I've been genetically modified to be what... a vampire snack bar?'

Fletch grimaces. 'Would have used a slightly better description myself, but I guess that's accurate. I'm not going to lie to you. This is so far beyond my level of expertise. I'm going to have to get Ethan's guys involved. What I can say is that you are healthy, Court. Apologies for the way this is going to sound, but you were... looked after for the most part. Whatever they did to bring on these changes, they wanted to keep you alive.'

'Not sure that makes me feel better. Did whatever they do to me mess with my eyes or could I always get into heads and pull memories out?'

'What do you mean by pull memories out?' Fletch asks.

'I did it a few times to Thea. Not intentionally, but it happens when I'm tired or my own memories are trying to break through. But when I did use the fucked up skill on her I was able to go through her memories and make her relive them.' Court looks down at the table in front of him and shakes his head. 'It was horrible for her to go through.'

Fletch glances at Nix then back at Court. 'Well, that's a new one. This new addition could have something to do with whatever they did to you. Prime abilities are far more enhanced than Hybrids. Their pure blood combined with their wings - which kind of act like an amplifier - ramps up their senses and any other little tricks they can do. I'm guessing by enhancing the Prime alterations in your DNA, they've also ramped up your abilities. Your eyesight was scary good before and you could get in people's heads, which is always a fun party trick, but pulling memories out is a whole new trick.'

'Not quite a trick.'

'It could be,' Nix says. 'The problem at the moment is you don't have a clue how to use it. We don't even know its full capabilities.'

'Yeah, and that suits me just fine,' Court says. He has no interest in exploring his new ability in the slightest. 'What about my memory?'

Fletch sighs as he leans back in his chair. 'Ah, well that's still a bit of a mystery. Unless I know exactly what they did to you, I can't know if that was as a result of what they did or if it was intentional. We're not finished trying to figure all of this out, Court. Every piece of the puzzle helps bring us closer to whoever did this to you. There's no way we're backing down from this.'

'So why would you bother to go to all this trouble? Not you. I mean whoever did this. Can the Primes not feed each other? Why do they need to alter my blood so they have a food source?'

'Vampire blood is highly addictive,' Nix says, 'Addiction runs rife in the older generations. The more blood a vampire consumes the higher their chances of becoming addicted. The chances of becoming addicted increases tenfold for Primes. That's part of the reason they're a dying breed. Primes can't drink Prime blood. It's like a heroin addict taking a massive hit of pure heroin. But, drinking Hybrid blood doesn't give them everything they need to thrive, so they generally mix the two. It's only going to work for so long though. The addiction will hit eventually. What the Primes need is something less harmful than Prime blood, but with the same kick.'

'But what about all of you? Are you going to become addicted too?'

Nix shrugs. 'There's a chance, that's why we keep an eye on each other. We can all recognise the signs so we know when to pull back. We each know how much we can take without risk. We're all descended from Primes originally, but the connection is so weak we don't have the same issues they do. It's been bred out of us.'

'But what about me? Am I Prime or Hybrid?'

'You're Hybrid, Court. Absolutely.'

'So that's good?' He feels completely lost at the best of times, but this conversation is pushing him towards a whole new area of lost. He hears what they're saying, and he understands it. Doesn't mean it's sinking in or that he wants it to. It was difficult enough accepting he needed to consume blood to survive, but this is so much more fucked up. Now he's a blood bank for the original vampires. And that's not something he has any interest in being.

'You can drink from a Hybrid vampire, so yes, that's good,' Fletch says. 'But you're also going to be very enticing to our Prime friends, so no, that part's not good.'

Court smiles sarcastically. 'Great. Fucking perfect. Thanks!'

'Okay, try not to think about that part too much.' Fletch curses and slams his hand against the desk. The room of vampires look up at his outburst. Nix swivels her chair towards Fletch. 'Are you all right?'

'What? I'm sorry. I'm just a little... well a lot pissed off. I wish I knew what they were up to.'

'Maybe you should take some time off, Fletch You look exhausted.'

He shakes his head and tries to smooth his hair. 'No. This is serious. Forty-seven vampires haven't been as lucky as Court here. They're still missing. Or worse. Taking some time off isn't going to help them.'

Nix nods and looks around the table. They all look exhausted. 'Okay. Court, you mentioned a farm when you woke up.'

'Well, yeah, but I haven't got a clue where it was.'

Shep shrugs. 'Not a problem. We'll just work back from what you do remember. Sit down with me when we're done and I bet we can narrow down the area.'

'You really think there could be something there?'

'Maybe. Maybe not. But it could trigger something. Some memory of what happened. If you made it out on foot, we may even find where you were.'

'How are you all so calm about this?' Court asks. 'You've just found out someone did something to my blood. I'm like Frankenstein. You should all be freaking out.'

'Actually, you're Frankenstein's monster,' Shep says. 'Frankenstein was the doctor. What?' he asks when everyone glares at him. 'There's always time for factual accuracy.'

'Thank you, Shep. After your lesson, can you find some time to trawl the system? Look for any mention of a cure or control for blood fever.'

'Yeah, sure. Like that's not looking for a needle in a haystack.'

'You saying you can't handle it?' Fallon snarks.

Shep glares at Fallon and smiles showing his fangs. 'Don't you go worrying about me.'

'Okay,' Nix says. 'So let find this place Court went after he escaped. Hopefully something there will tell us what the hell we're dealing with.'

Thea opens her door and is surprised to see Fallon standing outside it. The tall, auburn-haired vampire intimidates her without having to say a word or do a thing. 'Hi.'

'You want to train?'

Thea blinks a few times unsure what to say. Fallon leans against the door frame and crosses her arms but doesn't say anything else.

'I'm sorry. Do I want to what?'

'Train. Your father is second command of the group. He's been missing for three years. Why do you think that is?'

'I don't know what you want me to say.'

Fallon takes a step inside the room and rests her hands on her hips. 'He's a target. We all are. I don't know who took him or why. But someone did. As his daughter you're under our protection. Each and every one of us would give our lives to protect you.'

'Fallon, I appreciate that but no one is going to come—'

'Court is one of the best trained fighters I've ever come up against. They managed to overpower him and take him. How exactly are you going to hold back a team of vampire fighters intent on taking or killing you when he couldn't?'

Thea's mouth drops open as Fallon's blunt words sink in. She's right. 'But I can't train with you. I wouldn't know where to start.'

Fallon smiles and Thea relaxes a little. The woman is a lot less terrifying when she smiles. 'That's why you need my help. You're human. The people you'll come up against more than likely won't be. That doesn't mean you should be at a disadvantage. And it doesn't mean you won't be able to put up one hell of a fight. Get changed.'

'What? Now?'

'Yes. Now.' She softens her stance a little and looks away for a moment. 'Between you and me, I'm doing this for selfish reasons. I want Court to stay. We all need Court to stay. If he thinks you're at risk he'll leave. That puts the Blackjacks at a disadvantage. Puts you and Court at risk too. No one wins. However, if you learn how to protect yourself, he'll be less inclined to want to bundle you away from all this. He stays and we all win.'

Thea has serious doubts about what Fallon is suggesting but can't fault her logic. Besides, it would be useful to be able to defend herself in this crazy new world. 'Okay. Give me a few minutes to get changed.'

~

Nix pauses to check her surroundings. Apart from the person she's here to meet, she can't sense anyone else in the vicinity. She opens the car door and slips inside, sinking into the plush leather seats of the Mercedes. The driver turns to face her, a crooked smile on his lined face.

'Phoenix.'

'Vincent. How've you been?'

He nods and purses his lips. 'So, so. And you? I hear good things about you and your... comrades. Quite impressive.'

Nix laughs. 'From what I remember you were quite vocal about how much of a scourge on the vampire world we are.'

Vincent chuckles softly. 'Times change, my dear. Our world is changing. I fear we must conform, or risk being left behind. So, how are your parents? Still fervently against your current profession?'

'They have no problem with the Blackjacks. They'd just prefer I wasn't putting myself on the firing line.'

Vincent smiles sympathetically at her. She's known Vincent for as long as she can remember. The Prime elder had been a close friend of her father's until the Blackjacks were created. Although less than thrilled about her leading the team, her father had been protective of his daughter. He had been quite vocal about the need for the Blackjacks at the detriment of too many close relationships. He had never forgiven Vincent for trying to dismantle the Blackjacks after they started. Nix hasn't either, but she's all out of other options. As a well-regarded Prime with fingers in many pies, she can't afford to alienate him.

'So, Phoenix. As much as I enjoy seeing you, why don't you ask what you've come here to ask.'

'We've heard rumours about vampires being taken off the streets.'

'Taken where?'

'That's why I'm here. I don't suppose you've heard anything?'

Vincent sucks in a breath. 'You know I can't discuss business dealings with you. It's more than my life is worth. And I mean that literally. I can't help you Phoenix. I'm truly sorry.'

'Don't give me that sorry bullshit, Vincent. You seriously can't condone vampires being kidnapped. A few of your grandchildren are Hybrids. What if they disappeared from school one day and were never seen again? You really going to come back with the same response.'

Vincent turns his head, and she swears he snarls at her. 'You're walking a very fine line, Phoenix.'

'And it's a line I intend to keep walking. We have reason to believe these vampires are being used to create something which could counteract The Fever.' It's a theory but worth throwing out to see what reaction she gets.

Vincent's breathing halts momentarily before he composes himself again. 'Can I ask how you came to that ridiculous conclusion?'

'Is it ridiculous?'

He remains silent for a good few minutes, but Nix doesn't make a move to leave the car. If he wanted her to go, he wouldn't have been shy about telling her. Eventually he licks his lips and smiles at her. 'Hypothetically.'

'Of course.'

'If this is indeed happening and males are being taken, to what end?'

'So it is just males. Interesting.'

His face hardens when he realises his slip up. 'Very well. I repeat my question, to what end?'

'Like I said, controlling symptoms brought on by The Fever.'

'Any other reason you can think of?'

'Is that not reason enough, Vincent? I'm fairly sure The Fever is still quite prevalent among Primes.'

'That it is. And while I agree being able to control that would be highly beneficial, what else could an altered vampire bring to the table - long term of course?'

'You're going to have to tell me.'

He sighs dramatically. 'If, hypothetically, a cure could be found, Prime numbers could increase. Being pure blood brings its own set of issues, as I'm sure you are aware. If The Fever was no longer an issue, the bloodlines could be reinforced again.'

Nix pauses, then she realises what he's talking about. 'You're trying to purify the bloodlines. Get rid of the need for Hybrids.'

His sickly-sweet smile is all the confirmation she needs. 'Imagine what this could mean for the race. We would be stronger than ever. There would be no such thing as males without wings. Balance would be restored.'

'Balance? Are you really saying someone is going to all this trouble so all males can fly?'

'Not as the main reason, no. But it would be a long term result. Why should you females have wings and the males suffer without.'

'I'd hardly call it suffering. I work with males who don't have wings. They're more than capable of handling themselves. Better than some Primes I know.'

'Perhaps, but the Blackjacks are the exception rather than the rule. I have no doubt most Prime males would fail the initial training process.'

'Why don't you send some volunteers my way and I'll see what they can do.'

He doesn't reply. He's not about to actively increase Blackjack numbers. Nix sits back and stares out the window. What Vincent is alluding to has just confused her even more. She understands the need to control Blood Fever. The method is far from something she agrees with, but the reasoning for attempting to find a cure is sound. Increasing Prime numbers while ensuring Hybrids are wiped out is an entirely different kettle of fish. One she is loath to think about. 'Would you think the two sides are working together or is one a side effect or the other?'

'A little of both perhaps. I would imagine the Blood Fever issue was the dominant one and the wings...' his voice trails away and his eyes narrow as he looks over at her. 'Have they been successful?'

'How would I know?'

'Phoenix.'

'Vincent, I'm working on rumours and speculation. I came to you for a little clarification not the other way around.'

He grunts but looks far from convinced.

'I don't suppose, hypothetically, you know who would be involved in something like this?'

'No.' His reply is firm and absolute. 'I cannot say more than I already have. What I can and will say however, is that you and your band of miscreants should steer clear of anything to do with this. I mean it, Nix. If you stick your noses where they don't belong, I will not be able to protect you.'

'I don't need protecting, especially by you. If you're involved in this, you're going to be the one that needs protecting.'

'How dare you!' Vincent spits back at her. 'Who do you think you are? You have no right to speak to someone of my station like that.'

'You're missing the point, Vincent. I'll all about vampires being equal. The fact you're a Prime doesn't determine how I treat you.'

His laugh grinds on Nix's nerves. 'I fear you underestimate your position in our world. You and your pesky team are on borrowed time.'

'Don't worry about us, Vincent. We'll give as good as we get.'

She opens the door and climbs out of the car. The urge to fly from Vincent is strong, but so is staying out of his line of sight. She ducks behind the bridge support and waits until his car disappears before she risks taking to the sky.

27

Thea wanders back down the corridor towards her room. The training session with Fallon had been gruelling but surprisingly productive. It helped to repeatedly hit something for a while. As she'd attacked the punch bag, she had repeated to herself, 'Court is your father' over and over in time to each swing of her fist. She lost count of how many times she had said it, but the words still didn't sink in.

She knows he's the same person. She knows she still loves him. None of that has changed. But for some reason knowing he's her father and that he had, for whatever reason, decided to lie about it, is pissing her off. He doesn't know why he did it. No one does. And that just adds to her frustration.

She stops at her door and rests her forehead against the smooth wood. Maybe after a shower and a good night's sleep, her head will be clearer.

Thea reaches for the door handle to her room, but stops when she hears music coming from the opposite corridor. Davyn and Shep's room are down there. She'd heard Shep in the kitchen talking to Gwen, the housekeeper, when she was on her way back from the pool so the music must be coming from Davyn's room.

Instead of ignoring it and going to her room, she moves towards the music and stops at the heavy door at the end of the adjoining corridor. She's not ignoring Fallon and Shep's warning to keep away from Davyn. Thea has always preferred to make her own mind up about people.

Davyn had done nothing but keep both her and Court safe when he was driving them from the apartment. But that's not the real reason she's here. The more people who warned her away from the fighter, the more she found her thoughts heading in completely the opposite direction.

Not that she was going to do anything about it. Thea was not exactly brimming over with confidence when it came to men, especially broody vampires. She had limited knowledge when it came to the vampire world. Court had told her a little before he disappeared, and she had picked up additional bits and pieces after living with him for the last year.

Controlling and managing the need for blood was a difficult battle. She had seen it first hand with Court. His temper would flare at the smallest thing, usually resulting in more than a few bloody knuckles from slamming his fists against any available wall. Perhaps Davyn has difficulty managing that need. Maybe that's why they warned her to keep away.

Then why was she standing alone outside his room? Probably not her best idea.

Instead of leaving, she stays where she is, listening to the music blaring through the heavy wood. She wants to knock, wants to talk to him, but can't do it. She curses her stupidity and turns away from the door, stopping when she notices it's slightly ajar. She takes a step closer and peers through the narrow crack to the dark bedroom beyond.

She gasps as Davyn steps out of the bathroom, a bottle of something in his hand. Apart from the pair of black leather trousers he was wearing earlier, his chest is delightfully bare. The intricate Celtic tattoos circling his arms stretch up to his shoulders and across the top of his chest.

He takes a long swig and shudders, then turns his back to the door. Thea gasps and slaps her hands over her mouth. His back is horribly scarred. Deep, badly healed, angry jagged lines criss-cross his upper back.

He takes another long drink then drops the empty bottle to the floor before he leans over and rests his hands on his bed.

Thea stumbles back in surprise as an enormous wing slides out of his back. Thea hadn't watched closely as Nix's wings had come out. It's a mesmerising process. Davyn's wing grows as it unfolds. The thick bones appear to slide in place, twisting and realigning until the wing reaches its final form.

Davyn fists his hands in the covers and curses loudly, his shout barely audible above the music. He twists the covers in his fists as he buries his face in the bed then releases an agonised scream as another wing tears out of him. The second wing is badly deformed - twisted and bent at the wrong angle. As with the first one, it tries to reform, but doesn't complete the process. Instead of reaching to the side, it stretches behind him. The webbed skin is torn and ripped away from the main wing bone, hanging in tatters down his back.

He leans heavily on the bed and stretches the undamaged wing. His bat like wings are smooth and sleek, the red webbing a contrast to the black skin covering the bones. He looks incredible. Even with the damaged wing, seeing him like this leaves her speechless. It hits her slower than it should. Davyn is a Prime.

No one mentioned that he's a Prime. Bastian had included Davyn when he told her the guys in the team are all mixed-breed vampires.

Does that mean no one on the team knows he's a Prime?

Thea steps back from the door and turns away. Not only is she invading his privacy, but she's also witnessed something he's kept from the people he shares his life with.

'What the hell are you doing here?' She turns around and meets his glowing green eyes. She stumbles back as he pulls the door open. Her clumsy escape down the corridor is no match for Davyn's speed. He wraps a thick arm around her waist and hauls her inside his room, slamming the door. One of the razor-sharp talons at the tip of his wing embeds itself in the wall over her head as his large body pins her against the wall. 'Why the fuck are you spying on me?'

His piercing green eyes glow as they stare down at her. 'I'm not—'

'Yes, you are.' He slams the talon in the wall with greater force. The thick black claw tears through the concrete like it's butter. 'Why?'

'I heard the music. I was just curious. I'm sorry. Really.'

'This is my room. My space. You have no fucking right to be here.'

'I know. I'm sorry.' She looks in his green eyes and instead of cowering and trying to get out of here as fast as possible, she continues to look up at him. He smells of leather, soap, and whiskey, and it's seriously intoxicating. His usually brushed back hair has fallen over his face and tickles her cheek as he leans over her, caging her with his large body.

Thea turns her attention from his face to the red and black wing creating a barrier between her and the door. She hadn't seen vampire wings this close. The red skin is scarred and torn in places even on the good wing. He slowly pulls the talon out of the wall and Thea stares as he stretches the wing before folding it neatly behind him.

'You get a good look or do you want me to turn around for you?'

In spite of the situation, Thea smiles. 'You've got an Irish accent.' It's probably not the smartest thing she could have said in the current situation, but it just popped out before she could rein it in. She's barely heard him say more than a few words at a time since she got here. It wasn't until he said a full sentence that she picked up on the accent.

'I'm Irish so yeah, I have an Irish accent. What the hell does that have to do with you spying on me?'

'Nothing. I just... I like it.'

He moves his wings again and Thea is transfixed. The sight of the two stunning wings is seriously adding to whatever irrational feelings she has for Davyn.

He folds his arms over his chest and stares down at her with a blank look on his face. 'You going to run back and tell the others about this?'

'That you're Irish?'

'They're figured that bit out a few years ago.' He leans closer exposing his large fangs as he sneers at her. 'I meant about my wings.'

'Do they not know?'

'My wings are my fucking business.'

'Yeah, but—'

'You've been here five minutes. What the fuck gives you the impression I give a damn about your opinion?'

She's beginning to see signs of the person she's been warned about. 'Nothing. You're right. It's none of my business.'

'Too fucking right.' He opens the door and steps aside to let her out. 'Forget you were here, and you'd better forget what you saw.'

She slips under his arm and steps outside. The warm air is a pleasant relief after Davyn's cold room. 'I'm not going to say anything. I promise.'

'That's a promise you'd do well to keep. Court may have been one of us years ago, but he's got a lot to do to prove himself again. I get a vote on whether he gets to stay with the Blackjacks. You need to mind your damn business. It's not a good idea to piss me off.'

She turns away, then stops a few steps from his room. 'Davyn?'

He stands in the doorway and looks at her. Then his eyes leave hers and slowly travel down her body. Thea licks her lips as the intensity of his glowing eyes sends her pulse racing. Davyn's lips part slightly and she catches a glimpse of the tips of his fangs. The image that's in front of her right at his moment will be burned in her mind for a long time. When he speaks it's more of a growl than his usual voice. 'What?'

She clears her throat and desperately tries to remember what she was going to say. Davyn rests both hands on the door frame above his head and waits for her to answer. 'Right. Yeah. Sorry. I was just going to say there's still some food left after dinner. You look like you could do with a good meal.'

Instead of responding, he pushes back from the door and slowly closes it in her face.

Court shouts and sits up in bed. It takes a few seconds for his enhanced night vision to kick in. He blinks and looks around the strange room. Remnants of his nightmare still assault him as he tries to steady his breathing and figure out where the hell he is. He rubs his eyes then realises Thea is missing. He scrambles across the wide expanse of his bed and places his feet on the thick carpet. After a few attempts, he finds the light switch. He instantly recognises his room in the Blackjack compound. Thea is no doubt in her own room next door.

He shivers as the nightmare fades to the back of his mind with the rest of his memories. His wrists ache as they always do after a nightmare. All he remembers is fighting to free himself... but from what he's still clueless. He slams his fist against the wall, cracking the plaster. Just his damn luck to lose his mind as well as losing Thea.

Court opens the wardrobe and finds some t-shirts and joggers for working out. Just what he needs to do right now. He dresses quickly and, after checking the basic hand drawn map Nix gave him, finds the training room without meeting anyone. He breathes a sigh of relief when he finds it empty. Old pals or not, he's not in the mood for a one-sided catch up with anyone.

He decides to head for the treadmill first. Pounding his problems into the track sounds pretty damn good right about now. He starts slow and builds to an impressive pace, focusing on the wall opposite as his feet carry him mile after mile, but no further from his problems.

Knowing this was his life years ago is hard to believe. One part of him accepts he is the fighter they say he is. He had managed to stand up to the vampires sent to capture him a few days ago. But it's the other part of him that's struggling. The part that's still coming to terms with the fact he's a vampire - let alone a warrior.

The compound, the weapons, the vehicles, this war with the True Order - he can't imagine ever getting used to it. He thinks back to their dramatic escape in Davyn's car. He'd held his own without getting Thea or himself killed. Was that down to dumb luck or past training coming out when he needed it? He picks up the pace, wiping sweat from his forehead with his arm. Putting him in the field could just endanger the others. It could endanger Nix.

He pumps his arms and pushes his legs harder. That woman is driving him crazy. Ever since he saw her, he's struggled to keep her out of his thoughts. She's his boss. Thinking of her like he has been would probably get his ass kicked from the group. Not that he's sure he wants his ass in the group in the first place.

Something about her has captured him and refuses to loosen its grip. She's without a doubt the most stunning woman he's ever seen. The thought of seeing her naked with those magnificent purple wings gets him hard. He closes his eyes and runs faster, hoping to kill his body's response before he needs to deal with it in private.

'Might want to take it easy buddy.'

Court stumbles as the voice disturbs his thoughts. He jumps to the side of the track and discretely looks down, but thankfully the interruption killed the mood. Shep smirks at him as he leans on the weight bench opposite the treadmill. 'Sorry. Do you want me to go?'

'No.'

With everything else that happened when he first met Shep, he hadn't realised how big the Blackjack is. He could easily have taken Court down without much effort when they met in the alley. The shock of seeing his lost teammate must have tipped the scales in Court's favour. He's got to be six foot six, with the kind of body it would take most guys decades of daily training to achieve. Both arms are tattooed which only emphasises his biceps. His hair is tucked under a backwards facing baseball cap leaving his unusual chocolate brown eyes uncovered.

'I guess I owe you an apology.'

Shep waves his hand dismissively. 'No worries. I would have done the same. Two guys jump out of nowhere and ambush me I'm going to fight back.' Shep gestures to the treadmill. 'You usually go at that pace or is something up? I'm more of a talker than a listener, but I'll do my best not to talk for a bit if you want to offload.'

Court shakes his head. 'I'm good.'

Shep shrugs and lowers onto the weight bench. 'Suit yourself.' He lifts a barbell loaded with weights from the rack and begins his workout. Court tries to get back to his run, but the arrival of Shep has thrown off his rhythm and his train of thought. When it comes to stray thoughts of Nix, that's a good thing. 'Would you want me out in the field with you?'

Shep rests the barbell back on the rack and sits up. 'Of course. Why? Someone say otherwise?'

Court sits on the end of the treadmill and clasps his hands together. 'But you don't know me. You haven't worked with me for years. You don't know what they did to me. What if they did something that makes me a threat?'

Shep shrugs as he takes a drink from his water bottle. 'Firstly, I know you. Secondly, you don't unlearn skills like you had. You may be rusty, but it's still there underneath. Just gotta give it a chance to come out again. I saw the footage of you taking on the Order. That was impressive. And from what I hear, you managed just fine in Dav's car. Thirdly, you're right, we don't have a fucking clue what they did to you. I get that's scary as hell, but we're here for you. We'll deal with it like we always do. As a team. Lastly, if you do anything to hurt the group, I'll kick your ass.' He winks and smirks at Court.

'Thanks. That's a great help.'

'That's what I do. So, you been training much since you...' He pauses and scratches his head. 'No nice way of saying it, is there?'

'What? Since I can remember?'

'Sorry, man. It's a hard one to navigate around.'

'How do you think I feel? I'm guessing that I've known you for a while?'

Shep nods and smiles at him. 'Going on two decades now. You convinced me to join the group. Kept an eye on me. Made sure I didn't fuck up too many times.'

'I don't remember you. I'm pretty damn sure I wouldn't forget you easily.'

Shep smirks and wiggles his eyebrows. 'I'm not easily forgotten, I'll give you that. Then again, you forgot you're a vampire. Doubt you'd forget that either. You know what I'd recommend?'

'You a doctor too?'

'Nah, I'm not just a pretty face though.' He nudges Court in the arm. 'Seriously though, I reckon you should get back to it.'

'To what?'

'This. The Blackjacks. How are you going to know if this is the life you want if you don't immerse yourself in all the wonders this job brings? And I'm not just talking about the weapons. We're a fucking formidable team, Court. Even more so with you. We make a difference. We save lives. Every single time we take down a member of the Order we give a Hybrid back their life. I don't know about you but that makes me all warm and fuzzy inside.'

'You're a little strange, you know that?'

Shep laughs loudly. 'I'll take that as a compliment. So, you going to answer my question about training?'

'I spent most evenings in the gym near where we used to live. It was the only way of working off all the nervous energy.'

'Why do you think we have all this cool training stuff? We're all like that. Makes for a fun time when we're cooped up together for too long. I want you to train with me.'

Court takes in Shep's impressive physique alongside his in the mirror opposite them. Shep is huge, but seeing the two of them side by side, he's not that much smaller. A few weeks of serious training and he'd bulk up. 'You'd kill me.'

'Not intentionally. Without wanting to blow my own trumpet, I'm kind of the bees' knees when it comes to combat. Well, Dav is marginally better, but you won't get much help outta him. Train with me. Let a master see what you've got.'

'You always have such a high opinion of yourself?'

Shep beams widely. 'It's justified. I'm on rotation tonight but I should be back by six am. Meet me here around then. I'll put you through your paces then finish with a hundred or so laps of the pool.'

'The pool?'

Shep frowns. 'Hang on. You telling me you didn't get the grand tour?'

Court shakes his head. 'Nix gave me a rough map to the kitchen and here.'

Shep snorts loudly. 'Yeah, well that's not going to fly.' He gets up and walks towards the door. 'C'mon. I'll show you around properly.'

29

Rhain lowers the weights onto the stand and wipes his face with the towel Geraint passes to him. He examines the man Geraint brought to him as he takes a drink of water. Vincent looks nervous. He should. Being called in to see him usually brought about an unhappy ending for the other party. He only had one rule for those he associated with on a business level. Don't fuck with him. Nice and simple. Any deviation and there could very well be an opening for a new associate.

Rhain stands up and slowly approaches the older vampire. Vincent had done business with his father many centuries ago. He had many contacts, but with Rhain's bloodline, he didn't need much help with that.

'Thank you for coming at such short notice.'

He takes Vincent's hand and shakes it with more force than necessary. Vincent winces and rubs his hand. 'Of course. I have to admit, I was surprised to hear from you. Is everything all right?'

Rhain steps up to the treadmill and begins the program. He waits until he's picked up the pace before he answers Vincent. 'Not sure. I heard you had a chat with one of the Blackjacks.' He glances over his shoulder when his comment remains unanswered. 'Vincent?'

'I'm not sure where you heard such a thing.'

'So it's not true?'

'Of course not.'

Rhain increases his pace. 'How about you try that again. I already know the truth so stop wasting my time by lying.'

'She asked to meet with me.'

'Who?'

'Phoenix.'

Rhain clenches his jaw and ups the pace again. 'And? Come on, Vincent. Don't hold out on me now.'

'She was asking about vampires disappearing.'

'She was? What did she say?'

Vincent wipes his forehead on a pristine white handkerchief. 'She wanted to know who was taking them.'

'I presume you told her enough to get her off your back without giving away any details.'

'I had no choice, Rhain.'

'I don't suppose you mentioned me?'

'Of course not.'

'That's something I guess.' Rhain releases his wings and rams one of his talons through Vincent's chest. He steps off the treadmill and slowly lifts him from the ground. Vincent's mouth opens and closes silently as his hands tear at Rhain's wing.

Rhain wipes his face with a towel as Vincent struggles to free himself.

He lowers Vincent, holding him at eye level. 'You should know something about me, Vincent. I'm not a fan of liars. You should have told me the truth the first time I asked.' He dumps Vincent on the floor and stabs his talon through the man's neck, separating his head from his body.

Geraint looks down at the body with disdain. 'I am just glad you did not deal with this in the living room. Blood is so difficult to get out of a beige carpet.'

'Make sure he's never found. I'm going to grab a shower.' He leaves Geraint to deal with Vincent and takes the lift to the upper floor. He can smell Vincent's blood on his wing and it's calling to his Prime side. Right on schedule, the cramps twist at his gut. The pain mixes with the irritation at Vincent and the damn Blackjacks.

He's never dealt with the illusive Phoenix personally, but he's heard plenty from the ones running the True Order. The Blackjacks were thought of as nothing more than an irritation, a bug to be swatted away. Fucking idiots didn't realise how dangerous they really are. If even one of the stories he's heard is correct, the Order will have their work cut out for them trying to keep the Blackjacks under control. Rhain couldn't care less if the Order lost to the Blackjacks or vice versa. His only priority is his little project.

That doesn't mean he wants to get up close and personal with Phoenix and her band of fighters. Vincent didn't know enough about what he was doing to cause him any concerns, but the fact the Blackjacks are sniffing around isn't sitting well with him.

Another cramp hits as the lift doors open to his private suite on the top floor. His talon scrapes along the wall, leaving a trail of blood in the paintwork. In a dignified display, Rhain crawls the last few feet to the dresser in his room and pulls the case of preloaded syringes to the floor. He bites his lip as another spasm hits, driving the air from his lungs and causing the syringe to drop to the carpet beside him.

As soon as the pain fades a little, he grabs the syringe and manages to inject its contents in his vein. A quiet calm settles over him as the drug takes effect. He looks up at the top of his wing, still smeared with Vincent's blood. He's so close to finding a cure. He just needs more time.

The problem is he also needs more not-so-willing-volunteers and that's where he'd have issues with Phoenix. If he allowed himself to think about it, he'd probably fully agree with her objections. But this is bigger than the lives of a few Hybrid males. Finding a cure for The Fever could pull the Primes back from the brink of extinction.

The disease has been killing Primes for centuries, but was only acknowledged in the last hundred years or so. No one wanted to admit being a Prime meant you'd eventually lose your mind. It didn't paint an impressive picture of the first bloodlines of the vampire race. One by one, the old lines were dying out. Breeding with humans had diluted the bloodlines until only a few dozen true Primes existed. His own line was heading towards extinction. He was the last and he was going to go like all the others before him.

He could take a mate and assure his line continued, but he's not a monster. There's no way he was going to sire a child who would end up just like him. If there's still time for him to continue his line when he finds a cure, he may consider it. There may not be any Prime females left to mate with by then. He needs to find a way to keep the Blackjacks away until he's closer to a solution.

Rhain uses the dresser to pull himself to his feet and shuffles to the bathroom. He glances at his glowing silver eyes as he passes the mirror. They should be back to normal by now. He'll have to up his dose... again. Rhain steps in the shower and struggles to turn on the water as his hand trembles. He clenches his fist, forcing his muscles to obey. The trembling subsides, but it takes more effort than it should.

He's not going to let this disease cripple him. He's not going to become an uncontrollable savage. He hasn't lived this long to end his days chained to a wall like a fucking animal. If Phoenix or any of her mongrels get in his way, he'll have to show them why it's not a good idea to fuck with him.

Court follows Shep to the garage and stares at the impressive array of vehicles. Land Rovers, a DB7, a few bikes, the Mercedes truck, and even a helicopter. These guys aren't short a bob or two if these vehicles are anything to go by. He wanders over to the black Defender 110 and runs his hand over the matte paint.

'Like it?' Shep asks.

'I've always wanted one of these. Well, for the last year anyway.' He turns at Shep's loud snort. 'What?'

'That's your car, mate. You got it about a year or so before you did your vanishing trick.'

'Really?

Shep holds out his arm. 'I've got the goosebumps to prove it. That was spooky. You can take it for a spin later.'

'Which is yours?

Shep points to the black Harley. 'That's my baby. I've never been a fan of four wheels. Not entirely practical for UK weather but hey, I love it.'

'Who funds all this?'

'Mix of sources. Ethan was left a hefty inheritance. He paid for most of what you see. We get a salary for what we do, and over the years Ethan has invested it for us. Not a lot to spend it on out here. We do all right out of it.'

'How many Blackjacks are there? Are you all over the world or just here?'

'Just us. Six lone warriors against an unknown number of baddies. Well, seven now that you're back. And no, it's not a franchise.' Shep laughs as he leads Court back through the garage to the main training area. 'Can't see us headlining the next franchise expo next to McDonald's. Anyway, this is the main training area. When Ethan found this place there were a few houses already here. He just tucked them under the external building. Everything else was added over time. Cool right?'

Court absolutely has to agree. He's never seen anything like this, which probably doesn't mean much. Shep wanders over to a burnt-out car and leans on the bonnet. 'It's a killer training here with the girls. The height gives them an advantage. Plenty of places they can swoop down from and kick our asses.'

'How the hell do you fight against someone with wings?'

Shep smirks. 'Skill my friend. That's why this place is so damn important. The Order is made up of Prime males. That leaves you, Bas, Dav, and me the only ones with our asses on terra-firma while everyone else has the advantage. Nix makes sure we even the odds. She's a fucking great trainer. By training with the girls we learn the pros and cons of fighting with a pair of awkward wings sticking out of your back.'

'I can't imagine there would be many cons.'

'You'd be surprised. True they're handy if you're fighting mid-air, but once you get the fuckers on the ground, we have the advantage.

Especially if we distract them so they don't get a chance to pull their wings in. Wings are awkward as fuck on the ground. Not so manoeuvrable with a couple of skis wrapped in a sheet attached to your back. Shit imagery, but you get my point. Us wingless guys hold our own in here. Nix makes sure of that.'

'And your sister is one of the team?'

Shep's smile drops a little as he nods. 'Whoop-de-do. Sorry. Not top of my list of things I had planned for her. No stopping her though. I suppose she's good, but between you and me, seeing her facing up against someone the size of Dav freaks me out. Fallon is training her, but she's my kid sister. Don't want this for her.'

Court nods. He knows exactly what Shep means.

'C'mon.'

He looks around the training room one more time wondering how the hell he would survive ten minutes in this place training with someone like Shep or Davyn. Lasting ten seconds would be a miracle.

They enter the main house again and Shep shows him the kitchen. A short woman in her early sixties is preparing vegetables at the enormous island sitting in the centre of the room. 'This is the all-knowing Gwen.' Shep leans over the woman and kisses her on the cheek. 'She looks after the house.'

'And your stomachs.' She hands Shep a piece of carrot which he accepts.

'The most important bit.'

Gwen wipes her hands on her apron and grasps Court's hands in hers. 'I can't tell you how happy I am to see you again, Court. I missed you.' She wipes a tear from her eye and smiles. 'I am so sorry to hear about your memory.'

He returns her smile. He can't help but like Gwen. She instantly makes him feel relaxed and adds a homely feel to the compound. Shep reaches out for another carrot but she slaps his hand away, something that makes Court laugh out loud. Seeing a six-and-a-half-foot vampire being reprimanded by someone half his size is priceless.

Shep rubs his hand and leaves Gwen to prepare dinner. He points to the fridge. 'Help yourself whenever you want. Gwen and her team keep the place stocked. But no touching the top shelf. That's mine. I don't share food. Consider yourself warned.'

Shep brings him back to the living room and settles on one of the five plush leather couches in front of the cinema-sized TV. The fire is lit in the wide fireplace, the crackling of logs filling the silence as Court processes everything. He has too many questions but doesn't know where to start. It's all so surreal.

'Can I ask you something?'

Shep lifts his head from the back of the couch. 'Shoot.'

'How old are you?'

Shep laughs. 'Straight to the point. I'm ninety-four.'

'Seriously?'

'I'll take that as a compliment from an old guy like you.'

'Are you the youngest? I don't get how the age thing works.'

'Okay, so Willow is the baby. She's sixty-three. Same age as Gwen. Mad huh? Anyway, Bas is next. He's eighty-four. Then me. Fallon is one hundred and ten, Nix is a smidge older than you I think - no way I'm asking her that - and Dav is the granddad. He's heading towards two hundred as far as I know.'

'But he looks the same age as me.'

'Bonus of these wonderful vampire genes. The physical ageing process slows down massively when we hit our mid-thirties or early forties. We'll still age but it takes hundreds of years. Any vampire you see who looks older is probably hitting close to four or five hundred years old. Everyone in the team looks the same age, but there's decades between us. Hell, Dav is about a century older than me.'

Court leans back on the comfortable leather and takes a deep breath. He never thought about how long he could live for like this. It was unbelievable enough knowing he was nearly a century and a half old. Potentially living for five hundred years is too much to get his head around.

'You okay?'

Court nods then shrugs. 'Not sure.' He lifts his head and looks over at Shep. 'Why do you do this? The Blackjacks I mean. You said you're worried about Willow being part of the team so why not take her way from this? Do something else?'

Shep pulls off his cap and runs his hand through his hair, ruffling the soft spikes. He leans forward and rests his clasped hands on his knees. For the first time since this tour started, Shep's face is serious. His dark eyes are hard and cold, but it's not directed at him. 'There's something you've got to understand about the Blackjacks. Each of us came to the team because of some personal shit. We each have a past, and it led us here. We don't have anything else. Nix and Ethan... they gave us something to belong to. We're family. A fucked-up family with a hell of a lot of issues, but we work.'

'What do you mean personal shit?'

Shep smiles briefly, his eyes focused on the floor. 'We train together, live together, bleed together, but we don't talk - not like that. I know Bas better than anyone else, but he hasn't told me everything about his past. As for Dav and Fallon - I know two things about them. Fuck and all. Doubt Fletch knows everything about his sister.'

'And you? Sorry, I should mind my own business.'

Shep breaks eye contact with the floor to look at him again. 'There are people out there who don't think Hybrids deserve to be here. We're considered lesser beings. Tainted by human blood. Some feel they can treat us however they want, treat us like property, and not face any consequences.' His reply doesn't directly answer Court's question, but he's not going to push him. He shouldn't have brought the subject up in the first place. He gets the feeling he wouldn't like the answer. 'We need to stop them. We need to make sure Hybrids get a fair shot at living.'

'So you make a difference?'

Shep shrugs. 'Sometimes. We need more in the team, but what we do is not for everyone.' He seems to shake himself out of his dark thoughts. 'So, you thinking of sticking around or want to run for the hills?'

'Fuck knows.'

Shep laughs and grabs the remote from the arm of the chair. 'Good answer.'

Thea opens her door to find Nix outside. 'Oh, hi.'

Nix leans against the door and crosses her arms. 'You look a little disappointed. Expecting someone else?'

Thea smiles and shakes her head. 'No... well, maybe. I don't know.'

'Gwen said you wanted to see me.'

'I did. I just...' She shakes her head. 'Forget it. Ignore me.'

Nix leans against the door frame and nods slowly. 'Ah. I see. I thought you didn't want to see Court.'

'I don't. Like I said, ignore me. I don't know what I want.'

'If you want to see him, he's in the training room with Shep. From what I can tell, he's been there since first thing this morning.'

'Are you sure it's safe to leave them alone together after what happened the last time?'

'happened the last time?'

Nix laughs. 'They're both big boys. I'm sure they can train together without resorting to stabbing each other... again.'

Thea nods as she steps backs away from the door and sits on the side of the bed. 'I hope so. Is he… How is he?'

Nix closes the door gently behind her. 'He's worried about you.'

'I'm fine, really.'

'Is that why you're not talking to him?'

Thea shrugs. 'I just need some time, I guess. It's a lot to take in.' She laughs and shakes her head. 'Getting to grips with the vampire thing was easier than this. How does that even make sense?'

'You just need time to adjust. I can't imagine what it's like for either of you. It's not surprising you're finding it hard to accept.' Nix sits on the couch and leans forward. 'I just want you to keep something in mind. I'm not going to tell you what to do about your relationship with Court.' She needs to deal with her own relationship him before she can attempt to go there with someone else. 'It's going to sound like a line I know, but this isn't his fault. I understand why you feel hurt and confused, but from what Fletch can tell, something or someone took all of us from his memory. He didn't forget by choice. Someone decided they didn't want him to remember any of us.'

Thea nods and smiles. 'I know. It's just… I know I'm coming across as unsympathetic. I'm not, really. I think it's just the fact he decided, for whatever reason, to lie to me that first time we met. And my parents played along. Well, my pretend parents. I mean, why would they do that?'

'I don't know, Thea.'

'No one knows! That's the problem. And do I have a mother out there somewhere? Is she dead too? Was she human or a vampire? Court lying like he did and not being able to remember why is seriously messing with my head. When my parents died in that car crash I thought I was an orphan.' She pauses and looks across at Nix. 'But he's my father, Nix. Why didn't he tell me?'

'I can't answer that. What I do know is that he lied to you for a reason. Perhaps in time he'll remember why. Whatever his reasons, that trustworthy, loyal, protective, fierce, downright unflappable fighter is your father. I didn't make him my second in command for no reason. He's...' Spectacular, stunning, the best damn lover she's ever had. Nix clears her throat when she remembers she's in front of his daughter. Shame kills any heat that had risen in her body at the thoughts of Court in her bed.

She forces herself to look up at Thea and hates herself and her thoughts. This girl is worrying about her whole life being turned upside down and her newfound relationship with her father while Nix is thinking about getting him into bed. Not helpful.

'What I'm trying to say is that it didn't matter what was going on around us, Court was always composed and thinking straight. I can think of a lot worse people to have as your father.'

Thea takes a deep breath and nods slowly. 'I guess you're right. So, what about you? Are you okay?'

Nix freezes slightly. 'What do you mean?'

'Well, you and the rest of the Blackjacks thought he was dead for years. It must be strange to have him back after all this time.'

Nix releases a breath, hoping she keeps the relief hidden. 'It's going to take us time to get used to him being back. The fact he came back with no memory and these enhanced powers isn't helping the happy reunion.' She shrugs. 'It's a learning curve for everyone.' She sits up and smiles again. 'So, what can I do for you?'

Thea frowns for a moment before she nods. 'Yeah, sorry. I got distracted with all the father talk. I need to ask a favour. I need to get some things for myself.'

'What sort of things?'

'I didn't get a chance to pack much before I left by the window. I know Gwen organised some clothes and toiletries for me, but I'd prefer to have my own things. I'm not really a fan of using other people's stuff. Would I be able to go home and pick up some things?'

Nix slowly shakes her head. 'I'm afraid not. The Order destroyed the place. Davyn and I checked it out and it was just a shell. There's nothing left. Do you want to give Gwen a list of what you need, and she'll sort it out for you?'

'I'd prefer to pick my own underwear and products. Having a stranger do it is just a bit weird. No offence. Are we near any shops? I could just pop out and grab some things.'

'Probably not a good idea to have you wandering around alone, especially now the True Order knows about you.'

'I understand.'

Nix pauses for a minute before turning back to Thea. 'Can you wait until tomorrow? Everyone is tied up with training or out on patrol and I've got to go to a meeting with Ethan. Except...' She shakes her head. 'Forget it.'

'What?'

'Davyn's probably free. He just got back from checking out a few leads.'

'Perfect. I'll go with him,' Thea replies quicker than she meant to.

Nix frowns as she stares at her. 'I don't know. I'm not sure that's such a good idea.'

'Is he a good fighter?'

'He's our best,' Nix replies without hesitation.

'Then there's no problem. We're just going to the shops and coming back.'

'We're about thirty minutes from anywhere decent.'

'I've been able to deal with Court's moods, I'm sure I can cope with Davyn's.'

'This has nothing to do with moods. I trust Dav with my life. He will do everything in his power to protect you and bring you back in one piece. I have no doubts on that. My issue is that he's not really a people person. If you're looking for little-to-no conversation mixed with big doses of awkward silence, he's your guy.'

'I just want to get some clothes. To be honest, I don't want to talk to anyone, especially about what's happened. Awkward silence sounds pretty good right about now.'

'If I agree to this you are to stick by him no matter what. The True Order may not be hiding out in the local women's clothes shop on the off chance you or Court pop in, but I'm not taking any chances. They found you once. I'm not going to put anything past them.'

'I promise I will do exactly what he tells me to do. Please Nix, I just want some underwear that belongs to me.'

Nix blows out a breath then nods once. 'I can't exactly say no to that, can I? I'll let him know. You okay to meet him in the garage in five minutes? He's not a fan of waiting around.'

'No problem. Thanks for this, Nix.'

'I wouldn't be so quick to thank me just yet. You step out of line at all, and I'll give him permission to drag you back to the compound. If Dav feels something is off you don't argue with him. I need your word on that, Thea.'

'I promise I won't take any chances.'

She's still not completely sure this is a good idea but she knows she'd feel the same as Thea if the roles were reversed. 'Fine. Oh and make sure you let Davyn pay for everything.'

'I've got my own credit card.'

'Which the Order could very well be monitoring. Dav has a card that doesn't link to us. I'll organise one for you too, but for now let him pay. No personal credit cards, okay?'

'Of course. I didn't even think about that.'

'It's my job to think of these things. Buy what you want. You'll be staying here until we can figure out exactly what's going on with Court.'

'Thanks, Nix. I better get ready.'

She leaves Thea's room and heads towards the kitchen where she last saw Davyn. This is going to be a fun one-sided conversation. He's going to hate every minute of this shopping trip as much as Thea is going to enjoy it. You'd have to be an idiot not to have noticed Thea's obvious excitement about spending some time alone with Davyn.

Let Thea have her crush or whatever she feels for him. She's known

Dav long enough to have no doubt he won't reciprocate. She can't remember ever seeing him with someone. But if a few hours with Dav helps distract her from everything going on with Court, Nix isn't going to deny her.

She takes a deep breath before she enters the kitchen. Dav is sitting at the counter with a cup of coffee in front of him. He looks up as she walks over to him. 'Hi.'

He doesn't respond. Yeah, Thea is in for a fun filled car ride.

'I want you to take Thea to Hereford. She needs to get some clothes and toiletries.'

He frowns at her and straightens. 'You want me to what?'

'Everything she owns was destroyed. You saw that. It'll take a couple of hours. Just there and back.'

Nix bites the inside of her cheek to stop herself from smiling. She'd get a better reaction if she'd asked him to face two dozen Order fighters single handed.

'Think of it as protection detail.' His frown deepens and his hand tightens around the cup. 'She'll meet you in the garage in five minutes. Use your credit card to pay for everything. I don't want her to use her own in case the Order is tracking her.'

He slowly pushes to his feet and dumps his cup in the sink with such force the handle breaks off.

Davyn prowls from the room without a word. 'Dav?' He stops and turns to look at her. 'Please be nice.'

He glares at her for a moment then turns and walks away. 'I'm always fucking nice!'

32

As soon as Nix leaves, Thea throws open the bathroom door and grabs the brush she borrowed from Fallon. She quickly pulls it through her dark hair then cleans her teeth. The borrowed t-shirt isn't the most flattering and hangs off one shoulder. Unfortunately for her, the other women in the house are a lot bigger than her. The jeans are her own at least as are the boots. She waves a dismissive hand at her less-than-ideal attire, takes her bag from the stool beside the bed and goes downstairs to meet Davyn.

She hurries along the corridor and through the door between the kitchen and the large lounge area. After pausing for a moment to get her bearings, she takes the second right and follows it to the end of the corridor. She cracks open the door and peers inside, breathing a sigh of relief when she sees the vast garage filled with cars. She steps inside and jumps as the door slams behind her. She tucks her hair behind her shoulders and makes her way over to where Davyn had parked his car when he brought them here. Thea walks around the large black truck and stops as she comes face to face with an impressive helicopter. What do these people do that requires a helicopter?

She slowly circles around the large craft and stumbles to a stop, just managing to keep herself upright. Davyn's sitting on the bonnet of his car wearing dark jeans, a black t-shirt, and black boots. His hair is tucked under a baseball cap, the peak hiding his face from her. She brushes her hair back behind her shoulders again, then pulls it forward before stuffing both hands in her pockets.

For heaven's sake. You're a grown woman. Pull yourself together.

She steps out from behind the helicopter and her pep talk disappears from memory as he looks over at her. His green eyes lock on her for a second then move back to the ground in front of him. He slides off the bonnet and opens the passenger door. Without waiting for her to get in, he walks around the front of the car and gets in. Thea climbs up and looks over at him. The thick black lines of his tattoo twist around his toned arm as he grips the steering wheel. Everything about this man... vampire, is seriously impressive, including his clear dislike of her. Knowing his secret probably isn't helping him develop any fuzzy feelings for her. 'Thank you for doing this. I really appreciate it.'

'Nix ordered me.'

He starts the engine and drives down the tunnel towards the metal gates. Thea keeps her eyes firmly fixed to the road ahead of them and tries to breathe through her mouth. He smells incredible. She wracks her brain, desperate to come up with something intelligent to say, anything to spark up a conversation, anything to brush over his harsh comment, but her brain is letting her down. She risks a quick glance over at him. His eyes are fixed on the road, one hand resting on the steering wheel and the other on the gear stick.

He's as far removed from her usual type as he can be, and she's tried to stop thinking of him like that but is failing miserably. She's attracted to him. Her feelings are completely irrational, especially with everything else going on in her life. She glances at him again. In the confines of the car, he appears so much more imposing than he did in his room. The muscles in his thick arm move as he adjusts his grip of death on the steering wheel.

She turns her attention back to the road before he notices her staring. Common sense seems to have taken a break along with any spare topics of conversation that may have been present in her head. After everything that's happened since Court came back, it's not surprising she's acting out of character. Not that she's arguing against it. Whatever the reason, Davyn's hooked her, turning her to a teenager lusting after someone completely inappropriate.

Twenty minutes later, she's still trying to come up with something to say to break the silence in the car. If it wasn't for changing gears and steering, she'd think he was asleep. With another ten minutes or so left, this car trip will go down as the most awkward and infuriating, but exciting drive of her life.

'What?'

She looks over at him, not quite believing that she heard him speak. 'I'm sorry?'

'You keep looking at me. What's wrong?'

'Nothing. Everything's fine.'

'You can turn the radio on.'

'Sorry?'

He sighs and looks at her for the first time since he pulled out of the garage. 'If you don't like the silence, turn on the radio.'

With no idea how to respond, she looks at the dashboard, finds the radio and turns it on. She scans through the stations, stopping at a station playing Christmas songs.

Davyn looks over at her again. Twice in two minutes. She's on a roll. 'Really?'

'After twenty minutes of silence. Yes, really.'

He blows out a breath and focuses on the road again. 'Fine.'

That one word marks the end of the conversation until they reach Hereford. Davyn picks a parking spot at the far side of the car park. He reverses between two cars, turns off the engine and closes his eyes. His brow scrunches as he tilts his head to the side.

'What—'

He holds up his hand, cutting her off. Thea holds her breath, afraid to disturb whatever he's doing. He opens his eyes again and reaches under his seat. He pulls out a gun and a thick bladed knife. 'Can't sense any other vampires... for now. You ready?'

'We're going shopping not into battle. Why do you need a gun?'

'So I can shoot vampires.'

She stares at him, waiting for even a small smile to break free, but there's nothing. 'You're being serious.'

'I'm here to protect you.'

'I know that, but it's a shopping centre.'

He slips the weapons into the holsters on his belt then reaches into the backseat to grab his leather jacket. She breathes in his cologne, already addicted to whatever it is. His broad chest looms over her and she barely resists the urge to touch him. Thankfully, he moves away before she does something stupid.

Thea watches as he puts on his jacket before getting out of the car. It's not much of a consolation, but she is more than relieved that the weapons aren't visible with his jacket on.

'You getting out or what?'

'Eh, yeah. Sorry.' She puts on her own jacket and picks her bag off the floor.

Davyn walks around the front of the car and towers over her. 'Stay in my sight. Do exactly as I say. No questions and no arguments. Got it?'

She nods, not put at ease by the seriousness in his tone and expression. Thea follows him to the paved walkway running between lines of shops and her mood instantly lifts. Hundreds of lights are draped across the street which is packed with vendor carts selling hot chocolate, roasted chestnuts, and thick rolls filled with turkey, stuffing and cranberry sauce. The inviting aromas mingle with the fresh smell of the enormous Christmas tree in the centre of the walkway. Brightly wrapped boxes are piled underneath, and a sprinkling of snow sits on the ground around it.

She always loved this time of year. Growing up her parents celebrated Christmas with zeal. From the first of December until mid-January, the house was always filled with decorations and the smell of freshly baked mince pies. When they died six years ago in a car crash, she never thought she'd celebrate again, but all that changed when Court came back into her life. They may have only been in a derelict apartment with a sparse dusting of cheap decorations but having Court with her made last Christmas that much more special.

She stuffs her hands in the pockets of her coat as thoughts of the latest revelations threaten to dampen her mood. Being reunited with her birth father should give her more than enough reasons to celebrate in style this year, but she is far from being in the mood.

Knowing that Court is her father and not her brother is devastating her. Her entire life had been a carefully crafted lie. Not only was Court involved but her adoptive parents were in on the big deception. They'd lied to her every single day. Thea discreetly brushes a tear away. It's not even like she can confront them about it. They played along with the lie then died before telling her the truth. The whole situation is so unfair. And now she has a vampire father and a mother that no one knows anything about. That's one hell of a Christmas present.

It suddenly hits her that Christmas this year will probably be spent with the Blackjacks in their compound. She doubts this thing with the Order will be sorted in the next fortnight - whatever the thing is. Nix will probably want them to stay until it's safe. She glances sidelong at Davyn. She can't imagine the stoic vampire wearing a paper hat while enjoying a roast turkey dinner. Come to think of it, she can't imagine any of the Blackjacks doing that - well except maybe for Shep and Willow. Of all the vampires, those two seem the most relaxed.

She turns her attention from the Christmas extras to the actual shops. She'd never been to Hereford before and has no idea what's available to her. She spots at least three shops that will have everything she needs and heads in that direction. With only two weeks left to Christmas, the store is busier than it usually would be this late at night, but it doesn't cause them any problems. The crowd parts before Davyn gets close, leaving her plenty of room to move comfortably through the shoppers. Davyn sticks to her side, interrogating each of the unsuspecting Christmas shoppers with his gaze.

She unzips her coat as the heating over the door of the store blasts her. Thea does her best to ignore her bodyguard and rifles through the racks of clothes. She picks out three pairs of jeans in her size then moves over to the shirts and tops. She glances at Davyn thankful that he's giving her space. Instead of shadowing her, he's standing just inside the door, his arms crossed and his eyes scanning the other customers. She's irritated by the twinge of jealousy that hits when she notices more than one of the shoppers stopping to give him a second look. Not that she's surprised, he is worth looking at.

She wanders to the back of the shop to the underwear and glances over her shoulder at him. Seeing that he's still visually interrogating the other innocent shoppers, she chooses a few pieces and hides them at the bottom of her basket. After adding a few tops to her basket she goes to the changing room to try everything on. She doubts Davyn would be jumping to take her back here to change for a different size.

She has just pulled off her top when the curtain pulls aside and Davyn peers in at her. She yelps and pulls a shirt off the hanger, holding it over her bra. 'What the hell are you doing?'

'What part of stay in my sight did you not get?'

'You can't just barge in here.'

'Is everything okay?'

Thea peeks out of the cubicle and smiles at the shop assistant. 'Yes, yes. Sorry. My, eh... boyfriend just startled me.'

Davyn keeps his eyes on the assistant and smiles at her. Thea manages to keep the shock off her face and smiles at her too. 'Her Christmas party is coming up at work. She wants to impress them.'

The assistant doesn't look entirely convinced so Thea reaches out and wraps her arm around Davyn's waist. She ignores the way his body tenses at her touch as she cuddles against his chest. The awkward silence stretches on until Davyn returns her gesture and pulls her close to him.

The shop assistant's suspicion disappears, falling prey to a combination of his smile, and the clearly loved-up couple in front of her. 'Of course. Christmas parties certainly call for a new outfit. If you need anything just shout.'

She disappears along with Davyn's smile. He steps away from her, ending the embrace. 'Boyfriend?'

Thea shrugs. 'What else was I supposed to say? Vampire bodyguard wouldn't have gone down very well,' she hisses, trying to keep her voice down. 'And you played along.'

'I didn't have a choice. It was either that or kill her. Are you done in here?'

Thea stares at him open mouthed. As much as she doesn't want to believe he means what he just said, she has a horrible feeling he meant every word. 'No. I need to try these on. If you want to make sure I'm not attacked by an over helpful shop assistant you can stay, but outside the curtain.' She pulls the material out of his hands and draws it across the cubicle again. Davyn stays but lets her get changed in private.

When she's finished, she steps out and makes her way to the till. The same assistant idly chats to her as she scans each of the items. When she tells her the total, Davyn reaches out with a credit card to pay for her clothes.

Thea mutters her thanks, takes her bags, and leaves the shop and the smiling assistant behind. Thea goes into the chemist, buys much needed toiletries under his watchful gaze and steps back outside into the cool evening air.

'You done?'

'I think so. I'm going to grab a coffee from one of the stalls. Do you want anything?'

'No.'

'Are you sure?' He slowly turns his head and gives her one of his 'stop bothering me' looks. 'Great. Fine. I'll just be a minute.

She picks the closest vendor so she doesn't irritate Davyn more than she already clearly is. Thea breathes in the rich aroma of coffee, chocolate, and freshly baked pastries. The roast chestnuts on the stall next to the coffee stand smell incredible but there's no way she's going to suggest queueing at another stall and taking up more of Davyn's time.

She finally orders her coffee and pays for it with the small amount of cash she has in her wallet. Thea thanks the vendor and wraps her hands around the steaming cup.

'Done now?' Davyn growls from behind her, startling her.

She nods. 'Yeah. It'll do for now. Thanks.'

Without a word he nods towards the car park. Thea falls into step beside him, struggling to keep up with his long strides. She loads her bags into the backseat and climbs in. She fastens her seat belt as Davyn throws his jacket in the back and gets in beside her. He holds out a white paper bag.

'Here.'

She takes the bag and the aroma hits her before she's even opened it. 'Chestnuts?'

'You smiled when you smelt them at the stall.'

She stares over at him, completely speechless. It's a small gesture, but probably one of the nicest things any guy has done for her. The fact it came from someone like Davyn makes it all the more special. 'Thank you. Really. I love roasted chestnuts.'

He nods then starts the car and pulls out of the car park.

Thea opens the bag and breathes in the incredible smell. It brings her straight back to her childhood. 'Would you like one?'

Davyn shakes his head without looking at her. 'Fucking rotten things.'

Thea laughs as she digs into the treats. 'All the more for me I guess.'

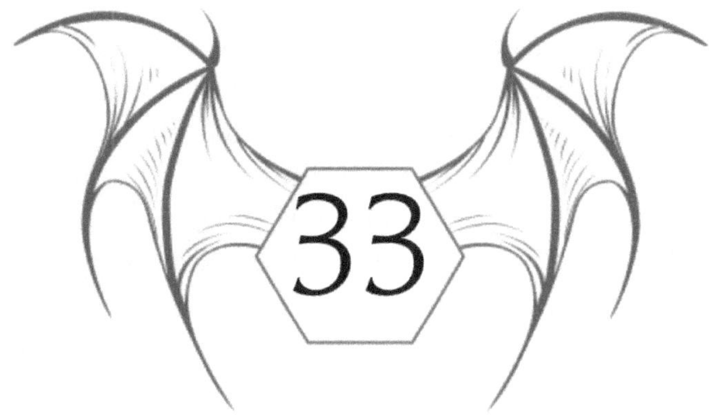

A heavy dread settles on Thea the closer they get to the compound. It may just have been a rushed shopping trip to Hereford, but the few hours away from Court and having to think about what's going on between them was just what she needed. Spending that time with Davyn hadn't been too much of a hardship either. Even if he had been less than thrilled about spending the time with her.

As with the journey to Hereford, he hadn't said anything on the way back. His comment about chestnuts had been the last thing he said, but Thea doesn't mind. His silent company is strangely comforting.

'Davyn?'

'What?'

'Do we have to go back to the compound straight away?'

'Yes.'

Thea looks over at Davyn. 'I've been cooped up in there for the last two days. I just want to get some fresh air.'

'You've just had fresh air. You're a target. I need to get you back.'

'I'm just asking for another five minutes away from all this mess.' She points out the window. 'The river is just there. Please, Davyn. Just five minutes.'

He drums his fingers on the steering wheel then curses and turns the car around. He drives through the narrow entrance to the car park and shuts off the engine. 'Five minutes. That's it.'

She opens the door, climbs over the gate, and shimmies down the mud bank to the small beach at the side of the river. Thanks to the recent rain, the river is quite full, sending the water rushing around the bend as it makes its way downstream. She sits on a fallen tree trunk lying on the beach and watches the bats darting through the trees, searching for bugs to eat.

This is exactly what she needs. She knows Davyn is somewhere behind her but right now she couldn't care. Right now she just wants to forget everyone and everything.

She opens her eyes when she hears Davyn stopping beside her. The large vampire looks completely out of place in this setting. His hands are jammed in the pockets of his jeans and he keeps looking around, like he's expecting a surprise attack from a deranged owl.

'This is heaven. Thank you. I guess I'm just finding all this a little hard to adjust to. Up until a few days ago it was just me and Court. Now there's the Blackjacks and the True Order and… my father…' She closes her eyes and stops before she makes a complete fool out of herself. 'Sorry. I didn't mean to offload.'

Nothing from the stoic vampire so Thea gives up trying to convince him to talk. After a few minutes of looking at his leg she finally breaks. 'Are you going to sit or just stand there like a bodyguard.'

'I am your bodyguard.'

'Can you please just sit?'

He lowers on to the tree beside her and leans forward, resting his arms on his legs as he continues to scan their surroundings. In the quiet, the enormity of the revelation about who her father is, hits her.

They'd talked like brother and sister. There were things she told her brother that she probably wouldn't want her father to know. And that's something she can't begin to figure out how to deal with. She quickly wipes an escaped tear from her cheek.

'What's wrong?'

Thea sniffs, which doesn't help her hide the fact she's crying. 'Nothing.'

'You're not crying over nothing.'

This is the last conversation she wants to have with Davyn. She looks over her shoulder at him and attempts a weak smile, but as soon as she sees his face, she knows he's not convinced. He clasps his hands together and raises his eyebrows in a silent question. 'I'm fine, really.'

His eyes glow in the darkening light. 'Not buying it. If I take you back crying, they'll think I did something to you.'

'It's not you.'

'I know that. It's finding out Court's your father.'

She turns to face him and takes a deep breath. 'That transparent, huh?'

'Common sense.'

She toys with throwing him a line and changing the subject, but something in his expression convinces her to take a chance. She may not know much about Davyn, but she is pretty damn sure he wouldn't ask a question if he honestly didn't want or expect an answer. 'I feel like I've lost my brother and my parents in one blow. Not that they were my real parents. But I thought they were and now Court is which is just weird.

'I know he's still alive, but he's not my brother anymore. He's my father, which is a whole other issue, but I miss my brother.' She shakes her head and frowns. 'The whole situation is driving me crazy. I just wish they were still alive so they could tell me why? Ignore me. I'm not making any sense.'

'You're grieving.'

Thea stares up at him and nods slowly. 'That's it. That's exactly it.' She hadn't thought of it like that, but grief is the perfect word to describe what she's feeling.

'So mourn your brother with your father's help. He's lost his sister.'

She shakes her head then looks out over the river. 'I don't know if it's that simple.'

'It can be. You're blaming him for forgetting he has a daughter. For telling you he's your brother.'

'Well, yes.'

He turns to look at her and his green eyes finally meet hers. 'You really think that's fair?'

'Excuse me?'

'Something fucked with his head. He doesn't know why he told you he's your brother. He doesn't know anything. At least he remembered you existed. Court fought side by side with all of us for years. He still doesn't have a fucking clue who any of us are. You don't see us getting all emotional with him. What we need to do is figure out what happened to him and tear whoever is responsible limb from limb. This isn't his fault so stop blaming him. Stop making this about you. It's about him.'

Thea blinks a few times as she digests what Davyn said. Apart from the fact she's never heard him say so much in one go, irritatingly, some of what he said made sense. Well, maybe most of what he said made sense except for the limb from limb part. 'Great. So, I'm getting emotional, huh? Being selfish?'

'Yes. That's not a criticism. The situation is fucking with all of us. Especially Court. But I'm guessing he'd prefer some support instead of the cold shoulder from his daughter. He's still Court. Does it really make that much of a difference that he's your father?'

Davyn's right. Whether he's her father or her brother, he's still the same person. She still loves him. If she's struggling with the truth, he must be too, especially when you add the vampire thing to the mix. 'Do you think he'll be okay? What if he never gets his memory back?'

He looks sideways at her. 'Seems like that would be a bigger problem for him than for you.'

She glares at him. 'You know, you don't always have to talk sense.'

He smirks. It makes the briefest of appearances, but she sees it. And it's something she would give anything to see again. Then the frown returns, almost like he dropped his guard for a moment then remembered and put it up again. 'The Blackjacks have his back. Always will. He needs you too though.'

Thea nods and gets to her feet. 'I'll think about what you said. And thank you for bringing me to Hereford. I'm looking forward to having my own stuff again.'

'Bit different to training and rotation.'

Thea laughs at that. 'Yeah. Sorry. To be honest, I'm surprised you agreed to take me. I thought after the other night you wouldn't want to have anything to do with me.'

Davyn nods and examines the trees surrounding them.

'Can I ask you something?'

He looks at her again. 'What?'

'Can Fletch not do something for you. To fix your wing I mean. You shouldn't have to go through that when you release…' The growl she hears from Davyn stops her from finishing the sentence. His glowing green eyes lock on her and the temperature drops by a few degrees.

'I told you my wings are my fucking business.'

'I know, but I just thought if he could fix it that would be a good thing. For you and the team.'

'You know fuck all about me. My wings have brought me nothing but pain. If I could cut them off my back I would. I've hated them since the day they broke out of me and I'll hate them until I die.' He clenches his fist, but not before Thea notices his hand is trembling slightly.

'I'm sorry. I didn't mean to upset you.'

'Time to go. Get in the fucking car.'

Thea nods and silently walks back to his car. The hostile, seriously pissed off Davyn follows behind her so she keeps to a brisk walk. He pulls open the driver's door, nearly separating it from the car. Thea quickly jumps in before he leaves without her and fastens her seatbelt. She risks a quick glance at Davyn as he starts the engine.

Whatever warmth she had seen while they were together is a distant memory. This is the fighter she was warned about. She's not scared of him, but she has no intention of trying to smooth things over with him either. It's too late for that. He told her to mind her own business when it came to his wings. Put it in clear, simple to understand terms. What in the world possessed her to stick her nose in again?

He slams the car in gear and accelerates out of the car park. The twenty-minute drive back to the compound passes in a hostile and seriously uncomfortable silence. Thea passes the time by concentrating on the view out the window. She bites the inside of her cheek trying to keep the angry tears at bay. What had started as a slightly awkward, but nonetheless enjoyable few hours, was now forever tainted by her dumb question.

He drives through the large gates to the compound and screeches to a stop in the underground garage. He takes her bags from the backseat and drops them in front of the car before opening the compound door and, without even a causal glance in her direction, steps inside leaving her next to his car.

Court stops at the door and checks the hand drawn map before stuffing the paper in his back pocket. He knocks, turning the handle when he hears a mumbled 'yeah' from inside.

Nix looks up from her desk and freezes with her hand hovering over the keyboard. 'Court, hey. This is a surprise.'

'Got a minute?'

She closes her laptop and pushes it aside. 'Of course.' She gestures to the chair at his side of the desk. 'Take a seat. What's up?'

'I've been thinking a lot the last few hours. There's still so much I don't know or don't understand about this world, but I think I need to stop hiding from what I am. My memory may never come back, and I don't have time to wait on the off chance it will all come flooding back. It's time I accept this could be the way things are for me from now on.'

'What are you saying?'

'I need to know everything. The Primes, the True Order, the

Blackjacks, my place in the group. It's killing me knowing that you know things about me I don't remember.' She leans back in her chair and doesn't immediately respond. 'Please Nix. I need to know.'

'Then what? We fill in all the blanks and you go after whoever did this to you?'

'If I find out who it was, yes.'

'What happens to Thea if you go off on a one-man crusade? She's already indirectly lost her brother. Her father just exploded into her life. You really want to risk leaving her alone?'

He pushes to his feet and paces her office, his boots keeping time with the fan spinning over her desk. 'They took a fucking big chunk of my life, Nix. I need to know how and why. You have to understand that.'

'I do, Court. Believe me, I want answers as much as you do. But charging in with guns blazing will only get you killed.'

He comes to a stop and rests his hands on the desk, letting his head drop. 'I need to do something.'

He looks up when Nix's chair is pushed back. She sits on the edge of the table beside him. 'You want to join us again?'

Court frowns at her, sure he's misheard. 'You being serious? Even with everything that's going on with my head.'

'You're one of us. Memory or not, I'm sure your instincts are still there. And I hear Shep is going to take you under his wing so to speak. He's an incredible fighter.'

'Yeah. He told me.'

Nix laughs. 'I'll bet he did. You know what though? He's only great because you taught him. Court, you were a damn impressive fighter. One of the best. We could really use you on the team again.'

'I've got all this stuff with Thea. How can I possibly think about doing what you all do? I don't understand enough about what you do.'

'There's only one way to fix that. You're right though. To be part of the Blackjacks you'll need to know everything. I'll give you access to all our reports. Every file and document on the system - with Fletch's okay of course. The last thing we want to do is set you back by overloading you with information.'

Court straightens and nods. 'Deal. So I'm a Blackjack again?'

'You've always been a Blackjack. That never changed. The second in command seat has been waiting for you since you disappeared.'

'Not sure I'm ready for that.'

'First bit of advice I'm going to give you. Stop doubting yourself. I saw that footage from the alley. The training, your instincts - it's all still there. It just needs a gentle push to get it out. Not that I'd call Shep a gentle push.'

She sits back behind her desk and opens the laptop again. 'I heard back from Ethan. His people have found the farm you stayed in after you woke up. Well, they think it's the farm. Only you can tell us for sure. How about you tag along? First time out with the team.'

Court's first reaction is to politely refuse but he stops himself in time. Shep seemed more than happy to have him back on the team. He doesn't doubt Nix would have told him if she felt it wasn't a good idea. Maybe he should trust the people who have known him for nearly two decades. They probably know him better than he knows himself.

'Yeah. That would be good.'

'Perfect. I'll send Shep to your room once we're done here. He can make sure you have everything you need. So, should I ask how things are between you and Thea?'

Court sighs and drops onto the chair.

'Ah, that good, huh.'

'I don't suppose you have any tips on how to deal with this?'

'I wish I did, Court. You've both have a lot dumped on you over the last few days. She'll need time to process everything. You both need time.'

He nods as he rubs his hand over his beard. 'I know. It's the great answer to everything isn't it? Time. Can't really argue with it.'

'It's shit. I know that, Court. But it will get better. I promise. We've got your back, okay. Each and every one of us is your family. Thea's family too. We're here for both of you.'

'Thanks, Nix.' He gets up and smiles at her. 'I'll leave you to it. See you in a bit.'

He closes the door behind him and stands in the corridor outside her office. The feeling has come back. Every single time he sees Nix, he gets a strange niggling feeling somewhere in the back of his mind. Like a memory trying to resurface. But like every time he tries to force the memories out, they only move further from his grasp.

He can't explain why it only happens with her. If he worked with all the Blackjacks, he should get the same niggle thing with them all - shouldn't he? Are there rules when it comes to having your memory taken from you? He could do with a manual of some sort. 101 tips to dealing with an artificially removed memory.

Davyn pulls his car off the main road and continues along the dirt track not taking his foot off the accelerator. Court grips the handle over the door as he gets thrown around the back of the car. Nix doesn't seem to be faring much better but doesn't say anything.

He glances over his shoulder and sees his black Defender 110 emerge from the trees behind them. Right now, Shep is behind the wheel with Bastian, Willow and Fallon. Fletch had agreed to stay at the compound with Thea. Court didn't want her anywhere near this place. He's not even sure if it is the place. He's only got a satellite image to go by. It looks about right, but there's no way of knowing until he sees the farm.

'Hey, you okay?'

He nods at Nix. 'Just hoping this isn't a wild goose chase.' He winces as his head hits against the headrest. He swears Davyn is doing it on purpose.

'We'll find out... well, now.'

The track opens to a large field. The grass is unkempt and the fence is in serious need of repair. Davyn guides his car down the track running the perimeter of the property. Court looks out the window, but nothing is familiar. They continue along the track until they reach a heavily rusted gate separating the field from the house further down the path.

'Want me to ram the gate, Nix?' Davyn asks.

'How about we leave the destruction of private property for another day. We'll leave the cars here. Walk the rest of the way.' Davyn pulls the car off the track and parks under a line of oak trees. Shep pulls in behind them and kills the engine. Court walks over to the gate as the rest of the team checks out the area. The hairs on the back of his neck prickle as he stares over at the derelict farmhouse.

'This is it, isn't it?' Nix asks as she joins him at the gate.

'Yeah.'

'Shep?'

'No vampires for miles. No humans either. Place is empty.'

'Davyn and Willow check the outbuildings. Fallon, Bas, and Shep you take the grounds. We'll have a look around the house.' The others break up, leaving Court and Nix standing at the gate. 'You ready to do this?'

'Don't know why I'm so nervous. I just slept here for a few nights. Nothing was done to me in there.'

Nix tries the door finding it unlocked. She steps inside and walks around the kitchen as he stands in the doorway. Everything is covered in a layer of dust. Apart from Nix's footprints, the floor shows no signs of anyone visiting since he left.

'You said you were wearing boxers when you escaped. Did you leave them here when you changed?'

Court doesn't register her words. He's still staring at the room.

'Court?'

He jumps as she touches his arm. 'Sorry. What?'

'The boxers you were wearing when you found this place. Did you leave them here?'

'Upstairs probably. I took some clothes from the main bedroom. I think I left them in the bathroom.'

They climb the creaky staircase to the first floor and Court takes the second door on the right. On the windowsill next to a dusty towel is a pair of black boxers. Nix goes back to the kitchen and returns with a plastic bag. She picks up the trousers and towel then places them in the bag and ties the handles. 'You really think you'll find something on them?'

'We won't know unless we look.' She touches her earpiece. 'Dav, you got anything?'

'Buildings are clear. Nothing's been touched in years.'

'Same here, Boss,' Shep reports. 'Think I may have found something else though. I'm in the field to the back of the house.'

'On our way.' She turns to Court and her brown eyes glow in the gloomy room. 'You head down. I just want to make sure we haven't missed anything.'

Court leaves her to check the rest of the house while he waits on the porch. He can feel the others near him. It's something he thought he'd hate, but if anything the feeling gives him comfort. He may not be able to see them, but the team are nearby. The team he's part of. He smiles to himself as it finally hits him. He's part of the team. Not a fully operational one yet, but he's a Blackjack.

'Nothing else up there.' Nix steps outside and points to the side of the building. 'Let's go see what Shep found.'

He closes the door behind him and picks his way through the overgrown yard. They find Shep and the rest of the team at the edge of the field to the back of the house. The entire property is surrounded by forest and that's what seems to have attracted Shep's attention. Court follows Nix over to him and realises that Shep isn't actually looking into the forest. He may be facing the trees, but his eyes are closed and he's frowning.

'What's he—'

'Shush,' Shep hisses at Court. 'Working here.'

Nix leans closer to Court. 'He's trying to isolate a scent. The master prefers to work in silence.'

'The master can hear you,' Shep replies. He walks towards the forest and the rest of the team fall in behind him. Court takes his weapon out, surprised to see the others have done the same. Seems their instincts are in tune with each other.

He doesn't know how, but Shep continues to walk through the forest without tripping or knocking himself out on a tree. He keeps his eyes closed, the only change to his face when he frowns and alters direction. Forty-five minutes later he stops and runs a hand over his face. 'Yeah, this is it.'

'This is what?' Nix asks.

'Our boy started here and went the way we just came.'

'You can pick up on my scent? It was a year ago.'

Shep makes a face. 'No offence, but the scent is strong.'

'What do you mean 'no offence'?'

Shep turns to face him. 'How can I put this. You stank. Stale sweat. Blood. More stale sweat. As I said, no offence intended. But, hey! It's all good. It led us here, wherever here is.' Shep turns in a circle and scratches the back of his neck. 'Eh, where the hell are we?'

Nix moves in front of Court and meets his eyes. 'Is anything ringing a bell for you?'

Court is about to say no when an image flashes to his mind. He closes his eyes, desperately calling it from the back of his mind. He concentrates, but all he gets is a whole load of pain. 'Fuck!' He falls to his knees as the pain increases.

Nix crouches down beside him and puts her hand on his shoulder. 'Try to hold on to it.'

He shakes his head. 'Fuck! It's gone. Why can't I remember?'

'Because someone doesn't want you to.'

The pain fades and he looks at Nix. 'I'm not sure how useful I am to you like this.'

'Hey, I'm the boss, remember. I'll make that call.' She squeezes his arm and gets to her feet. 'Fallon, take a look will you?'

Nix helps Court up as Fallon takes to the sky. She disappears for a few minutes before landing in front of them and tucking her wings away. 'We're on something. Can't tell from down here but it's a fort or something like that. Ground looks different.'

Bastian crouches down and digs in the dirt with his gloved hands. 'Find a contact point for me.'

Court watches in confused silence as the Blackjacks drop to their knees and join Bastian on the forest floor.

'What the fuck you looking at?' Davyn asks gruffly. 'Dig.'

With no idea what he's digging for, Court decides it's better to join in than piss off Davyn. He pulls handfuls of soil and leaf debris away but doesn't get far. His fingers hit stone. He tries to dig around it but it's a lot bigger than a rock. It's a wall or structure of some sort. 'I think I got something.'

Bastian crouches down behind him and wipes more dirt aside. 'It should do. Get out of the way.' Court moves aside as Bastian pulls off his gloves. He places his tattooed hands on the stone palm down and closes his eyes. Court knows better than to ask what he's doing.

Bastian opens his eyes and smiles at Court. His chocolate brown eyes are glowing, the irises swirling with browns, golds and greens.

'What is it?' Court asks.

'A door. About twenty metres behind Nix. It's locked but nothing I can't handle.'

'I'm afraid to ask.'

Bastian grins as he gets up and brushes off his leathers. 'I have a heightened sense of touch. I can read a structure or an item by touching it.'

Court follows the team in the direction Bastian pointed to. 'Read?'

'It's hard to explain. Take a building for example. By touching it I can tell how large it is, get a plan of the layout in my head. I can even tell if there is movement inside, like someone walking around.'

'That's incredible. Must come in useful in this line of work.'

Bastian nods. 'You could say that. You see, I can also see a map of locks and security panels I touch.'

Shep slaps Bastian on the shoulder as they catch up with the others. 'Bastian is one of the best thieves you'll ever meet.'

Bastian sneers at Shep. 'Was, my friend. Was. I'm retired,' he explains to Court. 'But yes, I made a living from it.' He shrugs and grins again. 'All in the past now.'

'Found it,' Davyn says, cutting off the string of questions Court wanted to ask. He would never have guessed Bastian's past was anything like that. He glances at the heavy tattoos on his hands and realises there's quite a bit he doesn't know about Bastian. Hell, he barely knows anything about any of the Blackjacks. He did though. He worked with them for over a decade. He must have known what Bastian did before the Blackjacks.

They wipe the debris away from a steel door embedded in the ground behind a rocky outcropping. Court stares at the door then stumbles back as an image hits him like a physical blow to his gut. He's been here before. He knows he's been here. 'There's a set of metal stairs.'

Nix appears in front of him. 'Close your eyes. Tell me what you see.'

Court tries to focus on the stairs, but the memory is shoved from his head by a ball of pain. 'Fuck!'

Nix grips his arms firmly and squeezes. 'Hey. Look at me.'

He breathes past the pain and focuses on her face. The pain eases, taking the memory with it. 'I could be leading you all into a trap.'

She smiles and let's go of his arm. 'How about we go find out?'

Bastian waits for Nix to nod at him before he places his palm over the control panel. He closes his eyes and frowns. A few seconds later he nods. 'Got it.' He taps in the sequence and the locks disengage. The hatch slides to the side showing metal stairs.

Fallon grimaces as she leans over the edge. 'Air is stale. Doubt there's anyone down there.'

'It's empty,' Bastian confirms.

Nix moves to the edge of the stairs with Court. 'You can stay here.'

He shakes his head. 'Not a chance.'

'Thought you'd say that. Dav, take the lead with me. Shep and Fallon follow the others.' Court watches as she disappears down the stairs followed by Davyn. He said he's going, but that doesn't mean he wants to. He knows without a doubt he spent some time here. Willow and Bastian go next leaving Court standing at the top of the steps.

'You good, buddy?' Court forces a smile, but Shep isn't fooled. 'We've got your back.'

He adjusts his grip on his gun and steps down.

After a few steps Nix's enhanced night vision kicks in. They reach a fork in the tunnel and wait while Bastian does his trick. 'Left. It opens up a few metres ahead.'

'Still alone, Shep?' Nix asks.

'No vamps. We're good.'

They follow the corridor to a central room. Court stops at the entrance, clearly not keen on stepping inside the room. Twelve glass containment cells take up the far wall. Each one is damaged, either by time or intentionally. Banks of computer screens fill the left wall, but like the cells, they haven't been used for a while.

Bastian walks to the centre of the room and crouches down to place his palm on the stone floor. 'There's a smaller room back at the right fork, but it's empty. This seems to be the heart of whatever this place was.'

'Our boy spent some time here,' Shep says as he checks out the screens. 'Your scent is strongest on the far left cell.'

Court slowly approaches the cell Shep mentioned. Compared to the other eleven, the damage to his cell is severe. It looks like he shoved his fist through the screen. 'I broke out of here.'

Nix picks up a thick shackle from the floor of the cell. 'It looks like it was powered.'

He looks down at the scars around each wrist. 'It burnt if I pulled against it.'

Her throat dries at the thought of him secured in that glass container like a specimen in a jar. 'They must have electrified it so you couldn't break out.'

'So how did I get out?'

'Maybe there was a power outage,' Nix says. 'Maybe someone let you go. The important part is that you did get out.'

'I don't understand why they abandoned this place. I wasn't here alone so where is everyone else? Can't see them letting them go.'

Nix shrugs. 'We may never know. That doesn't mean we're not going to try to find out. Shep, do your thing on the system. Take anything that could be of use. Dav and Bas, check out the other room just in case. Willow and Fallon, head back outside. See if you can spot any other structures like this from the air. Keep to within a few miles.'

The teams head off and Shep disappears behind the bank of screens against the far wall. Nix examines Court as he stares at the cell that held him. She's trying so hard to keep her walls up, keep her feelings for him buried deep within, but after seeing this place she's having a hard time remaining emotionless.

Every time she looks at the cell, she pictures him in it. What the hell did they do to him and why? 'Is anything else coming to you?'

He shakes his head. 'Fletch is right. It's like there's a block or wall up. Someone doesn't want me remembering what happened. Kind of on board with that after seeing this place.'

Nix stops her hand from taking his, stuffing it in her pocket instead. 'Anything Shep?'

'Nope,' he mutters from behind the screens. He gets up and dusts himself off. 'Except for a few spiders that I'd rather kept to themselves there's nothing. Hang on.' He ducks down and reappears with a cigarette butt in his gloved hand. 'What do we have here? Don't they know smoking is a nasty habit?'

Nix smiles and fishes in her pocket for a tissue. Shep wraps the butt in the tissue and hands it back to her. 'Nasty habit, but hopefully it'll give us some answers.'

'You really think you can find a match from that?'

Shep yelps and swipes frantically at his hair. 'Fucking spider.' He pulls out his gun and directs it at the creature scuttling to the safety of the shadows. 'Do that again and I'll put a bullet in your hairy ass.'

'What the fuck are you doing?' Bas asks as he comes back with Davyn.

'Spider. Big ass spider.' He holds his hands out to show him how big it was. Bas frowns at him, clearly not believing for one minute that the spider in question was the size of a small dog. 'Okay, so it may have been a smidge smaller than that, but it was hairy. Anyway, Ethan and his team have access to a substantial database. There's a chance he'll find a match to the owner of the butt on his system.'

'Did you guys find anything?'

Davyn shakes his head. 'Storage room. Nothing in it.'

'Time to go,' Nix says.

'We gonna blow this place?'

She shakes her head. 'Love to, Shep, but I'd prefer we didn't announce we found this place. Bas, I'll leave you to lock up again.'

Shep stops in the doorway, his usual grin gone from his face. 'We got company heading our way.'

37

Court pulls out his gun again as he steps out of the tunnel. Davyn and Bastian are standing to either side of the entrance, scanning the sky for their unwanted company. He can't see anything yet, but Shep's abilities must be accurate. The team had moved out without question.

Shep joins them and closes his eyes for a second. 'West, Boss. Coming from there,' he says, pointing up.

Nix shakes her head and gestures back towards the farm. 'Just what we need. True Order fighters dropping in on us. Everyone move.'

Fallon, Nix, and Willow take to the air while the rest of them cover as much ground as possible. The farm appears on the horizon just as Nix shouts that the Order have arrived. Before any of them can react, Fallon crashes to the ground in front of Court with a large vampire on her back.

Shep, Davyn, and Bastian split up as Court moves towards Fallon. She's on her back on the ground fighting the Order male in a tangle of limbs. Court doesn't get a chance to check on her. Another male lands in front of him, knocking the gun from his hand. The Order fighter smiles widely. 'You're him.'

'Not sure who 'him' is, but let me guess. You want me to come with you?'

'Yes.'

Court shakes his head. 'I'm good, thanks.' He ducks behind the vampire, and drives his knife into the guy's wing, burying it deep in the main bone. His opponent snarls in pain and lashes out with his other wing. Court smiles to himself. Shep was right. Keep the fuckers on the ground and you've got the advantage. Court kicks out, striking him in the chest. The injured fighter crashes back against a tree. Before he can convince his body to move, Court rams his knife in his heart. He pulls it free, locates his gun, and hurries over to help Fallon.

She's got the fighter in a headlock, but his wings are doing their best to decapitate her. Court lowers his gun as Fallon breaks the guy's neck and dumps his body on the ground.

She wipes her auburn hair away from her forehead and looks around. 'Where's everyone else?'

'Back at the farm hopefully. You okay?'

She nods. 'Never better. Nothing like taking out a few Order fighters to brighten up a girl's day.'

They follow the others, Fallon keeping to the ground thanks to a damaged wing. They pick up the pace when they hear gunshots up ahead.

Court growls and raises his gun as a tall vampire steps out from behind a tree. The man's eyes lock with his as the vampire's green wings spread wide behind him. He smiles as he raises his weapon to point it at Court.

'You're not leaving here.'

Court's jaw pops as he clenches it tightly. 'That's not your decision I'm afraid.'

He walks around Court, slowly turning him so his back is up

against a tree. 'There's nowhere for you to go. You come with us and I promise I won't hurt your mongrel friends too much.'

Court is vaguely aware of Fallon and the others engaging with different True Order fighters, but at the moment Court's attention is on the brute in front of him. He's familiar. Court doesn't know how, but he remembers this vampire.

The green-winged guy rushes Court. The first punch glances off Court's chin. The second punch doubles him over and expels the air from his struggling lungs. He drops to his knees and looks up at the large vampire in front of him. He tries to get a clear lock on his eyes, but this guy is no fool. He laughs and backhands Court. 'You think you can pull that eye trick on me?'

He smiles down at Court. He has every reason to smile. He's one strong fucker.

Court pushes the pain to the back of his mind. He ignores the protests from his body and stands up straight. His eyes glow with rage as he stares at his opponent. In those brief few seconds, Court sees everything he needs to. Surprise. His opponent didn't expect him to get up again. The vampire tries to stand tall, but it's too late to redeem himself. Court has him where he wants him.

'You're... in... my... way!' Court takes a lurching step forward with each word, striking the green-winged vampire wherever he can hit. On the fourth step, he swings his fist at the man's face.

The blow strikes home sending him crashing back against a tree. Court wants to finish the job, but Fallon is in trouble. One of the Order's fighters has her pinned to the ground. He races over to her and pulls the guy away then helps her up. The fighter pushes to his feet and draws his gun then fires. Before Court and Fallon can react, an imposing figure leaps in front of the gun.

Davyn drops to the ground followed a few seconds later by the fighter when Nix appears from behind him and fires. Court hurries over to Davyn. Blood is darkening his t-shirt where the bullet entered his upper chest.

Court keeps pressure on the wound as Nix hurries over to the others. She comes back over and crouches down beside them. 'Shep and Willow are going back for the cars. The Order has fled. We took out all but one of their fighters.'

'The green-winged one. He's...' Court looks around. There's no sign of him. 'I thought I knocked him out.'

She shakes her head. 'He's gone.' She kneels down beside Davyn. 'You okay?'

Dav nods, but he's losing blood fast. 'Everyone okay?'

'Bas was hit too. Shep and Willow were taking him back to the cars when you were hit. Fallon?'

'I'm okay, Boss. One of them got a lucky hit on my wing. Knife wound. Dav saved me and Court by launching himself in front of the fucking bullet. Idiot! Why the hell did you do that?'

'I'm regretting it,' he replies as he presses his hand to the wound.

Court takes the field kit from Nix and tears the wrapping off the thick bandage. He curses as Davyn falls back, hitting the ground with a thump. Fallon scrambles over to them, the knife wound in her wing still oozing blood.

'You didn't feed again, did you.'

Davyn glares at her, but doesn't bother replying as she pulls down the front of his t-shirt. Court presses the bandage over the bullet wound and Davyn curses in pain.

'I've got him,' Court says to Nix. 'You fly back and grab one of the cars. There's no way he can walk like this.'

She nods and takes to the air, disappearing above the trees. He takes another bandage from Fallon and tapes it in place. 'I can't stop the bleeding.

'He's just lost consciousness,' Fallon says as she checks for a pulse. 'Fuck. It's weak. Bastard needs to feed more often. That's why the wound is still bleeding. He's going to get himself killed if he keeps this up.' She unzips a pocket in her jacket and takes out a transfusion kit.

'Turn his head to the side.'

'Are you sure you're okay to do this?'

'No way we're going to test your blood on him.' She attaches a needle to both ends of the tube, slides one needle into her arm and the other into Davyn's neck. 'That should give him a boost.' She grunts in pain as her deep rust-coloured wings slowly retreat inside her.

'Do you not need to treat the wound first?'

'A few hours in my body is better than anything Fletch can do for them. Feels like there's a damn knife in my shoulder though. Fucking Order bastard.' She leans against a tree and watches her blood travelling down the tube to Davyn. 'We did figure out something though.'

'What?' Court asks as he checks Davyn's pulse. It's not great but at least it's still there. Fallon's blood must be helping him.

'We're on to something. Something they don't want us knowing about.'

Court nods but doesn't feel encouraged in the slightest. Bastian, Davyn, and Fallon were injured trying to figure out what happened to him. If this is the result of prying in whatever is going on, maybe they'll be best to leave well enough alone.

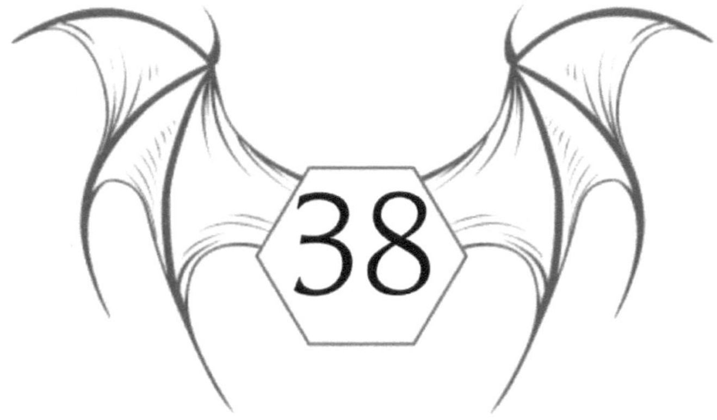

As soon as Fletch comes back to his examination room Thea knows something is wrong. Her thoughts instantly go to Court. He went out with the others a few hours ago and she hasn't heard from him since. Not that he would contact her anyway. She hadn't spoken to him yet. He probably still thinks she's angry with him.

'What is it?'

'Can you grab my bag from the cupboard to your left. I just got a call from Willow. They were attacked. Fallon, Davyn, and Bastian are injured.'

Thea freezes for a second at his words, then jolts into action. She grabs his bag and follows him out of the room and along the corridor to the garage. She stands beside Fletch and stares at the ramp leading to the darkness beyond. She wants to ask Fletch for more information, but a part of her doesn't want to know. If Fallon rang him does that mean Davyn is unconscious?

Time crawls as they wait to see what's about to arrive. It's only been a few minutes, but it feels so much longer. The breath she was holding releases a little when headlights appear further along the tunnel gradually growing in intensity as they near. The roar of an engine echoes down the tunnel and eventually Davyn's car bursts out of the darkness and screeches to a stop a few feet from Fletch and Thea.

Fallon climbs out of the driver's seat and pulls open the back door. Fletch gestures for Thea to bring his bag around as he leans inside. 'What happened?'

'Fucking macho idiot put himself in front of a bullet meant for me. It's in his chest but there's no exit wound. He lost consciousness pretty fast. Must not have fed recently. I had to give him blood. His pulse was all over the place.'

'Are you okay?'

'Knife wound to my wing. Managed to get it back inside so it's not too bad. Should heal in me but I'll check it later. The others are on their way back with Bas. There were still a few Order fighters hanging around, so we split up. Shep and Court are trying to lead them away. Willow and Nix are a few minutes behind with Bas.'

'Okay. We're in for a busy night. And I will be checking your wing once Dav and Bas are dealt with. Thea, bring the gurney over.' Thea spots it against the side wall and quickly wheels it over to the car. 'Okay, sis, get him out.' Fletch stands aside as Fallon drags Davyn onto the gurney. He helps arrange him on the trolley then sets about cutting his top open so he can check the wound.

'Get him on his side, sis.' Fallon holds Davyn up while Fletch finishes cutting his top off. He runs his hands over Davyn's back. 'Fuck. There's definitely no exit wound. I need to get him into surgery.' He frowns and his hand stops moving. Fletch crouches down and his frown deepens. 'Fuck me.'

'What?' Fallon asks.

Thea doesn't know why but for some reason Fletch glances at her before he answers Fallon. Thea shakes her head, silently begging him not to say anything to Fallon. 'Nothing. Just hoping there would have been an exit wound. Would have made everyone's life easier. So, Fallon, can you get the theatre ready? I'll bring him up. Are you okay to look after Bastian?'

'Sure. I'll shout if I need help.'

As soon as she leaves the garage, Fletch straps Davyn down and crosses the garage, pushing the gurney in front of him. 'So, you going to tell me how long you've known he's a Prime?'

'Only a few days. I saw him with his wings out. He really doesn't want anyone to know about them. One of them is deformed. He made me promise... well, he threatened me if I'm being honest. He's adamant no one finds out about them.'

'Fucking stubborn fool,' Fletch mutters to himself.

'Are you going to tell anyone?'

'How about I make sure I get that bullet out first. Once he's awake we'll see what he says about his wings.'

39

Court sits next to Nix's empty chair and looks around the room. It's the first time he's been at a briefing with the team, but Nix insisted he take part. He feels like an impostor even being here, let alone being included as a member of the team.

A man he doesn't recognise sits opposite him. Probably not a statement he needs to use. Everyone is unrecognisable. He holds out a well-manicured hand, but there's no mistaking the strength behind his grasp. 'I'm Ethan. Nice to finally meet you in person - again.'

'You too,' Court says. Court may feel completely out of place with the other Blackjacks, but Ethan couldn't be more of a contrast himself. His shirt is immaculately pressed, not one hair is out of place and his hands are free of callouses and scars. He loosens his tie and takes some files out of his bag.

Shep slaps Ethan on the back as he sits in the chair beside him. 'Gracing us with your presence?'

'How could I keep away from you and your wit for another

second?'

Shep grins. 'I get it. I have that effect on a lot of people.'

Court zones out of the banter as each of the Blackjacks take their seats. His attention moves from the group to Nix as she appears at the end of the corridor. Not for the first time he finds it difficult to take his eyes off her. Dressed in figure hugging jeans with ankle boots and an off-the-shoulder jumper, their leader is beautiful. Everything he's seen of Nix so far impresses him. Not only is she stunning, but she also manages to bring this group of mismatched fighters together.

That's no easy task. She meets his eyes as she nears the room and smiles at him. Something about the action stirs a memory followed by the inevitable pain in his head. He ignores it and tries to focus on the memory. It feels like deja-vu, but also so much more.

He closes his eyes and concentrates on the image, but it's like trying to grasp a handful of mist. Along with the memory, the pain subsides, leaving the familiar hollow feeling. He opens his eyes to find Nix crouched beside him and the whole room staring at him.

'Are you okay?' she asks.

'Yeah. I'm good.'

'You sort of zoned out on us for a bit. You looked like you were in pain.'

Fletch offers him a bottle of water. 'Presume that was another memory trying to break through.'

'Whatever is stopping them is effective. I'm about done with it though.'

Fletch smiles and sits back down. 'No one could blame you.'

Nix takes her seat, but her eyes are firmly locked on him. 'Are you sure you're okay to continue? We can do this without you and I'll brief you when we're done.'

'This is my fucking life they messed with. I'm staying. I'm fine. Really. Just feels like I've been punched in the head. It'll ease in a few minutes.'

'As long as you're sure. I've got two fighters under Fletch's care. I could do without adding you to the list.'

'Who's been injured?' Ethan asks, looking around the table.

'Bastian and Davyn. Fallon was hit too but thankfully it was a minor knife wound to her wing. It should heal inside her.'

The colour drains from Ethan's face as he spins his chair around to face Fletch. 'Bastian is injured? Is he okay? I mean are Davyn and Bastian okay?'

Fletch scratches his beard as he nods slowly. 'It took a bit of work to get the bullet out of Dav, but it eventually gave in. Fallon dealt with Bastian's shoulder. The bullet made a right mess of it, but it should heal. They were both sedated for surgery so they'll probably be out of it for another hour or so. They both lost a lot of blood and will need a good feed once they've come to.'

Ethan runs a hand over his face then adjusts his tie again. 'That's good. Do you need me to organise some donors?'

'Might not be a bad idea. We have plenty of blood in stock but Bas would probably appreciate a donor instead,' Fletch says. 'Doubt Dav will take much from our stock. Awkward git never does. '

'No problem. I'll send someone over for Bastian. Keep me posted on their progress,' Ethan says, but he looks far from happy. If Court had to guess, he'd say Ethan looks downright worried sick. If he doesn't stop messing with his tie, he's going to choke himself

'So,' Nix says, trying to move the meeting on. 'What do you have, Ethan?'

Ethan turns on the screen, and Nix spins her chair around. 'The cigarette Shep found had DNA from a well-known mercenary called Maddox. According to the sketchy and plentiful reports, Maddox likes to dabble in private security.'

'Mercenary?' Fallon asks.

'That's putting it nicely. He'll do anything as long as the pay is right.'

'Are you saying he's behind what happened to me?' Court asks.

Ethan shakes his head. 'I seriously doubt it. He's more the muscle than the brains of the operation. Not saying for one moment you shouldn't take him seriously. He's lethal and so are the men he leads. If he's involved at all it will be from a protection aspect.' He pulls up another file and points to the screen. 'We've only got a blurred photo of Maddox, but it was taken recently.'

'Any way of tracking him?' Nix asks.

'It won't be easy. Like I said, he's trained to protect whoever is paying him. That's the person we need to find. I've got my team on it, but we're going to have to take a few grey paths if we want to track down his funding.'

Shep nudges him. 'Aw, taking a walk on the dark side with us.'

'I'm a Sith lord at this stage.'

Shep feigns surprise. 'Did you just Star Wars me?'

'I know, I hate myself. Anyway, we're on the case. There's something I need you all to be aware of. Maddox isn't cheap. I'm talking seven figures minimum. Whoever is bankrolling him has deep pockets. Court, if they took you for a reason, there's a strong chance they're not going to give up looking for you.'

'There's also a strong chance they have others like me.'

Ethan nods. 'Absolutely.' He pushes the files he brought with him to the centre of the table. 'I gave Nix a list we compiled. There are forty-seven vampires unaccounted for. The first one vanished four years ago. The last was two weeks ago.'

'Who are they targeting?' Bastian asks.

'Males and only those with a similar blood group to Court.'

Nix looks up from the list. 'Do you know how they're finding out that information?'

'I think they're looking at specific family lines. There's no other way. Take Court for example. His blood group isn't on record anywhere that I can find. Unless you've been tested, you're not going to know. While you're not a Prime, your bloodline is relatively pure until the last generation.'

'So they're targeting males with a similar heritage?' Court asks. His thoughts immediately go to Thea. 'Are you sure it's just males?'

Ethan smiles and nods. 'Thea's perfectly safe. Not saying it's a good thing, but from what I can find, no females are missing. And Thea's human. That would rule her out anyway. Nothing to worry about.'

Court returns the smile, but he's not taking Ethan's deduction as solid fact. With everything he's heard since the Blackjacks threw his life upside down, nothing is impossible. 'Have you any idea who is behind Maddox?'

Ethan straightens his tie again before he answers. 'Yes and no. Fletch and I were talking about it before you left for the farm. If whoever is behind this is trying to find a cure or something to slow down the effects of the illness, they'll need a lot of funding.'

'Does what we found near the farm help to backup Vincent's claims?' Nix asks.

Ethan looks across at Fletch. 'I'll let you do this part.'

Fletch grins and tucks his hair behind his ear then rolls his sleeves up. 'Okay, so, the cells you found at the facility were clearly designed for vampires. The cells themselves and the electrified restraints were custom made. No getting out. From what I can tell from the photos Shep showed me, there was a transfusion station there at one stage. Each of the cells had access points for medical equipment - like IV tubes and the like. Some of the tubes were still hanging out of the less damaged cells.

'That, together with the males that are being taken... well, it all helps to verify what Vincent said. Someone is harvesting blood and doing something with it to try and deal with Blood Fever. As to what exactly they're doing, I haven't got the first fucking clue if I'm being honest, and that's pissing me off quite a bit.'

Nix squeezes his arm, and Court feels an irrational twinge of jealousy. 'It's a new one for all of us. So, there's clearly money behind all this. I'm presuming you can't pop down to the local supermarket and pick up what you need.'

Fletch shakes his head. 'No way. Like Ethan said, deep pockets are involved. I'd hate to guess how much the cells themselves would cost.'

'Don't suppose you've tried to trace the cells back to whoever made them?' Shep asks.

'Funny you should ask,' Ethan says. 'I'll need your help on that one if you're up for it.' He passes Shep an external hard drive. 'That's an enhanced copy of the details we could make out from the images you sent. Think you can work some of your magic?'

Shep grins and slips the hard drive in his pocket. 'Of course, but only because you asked so nicely.'

Court pulls the file towards him and looks at the faces staring up from the page. It kills him that he's the only one who made it back to their family. 'Is there a chance they're still alive?'

The hum of conversation dies down. No one answers for a few minutes and it's Ethan who finally breaks the silence. 'I don't know, Court.'

'You don't think they've finished though, do you?'

Ethan shakes his head. 'No. Judging by the dates on some of these reports, they're still very much active.'

'So what's the plan?'

Ethan excuses himself as his phone rings. As he leaves the room, Nix looks back at Court. 'The plan is we keep digging. Get the word out to the community too. Make sure males go out in groups. Try to make it more difficult for them to be picked up.'

Ethan comes back, his face serious as he squeezes his phone in his hands.

'Oh, I know that look,' Shep says. 'What's up?'

'Apparently Vincent is missing. His wife hasn't seen him for nearly a week. Actually, she hasn't seen him since the day after he met with you, Nix.'

'I presume this isn't usual?'

Ethan shakes his head. 'I think someone found out Vincent spoke to you and took care of him.'

'Fuck.' Nix rubs a hand over her face then shrugs. 'I'm not going to waste any time mourning that man. Clearly, he knew a hell of a lot more than he told me. He wouldn't have been taken out unless he was a threat to whoever is behind this.'

'I agree,' Ethan says. 'I've told his family to lay low for a few weeks. They're heading off to the country residence. I thought you'd prefer to have a look around without them getting in the way.'

'Thanks.' Nix gets up and closes the file of names. 'Shep, you concentrate on sourcing the manufacturer of the cells. Willow, I want you to escort Ethan wherever he wants to go.'

'I don't need—'

'You're a Blackjack as much as everyone else. I'm not going to let anyone out alone. No chances. Court, will you come with me to Vincent's house? I don't really want you out in the field, but there could be something at Vincent's house that triggers a memory for you. I don't know. I'm grasping at straws here. Fallon, I want you to come too just in case someone does try to get to Court again.'

'Sure thing, Boss.'

'Fletch, you get our two boys back on their feet ASAP. We're going to need everyone fighting fit.'

'Will do.'

'Let's get to work.'

Thea checks her watch for the tenth time in as many minutes. Davyn was brought to the recovery room an hour ago and so far, hasn't stirred. The bullet hadn't damaged the bone in his wing, but he'd lost a lot of blood. Fletch had a hard time taking it out but he's confident there won't be any problems with Davyn's recovery.

She glances over her shoulder at the bed opposite his and the sleeping Bastian. She'll never get her head around the accelerated vampire regeneration. Both men had been seriously injured, but according to Fletch, they should be on their feet in an hour. After a good feed, they'll be back to their old selves by morning.

Thea slowly gets to her feet and approaches Davyn's bed. He looks a lot different in his sleep. Some of the lines that give a harsh edge to his face are gone, as is the constant frown he always seems to be wearing.

'What the hell are you doing?' she mutters to herself as she backs away and sits down again. Just in time too. The door to the clinic opens and Fletch comes in.

'Sorry. The meeting ran on a bit. Thanks for keeping an eye on them. Anything from our Sleeping Beauties yet?'

She shakes her head then turns towards Davyn's bed when she hears a low groan. 'Speak of the devil.'

Fletch leans over the bed and smiles at his patient. 'You back with us Dav?'

Davyn slowly opens his eyes. He winces and touches his chest. 'Fuck that hurts.'

'Getting shot in the chest usually hurts,' Fletch replies as he pulls a chair up beside Davyn. 'Listen, I owe you a big thank you, Dav. Fallon said you saved her by taking that bullet.'

Davyn nods but doesn't say anything.

'So,' Fletch continues when he gives up on getting a response, 'We had to operate to get the bullet out. You were unlucky I'm afraid. The bullet lodged in a bone in your back. Which is strange because there isn't meant to be a bone where the bullet ended up. It should have gone through.'

Davyn clenches his jaw but offers no explanation.

'Really? Still not going to fess up? Credit me with a smidge of intelligence, Dav.' Fletch glances over at Bastian, but the vampire is still out of it. 'I know you're a Prime.'

Davyn's eyes glow as he glares at Thea. There's so much contempt in his look, she takes a step back.

'You can get yourself under control. It had nothing to do with Thea. I was looking for an exit wound and found wing ridges instead. Doesn't take a genius to figure it out. What you need to be doing is thanking that girl over there for keeping your secret. I was all ready to blab it out to Fallon, but she stopped me.

'Apparently, you were pretty damn insistent on keeping your wings to yourself so I sent Fallon on her way and Thea helped me. So, like I said, drop the angry vampire, glowing eye thing and try a simple thank you. I did it a few minutes ago with you. It's straightforward enough.'

Thea isn't the slightest bit surprised when he doesn't thank her.

Davyn pushes onto his elbows, his breath hitching as the movement jars his injury. 'Can I go?'

Fletch crosses his arms as he glares across at Davyn. 'I'm sorry?'

'Can I go?'

Fletch rubs a hand over his jaw. 'Let me have a think about that. I'm going to say no, you can't go.'

'Why not?'

'You've just had surgery, Dav. You also lost a hell of a lot of blood. No doubt you're feeling less than fighting fit. You need to rest and feed.'

'I'll feed in my room.' He pushes up and swings his legs out of the bed. He squeezes his eyes shut and steadies himself on the bed.

'And you really think I believe that? I want to see you feed.'

'I feed in private.'

'Yeah, because you don't feed. Not as much as you should. And that's before you add the fact you're a Prime into the equation. Where are you getting your Prime blood from?'

'Back off, Fletch.'

'I'm just trying to keep you on your feet, Dav. I worked damn hard to save your ass. I can get Prime blood in for you – off the record of course. No one has to know.'

'I need a t-shirt.'

'What you need is to lie back down and let me help you.'

'I've survived this long without you interfering. I need a t-shirt, Fletch.'

Fletch gets up and opens the cupboard against the far wall. He takes out a scrub top and throws at Davyn. 'You're going to undo all my good work, stubborn git.'

'Are you going to tell Nix?'

'About your wings? No. Thea mentioned the whole 'don't tell

anyone on pain of death' threat.'

Davyn stumbles over to the door and slams it loudly behind him. Fletch stares at the door for a few minutes after Davyn left. 'Well, nice to feel appreciated in your work, isn't it? I'll give him ten minutes then make sure he's not bleeding out somewhere between here and his room.'

'Can I check on him? I need to explain why I told you.'

'There's nothing to explain. Even if I hadn't noticed the ridges, I would have noticed the wings when I opened him up.'

'This isn't meant to sound like a criticism, but how has no one noticed them before now?'

'Ridges on Prime males are less noticeable. I've seen his back before. It's a fucking mess if you'll excuse the language.'

'Yeah, I saw all the scars.'

He smirks across at her and winks. 'Is that right? Probably best you don't elaborate on how you saw them. The least I know the better, thanks all the same. Anyway, it's easy to lose the ridges among everything else going on with his back. Until I felt them, I had no idea they were there. He's done an outstanding job of keeping them hidden.'

'Can you do anything for his damaged wing?'

Fletch shrugs. 'Until he asks me to help, I can't do a thing. I'm a mere mortal, Thea. No way I'm going to try to force a vampire like Dav to let me examine him. I'll talk to him, but I'm not going to get my hopes up.'

'I don't understand why he's being like this about his wings. Why wouldn't he want everyone to know?'

Fletch leans forward and clasps his hands together. 'There's something you need to understand about these delightful vampires we share a house with. As well as being stubborn, they've been around the block a few times. My sister is twice my age for fucks sake. Nix, Court, and Dav have a century or more on me. You don't live that long without picking up a few scars along the way. And I'm not talking about ones you can see. Fallon means the world to me and we have a decent enough relationship, but I know she keeps things from me.'

He shrugs and looks over at the still sleeping Bastian. 'It's what they do. Whether it's self-preservation or protecting the humans in their lives I can't say. Whatever the reason I know to leave well enough alone. She'll talk when she's ready. I'm sure Dav will—' he stops speaking abruptly to laugh at himself. 'Scrap that. I'm not sure of anything when it comes to him. Or Shep. Or this one,' he says, nodding over to Bastian. 'But hey, life would be incredibly boring otherwise, right?'

'Is that so bad?'

'I'll give you that. A little boring would be nice from time to time.' He gets up and hands her a small pouch. 'There's a fresh dressing in that. Check the stitches are still in place. They'll need to stay in for a few hours until the wound heals.' He opens the fridge, takes out a bag of blood and places it in a small cooler. 'He'll probably refuse it, but see if you can convince him to drink this. It'll speed the healing process. I'll try and get some Prime blood in stock for him. He's not going to be at full strength otherwise.'

'You're happy for me to see him alone?'

Fletch snorts. 'I'm not your babysitter. Listen, I know there are stories going around about each of the team. Believe me, I've heard some impressive ones that would give the best-known fairy tales a run for their money. The team is lethal, but that applies to when they're doing their job. You can ask Gwen. She's been here a hell of a long time and she has never had a problem with anyone, including Dav. The guy doesn't like talking. So what? Shep doesn't like anyone touching his food. They all have their quirks. Doesn't make them unsafe to be around.'

'Thanks, Fletch.'

'I wouldn't thank me just yet. He's still a rude arsehole.'

Nix pulls off the road and onto Vincent's driveway. Gravel crunches under the car's tyres as she weaves through the imposing line of trees standing guard on each side of the drive. Each tree is pruned to perfection. Not a branch or leaf daring to grow outside the defined silhouette.

After navigating the ridiculously long entranceway, the house finally appears from behind the trees.

Court leans forward to get a better look. 'I thought you said this is his holiday home?'

'It is. Vincent is from the old money version of old money.'

'I get that, but this is bloody ridiculous.'

Nix couldn't agree more. The mansion is monstrous in every sense. Numerous stone statues of half-naked women are dotted around the stone courtyard, and two enormous fountains decorate the lawn. Each one is topped with another scantily clad woman holding a large vase from which the water would pour. Now, they're silent. Just like everything else around the house. There's an eerie quiet about the place that unsettles her.

Nix shakes her head as she looks at the gawdy statues. 'I'm sensing a theme with his garden ornaments. I'm just hoping it doesn't continue throughout the house.'

'Couldn't agree more,' Court replies. He nods towards the house. 'You feeling brave?'

Court gets out of the car and stands beside her and Fallon at the bottom of the steps. The two hour journey had been pleasant enough. She tried to keep the conversation going, but struggled. Court was clearly still processing everything he'd heard at the meeting and she can't blame him. He's had too much thrown at him over the last few days - let alone since waking up in the middle of nowhere with no memory. It doesn't surprise her that he's holding it together as well as he is. That was Court. No matter the situation, he was her rock. Fallon hadn't been much help with the conversation either. She wasn't one for chit-chat.

Court looks over his shoulder at her and smiles. She missed him so much. Having him back and less than a few feet away from her hasn't diminished that feeling one bit. If anything, it's so much worse. She knows what she could have with him. Knows what she can never have again. The pain from that is unbearable.

'Fallon, can you keep an eye out for any unwanted company?'

Fallon spreads her wings and pushes off the ground. Nix waits until she lands on one of the many impressive chimneys and has a look around.

'All clear, Boss,' Fallon says in her ear-piece.

Nix looks up at Court. 'Ready to poke into Vincent's life?'

'Can't wait.'

They climb the impressive stone staircase at the centre of the façade and stop in front of the heavy wooden door at the top. She can't figure out if the place has more chimneys than windows or vice versa. As with quite a few of the older families she's met over her long life,

Vincent's family liked to show their wealth. It was all about who had the biggest house, the fattest bank account, the plushest cars. Appearance was everything to them.

She pushes open the door and steps into the highly polished hallway. The whole place reeks of furniture polish and expensive perfume. 'We'll start in his office. Ethan said it's the third door on the left.'

He follows her down the corridor and to the office. Three plump leather couches sit facing an impressive fireplace which must easily be six feet tall. Three walls are lined with bookcases full of leather-bound volumes. An enormous wooden desk sits against the far wall with an equally obnoxious leather chair behind it. The wall behind the desk is covered in photos framed in gold along with certificates for various business achievements. 'Makes my office look like a shed.'

Court laughs. 'Think I'd prefer that to this.'

She begins with the paperwork on the low coffee table in front of the fireplace. It may have been the last stuff he was looking through before he vanished.

Court wanders over to the desk and looks at the photos hanging on the wall. She glances up at him and frowns. He's staring at one picture in particular. 'Find something?'

'I don't know. Do you recognise him?'

Nix gets off the couch and joins him at the wall of photographs. The one that's got his attention is of ten or so males in crisp tuxedos standing on the grand staircase in the main foyer. She has no doubts the champagne in their glasses is the best money can buy. 'Which one?'

Court points to the end of the back row and an imposing blond man. He's quite a looker, but not someone she recognises. 'He's not familiar. He's younger than the others though by a few centuries maybe. Do you recognise him?'

Court frowns at the photo. 'I don't know. I don't think so, but there's something—' He gasps and clutches his head as he falls back against the desk.

'Court!'

She manages to stop him from hitting his head as he slumps to the ground and leans against the side of the desk. He buries his head in his hands and tears at his hair. Nix grabs onto his arms, trying to stop him from doing any more damage to himself, but he catches her off guard and throws his head back, whacking it off the desk.

He suddenly opens his eyes and looks at her, locking on to her with his glowing eyes. The assault takes the breath from her lungs as Court invades her mind, throwing images at her like she's watching a film on fast-forward. She can't make sense of anything, but they keep coming until she loses consciousness.

Court groans and licks the blood off his lips. He feels like he's gone a few rounds with a wrecking ball. Damn thing is still trying to get out of his head. He pushes onto all-fours and squints, trying to get his eyes focused again.

'About fucking time.'

He looks over his shoulder and sees Fallon sitting on the floor between himself and Nix. 'What happened?'

'Presume you did your eye thing. Knocked the two of you out.'

His breath hitches in his throat. 'I hurt Nix?'

'She's still out for the count. Steady pulse though. How are you doing?'

'Impressive headache, but okay.' He sits back against the desk and stares over at Nix, sprawled on the floor. He did that. It was his fucking creepy eye thing. He'd attacked Thea with it a few times, but she never lost consciousness. Thea had tried to tell him it wasn't an attack, it was just something he couldn't control, but fuck that. What else would you call forcing yourself inside someone's head? Into their memories. It was an attack and a brutal one. He scrubs his hands angrily through his hair, wincing as he brushes against fresh cuts on his scalp. 'Damn it! I'm so sorry, Fallon. I didn't mean to hurt her.'

Fallon crouches down in front of him. 'Hey, I know that. She knows that. Seriously though, you could do with getting a grip on whatever you do. Hell of a powerful weapon.'

'Any ideas how I do that?'

She shrugs. 'I've got wings so no special powers for me. I'm sure Bas or Shep could help you.'

He takes his phone out of his pocket and finds Ethan's number. The Blackjacks are going to kick him out of the team for this. He's too much of a liability. He looks down at Nix. He doesn't care. She's more important. He taps the screen, but Fallon reaches out and takes the phone. Before he can react, she places it to her ear. 'Hey, Ethan. Yeah, we're fine. False alarm. Yeah, I'll ring you when we're done here.' She disconnects the call and hands the phone back to Court.

'What the hell did you do that for? She could be injured.'

'All that'll come of that is Ethan in a state because you worried him.'

'Besides, I'm fine.'

They both turn to look at Nix.

She opens her eyes and winces. 'Apart from the mother and father of all headaches, I'm fine.'

'I could have killed you, Nix.'

'I'm fairly sure I'm still alive.' She pushes herself up and holds her head. 'Well, most of me is. You pack one hell of a punch.'

'I'm sorry, Nix. I... fuck it. Anything I say is going to sound hollow.' Like every single time he's said the same words to Thea.

She squeezes his hand but lets go too soon. 'I know you didn't do that intentionally. We need to seriously figure out how to stop it or some way for you to control it at the least.'

'Exactly what I just said,' Fallon says as she helps Nix to her feet then pulls Court upright. 'So I don't suppose either of you know what triggered that little episode?'

He looks over at the picture on the wall of the man who triggered this attack. 'That blond guy did. How do you know him, Nix?'

Nix leans on the edge of desk beside him. 'I don't. I haven't got a clue who he is.'

'But I saw him. In your memories when I... you know.'

She shakes her head then quickly stops and rubs her forehead. 'Bad idea. I don't know him Court. I have no idea how you did it, but you shared your memories with me.'

'What?'

'I saw that man because you know him from somewhere. I felt cold and my wrists were painful. There was a glass panel in front of me. No, it was the wall of a cell. Just like the ones we found in the old facility. I was in one of the cells. But it wasn't me. I was you.'

His frowns deepens as he takes in what she just said. This is so much worse than taking her memories. He doesn't want her to experience any part of what he went through. Not remembering the details didn't make him any less convinced he wanted her as far from it as possible. 'I don't understand any of this.'

'Neither do I. All I know is that whoever the man is, you know him. We'll bring the photo with us. Ethan should be able to tell us who he is.'

Fallon gestures to the couch. 'You two sit and get yourselves sorted. I'll gather up any paperwork I can find.'

Court looks across at Nix as they both settle on the couch. 'Are you sure you're all right?'

'I'm fine. Just do me a favour.'

'What?'

'If you find any more photos, please don't look at them. Being punched in the brain once today is enough.' She smiles to soften her words, but it does nothing to ease the guilt sitting in the pit of his stomach.

43

Nix pulls in beside Ethan's BMW and kills the engine. She looks over at Court. He didn't say much on the drive back. After half an hour, she gave up engaging him in conversation. His head was somewhere else. And now she knows where. The brief flashes of memories he shared were enough. Whatever happened, he was cold, in pain, alone... and afraid.

He lost something during the years he was missing. She's not sure if it's the too many questions thrown up by his amnesia, or the brief flashes of memories, or his enhanced talent. Maybe it's a mix of all three, but he's so unsure of himself. Since the first day he stalked into her office as a new recruit, he was confident. Not overly so like Shep, but it was there. Whoever took him, whoever did this to him, took part of his essence from him.

He's back to training regularly with Shep and Fallon. His broad shoulders are filling out and, apart from the beard, he looks like he did a few years ago. His body is back in shape, but she can't do anything about his mind, and that's killing her. She wants to help, but she doesn't know how.

If that blond man was in any way involved, she would personally make sure hers' was the last face he ever saw. Hopefully Ethan would be able to shed some light on who he is. Any piece that can be added to the puzzle is one step closer to retribution.

'You okay?'

He jumps slightly at the sound of her voice. 'What? Yeah. Sorry. I was miles away.'

'You sure? You can stay here and I'll speak to him with Fallon.'

'Seriously, I'm fine. Let's see if Ethan knows who that mystery guy is.'

'Okay. Fallon, you stay here. We won't be long.'

They get out of the car and head towards the lift. She pushes the button for the tenth floor and the door closes silently. 'Does Ethan own the building?'

She nods. 'His family is very well off. And I mean very. Ethan started Croft Holdings a few decades ago - well, according to the outside world, his father did. Best way to explain the fact he hasn't aged. Anyway, most of the people he employs are vampires, but there are quite a few humans too.'

'Do they know about vampires?'

'Some do. It's an international investment company. He has two teams, one day and one night. The majority of the staff work on legitimate investments, but he has a team dedicated to helping us.'

'I presume he's not the only one operating like this.'

'We have to make a living just like humans do. I know you haven't seen much evidence lately, but we're not all intent on wiping out the human race. Some of us have mortgages to pay.' She smirks and gestures for him to step out as the doors open.

She steps out onto the polished wooden floor and walks over to the reception desk. Court glances over at the floor to ceiling windows which make up the entire wall beside the lift.

The receptionist smiles widely when she gets an eyeful of Court. The female's smile grows ridiculously as he nears. Nix gets a small kick when she notices there's a smear of lipstick on the female's teeth.

'Hello. Welcome to Croft Holdings. I'm Amber. And you are?'

Nix leans over, putting herself between Amber and Court. 'We're here to see Ethan.'

Amber's glare makes a brief appearance before she reins it in. 'And you are?' she repeats, directing her question at Court.

'Tell him Nix is here.'

Amber picks up the phone, never taking her eyes off Court. Nix looks over her shoulder at him and understands why Amber is drooling all over her handset. She may understand the attention he's getting, but that doesn't mean she's in any way happy about it. She smiles sweetly at Amber, showing a little of her canine. That together with a 'back-off' look does the trick. It's pathetic, but she's not going to apologise.

She's still asserting her dominance when Ethan steps through the double doors. 'Nix? You want to come through.' He taps her on the shoulder and she finally turns away from Amber. She follows Ethan through the door and has to stop herself from having a private word with Amber when the receptionist wiggles her fingers at Court as he passes.

'What the hell is wrong with you?' Ethan hisses at her.

'What?'

'Do I need to send Amber home with a security detail?'

'Don't be dramatic.'

'And don't visually threaten my staff because they noticed Court. He's someone you would notice. Don't look at me that way.'

'What way?'

'The same way you looked at Amber. I'm just saying you made your feelings about him perfectly clear. Or at least that's what you told me. Which is fine. But you have to realise he will be drooled over, and no doubt find someone to mate with sooner or later. You're going to have to get used to seeing him with other females.'

'Will you shut up!' Nix hisses as she glances over her shoulder to Court. 'He could hear you.'

'And what a shame that would be.'

Court follows after Ethan and Nix in a bit of a trance. His head is still firmly back in Vincent's house waiting for Nix to come round. All this vampire and Blackjack stuff he can handle. Well, sort of. It's whatever the hell is going on with his head that's scaring the fuck out of him. He could have killed her. If he can't get a leash on whatever it is, he's going to be too much of a liability.

He shakes himself back to the present and grimaces when he notices Nix and Ethan have stopped at a set of doors and are looking strangely at him. They're actually looking at him the same way too many people have been looking at him lately. And he's getting really tired of it. In yet another award-winning performance, he smiles, but he must be losing his touch. They look far from convinced.

Ethan opens one of the doors and steps aside to let them in his office. While Vincent's office was styled for form over function, Ethan's is all business. The glass topped desk is large but simple. The bookcase lining one wall contains a few books, but they're clearly there because he uses them and not just for show. He gestures to the black leather couch and opens the mini fridge filled to bursting with at least half a dozen different juices and flavoured waters. Nix goes for a regular water while Court just shakes his head. He doesn't trust his stomach just yet. It's still churning after the episode in Vincent's house.

Ethan places her bottle of water on the low table in front of the couch and sits opposite them.

'So, I presume you found something at Vincent's?'

Nix places her bag on the table and gently slides the contents onto the table. She passes the framed photo to Ethan. 'The young looking blond at the back. Do you know who he is?'

Ethan examines the picture then nods. 'That's Rhain.'

'What do you know about him?' Court asks.

'For starters, he's not exactly young. He must be three centuries old. He's the last surviving member of one of the oldest Prime bloodlines. His parents were well respected and had their fingers in any pie worth having your fingers in. It was all left to Rhain when they died.'

'What sort of pies?' Nix asks.

Ethan shrugs. 'Take your pick. I can possibly get you a full list, but I do mean possibly. His bloodline isn't known for airing their laundry - dirty or pristine - in public. They have always kept to themselves, but I'll have a look for you.'

'So he's got a healthy bank balance?'

Ethan frowns across at Nix. 'Of course. Hold on. You're not suggesting Rhain is the funding behind Maddox and his men.'

Nix glances up at Court and he knows he has to come clean. 'When I saw him, he felt familiar somehow. Then the pain hit, and I knocked Nix unconscious.'

Ethan's eyes darken as he looks back at Nix. 'That call earlier. He rang because you needed help and Fallon just brushed it off.'

'She brushed it off because I was fine. I came round with a bit of a headache. There was nothing to worry you about.'

'I'll be the judge of that.'

'Anyway, that's not the point. Instead of bringing my memories out, he shared some of his with me. He was in the cell we found and Rhain was there.'

Ethan turns from Nix to Court, then to the photo, then back to Nix before sitting back in the chair and shaking his head. 'You must be mistaken. Rhain is from a respected line. He's never been linked to anything remotely suspicious.'

Court buries his head in his hands. He needs to rein in his frustration before Ethan gets the brunt of it. He takes a long breath and looks up again. 'You don't think he's involved. Fine. So why— how do I recognise him? I've seen him before. I don't remember anyone else from my past so why him? Why did seeing him trigger this block in my head?'

'I don't know—'

'I need to know! For fuck's sake this is driving me insane!' Court jumps to his feet and walks over to the wall of windows behind Ethan's desk. He can see the reflection of his glowing eyes in the glass. If he doesn't calm down, he could share more of his fucked up memories with not only Nix, but Ethan too.

Ethan waits a few minutes until he comments on the pathetic outburst. 'I'm not dismissing what you said, Court. I promise. If you say you know him, I believe you and I will find out as much as I can about him.'

'I'm sorry. I know I'm coming across as an ungrateful ass. You're all doing so much to help, and I keep adding more questions to the pile.' He looks over his shoulder at the pair and attempts another smile. 'I do appreciate everything. I mean that.'

Nix joins him at the window and it doesn't escape his notice that she checks his eyes before she speaks. He can hardly blame her. 'More questions isn't a bad thing. All the questions lead to the same person or group. Once we find them, you'll get the answers. I'm with Court on this Ethan. I saw Rhain in the memory. I don't know in what capacity, but he has something to do with this. Or knows something about it at the very least.'

'If that is the case, I wouldn't recommend approaching him about it without some serious evidence. My grandparents know him. All their friends know him. Everyone of any importance in vampire society knows him. His connections have connections. I know for a fact I'll hit a wall. It's the same when I delve into my dear grandmother's affairs when I get bored. Money means anonymity - and he's got enough funding to pay for plenty of that. Doesn't mean we're not going to give it a damn good try.'

'Thank you,' Court says. 'I don't want you to do anything that'll get you noticed by the wrong people.'

'Don't worry about that. Rhain isn't the only one with connections. Leave it with me. I'll give you a shout if I find anything.' He looks at the other files on the table in front of him. 'Anything else of interest in this lot?'

Nix squeezes Court's arm before she joins Ethan on the couch again. 'Just some financial documents I can't make sense of. It seems dear, departed Vincent was receiving cash deposits ranging from five to twenty thousand for over a year. When we spoke, he mentioned a by-product. Could this be something he's selling?'

Ethan shrugs. 'Couldn't say for sure. I do know we've noticed a rise in vampire attacks lately. We know whatever they did to Court helped to enhance the Prime side of his bloodline. We also know it can't have worked for everyone or we would have heard about it before now. What if it did something else to the males they tried it on - something the order saw a profit in? If it has the potential to enhance the Prime side of a bloodline, maybe it can also bring out other traits that perhaps weren't wanted.'

'Like what?' Court asks.

'Well, don't quote me on this but I have heard some talk about a new drug.'

'What kind of drug?' Nix asks.

'That's the problem. It's only rumours. We haven't been able to get a firm handle on exactly what it is. From what we can make out it's only being offered in certain circles. It sounds very much like a vampire version of heroin. Equally as addictive too.'

'But that's impossible,' Nix says. 'Apart from blood, vampires can't get addicted to anything.'

Ethan leans back in his seat and straightens his tie. 'Well, whatever this drug is, it is addictive.'

'Can you get your hands on some of it?' Nix asks.

'Unlikely, but I do have my people on the case. If we can get some and test it, we will. Until then I have no idea what we're dealing with. Or even if this new drug is linked to what happened to Court. It might just be an unpleasant coincidence.

'Could be any number of things. We're a volatile race.. Especially Primes. Emotions are ramped up most of the time and it takes a lot to restrain and control our urges. Well, I probably shouldn't include myself in that. There's a chance some of our less desirable traits may be amplified as well as the more desirable ones.'

'So he could be creating a bunch of hostile vampires?'

'Could be. Blood Fever could also be part of that. I've got no proof, but I'm not overly keen on having the theory proved.'

Court leans on the edge of the desk and looks over at the photo of Rhain. He still hasn't got a clue where he fits in to all of this or even if he wants to know, but one thing is clear. If Rhain is altering vampires in any way for whatever reason, it has to end. Even if that means he has to go back to the lab to get answers.

45

Thea takes a step back as Davyn yanks his door open. He glares down at her and her bag of supplies. 'What the hell do you want?'

'You left in such a hurry you forgot to take the blood with you. Fletch also wants me to check you haven't opened your wound again.'

He looks down at his chest then back at her. 'It's fine and I don't need the blood.'

'I know I've only been in this world a short time, but I do know two things. One, you won't heal unless you feed, and two, your wound still needs to be taken care of until it heals. I can help on both those issues.'

'I'm not feeding from you.'

Thea ignores the unexpected tightness in her throat. Nice to know he was so turned off by her. 'I have a bag of blood with me.'

She waits while he tries to make up his mind about what is clearly a difficult decision. He finally shoves his door open and moves aside. Thea steps inside and turns on the light. She lays the bag on the end of his unmade bed and looks around the room.

It's the same size as Court's but not as well looked after. He lives here, but it's clear he doesn't care about the place. Davyn sits in the chair beside his bed and slouches down, his legs spread out in front of him as he watches her in silence.

'Can I check your wound?'

He raises his pierced eyebrow but doesn't say anything. Thea stands in front of the chair and realises she's going to have to kneel between his legs to get anywhere near the wound. If Davyn has an issue with that he doesn't say, he just keeps up his silent staring as she gets to her knees on the carpet and leans over him to gently peel the bandage away from his skin. 'The stitches are still in place. You're lucky you didn't rip them out when you took off like that.'

He rests his head on his hand and quietly stares at her as she fixes the bandage over the wound again. His eyes drop to her chest and Thea blushes when she realises he can see down her top. She moves away from him and sits back on her legs.

'Did you guys find out anything about who took Court?' she asks.

'Ask your father.'

'I was asking you. You know how things are between Court and I.'

'Not my problem.'

'Right. Thanks.' With a sigh she gets up and washes her hands in the bathroom, cursing herself under her breath. What exactly did she hope to achieve by coming here? Davyn is never going to be anything more to her than a gorgeous, completely out of reach man... male. Whatever. What she needs to do is leave him the hell alone and stop torturing herself.

When she comes back out, he's still where she left him, his green eyes looking coldly at her.

'What's that look for?' she snaps, her irritation at the entire situation impossible to hide.

'No point getting shitty with me.'

His comment makes her snort in disbelief. He's one to talk. 'I'm not getting shitty with you. You don't have to be so...'

'So what?'

'Blunt. This isn't easy for me, okay. The whole situation with Court isn't easy.'

'For either of you.'

'Yes, thank you for pointing that out.'

He shrugs but doesn't say anything, so Thea gives up on the conversation. He's not going to see it from her point of view. After their last chat she knows that much. She goes back to the bag and takes out the blood. 'Do you want this now?'

He shakes his head. 'Leave it on the bed.'

'You need to drink it.'

'I said leave it on the bed.'

Thea does as she's told and looks down at the blood. 'Do you drink it straight from that?'

'What else should I do with it?'

'I guess, it's just a little... I don't know... it doesn't seem right. I suppose it's like me eating a microwave meal out of the plastic tray it comes in.'

'You're comparing a bag of blood to a microwave meal?'

'I just mean... forget it.'

Davyn takes a deep breath as he frowns over at her. He seems to do that a lot. Eventually he rubs his forehead and eases up on the frown. 'Ethan has a database of vampires we can feed from. Some of the others use them. I prefer this way.'

'Oh. And they volunteer to feed you guys? Does it not hurt when you... you know... bite them?'

He sighs again. He'd do well in a lecture hall. He's got that whole stop asking stupid questions vibe about him. 'No.'

'It doesn't?'

'I just said it doesn't. They wouldn't do it if it did.'

'Do you not feed each other within the team?'

'What's with all the questions?'

'I don't know. I guess I'm just curious.'

'Why? You want to go on the list? You want a Blackjack to feed from you?'

She frowns as his words sink in. Is that what she wants? She'd be lying if said she didn't wonder what it would feel like. Knowing there's a database of willing volunteers just added to the curiosity. There's only one sticking point. She has no interest in being added to a database. The one she wants to feed is sitting in the chair opposite her with a strange look on his face.

'Fuck.' He gets to his feet and runs a hand through his hair. 'You do, don't you?'

'Would feeding from me be better for you than that bag of blood?'

'Fresh is always better, but we're not going there. And you're human.'

'But you can drink human blood, can't you?'

'Yes, but we can't survive on it. Weak human blood won't keep us going for long. Fuck. I'm not doing this. Not with you.'

The guy really knows how to make a woman feel wanted. 'Why not? I'm here and I'm offering.'

'And I'm refusing. You need to get the hell out of my room. If the others find out you even asked me... Just go!'

'I don't understand. Why would the others have a problem?'

'They'd have a problem with you asking me. You telling me they didn't warn you off me?'

'Well, yes, but-'

'But nothing. They did that for a reason. You need to go. We didn't have this conversation.'

'Fine. How about I just add it to the other conversations we didn't have in this room.'

Davyn stalks towards her, his glowing eyes locking on to her. 'You threatening me now?'

'What! Of course not.'

He leans closer and tilts his head as he looks down at her. She can feel the heat coming off his bare chest. His tattoo is at her eye line and she follows the winding Celtic design across his chest. Time slows as she focuses on the dark lines rising and falling as he breathes.

'Why'd you stop Fletch from telling Fallon about my wings?'

She keeps her eyes on his chest as she replies, 'You made it painfully clear you wanted them kept a secret. Finding out like that - when you're injured - it didn't seem right. I know I've stuck my nose in it about your wings more times than I had a right to. I guess it was my way of apologising. It's your body. It's one hundred percent down to you to tell or not tell whoever you want.'

'Look at me.'

His no nonsense command does the trick. She tilts her head back and meets his eyes. Davyn crosses his arms and takes a deep breath as his eyes refuse to leave hers. The silence heads towards seriously uncomfortable and Thea has no idea if she should leave.

Just as she's about to try and extract herself from his gaze and excuse herself from another embarrassing moment - she's on a roll with those at the moment - he finally decides to talk.

'You should ask one of the others. Not me.'

It takes longer than it should to realise he's talking about feeding one of them. His eyes are still glowing, but for once he's not frowning. 'I don't want to make a big deal out of this. If I ask Shep he probably would never let me forget it. Bastian... I think he'd refuse. I don't know much about him, but I get the feeling he wouldn't be on board. Court, well, he's family and that's not allowed, right. I remember him telling me that before he disappeared.'

'No. We can't feed family. Feeding... it can sometimes be...' he looks away from her and frowns at the floor. 'It's not something you do with a family member.'

Thea nods and swallows to moisten her dry mouth. 'Right. So like I was saying, the girls are out - it would just feel weird.'

'Which leaves me. No other option, right?'

Thea mentally kicks herself. Not the best way to give him a confidence boost. 'I didn't mean that like it sounded. What I was trying to say, incredibly badly, is that I know if it was you, you'd feed then not mention it again. No awkward conversations... Well, apart from this one. I just thought you'd be the obvious choice, not the last one.'

The frown appears again but instead of directing it at her, the floor gets the special treatment.

Time to put an end to this. Thea ducks around him and goes over to the bed to collect the bag of supplies Fletch gave her. 'You were right. I shouldn't have said anything. Can you please forget this conversation? I'll leave you to... whatever.'

She grabs the bag and hurries over to the door, the weight of her stupidity pushing her away from him.

'Wait.'

Thea stops with her hand on the door handle. She turns and looks at him. He hasn't moved, his arms still by his side as he faces the wall. For a moment she wonders if her ears were playing a trick on her.

'You really want me to feed from you?'

'I wouldn't have suggested it if I didn't.'

'Okay.'

His reply seems to echo in the room. She never expected him to agree. Not for one second. 'Really?'

He steps closer and locks eyes with her. 'I need you to say I'm not forcing you to feed me. That you know you're safe with me.'

'What?'

'Say the fucking words, Thea, or this conversation is done.'

That was the first time he'd said her name. Shame it came after a curse and before a threat. 'Davyn, you are not forcing me to do this. I want you to feed from me. And I wouldn't ask unless I knew I would be safe with you.'

'Go over to the wall and turn around.'

'I'm sorry?'

'I can't do this with you looking at me. Face the wall.'

That's one way to put a dampener on the occasion. She drops the bag at the door and walks over to the blank wall opposite his bed. Nothing seems to happen for a long few minutes and Thea wonders if he might have changed his mind again.

And then he's behind her, his body caging her in. He rests his hands on the wall to either side of her head and Thea's breath hitches when she smells him. Just like in the car, he smells incredible. His breath is warm on her ear as he leans closer.

'Are you absolutely sure you want me to do this?' His voice sounds different, deeper and huskier than a few minutes ago.

She licks her dry lips and swallows trying to get some moisture back in her throat before she answers. 'Yes'

Her heart races in her chest as he lifts one hand from the wall and slowly slides her hair to the side before placing it back on the wall again. The anticipation is torturous. She knows it's just a feeding for him, but it's so much more for her. That's probably the best reason she has for calling a stop to this and getting out of his room. Instead she tilts her head to the side and closes her eyes.

Davyn's hair tickles her cheek when he leans over. His breath is warm on her neck and does things to her body she has no control over. As much as she'd prefer to be facing him, the thought of seeing him looming over her while his fangs drop would be too much.

He growls against her neck, and she holds her breath as his canines gently scrap her skin. His left hand leaves the wall and slides under her chin. He holds her head to the side, his skin against hers sending her heart racing again. When his other hand wraps around her torso, holding her against his hard chest she closes her eyes and tries to relax. But having him hold her like this is making that difficult enough without the anticipation of what's about to happen adding to it.

Davyn nuzzles against her neck, his growl deepening. Thea gasps as a sharp pain spears her neck, but it's gone as fast as it appeared.

Once he drinks, the initial pain becomes a distant memory. She can't tell exactly what she's feeling but it's beyond any words she could use to describe it. The combination of his body behind her, the feeling of his tongue against her neck as he sucks, the pressure of his fangs in her skin, his hands around her waist and her neck holding her in place, it escalates to something Thea doesn't want to end.

It feels so good. Really good. She knows why family members don't feed each other. She holds back a groan as Davyn's grip on her increases. He growls softly as his fingers dig into her skin. Thea wants to touch him. Desperately needs to touch him, but she's afraid he'll stop if she moves.

Far too soon, he stops and releases her. Thea rests her head on the wall, unable or unwilling to move. She smiles to herself as she lets the reality of what she just did sink in. She had just given Davyn what he needs to heal, what he needs to survive.

Davyn grabs a damp cloth from the bathroom and wipes the side of her neck, pressing it to the bite mark. 'The marks will go in a few hours. You okay?'

She turns around and smiles up at him. 'That was... I don't know how to describe it. It hurt for a second, but then the pain went. It was... amazing.'

'It can be intense.'

That's an understatement and a half. 'So, how about you? Are you okay? I mean did it help you?'

Davyn nods. 'Better than a microwave meal.'

She laughs and pushes off the wall. 'I'm glad.'

Davyn nods again, then his face changes. The frown comes back, and she can see the muscles in his arm tensing. 'You need to go now.'

'Are you okay?'

'Stop with the fucking questions. I fed from you. It's done. You can tick that off your list. Now get the fuck out of my room.'

At a loss for words, Thea grabs the bag from the floor where she dropped it and opens the door. She glances over her shoulder at him, but he's already in the bathroom with the door closed. It takes her a few seconds to realise he's retching. She stares at the closed door and considers going in to see if he's okay, but she can't bring herself to go anywhere near him. Knowing that her blood did that to him makes her feel terrible. Was there something wrong with it? He didn't seem to have a problem when he was feeding so what changed?

Whatever the reason, she needs to get out of here. She hurries down the corridor, feeling a little lightheaded and a lot embarrassed. 'Last time, Thea,' she mutters to herself as she rushes towards the safety of her bedroom. 'Last time you let him...' Let him what? He did nothing wrong. Nothing at all. This was all down to her. She was the one who let her head run away with her.

He didn't want to feed from her, but she was the one who pushed him. It's not hard to believe he gave in just to shut her up then had regrets over it. If anything she was the one who used him. She wanted a distraction from what was going on with Court and had used Davyn as that distraction.

She locks her bedroom door behind her and closes her eyes as she curses herself. Not only is she brooding over Court, but she's also involved Davyn in the problem and possibly made him ill. If Nix finds out, she'll have every right to be upset. She doubts Davyn will say anything about what happened. All she needs to do is stay here until his bite mark disappears from her neck.

Nix sits beside Court at the counter in the kitchen and pours herself a cup of coffee from the pot in front of him. 'So, I have a plan but I'm not sure how you're going to take it.'

Court glances sideways at her. 'I don't like it already.'

Nix takes a sip of her coffee and grimaces when she realises it's cold. 'How long have you been nursing that coffee?'

He looks at the clock on the far wall. 'About an hour.'

'You want a fresh one?'

He pushes his cup aside. 'I'm good. So, what's this plan of yours?'

She leans forward and rests her arms on the counter. She's fairly sure she only has one shot at this. 'I want you to link with me and try to project more of your memories.'

Yeah, that goes down as badly as she thought it would. The look Court's giving her would have been funny in any other situation. It's like he fully believes she's completely lost all common sense.

'Think about it.'

'Think about what? We don't have a fucking clue what I'm actually doing to you when I use my mind thing. What if I'm leaving long term brain damage? What if I'm messing your head up like mine is? There isn't a chance in hell I'll intentionally use whatever my power is on anyone – especially you.'

It takes a second for what he said to register. 'Especially me?'

'Yeah. If I hurt the boss, I'll have an angry group of vampires after me. No thanks.'

She smiles and looks down at the coffee cup. That's what she gets for letting her imagination run away with her. 'Hear me out.'

'No, Nix. I'm not going to do this. How can you even ask me? I could have killed you.'

And now she feels absolutely terrible. 'We need to unlock whatever's in your head. This is the best option.' He opens his mouth, but she holds up her hand to stop him. 'Give me a minute.' Court rests his head in his hands and looks utterly beaten. 'What I was proposing is that we have Fletch and Bastian with us. Fletch can monitor both of us and pull me out if something doesn't look right.'

'And Bas?'

'He can help you get a handle on your power. Shep's power is... well, I guess the best way to put it is that it's always on. Bastian is different. He has to concentrate, to consciously use his power. Like you can do.'

'I have no control over it.'

'Not yet, but you used to. You could stare in someone's eyes without getting inside their head.' He used to stare at her. She licks her lips and dismisses the memory. 'Bas can teach you to harness it.'

Court looks down at the table and runs his hand over his beard again and again.

'I know you're scared.'

His eyes move up to look at her and she knows without a doubt he's more than scared - he's terrified. Terrified of the memories. Terrified of his new ability. Maybe terrified of hurting her. Possibly a mix of all of them.

'I need to find out what happened to you. I need to find whoever did this to you. I will do anything I have to in order to protect my fighters, to protect our race from whatever is going on. But I need your help to do it, Court. Trust us to have your back.'

'Fuck.'

'Not quite the answer I was going for.'

He looks over at her and shakes his head. 'Can't believe I'm saying this... but fine. I want Bastian to stay in the room and I want him armed.'

'Of course.'

He gets up and walks to the door. 'C'mon then. Might as well get it over with.'

Court tries to get comfortable in the chair but it's like the damn thing is full of rocks. This is without a doubt the worst idea he's ever agreed to, but Fletch, Nix, and Bastian seem to be on board. Which either means it's not as crazy as he thinks it is or they're all as crazy as the plan.

He'd spent an hour with Bastian who talked him through trying to get a little control of his power, but he's not sure anything Bas said got through. The fear of frying someone's brain is stopping him from letting go fully. They'd tried without a guinea pig in front of him, but it didn't work. They'd even tried him looking in the mirror, but again - nothing. It seems his trick only works on a living being with a real brain he can fuck with.

Bastian crouches down in front of him and squeezes his arm. 'You good?'

'Far from it.'

'I'll stay beside you. Talk you through it. You just got to let it do its thing. You're in charge of it, not the other way around.'

Bastian smiles, but Court isn't convinced. Bastian's been using his powers for decades. That's a hell of a lot of practice. 'You ready to step in?'

Bastian reaches behind his back and pulls out a heavy gun. 'It's a tranq gun. I'd prefer not to kill you so soon after getting you back.' He smirks and pushes to his feet. He pulls a chair around and sits beside Court with his arms crossed.

With his backup in place Court looks over at Nix. Fletch is fixing monitors to her so he can keep an eye on her vitals during the process. He has no idea how the hell she can look so calm.

Fletch steps away and rubs his hands together. 'Well, I reckon we're all ready to go. Bas, you good?'

Bastian checks the gun even though Court has no doubt he's already done it numerous times. 'All good.'

'Nix?'

She settles back in the chair and smiles. 'I'm ready.'

Fletch faces Court and stuffs his hands in the back pocket of his jeans. 'Guess it's up to you now, buddy. You ready?'

He resists the urge to say no, leaving it at a quick nod instead. Court takes a deep breath and, ignoring Fletch and Bastian, looks over at Nix. She smiles reassuringly. 'It's going to be okay, Court.'

Nix holds up the photo that triggered the attack in Vincent's house. He licks his lips and focuses on Rhain. He's surprised how fast the pain builds. He follows his instincts and closes his eyes, putting up a block between himself and Nix.

'You're in control,' Bastian says. 'It's like turning your head or moving your hand. It's no different.' Court opens his eyes again and looks back to the photo. This time he doesn't pull back when the pain comes. Remembering what Bastian taught him, he concentrates on Nix, concentrates on getting inside her head. He grunts as the pain intensifies, but keeps his eyes locked on Nix's.

'Ignore the pain, Court. Focus on Rhain.'

Then it happens. Just like Bastian said it would. It wasn't as painful as the other times. But then he's back in the cell. He looks around, desperate to see Nix or Fletch or Bastian, but he's alone. He lifts his head and sees that's not the case. He's just one of many, suspended in a cell with wires and tubes trailing out of them. He tries to call to them but there's something in his mouth, stopping the sound from getting out. The vampire in the cell next to him has a metal gag in his mouth. So does the next. He knows this is just a memory, but the panic still rises to the surface. This is his memory. He was kept like this.

Then the man appears. Rhain. He approaches Court's cell and examines him through the glass. He says something, but Court can't hear the words. Then Rhain frowns and clutches his head. People race around the room they're in. They look like they're shouting, but he still can't hear the words.

He drops to the ground as his restraints are released and the door to his cell is opened. Instinct roars to the surface. Instead of waiting to see what they do, Court fights. He lunges at Rhain but is shoved aside by a dark-haired man. By Maddox. Court dismisses the two of them and makes for the door. A guard steps in front of him, but his face goes blank, and he steps aside letting Court push by.

He reaches the metal stairs and climbs to the top, finding the hatch is locked. Another guard approaches him, his gun raised. He doesn't have a clue what he does, but the guy climbs the stairs, keys in the code, and opens the door for him.

Without pausing, Court races through the forest, squinting at the light that hits his eyes after so long underground. He charges through the trees, trying to put as much distance between him and the guards.

He can hear them behind him. Hear their shouts. There's nowhere to hide. He spots an area of marshland and heads there. He looks over his shoulder as the shouting gets louder. He's running out of time. He slides down the bank and grimaces as the freezing mud soaks through his boxers and coats his skin. He ducks under the surface to cover his face in mud, then resurfaces, and pushes himself against the soft sides of the bank.

He ignores whatever is crawling up his bare chest, ignores the shivers working through his body, ignores the stink of rotting vegetation. The only thing he's focusing on is his breathing. Whatever was on his chest takes a tentative bite then changes its mind and decides to move on to something more appetising.

He ducks down as someone stands on the bank over his head, pushing the soft earth down, and him along with it. Panic threatens to take a hold as the muddy water forces its way up his nose.

Court shouts as strong hands grab him by the arms and squeeze hard. He turns around and lashes out, catching someone on the jaw. The curse that comes back sounds like it is in Spanish. He lashes out again, but this time the other guy grabs his wrists and holds them in his impressively firm grip.

'It's me Court. It's Bastian. You're safe.'

Court blinks and jumps as Bastian's face suddenly appears in front of him. 'What the fuck happened?'

'First, you gonna hit me again or are we good?'

Court frowns at the blood at the corner of Bastian's mouth. 'I hit you?'

'Got me good. Can I let you go?'

Bastian has both his wrists in his hands. 'What? Fuck, yeah. I'm sorry.'

Bastian grins. 'Not a problem.' He releases Court's wrists and stands up, but stays beside him.

'Nix?'

'I'm fine.'

Court releases the breath he was holding. The Blackjack leader is slumped in her chair smiling. 'I didn't hurt you?'

'It was far from pleasant, but no, not like the last time at all.'

Bastian squeezes his shoulder. 'You controlled it. You did good.'

'Control? Did you see what I did in the tunnels?'

Nix nods. 'You were able to control those guards.'

Bastian sits down again and wipes the blood from his lip. 'You saying he can compel people to do what he wants? I thought my gift was cool.'

'Is that what I did?'

'It looked that way.'

Fletch begins removing the monitors from Nix. 'Is that how you got out?'

'I think so. I do know one thing though - Rhain and Maddox were there. There were others with me. I was the only one who got out. I hid in a marsh until they stopped looking for me. I must have gone to the farmhouse after that.'

Bastian crosses his arms and traces one of his tattoos with his finger. 'It's not proof though, is it? Ethan will believe what you say, but we can't go to anyone else and say you saw Rhain and Maddox in his memory. We'll lose any credibility we have.'

Nix lies back in the chair and nods. She looks exhausted. Court did that to her. 'I know. There's no way we can take Rhain down in the public eye. We won't have a leg to stand on. From what Ethan said, he's got contacts in every corner of vampire and human society.'

'And there's the small detail about all this being a memory,' Fletch says. 'I'm not saying it didn't happen. Just playing Devil's advocate, I guess. Your memories have been well, fucked with for want of a better word. Whatever you can do now gift-wise is still a whole lot of unknown. Maths was never my strong suit, but a whole lot of unknown added to a whole lot of unknown equals a whole lot of unknown. There's nothing to say these memories are accurate.'

He's right. He might just have put Rhain in the memory because of the photograph.

Someone knocks on the door, dragging everyone out of their thoughts. 'Yeah. We're done,' Nix calls. Shep opens the door and whistles.

'Damn, Boss. You look like shit.'

'Thanks, Shep. What's up?'

He passes a piece of paper to Nix. 'I did my wizardry on the custom cells we found in that bunker. It took a hell of a lot of digging and, yes, I had to do some ingenious things I won't explain, but I did manage to trace the payments on one of the parts to a legitimate business with a legitimate address in a legitimate country. Well, they're all legitimate countries so that doesn't make sense. You're not going to make up a country. Anyway, it traces back to a subsidiary of a subsidiary of a shell company that operates as a division of a company—'

'Shep!' Nix shouts. 'I've got a fucking terrible headache. Please get to the point.'

'Way to steal my thunder, Boss. It's a company owned by Rhain's corporation.' Nix gets up and kisses Shep on the cheek. 'What was that for?'

'You beautiful male.'

'Won't argue with that.'

'Rhain was there in the bunker,' Court explains. 'You've just confirmed that I may not be completely losing my mind.'

'All good then,' Shep says with a grin. 'So we're making a move on him, and I don't mean in the good sense.'

Nix shakes her head. 'It's not that easy. He's not going to be wandering around in the open waiting for us to attack.'

'Yeah, he's also got sixteen properties that I found and that's just in the UK.' Shep takes the seat next to Bastian. 'I've been digging as much as I can, but this guy is good. And by good, I mean secretive. I don't even know which house he lives in. No idea of employees or even if he has any. He's one big fucking mystery.'

'Apart from one detail,' Nix says. 'He's Prime.'

Fletch smiles and nods. 'Yes, he is. And he's heading towards a few centuries old. He probably has Blood Fever. Early stages at least.'

'So he has an interest in finding a cure.' The pieces may be falling into place, but nothing he's hearing is giving Court a warm fuzzy feeling inside. 'So how the hell do we get to him?'

Nix, Fletch, Shep, and Bas look at each other then back over to him. 'That's going to be the problem,' Nix says as she looks down at the picture of Rhain. 'But we will. Whatever we do, we'll have to be smart about it. If he knows were coming for him, he'll disappear. Someone with his resources could vanish for decades if he wanted to.'

She smiles across at him. 'His cards are marked, Court. Believe me.'

Nix uses her override to open Court's door and rushes over to his bed. She stops beside the bed unsure what to do. She heard his moans of pain as she walked by his door and couldn't leave without checking that he was all right.

Court thrashes around, the sheets tangled around his legs. He arches his back and screams, then buries his head under his arms. Keeping out of striking distance, Nix calls his name. On the fourth attempt he stills, and his eyes fly open. He sits up and tries to push himself up the bed but doesn't get far thanks to his tangled sheets.

Nix tugs at the bottom, helping to unwrap his legs. As soon as they're free, Court pulls his legs to his chest and breaths heavily. Leaving him to get himself together, Nix takes the glass from his bedside table and fills it from the sink in the bathroom. She slowly approaches him and holds out the glass.

'Court. I've got water.'

He jumps slightly at her voice and looks at her as if noticing for the first time that she's in the room. 'Nix?'

'Hi.' She holds out the glass again and he takes it, emptying it in one go. She refills it and places it back on the table beside him, then sits on the edge of the bed. 'Are you okay?'

He smiles, but it doesn't reach his eyes. 'Yeah. Thanks. Sorry. Did I wake you?'

'I was coming to check on you when I heard you screaming. I used my override code to get in. Hope you don't mind.'

'No problem.' He scrubs a hand over his head, pushing his sweat soaked hair out of his face.

He looks scared. She's never known Court to afraid of anything. He was so level-headed no matter the situation. Whatever he was remembering through his dreams scares him. And that scares her. 'Do you want to talk about it?'

He runs a hand through his damp hair then drops his head against the headboard with a dull thud. 'I don't know.'

'Don't know if you want to tell me or—'

'Don't know what it was about. Besides, I think you've seen enough of my memories for now.' He smirks, but it doesn't last, fading to a frown as he stares at the end of the bed.

Nix keeps her hands firmly on her lap. All she wants to do it take him in her arms and hold him. 'Do you have the dreams—'

'Nightmares,' he interrupts. 'A few times a week. Sometimes more often.' A shiver runs through his body and he pulls his arms tight around his legs. 'I never wanted to drag you in to my memories.'

'I know.'

He nods, the frown still firmly in place. 'I've been thinking. Until I get a handle on my eyes, I shouldn't—'

'Stop.'

'But Nix—'

'I said stop, Court. If you are even considering saying you'll leave or you're not safe to be around or whatever else you can think of – I don't want to hear it. You are a part of the team. We can't lose you again.' She can't lose him again. Not after getting him back. Not that she really has him.

Ethan's words come back with a sickening jolt. Someone will claim him sooner or later. Someone like Court doesn't stay single forever. One day, Nix will have to deal with seeing another female standing beside him. Touching him. Looking into those pale eyes like no one else existed in the world apart from him. Maybe someone like Amber.

He glances up at her as she growls. 'You okay?'

Nix smiles. 'Absolutely.' If Ethan's receptionist came within a hundred feet of Court, she'd rip those lipstick stained teeth from her skull. *Yeah, that's helpful, Nix.* She can't spend the rest of her life warning other females off Court and not claim him herself, can she? He deserves to be happy. He's given so much already. Out of everyone she knows, he deserves a happily-ever-after. Even if it's not with her. But if someone else claimed him would she be able to handle it?

Nix prided herself on being cool and calm under pressure. It served her well as the leader. Unfortunately, when it came to personal issues, specifically Court, that cool and calm turned to a raging pool of lava complete with eruptions of hefty rocks of jealousy.

Now isn't the time for jealous rage at someone who wiggled her perfectly manicured fingers at him. What sort of a terrible person is she? He's suffering, trying to pull himself out of a terrifying nightmare and she's planning the demise of anyone who looks sideways at him. *Great leadership, Nix.*

She holds out her hand and he stares at it suspiciously. 'C'mon. I won't bite,' she says with a smile. 'Trust me, Court.'

He looks down at her hand again before slowly reaching out to take it. His hand is cold in hers as she guides him off the bed to the bathroom. She turns on the shower, takes a fresh towel from the cupboard then tests the water. Satisfied it is the correct temperature, she gestures to the steaming cubicle. 'Get yourself in there and I'll change your bedsheets. You'll catch a cold if you stay in a damp bed.'

He opens his mouth to argue, but she holds up a hand, stopping him. 'That's an order.'

She closes the door and turns towards the bed. 'What the hell are you doing, Nix?' she asks herself as she stares at the vast expanse of Court's bed. She pulls the damp sheets from the bed and takes out a fresh set from the cupboard.

Ten minutes later he still hasn't made a reappearance and Nix is done staring at his bed and remembering the long hours they'd spent there together. She knocks on the door.

'Court? You okay?'

Nothing. She takes a step back then glares at the door, willing it to open. If it doesn't open, she'll have to go in. If she does that, she risks seeing him naked. She scrubs a hand over her face and knocks again. Still nothing. Fuck! She has to go in. He could be mid-memory seizure and need her help.

Nix takes a deep breath and slowly cracks the door open. Through the steam she sees him, and her world stops for a minute. He's still in the shower, but clearly in a world of his own. He's facing the powerful jets, his head down and his hands braced against the wall. Water cascades down his back and powerful arms. She follows the trail of the water down his body and licks her lips as her mind tortures her by playing out a scene she has no right to be thinking about.

Feeling utterly ashamed of spying on him she slowly retreats before he notices her. 'Nix?'

Caught! She peeks around the door. Court has dropped one hand from the wall so he can look over at her. 'Sorry. I didn't mean to intrude. I knocked. You didn't answer so I...' Just decided to stare at your naked body for a few minutes. That's all. Completely normal.

Court doesn't say anything. Nix doesn't say anything. He doesn't ask her to leave, and she doesn't make a move to go. Nothing like torturing herself a little more.

He opens the shower door and her eyes instantly move down briefly before she forces them to behave and focus on his face. Nope.

She can't look there either. With nowhere else safe to look she focuses on the large wings tattooed to his chest.

'Can you look at me?' he asks.

No, she can't. Not without wanting to do something she really shouldn't. She takes a subtle – she hopes – deep breath and meets his eyes.

'I feel like... I don't know,' he says, shaking his head. 'I know my memories are all fucked up, but I feel like there's... I don't know if I'm remembering or wishing or what the fuck is going on.' He shakes his head a little more forcefully. 'Never mind. I'm all over the place. Ignore me.'

'What are you trying to say, Court?' Her heartbeat drowns out everything else. The pounding of the water on the shower stall disappears as she waits for an answer she wants to hear more than anything yet is terrified of hearing. What if he says he wants her? What if he doesn't? Both answers could crush her for very different reasons.

He pauses, then hits her with those eyes again. 'I want you to take off your clothes and get in here with me. Now.'

And there he is. The commanding Court she surrendered to when they were alone. Memory or not, his instincts are as sharp as ever.

Nix steps out of her jeans and pulls off her t-shirt. It is absolutely the wrong thing to do and certainly the worst timing in the history of worst timings, but she ignores common sense and goes for it.

Court doesn't respond, doesn't move. In reality it is probably only one or two seconds, but it feels like a lifetime to Nix. But then everything changes. His hand slips around the back of her neck and pulls her towards him. His tongue pushes her mouth open and hungrily attacks. Her hands take on a mind of their own, exploring his back and chest in a desperate attempt to touch everywhere at once.

His canines scrape her bottom lip as she drags her nails down the centre of his chest. He pulls away and his nearly white irises glow brightly in the dim room. His smile is predatory and something she missed more than she could ever put in words. It's the look he gave her before he asserted his authority.

As he towers over her, taking in every inch of her body with those cool blue eyes of his, she forgets the missing years. Forgets all those lonely days, lying on her bed, staring at the ceiling, wondering where he was and why he had left her. Being with him like this, it's like that nightmare never happened. He's familiar, how he makes her feel, how he touches her, how he looks at her. It's all the same, but also so much better than she remembers.

He feels so good against her, his firm body all hot and slick from the shower. He holds her tight, burying his fingers in her wet hair. His kiss takes away whatever breath she had left. With a deep growl he pushes her back against the tiles and moves his mouth along her throat to trace the path of water running between her breasts. The tips of his fangs graze ever so slightly against her nipple as he moves lower. Court's hands grip her hips as his tongue and mouth continue down her body.

'You taste so damn good, Nix.' She makes the mistake of looking down at him and groans in pleasure. His eyes are glowing softly. Water pours over his powerful body following every contour as it travels down his smooth skin. His wicked smile shows his fully extended fangs in all their glory. She throws her head back as he sucks gently at the sweet spot between her thighs. Court slides her leg over his shoulder and Nix cries out when his tongue joins the party, driving deep inside before a slow torturous withdrawal.

Nix thought being with him like this would be different. That he would be different. But whatever is going on with his memory hasn't affected how he is with her. This is her Court. Instinct or maybe some buried memory is taking over. He's touching her like he used to every time they had been together. His hands feel the same. His mouth feels the same. Everything is so familiar. 'Please...' She wants more. She needs more. She needs all of him.

As if reading her thoughts, he lifts a hand from her hip and pushes a finger deep inside. Then his tongue plays with her clit as his finger hits the right spot inside her.

'Oh, God.' She fists his hair, holding him against her. 'Please... please.'

He burrows deeper between her thighs, driving her further to the edge. She screams his name as her orgasm hits. Before she gets a chance to recover, Court stands up and lifts her off the ground. Nix wraps her legs around his waist and draws in a breath as the tip of his cock presses against her entrance. He holds her away from him, teasing her without letting her have what she so desperately wants.

She traces her nails down the side of his neck, feeling his strong pulse race beneath her fingers. She would give anything to taste him again, but his blood is off limits. Her nails leave marks as she pulls them down his neck to follow the wings across his chest and over his nipples. He sucks in a breath and growls, the deep rumble sending a flurry of goosebumps over her skin even though steam fills the room.

Court slams into her at the same time he buries his teeth in her neck. The explosion of sensations hits Nix at once. She digs her fingers into his shoulders, trying to hold herself steady as he thrusts, his pace increasing as he feeds from her. It was always incredible when she was with Court, but this is so much more.

She'd lost him. Grieved that loss for years. Nix runs her hand down the side of his face, almost like she's checking he's real and this isn't some twisted daydream. Then he rotates his hips the way he used to and Nix gasps.

His low growl is almost a purr as he feeds from her, and Nix's body tingles in response. He slowly pulls his teeth out of her and targets her with his glowing eyes. He moves her head to the side and draws his tongue along the wound he just left in her skin. Nix teeters on the edge, desperate for him to tip her over. And he knows it too. His tongue moves across his bite marks and his growl hits her deep in her core.

Court grips her by the jaw and slows his movements as he looks at her. 'I want you to come now, Nix.'

When he kisses her, his thrusts come faster and faster until she can't breathe from the onslaught of sensations. His strong arms tighten around her, holding her in place against him as her orgasm hits. Court doesn't miss a beat, keeping up the mind-blowing pace until he comes. His guttural growl mixed with him pulsing deep inside her, has her screaming in pleasure again.

Nix drops her head onto his shoulder grateful that he's still holding her against him. She doubts she'd be able to support herself after that. It was so much better than she remembers. He is so much better.

He lifts her head from his shoulder so he can look at her. His pale eyes are glowing softly, stirring something in Nix she thought she had control over. Then he kisses her and Nix loses herself in the moment again. She doesn't want this to end. Doesn't want him to let her go.

Court breaks the kiss and the emptiness Nix had with her since he left takes hold again. She looks away from his eyes, but he tilts her head back.

'Open your eyes.'

She didn't realise she'd closed them. She takes in the glorious sight in front of her. She runs her hand over his hair, and he smiles at her, his canines still on full display. Yeah, he's stunning and she's so deeply in love with him. And that's what terrifies her. That love is what took him from her the last time.

She comes down from her euphoria with a bump. What the hell is she doing? The last time she let her guard down he was taken. There's no way she's going to make the same mistake again. She can't risk him or any other member of the team. Not again.

'What's wrong?'

Nix removes her hand from his hair and pushes back from him. 'I'm sorry. I have no idea where that came from. Can you put me down?'

Court slowly pulls out of her and places her back on the ground. Nix turns off the water, which has turned to lukewarm. Just like her post-sex euphoria.

She steps out of the shower and grabs the towel from the chair, roughly wrapping it around her. 'You need to leave.'

He joins her on the heated tiled floor and pulls another towel from the rack. 'It's my room.'

Okay, that's more than a little embarrassing. Nix grabs her clothes off the floor and hurries back to the bedroom, desperate to put some distance between them. She ditches the towel and tries to wrestle her jeans over her wet legs while purposely avoiding looking at the naked male behind her.

'You're leaving?'

Nix sits on the chair and fights with her boots. 'This was a mistake. It should never have happened. I've worked damn hard to get where I am. To be taken seriously as the leader of this group. I shouldn't have... Fuck. What the hell am I doing?'

'So it was a mistake?'

'Of course it was. You have to know that.'

'I didn't force you. I'm pretty damn sure you wanted that to happen as much as I did.'

She fastens her bra and pulls her t-shirt on, glad to finally have a barrier of some sort between her skin and his. 'I didn't say you forced me to do anything. We'd had a tough day. We both got carried away in the moment. That will never happen again.'

'Has it happened before?'

Nix stops wrestling with her boots and makes the mistake of looking at him. He's still gloriously naked apart from the towel. His eyes are back to normal as he looks over at her with a mixture of hurt and confusion. That's her fault. 'What?'

'You and me. It felt...' Court frowns and rubs a hand over his jaw.

'Nothing in the compound feels familiar to me. Not my room, my clothes, not even my damn cologne. Nothing.' He locks on to her and his pale eyes glow again. 'Nothing except you. We've done that before. I know we have.'

Nix laughs, but it falls short sounding more like a snort. 'It was just sex, Court. Don't make this in to more than it is.'

His face hardens and the glow dies like the switch was shut off. 'So that's a no. Whatever I'm feeling... it's not true? I'm making up my feelings now?'

Nix shrugs, hating herself with each passing second. Denying what she had with Court is tearing her apart, but it's the right thing to do. No good can come of opening that wound again – for either of them. Well, after it closes again. Something tells her it's going to take a lot to close it this time.

'I can't say what you're feeling. All I know is that there's nothing here. There can never be anything between us. We're here to do a job, Court. We can't afford to blur the lines. When that happens people get hurt. We've just got you back. There's no way I'm going to do anything to jeopardise you or the team. As much as ...'

'As much as what?'

'Nothing, Court. The Order are taking innocent vampires from the street and doing who knows what to them. That's where my focus needs to be. I can't afford to have any distractions.

'So what the hell was all this? You just wanted a quick fuck, was that it?' he asks.

'We're both adults. We had a moment. It's best we put it behind us and move on. It was a mistake and I'm sorry for messing you around like that.'

'Give me a fucking break, Nix.'

'Excuse me?'

'I don't know what kind of obedience you got from the old Court. Maybe he liked being teased. Liked being used to make you feel better. Maybe he was quite happy to be at your beck and call, but I'll let you in on a secret. I'm a different model. I've got no interest in being a plaything.'

'You really believe that's what this is? You think I used you like that?'

'We have amazing sex and then you can't get away from me fast enough. What the hell do you expect me to think? My memory is gone, Nix, but don't treat me like a fucking idiot. I know that wasn't the first time we've had sex. I knew your body. Knew what you wanted. And I sure as hell know you knew my body. You going to tell me different?'

'It was a release we both needed. That's it. I'm not going to jeopardise the Blackjacks for a quick fling with one of the team.'

'Whatever you say. You're the boss. You can show yourself out.' He locks the bathroom door behind him, ending a conversation she wants desperately to go back and edit.

Nix stares at the closed door long after he's gone. Part of her is desperate to chase after him. Apologise over and over for what she said and beg him to forgive her. Beg him to hold her and not let go. But that's not the part she needs to listen to - no matter how much she wants to.

She let him in before. She fell in love, dropped her guard, and he was taken because of it. To keep the team safe she needs to keep her love life and her job as far from each other as possible.

With a last look over at the door to the bathroom, she tears herself away from the door and leaves his room.

Court finishes getting dressed then sits on the edge of his bed to pull on his boots. Time to have a one-to-one with Thea. It's absolutely the worst possible time to have this conversation with her, but he's done being a punching bag. If he has to face a slanging match with Thea to clear the air, that's what's going to happen.

He knows what happened with Nix is influencing this decision, but he's beyond caring about that. His relationship with Nix is doing his head in. So is his one with Thea. He can't do anything about the first, but he can sure as hell try to sort out the latter.

After Nix left his room, he'd stayed in the bathroom for nearly half an hour. He just sat on the chair by the bath and stared at the tiled wall opposite him. He thought finding the Blackjacks would put an end to some of the constant confusion, the ever-present fear that no one in the world knew who he really was.

He'd never told that to Thea. She had enough to worry about without adding his whopping case of identity crises to the mix. But the Blackjacks knew him. He'd realised that within a few minutes. They greeted him as they would an old friend. That's what he was to them. And it gave him so much comfort.

Whatever the hell is going on with Nix is successfully tearing that to pieces. He's either losing the little part of his mind that's still his and imagining this big romance between them, or she's lying about it which is fucking with him just as much. If it is the latter, why did she have sex with him then throw a bucket of ice on the situation? She clearly regretted the encounter. That had been damn near beaten into him while she got dressed.

'Promise you'll come back to me in one piece.'

'Always. I love you, Nix.'

The memory hits him like a punch to the side of his head. He buries his fists in his hair as something in his head rebels against the memory. He crashes to the floor as the words bounce around his head in a desperate attempt to break free. He can see Nix standing in front of him. See his hand reaching out to tuck her hair behind her ear. Hear him telling her he loves her.

Then it's gone.

Court takes a few deep breaths desperately trying to get control over his churning stomach. He uncurls his fingers from his hair, grimacing when he sees blood under his fingernails. Using too much effort, he pushes to his feet and stumbles back into his bathroom. The reflection that greets him in the mirror doesn't look too hot. His skin is pale and has an unhealthy grey tinge to it. There's blood dripping from his nose and his hair is a mess thanks to him trying to scalp himself.

He checks the damage, but apart from a few impressive gouges which have already stopped bleeding, it's not too bad. Court fills the sink and washes away as much of the blood as he can before dealing with his 'stuck a finger in a socket' hairdo. He examines his reflection and grimaces. Better, but Thea will know something is wrong with him. She always does.

He's had a few memories try to break through, but that was the most intense. He told Nix he loves her. There's no way he made that up. It was real. That doesn't help him in any way. If the memory was real, why is she denying there was anything between them? If the memory isn't real... he laughs at his reflection. Maybe he is losing his mind.

He beats his fist against the edge of the sink and glares at himself.

Between Nix refusing to be honest with him, and Thea blaming him for forgetting who she was to him, he's getting to the limit of his patience. Scrap that. He's reached the limit. Fuelled by frustration and anger at how helpless he feels, he barges out of the bathroom and pounds on Thea's door.

'It's me, Thea. Open the door.'

He can hear her moving around inside, but she doesn't open the door. He thought giving her space would have done the trick. Instead she'd just dug her heels in and refused to acknowledge him. Refused to talk to him. He hadn't admitted it to himself until now, but the fact she didn't even come to see how things went at the farm hurt him deeply.

He knows she still loves him, but unless she deals with what they are to each other, that means nothing. It's time to sort this out before it's too late for either of them. 'Open the damn door, Thea. I'm not going anywhere so you might as well talk to me.'

The door swings open and she crosses her arms. No invitation to step inside. Guess this will have to happen in the corridor.

'What the hell is wrong with you? Are you trying to bring the whole house down here?'

Court rests his hands against the top of the door frame to stop himself from storming in and making things worse.

'We need to talk, Thea.'

'I know we do, but not when you're pissed off.'

'I'm not pissed off.'

'Oh really? Cause you look a hell of a lot more than pissed off. I'll talk to you when you've calmed down, okay? I promise.' She tries to close the door, but he doesn't let her.

His eyes harden as he pushes the door back, jamming it open with his foot. 'No. Now, Thea. I've tried to give you time and space to get your head around this, around us, but I'm getting to the end of my patience. You need to get over this.'

He knows it's not the right way to go as soon as he says the words, but anger is taking the lead in this conversation. 'Excuse me? Get over this? Are you serious? This isn't something I can just get over. My brother is now my father!'

'Exactly! I haven't died. I'm still here, damn it. I'm still the same person. I still love you the same although right now I'm sorely tempted to strangle you. You're a grown woman, Thea. You need to stop acting like a selfish, spoilt teenager.'

'Well I'm sorry if my reaction to finding out my entire life has been a lie is irritating you.'

'You're only concerned with how you feel. Have you ever stopped, even for one fucking second to think how I feel about this whole bloody mess, huh? My entire life is gone. I'm one hundred and forty-five years old and I can't remember one hundred and forty-four years of that. Nearly a century and a half gone, just like that,' he says, clicking his fingers.

'I have a daughter I don't remember and I'm second in command of a team of vampire warriors. I have nightmares that terrify me because I know they're memories of where I was. And I've got a tattoo on my back that tells everyone who reads vampire that I'm pretty damn tasty. Someone took my life from me and I don't know why. That scares the hell out of me, Thea. I need... I need you. I can't deal with all this without you. I... ' He takes a deep breath trying to rein in his emotions when something hits him. He moves a little closer and Thea holds her hand up.

'What are you doing?'

Court growls as he focuses on her neck. 'Pull down your collar.' Thea's face instantly reddens, giving him all the confirmation he needs. 'Who was it?'

'Sorry?'

'You're going to stand there and tell me someone didn't feed from you.'

Thea licks her lips, but can't meet his eyes. 'You're getting worked up. Calm down, okay.'

'Who was it?'

'Court, please.'

He closes his eyes and focuses on the scent. When he realises who it belongs to, something inside him snaps. He heads down the corridor without saying a word to Thea.

Court doesn't bother knocking on the door - his boot makes the introductions for him. With rage in full control, Court launches at Davyn. He throws him against the wall and presses his arm under Davyn's neck. 'You fed from her?'

Caught off guard, it takes Davyn a few seconds to catch up. He swings at Court, catching him in the jaw, but Court doesn't feel it. All he's focused on is Davyn feeding from his daughter. Thea grabs him by the arm and shouts at him to stop. Not happening.

Davyn swings again and this time the blow registers. He loosens his grip on Davyn. Davyn pulls out from under Court's arm and rams his fist in Court's stomach, driving the air from his body.

Court is far from done though. He locks eyes with Davyn and in less than a second has the fighter under his control. He forces himself into Davyn's mind, urging him to back off. And he does. Davyn stands opposite him, his arms clenched by his side and his teeth bared. But he doesn't move to attack.

Thea thumps Court in the chest. 'Let him go! You're hurting him.'

Court only increases his hold, ignoring the blood dripping from Davyn's nose. Strong arms pull at Court and he's vaguely aware of

Shep telling him to calm down. Court's not interested though. Thea puts herself between them, trying to get his attention. 'If you don't let him go we're done, Court. I mean it! Let him go!'

He releases Davyn and the male falls back against the wall. He glares over at Court and wipes blood from his nose. 'Stay the fuck out of my head.'

'Stay the fuck away from my daughter and I'll think about it.' Bastian holds Davyn back, using his full weight to pin him against the wall.

Nix, Fallon, and Willow join the others holding the two males away from each other.

'Fallon, get Thea out of here,' Nix shouts, trying to get control of the situation.

'No!' Thea says, moving away from Fallon. 'I need to explain. Davyn didn't do anything wrong. Let me explain. '

'And I don't need you getting hurt. It's an order Fallon. Get her out of here.'

Fallon pushes Thea towards the door and closes it behind her. Nix steps between Court and Davyn. 'What the fuck is going on here?'

Davyn straightens and wipes more blood from his nose. A little guilt creeps in. Maybe Court had hurt him by doing what he did. Then he remembers the smell of Davyn all over his daughter. 'He fed from Thea.'

Court can feel the mood in the room taking a sombre turn. Nix turns on Davyn. 'You fed from her?'

'She wanted me to. She was curious what it felt like. I just fed a little and she left.'

'You had no right to touch her. She's my daughter. You had no fucking right! Shep gave me all the sordid details about you while we were training. You kill people you feed from.'

Davyn's face drops and glares over at Shep who looks anywhere but at him. 'You know nothing about me,' Davyn snarls. 'I didn't hurt

Thea.'

'Okay, calm down, both of you!' Nix stands between the fuming males, her arms outstretched. 'Davyn, exactly what happened?'

He shoves Bastian and Shep away from him and leans heavily on the wall. 'I just told you. I didn't hurt her and I didn't force her so keep your hands and fucking eyes away from me, Court.'

Nix gestures for Bastian and Shep to move away from Davyn, but they don't venture far. He pushes past the others, heading towards his door. 'We're not done here,' Nix says, but Davyn isn't listening.

He grabs his t-shirt from the chair and pulls it over his head.

'I'm not finished with you, Davyn!' Nix shouts.

'You all think I forced her to feed me. You've fought with me for decades and you still think I'd force myself on someone like that?'

'Davyn, we don't—'

'Spare me the bullshit, Nix.' He steps closer to Court and smiles, showing his canines. 'I'm better at restraining myself than you are. Your scent is all over each other. Fucking the boss is one way to stay on the team.'

'Enough!' Nix shouts.

Davyn wipes more blood from his nose. 'I'm going to the training centre. Talk to Thea. If you don't believe me maybe you'll believe her.'

Court stares after him as he storms away and disappears from view. 'You're just letting him go?'

Nix nods. 'Keeping the two of you in the same room won't help anyone. Shep, keep an eye on Dav. Make sure he stays put until we talk to Thea. Everyone else, out.'

Court runs a hand through his hair as he paces Davyn's bedroom. 'What the hell is that look for?'

'I thought you had more sense. He could have killed you.'

'He fed from Thea.'

'Yeah, I know. But he didn't hurt her. And what Shep told you about Davyn, that's just a rumour,' Nix says. 'When you're as old as he is you pick up a rumour or two along the way. He's never hurt any of us.'

'Does he feed from you?' Nix drops her gaze and doesn't respond. 'Exactly. You have no idea what he does so don't get on my case about wanting to protect her.'

'Okay, I get that, but it doesn't give you the right to get in his head like that. You're not in full control of it yet. You could have killed him. Did you see the blood pouring out of his nose?'

'Yes, Nix. I saw.'

'We are a team, Court. We don't fight each other. Hey, look at me.'

He slowly turns his head and glares at her.

'I'll sort this out okay.'

He nods and wipes a hand over his face. 'I didn't mean to get into his head like that. I really didn't. I'm angry as hell at him but I didn't want that.'

'I know that, Court.'

'The team know what we did too. I'm presuming you didn't want that to happen.'

Nix shrugs. 'We're both adults. It's none of their business what we did.'

'Yeah, you still regret it though, right.'

'I don't regret it, Court. I just don't think we should go there again.'

'You're the boss,' he replies sarcastically, not really giving a fuck how she takes it. He's more concerned about his daughter at the moment. Then another thought hits him. 'Fuck. We didn't use any protection when we-'

'It's fine, Court. Females only go into heat once a year. We also can't catch anything from sex like humans can. Nothing to worry about.'

He raises his eyebrows as that piece of information sinks in. 'Right.'

'How about you go back to your room and calm down. I'll talk to Thea and Davyn. Try to figure out exactly what happened.'

'She's my daughter. I'll talk to her.'

'No you won't. If you go anywhere near her in that mood, you'll make things a hell of a lot worse. Take five and calm down.'

Being ordered around like a child doesn't sit well with him, but even through the anger he knows what she's saying makes sense. Court leaves Davyn's room and goes back to his room, locking the door behind him. He sits on the bed, his fists clenched on his knees.

He needs to keep hold of the anger. If he doesn't, he'll let the images from Davyn's head get to him. And that's the last thing he wants. He didn't mean to go into his memories. It wasn't a conscious thing. He just wanted to hold him back.

But he got more than he bargained for.

Davyn had tried to keep him out but, unfortunately for Court, he wasn't entirely successful. The parts that slipped through are enough to convince Court never to try that again with him.

Whatever small memory Davyn had unintentionally shared with him had rivalled some of his own disturbing memories. It was cold, dark, and Davyn was in serious pain. But that wasn't the worst part. It was the fear that Court was struggling with. Whatever the memory was about, Court knows one thing - Davyn was terrified.

Court pushes to his feet and shakes his head. No. He's not going to feel sorry for him. Davyn fed from his daughter. Whatever happened in his past doesn't excuse him laying one finger on her let alone feeding.

He'll give Nix a few minutes to talk to Thea and use the time to get himself under control. Then he was going to talk to her himself. Find out exactly what happened.

Rhain ends the video conference and sits back in his chair. If he could he'd happily sell his father's companies and focus all his attention on his project, but they help play a part in his charade. Help to hide the fact he couldn't detest this world and his place in it more than he does.

He's weary of everything. Has been for well over fifty years at this stage. Envying humans and their easy lives is not something that is common among his race. They're weak, inferior, easily killed, and live for less than a century in most cases.

But it is a life he envies nonetheless. True, they're far from perfect, but they were permitted, for the most part, to live their lives as they chose. Thanks to his 'breeding' he can only mate with a Prime. He has no doubts had his family still been alive he would have been auctioned off to some prestigious female like a damn trophy. That wasn't a life he ever wanted. He'd stay single if that means he gets a choice.

The door to his office bursts open and a short, rotund vampire walks in and takes a seat on Rhain's couch. He doesn't bother acknowledging the intruder. Barton acted as spokesperson for the True Order hierarchy. Rhain detested him more than he detested a lot of people he'd met throughout his long life. The vampire was unable to think for himself - something which infuriated Rhain considerably.

He continues to ignore Barton and checks through his emails.

'Vincent is missing.'

Rhain takes another minute before he looks up from his screen. 'Excuse me?'

'Vincent is missing. We were wondering if perhaps you might know something about that?'

Rhain leans back in his chair and clasps his hands together. 'And why exactly would I have the first clue where Vincent is? He works for you. Surely you should know where he is?'

'We are only allowing you to continue with your project if it does not draw attention to us. We all want to increase Prime numbers, but the method won't help to endear us to many.'

Rhain stares at the vampire, suppressing a smile. Increasing Prime numbers may have been one reason the Order was behind the projects, but he knows the profits from the by-product drug is the main reason they're still working with him. 'I'm aware of your modus operandi,' Rhain replies, trying to stop himself from sending Barton out the fucking window with a talon sized hole in his chest.

Barton gets up and leans on Rhain's desk. 'We expect results, not complications. Having Vincent disappear is a complication. Either you killed him, or the Blackjacks did. Either option doesn't bode well for us.'

'Maybe he decided he wasn't cut out for this and left?'

'Or maybe you decided he was too much of a liability.'

Rhain frowns as he looks across at Barton. 'Did you think he was too much of a liability? By you of course I mean the True Order. I believe independent thought is above your pay grade.'

Barton smiles at him but doesn't react to the comment. Probably because he wasn't given permission by his masters to react. 'We're watching you Rhain. Do not deviate from the plan. The race must be purified.'

'I don't need you to tell me what the plan is. What I need is for you to stick to your side and provide me with vampires.'

'We are collecting them as quickly as we can.'

'One every week or so is far from quick in my mind. If you want more of the drug on the streets, you need to up your supply of vampires. It's not made from thin-fucking-air, Barton. It's made from blood. Not enough blood means not enough drug. Even you should understand that.'

'And what should I say about Vincent?'

'I honestly couldn't care less. If Vincent is dead, he's dead for a reason.'

'That's your response?'

'It is all you're getting from me. Now, I'd appreciate if you could kindly get the fuck out of my office so I can get back to work.'

Rhain looks back to his screen, ignoring the venomous look Barton is throwing in his direction. When he realises Rhain isn't going to acknowledge his presence again, he straightens his suit jacket and leaves the room. Rhain slumps back in his seat and stares at the door.

He's not worried about repercussions for Vincent. There's no definitive evidence linking him to his death. Even if there was, the idiot deserved to die. Not even the Order would hold him accountable for that. What isn't helpful is the fact they believe they can send Barton to his premises to attempt to strong arm him into a confession. That's the part irritating him more than anything. It may be time to consider winding down his partnership with the Order.

Thea had spent the last hour replaying every single mortifying second of Court attacking Davyn and her being banished to her room like a disobedient child. What the hell was Court thinking? He had no right to go off like that. Not only did he put his own life at risk by attacking Davyn - he'd also managed to completely humiliate her with his alpha male crap.

Then things got a whole lot worse when Nix and the others couldn't even be bothered to hear her out. It only would have taken a few seconds.

I asked him to do it.

Six little words and the whole thing could have been diffused. Davyn shouldn't be blamed for what happened and he absolutely shouldn't have been attacked by Court. It was like they had all decided he'd forced himself on her and they weren't interested in hearing any different. Instead, Fallon had forcefully escorted her from the room and told her in no uncertain terms to stay put and not leave.

Court may be happy to do what Nix says, but she's not one of the Blackjacks. After what just happened, she's not sure what she's doing here. Her opinions and her views don't matter. Court wasn't interested in hearing her out. That was the bit that hit her the hardest.

For as long as she can remember, she could always depend on him to listen to her. After the way she's been with him lately can she really blame him for dismissing her as he did? She hasn't exactly made it easy for him.

She grabs her bag off the end of her bed and quietly cracks the door open. No sign of Fallon. She closes the door behind her and glances down the corridor towards Davyn's room. Court and Nix are still arguing loudly with each other. There are definitely some unresolved issues there, but she can't think about that right now. All she wants to do is get away from Court, from Davyn, and from this place. Ever since she stepped foot inside this compound, her world has turned upside down. It's time she takes back control of her life.

She hurries along the corridor from her room and down the stairs, pausing at the bottom. No sign of anyone. She walks past the living room and slips down the corridor leading to the garage and training room. The vast space is empty. Everyone must be dealing with Court and Davyn. Thea races across the garage and stops at the line of cars.

When she left the compound with Davyn in his car, the gates had opened automatically as he drove up to them. She may not have been concentrating on details at the time, but she doesn't remember seeing him push a button or take out a remote. She's hoping that means there's something in the cars that triggers the gate. One way to find out.

She walks over to the far end of the line and smiles. Fuck it. It's not like he can get more pissed off with her at this stage.

Nix shuts her laptop and stares up at Court. 'What do you mean she's gone?'

Court leans on Nix's desk. 'I mean Thea's gone. I went to her room and it's empty. She took her purse with her. I've searched the whole place and I can't find her. I thought you said the compound is safe. How did she get out?'

'You can't leave without a code. It's impossible. Unless...' she pauses.

'What?'

Instead of answering she gets up from behind her desk and opens the door. 'We need to go to the garage.'

Court and Nix stare at the line of cars and the very noticeable empty spot at the end. Shep comes out of the small office to the side housing the cameras and rubs the back of his neck. 'Checked the footage. Thea took your car, Court. '

'Yeah, I sort of guessed that from the fact it's not here.'

Nix faces Shep with her hands on her hips. The usually mouthy vampire has the good sense to keep quiet. 'How did she take his car, Shep? I thought you'd locked the place down?'

'I did. But you need to walk through the garage to get to the training room so I left it open. The main gates are locked but they're programmed to open for our cars. I didn't think she'd nick one of them and make a run for it. My bad.'

'Yeah, well I don't think any of us could have planned for that.'

'Did she leave alone? Are you sure Davyn's still here?' Court asks.

Nix nods. 'He's here. Taking out a bit of pent-up aggression in the gym. Do you have any idea where she might have gone? Does she have any friends in the area?'

Court shakes his head. 'Not that I know of. I mean she must know people, but she never mentioned any names. I haven't got a clue where she'd go. Do the cars have locaters?'

Shep holds out the tablet. 'She turned it off. Probably should move it from the dash to somewhere a little harder to find.'

'Perfect. So you don't have any way of tracking her?'

'Not personally. Boss, is it okay if I contact Ethan? I'm sure his team have some way of finding Court's car. Unless she decided to take the reg plates off too.' Shep smirks and immediately wipes it off his face when Court glares at him. 'Yeah, well... I'll go do that.'

Nix nods. 'Thanks. Oh and tell the others to keep an eye on Dav.'

'Got it.' Shep disappears around the side of the bus leaving Court and Nix alone with a fair amount of awkward silence.

'Listen, Court—'

He walks away from her and opens the locker holding the keys for the cars. He takes the key to the spare Land Rover from the hook and unlocks the car.

'What exactly do you think you're doing?'

'I'm going after my daughter.'

Nix crosses her arms as she stands in front of the car. 'Not a chance. I already have to worry about Thea wandering around alone. Fallon and I will go and find her. We can cover more ground from the air than you could from the road.'

He slams the door shut and charges over to her. 'You don't get to tell me what to do. I may have been someone you could boss around, but not anymore. I haven't got a fucking clue what I am to you and right now I couldn't care less. Thea is my priority.'

'I understand that, Court. I really do, but you're my priority. Give us twenty minutes. If we can't track her down, then you can go search for her.'

His shoulders drop and he nods. 'Twenty minutes, Nix.'

She pulls her phone out of her pocket and calls Fallon. 'We're going after Thea by air. I need you in the garage in two minutes.'

Nix squeezes his arm relieved when he doesn't pull away from her. 'We know this area like the back of our hands. Trust us.'

~

Thea slows as she pulls into the car park behind their old apartment block. She peers out the windscreen at what was her home for over a year. It was far from where she envisioned herself living, but they had made it theirs. Over the first few weeks she had visited a few charity shops in the area and picked up a rug, some pictures, and cheap ornaments. It didn't take away from the fact they were living in an apartment that probably should have been condemned, but it helped make the place feel a little more homely.

It looks worse than condemned now. The True Order had destroyed it. Good luck to the vendor trying to sell it with all this damage.

It was probably stupid to come back here, but she didn't have anywhere else to go. She doubts the Order would still be hanging around waiting for them to show up at a burnt-out shell. Maybe Court wouldn't think of looking for her here either.

Thea glares at the purse lying on the passenger seat next to her. No cash. Just one credit card that was nearing its limit. While she'd give anything to tuck herself away in a hotel or B&B for the night, she's not going to risk using the card. She's caused enough problems without adding that to the list.

Thea looks around the carpark but there's no one else around so she gets out, making sure to take the keys out of the ignition first. The last thing she needs is to have Court's car stolen and be stranded here.

The cool night air is fresh and helps clear her head a little, but not nearly enough. Getting away from it all was the right decision, but now that she's by herself she doesn't have a clue what to do. Should she go back and try to put things right with Court? Realistically, how possible will that be. Unless she can get past the block between them, she's fighting a lost cause.

She knows the problem is with her. She knows hearing he's her father changed things and she's the one who can't get past that. But how to you get past the fact your entire life had been a lie? The people she thought of as parents weren't her parents. Court wasn't her brother. It was all a lie orchestrated by Court and there's no one that can clarify or explain his reasons. Until he gets his memory back, they're both lost.

Ever since he came back to her life last year, he's done nothing but protect her. Whether as her brother or her father he was still there for her no matter what.

And she has a father.

He's alive and has been watching out for her all her life. She lowers to sit on the wall running along the edge of the car park. Nix's words from a few days ago come back to her. If she had a pick someone to be her father, she could certainly do so much worse than Court. His reaction to finding out what happened between herself and Davyn was probably justified to a certain extent. As her brother he would have flipped out. As her father... well, maybe he felt his actions were justified. A little excessive but a vampire had just fed off his daughter.

And then there's this whole mess with Davyn. That's another relationship she's managed to destroy. Not that there was one in the first place. Talk about chalk and cheese. They couldn't be more different if they tried. So why can't she get him out of her thoughts? Why can't she stop wishing he went so much further with her in his bedroom? Why is she imaging his hands on her, that incredible body of his pressed against her as he feeds, his stunning wings adding a whole new level to her fantasy. That's certainly a new one for her.

She groans and buries her head in her hands. The thought of facing him again isn't appealing in the slightest. Getting him in trouble with Court and the rest of the Blackjacks wouldn't have helped that. She had no right asking him to feed from her. It was a stupid thing to do. All she's done lately is act like a spoilt brat and now she's backed herself in a corner she has no idea how to get out of.

Thea smiles when she hears footsteps behind her. She turns, thinking Court or Davyn will have tracked her down, but it's neither of them.

An imposing vampire with deep green wings smiles at her, showing his fangs. 'Well, well, well. What are you doing out here all on your lonesome?'

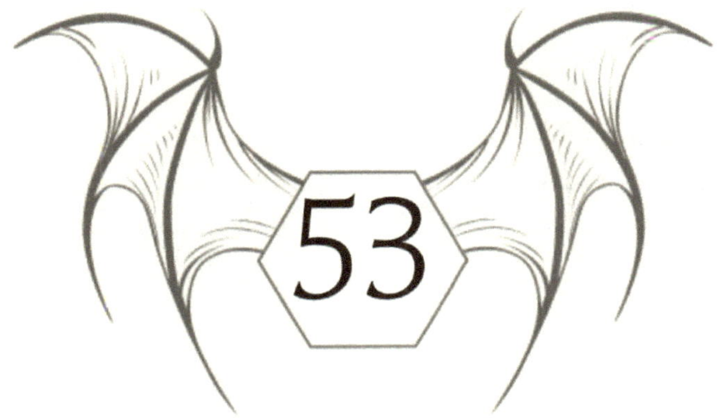

Nix lands on top of the old barn and scans the fields around her. Nothing. She's scoured the entire area and no sign of Court's car or Thea. She checks her watch and curses. Five minutes before Court comes after her.

She pulls her mobile out of her pocket and smiles when she sees Shep's name on the screen. He'd only be calling if he found something.

'Please say you have her?'

'I might, boss. I was able to track her mobile with Ethan's help. You're not going to believe this but she's back at their old place in Bristol.'

'Great work, Shep.'

'Yeah, well I wouldn't get too excited yet. I picked up on some chatter while I was putting out feelers for Thea. The Order is in the area.'

'Dammit. Does Court know?'

'Not yet, boss, but he's wearing a dent in the floor here. You need to set him lose or he's going to destroy something.'

Nix takes off, heading towards Bristol. 'Okay, move out. Two cars only. I don't want Court or Davyn to go off on their own or to be left on their own. There are too many emotions flying around right now. Contact Fallon. Tell her to meet us there.'

'Got it. Stay safe, Nix.'

She ends the call and slips the phone back in her pocket. If the Order have somehow linked Thea to Court, she could be in a world of trouble.

~

Thea's heart pounds in her ears as she runs back to Court's car and slams the door shut, locking it behind her. So much for thinking the Order wouldn't still be hanging around. Just like an idiot, she'd offered herself up to them on a platter.

She screams as something heavy lands on the roof, violently rocking the car. Another vampire appears at the window and smiles at her, baring his fangs. Thea reaches under the driver's seat, hoping Court kept some weapons there like Dav did. When her fingers close around the gun, she keeps the smile to herself. Thea pulls it from its hiding place and takes the safety off. Her attacker's smile disappears as she swings the gun up and shoots him in the chest through the passenger window.

Muttering a silent thank you to Fallon for insisting she learns how to shoot, she fumbles under the seat again and finds a knife so pulls it out and places it in the cubby hole between the seats. Thea drops the gun in her lap and grapples with the key, trying to get it in the ignition. The Defender growls to life but that's as far as she gets before a vampire tears the door from the car, and grabs her by the arm. He smiles at her, his fangs extended as he focuses on the side of her neck. He moves towards her but stops, his brows furrowing in confusion.

He takes a step back and looks down at the thick blade in Thea's hand covered in blood. He falls to his knees and Thea strikes him across the face with the gun.

Before the others get to her, she slams the car into reverse and, without looking behind her, pulls away from the building. She hits the brakes and puts the car in first gear, accelerating around the side of the apartment towards the main road. If she gets out in the open maybe the Order vampires will back off.

Thea screams as a fist punches through the windscreen narrowly missing her. Out of instinct she jams on the brakes. She fumbles for the gun, but when she braked like she had, the gun must have slipped off the seat. The green winged vampire smiles as he reaches through the hole in the windscreen and shoves his own gun against her forehead.

'I'm not sure what all that was but I'm impressed. I thought you'd come without a fight. I'm done playing though. Get the fuck out of the car human before I blow a hole in your pretty head.'

One of his friends drags her out and dumps her on the ground. Thea looks up at the green winged vampire as he jumps off the bonnet and walks over to her, his gun still pointed at her head.

'I'm going to enjoy draining you.' He slams his fist against her face and the world goes black.

Nix lands on Maddox's back and tears him away from Thea before he gets his teeth anywhere near her.

She slams her fist in his surprised face and he falls to the ground. He smiles as he pushes to his feet, wiping blood from his nose. 'Well isn't this my lucky night? I pop by to see if anyone is stupid enough to return here and not only get her,' he says, nodding towards Thea, unconscious on the ground. 'But I also get the famous Phoenix. I am truly honoured. I was hoping you'd show yourself. Bit harsh using that human as bait.'

'Maddox, I presume.'

He nods. 'My reputation precedes me I see. Guess I should be flattered.' He looks around at his fighters. 'Or maybe not. There's five of us. I'm a little insulted you thought you could take us on alone.'

'The others are coming.'

He laughs loudly. 'Yeah. Of course they are. Well, how about you and I have a little fun while we're waiting for your friends? A bit of a warmup. C'mon, little lady. I'm waiting for you to show me what you've got.'

Nix has fought her fair share of Primes, but Maddox is a whole different league. The little information Ethan could find on the male is enough to tell her he's going to be lethal. You don't stay off the radar as long as he has unless he could take care of himself and anyone stupid enough to get close to him.

Maddox charges at her, so she feigns a stumble and catches Maddox in the gut with a powerful punch. Maddox falls back and doubles over, gasping for breath. Nix doesn't give him a chance to recover and kicks him in the face. Maddox lands on his ass, spitting blood on the cracked concrete carpark.

'Bitch. You're going to pay for that.' Maddox slams against her before she can move out of the way. For someone as large as he is, he can move surprisingly fast. She lands on her back, the air leaving her body as his immense weight presses down on her. His thick hand closes around her neck.

Nix tears at his wrist, trying to ease the pressure but the bastard is unbelievably strong. Her vision swims as he increases his grip. Maddox smiles at her and something clicks in Nix. This asshole has to go down. Just before she loses consciousness, she slams her fist into the side of Maddox's head. He curses but doesn't let go so she repeats the move over and over until he finally releases her.

Nix shoves him to his back, planning on beating him to a pulp, but stops when one of Maddox's men stalks over to her, the prone body of Thea on his arms. 'Back off or I'll tear the head off your human friend.'

Nix looks at Maddox, the anger building at the victorious smirk on the bastard's face. She sits back on her legs and nods once. Maddox struggles to his feet and wipes blood from his face. 'Not too bad.' He turns to the other vampire holding Thea. 'Bring her with us. Might help this one remember who's in charge.'

The vampire holding Thea spreads his wings then disappears into the night sky. Nix tries to get to her feet, but Maddox shoves her onto her front, pinning her to the concrete. She watches helplessly as another vampire joins Maddox and roughly jams a syringe in the side of her neck.

Maddox leans over and breathes foul breath on her face. 'Sweet dreams.'

55

Court accelerates along the road, the powerful engine in the Land Rover covering ground quickly. Davyn is sitting behind him with Shep in the passenger seat. Willow and Bastian are following in the other Land Rover. Court wasn't happy about having Dav in the car with him but he wasn't about to let the guy take off in his own car.

The whole situation with Davyn and Thea is making his fucking head hurt. He's heard so many things about Davyn and none of them are making him any less adamant he shouldn't go anywhere near Thea. It doesn't matter if he's being an overprotective father or brother or whatever. The thought of Thea and Davyn together... of him feeding from her...

The drive to Bristol takes place in silence. Shep keeps his eyes locked on the tracker Nix wears on the back of her necklace. It's still showing her at the old apartment. She's either still there and hasn't been able to contact them or her tracker is still there and she's not.

'Court?'

He turns on his comms. 'Yeah Fallon. Have you found them?'

'They left her phone and necklace on the floor in your apartment. No sign of anyone here.'

'Fuck. Right. Stay put. We'll be there in a few minutes.'

He pulls the car into the parking area behind the building and shuts off the engine. Fallon lands in front of the car startling him for a second. He gets out and walks over to her. 'You okay?'

She nods. 'Didn't get here fast enough.'

'None of us did. Shep, can you sense anything?'

Shep is already out of the car, his eyes closed as he does whatever he does to track people. He growls and opens his eyes. He turns his glowing blue eyes to Court. 'That green winged fucker took Nix.'

'And Thea?'

Shep frowns again then nods. 'Her too. One of his men took her then he left with Nix.'

Court nods and gestures to the rest of the team. 'Split up. Check the area. Davyn, hang back for a minute.' Whether or not he's happy about being put on the bench he does as he's told and waits as Shep and Court check what's left of Court's car. The windscreen has an impressive hole in the driver's side and the side window. The driver's door is on the ground and splattered with blood.

Shep smiles. 'Way to go, Thea. It's not her blood.'

'Are you sure?'

'I'm positive, Court. It's from a male vampire. I'm getting five unknown males as well as Thea and Nix.'

'That's something at least. Do I keep weapons in here?'

'Under your seat. A gun and a knife.'

Court reaches under the seat but can't find them. 'Thea must have used them. Or whoever took her used them.'

Shep closes his eyes for a few seconds. 'I can't pick up any human blood. Nix was injured though. She put up a fight before they took her. No way she would have gone quietly.'

'Unless she let them take her so she could keep an eye on Thea.'

Shep nods. 'That works too.'

'Okay. Anyone have any fucking ideas on where they might have gone?'

'We have a way of tracking Thea,' Bastian says. He nods towards Davyn. 'He fed from her. There's a chance he can track her. We'll have to narrow the search area down first.'

Court stares over at Davyn. 'Hold on - he can do that?'

'We all can. You too.'

'But I've fed and never felt anything like that.'

'It's not something that is just there,' Bastian explains. 'You have to go looking for it. It's a skill you'll pick up with practice. You should be able to track your donor for a short while. As long as their blood is in your system, there is a link of sorts. There's a chance he can still pick her up.'

'I fed from Nix.'

As one they turn to face him. Shep clears his throat. 'You did? Okay, well. What Bas just said about Thea and Dav applies to you and Nix too.'

Fallon shakes her head and sits back against Court's car. 'No chance either of you can track them unless we're sure they're close. We're going to need to be within a few miles for you to pick them up.'

Shep crosses his arms and nods over to the stoic vampire. 'He'd have a better chance than Court. He's older and stronger. No offense.'

'I couldn't care less what you say. I just want to find them.'

Shep nods over his shoulder at Davyn. 'You going to hit him if I ask him to pick up Thea's scent?'

'I'll kiss the fucker if he can find her.'

Shep snorts loudly. 'Think he'd prefer you hit him. With the two of you trying to get a lock on them we may have a shot at this.'

Davyn frowns across at Court, his green eyes glowing as they glare at each other. 'Fuck. You stay here, Shep. I need to ask him myself.'

Court walks back over to Davyn and the destroyed car. 'I fed from Nix and you... you fed from Thea. If we narrow down the search area can you help me track them? I haven't got a clue what to do. I'll need you to help.'

Davyn silently looks at him for a few seconds as he runs his hand over the short stubble on his jaw. 'Fuck.'

Court frowns at Davyn. 'A simple yes or no would be just fine.'

'No.'

'Right. Perfect. Thanks. I get you're pissed off with me and believe me, I feel the same, but I need your help to find my daughter. To find Nix. Please, Davyn.'

'I mean I don't need you to narrow down the area. I don't need you to help either. I should be able to track her. Shite apology by the way.' Without an explanation he pulls off his jacket, dropping it to the wall beside him, followed by his t-shirt. Davyn takes a deep breath then nods once to himself. 'Get back and don't ask any fucking questions. This is about finding Thea.' He braces against the bonnet of the car and Court takes a step back as the first wing slides out of Davyn. The black and red limb grows as it realigns, the bones locking in place to form an imposing and seriously impressive wing.

Before Court gets a chance to react, Davyn's head hits against the bonnet as he roars in agony. His second wing tears out of his back with none of the grace of its companion. It attempts to reshape itself, but something is seriously wrong. Instead of stretching to the side, the wing turns back on itself. The bones are twisted at the wrong angle leaving the skin ripped and tattered.

Keeping his weight on the bonnet, Davyn takes a few shaky breaths. His large body is trembling from the effort of the release and, when Court steps closer to get a proper look at his back, he knows why. Nix had told him the skin covering the wing ridges which run down each side of their spine isn't regular skin. There are no pain receptors there and the skin heals quickly.

His second wing took a very different path out of his body. Thanks to the damage the wing tears out through regular muscle and skin.

The resulting wound is substantial and bleeding heavily. The pain must be unbelievable.

As one, the Blackjacks full attention is locked on their teammate. Court doesn't need to see their faces to know they're as shocked as he is. Leaving the whole damaged wing thing aside, Davyn is Prime. Someone they worked with for years, fought with, bled with. How had he kept it hidden from them all?

Shep gets the obvious statement out before anyone else does. 'You're a Prime? Why the fuck didn't you tell us?'

Davyn pushes upright and wipes a hand over his face. 'I said no questions.' He arches his back, spreading the impressive black and red wing to its full width. The damaged wing makes a valiant effort but gives up without really getting anywhere.

'Yeah, sorry mate. You can't spring those fuckers out of your back and say no questions. That's not an option.'

'My wings are my fucking business. Don't push me, mate.'

Court puts himself between Shep and Davyn. 'Okay, we don't need to add fighting amongst ourselves to all the other shit we have to deal with right now. There'll be time for that after we get Nix and Thea back.' Court turns back to Davyn. He looks terrible. His skin is pale and even though he's trying to hide it, he's in pain.

'You good to do this?'

'My wings will act like an amplifier. It should help strengthen my blood bond with Thea, but I'll need Fletch to bring the bus closer so I can follow it. I can't... I can't fly and I'm not able to pull them in and out. I need time to heal between. They need to stay out until I find them.'

Court swallows and nods. After seeing what he has to endure to release them, he's not surprised he needs time to heal. Even now, his arm is braced against the bonnet, helping to keep him upright. 'Of course. Willow, can you contact Fletch and bring him closer? The rest of you, spread out. The last thing we need is the Order coming back to see if we've shown up yet.' He looks over at Davyn, still leaning heavily on the car. 'Is there anything I can do to help?'

Davyn shakes his head. 'Not yet. I'll narrow down the search area. I don't know how long my connection with Thea will last. I didn't... there isn't a lot of her blood left in my system. You might have a better chance of finding them once we get closer.'

'No problem. What now?'

Davyn takes another shaky breath and gestures to the roof of the apartment. 'Height will help me find her.'

Without having to be asked, Fallon holds out her hand, offering to bring him up to the roof. Court leads the others over to the fire-escape. When they get to the roof, Davyn is standing on the wall surrounding the roof, his healthy wing extended to its full width. Fallon is in front of him, one hand on his chest, presumably to prevent him from falling over the edge.

The large wing shifts as he adjusts his balance with help from Fallon. Whatever his reasons for hiding them, Court can't help but be seriously impressed with Davyn's wings. The blood red skin between the black fingers may be torn in places and more than a little battle scarred, but they tell a story about Dav he didn't know. He didn't always hide his wings, so what the hell happened to change that?

Court leaves Davyn to do his thing and joins the others. 'What are the odds he'll pick up something?'

'The odds are definitely in his favour,' Willow replies. 'With one wing it might take him a little longer, but he will find her.'

'So,' Bastian asks, 'when he gets a trail what's the plan?'

It takes Court a few seconds to realise the question was directed at him. 'What?'

'You're second in command. What's the plan?'

'You're trusting me with this? I haven't come up with a plan... ever.'

'Bullshit,' Shep replies. 'Coming up with plans is what you do. You've got five highly pissed off vampires ready to kick some serious ass. You just got to point us in the right direction and set us free.

When you took down those True Order soldiers in the alley, did you see how the fight was going to play out?'

'How the fuck do you know that?'

'It's what you do. Something to do with your eyes maybe. You never explained it to us. You've always been able to see how a fight will play out, like planning a game of chess. We're not saying things always go to plan, but you can see it in your head.'

'I guess we need to find out where they are first.'

'That way,' Davyn says as he points over the city. 'She's at the edge of my range, but I can feel her.'

They look down as the bus pulls up in the car park below them. 'Perfect timing. We'll leave the cars here. Load up.'

Court looks over in the direction Davyn pointed as everyone makes their way from the roof to the bus. A strange calm settles over him. Shep is right. This is what he does. Instead of panicking, he's unemotional about the entire situation. Deep down he's worried about Thea and Nix but worrying about them won't get them out. These guys stole his memory from him, but it seems his instinct and training just need to be set free again. And he's looking forward to doing just that.

Nix groans and, after far too much effort, manages to open her eyes. She blinks a few times, but nothing happens. Just all-consuming blackness. Her night vision is impressive, so something is seriously wrong. It takes her a few seconds to realise the problem isn't actually with her vision. It's with whatever is covering her eyes. She attempts to take it off but hits another problem. Her wrists are locked above her head and supporting her full weight if the pain in her shoulders is anything to go by.

'Morning.'

Her head whips up at the sound of the voice. It's the male from the apartment. 'Where is she?'

Nix hears locks being disengaged and Maddox grips her by the chin, digging his fingers into her jaw. 'Safe and sound. Need some leverage to make sure you do what you're told. So you need to behave or I'll be paying her a visit.'

Nix's canines extend. 'Now you're dragging humans into whatever is going on here. You really are idiots.'

Maddox laughs and squeezes her chin painfully. 'Ouch. You just hurt my feelings.' She hisses as Maddox squeezes her arm. 'Feel those needles? We're draining you, lab rat.' He presses against another tube in the side of Nix's neck. 'And that... well, that's a special little something that turns your brain to a sieve.' She tries to turn away when she feels Maddox's breath on her ear. 'In a bit you won't care what I do to that human. You won't remember who she is.'

Nix slams her head to the side and connects with Maddox. He shouts and curses. 'You're going to pay for that.'

She screams as the electrical current hits both wrists and travels down her body.

'Knock it off, Maddox.' Nix barely registers the different voice through the ringing in her ears. She rests her head against her arm as she tries to catch her breath. Every nerve ending is on fire, every breath stretching skin that is suddenly hypersensitive.

'Maddox, I'll call you if I need anything. You can go.' The newcomer stays quiet for a moment as Maddox leaves. 'I apologise for my friend. He can get a little carried away.'

'He's certainly got a way about him. I would say it's a pleasure to meet you Rhain, but I'm not feeling the love right now.' Nix finally convinces her legs to do their job, releasing a little pressure from her wrists. 'From your accent I presume you are Rhain.'

The long pause tells her more than he probably meant it to. He wasn't expecting her to know his name. Small victory, but she'll take it.

'You're not honestly expecting me to tell you anything, are you?'

'Why do you need my blood?'

'I don't need it. I'm just taking it.'

'Why?'

'This isn't one of those moments in the movies when the bad guy, as you no doubt think I am, tells the captured good guy his plans.'

'Maddox said you're taking my memory. Why?'

'You probably won't believe me, but that is for your benefit as much as ours.'

'Is that so? I'm not so sure the people you've taken memories from would agree.'

'You stop fighting when you can't remember what you're fighting for. Take your colleague for example. In that messed up head of his, the first thing he remembers is when he escaped, am I correct?'

She doesn't bother answering. Something tells her Rhain knows the answer.

'That's because while he was here nothing that happened stayed in his memory. It's like we turned that part of his brain to... what did Maddox say, oh yes, a sieve. Nothing stuck. Nothing to point a finger to us, or so we thought. The tube in your neck is administering that same drug to you and will continue to do so until we're finished with you. That is what's going to make you forget all this just like your friend did.'

'His eyes. Was that you too?'

'His enhanced gift? It was an unforeseen side effect of what we did.' She hears the footsteps fade. 'The drug will take an hour or so to work through your system. When it kicks in you won't remember any of this.'

Nix pulls against the restraints but she's not going anywhere. She tries to release her wings but there's something heavy on her back, pressing firmly against her skin. They must have put a restraint on her to keep her wings inside.

Trapped in the dark, Nix tries to calm down, but it's not a fight she's going to win. She shouts and pulls against her restraints again, not caring if she dislocates both shoulders. She rubs her face against her arm, but the blindfold isn't going anywhere. All she does is tear the underside of her arm on the blindfold's hinge which adds to her level of seriously pissed off.

Every time she moves her head, she can feel the needle in her neck.

That's the part that's scaring her the most. That needle is going to take everything she knows and loves from her. Take Court and the Blackjacks from her. After just finding him again, the thought of forgetting everything about them, everything about her life with Court and the team is worse than anything else that Rhain can do to her.

Nix's eyes drift closed as a sudden tiredness takes over. No matter how hard she tries, her eyes refuse to stay open. Not that it makes a difference either way. Her legs give under her weight, but after too much effort, she locks her knees and forces them to hold her up. It's a futile battle and one she won't win for long. Her body isn't thrilled about the amount of blood it's losing.

Desperate to hang on to consciousness and her memories as long as possible, she tries to remember details of Court's face. She needs to remember him. They can't take him from her. She's still clinging to an image of Court when she finally loses her fight, along with consciousness.

Fletch pulls the bus over at the side of road and, after making sure there's no one around, Davyn gets out and sorts through the scents for Thea. This is the third stop since they left Bristol. Whoever took Thea followed this path. After five minutes he opens his eyes and gets back in the bus, manoeuvring his wings to get through the door. 'We're close. She's easier to track.'

Court checks the map on the table in front of the team. They're heading towards the Forest of Dean. Makes sense. If the Order have a secret lab of some sort like the one they found in the forest, it'll have to be hidden. That would be the perfect place. 'How close?'

Davyn doesn't bother opening his eyes as he replies. 'Few miles maybe.' He's exhausted. Tracking Thea after the trauma of releasing his wings is taking it out of him, which is not good news. Fallon had cleaned the wound on his back, but there isn't a lot else she can do for him. Once Davyn finds Thea, he'll have to go through the painful ordeal in reverse to pull them back in his body. If he's this wiped out after doing it once, Court dreads to think what he'll be like after he does it again.

If they're to have a chance of surviving an encounter with the Order he needs all the team to pull their weight. Fallon clearly is having the same thoughts. She crouches beside the seat Davyn is stretched out on and thrusts her arm up to his face. 'Drink.'

Davyn opens his eyes and stares over at her. 'What?'

'I know you're not a fan of feeding from us, but I don't see that you have a choice right now. We need you to fight. Drink or I'll force feed you.' Fallon smirks. 'If you think you'd win give it a shot. Could be a bit embarrassing for you.' Davyn doesn't make a move to drink so she kneels on the floor. 'You took a bullet meant for me a few days ago. Let me do this for you so we're even. Otherwise I'll have to save your ass at some stage and fuck knows what that'll do for your macho pride.'

Court hides his smirk as Davyn relents and takes what Fallon is offering. A part of him would have liked to see what she would have done had he refused. When he's had his fill, he pushes away from her and swallows deeply a few times, almost like he's convincing himself not to throw up. Fallon doesn't notice his reaction or couldn't care less and re-joins Court at the map.

She points to an area a few miles from them. 'Hey guys. Anyone else think an old mine sounds like the perfect place for a secret lab?'

Shep grins. 'Absolutely.' He checks the details on the laptop perched on his knee. 'Interesting. It's been out of commission for nearly a decade. Ownership transferred from the company who originally worked it to a private corporation. Hang on. Yep, it's one of the companies linked to Rhain... well, indirectly.'

'Shep, you need to be sure.'

'I'm sure, Court. He owns it.'

'Fletch! Stop!'

Court doubts Fletch would have needed the intercom to hear

Davyn's command. The bus screeches to a stop and Davyn climbs out, not caring if there's anyone around to see him. He walks to the edge of the road and looks down the valley in front of him. His wing stretches to its full span and he closes his eyes. Less than a minute later he looks over his shoulder, his green eyes glowing and something resembling a smile on his face. 'Got her.'

~

Thea presses against the corner as the lights go out in her room and the door opens. A tall man steps inside and the door closes behind him. 'Are you okay? I hope Maddox and his men didn't hurt you?'

'Who are you. Why did you turn the light off?'

He takes a deep breath and leans on the far wall. 'I've just had all the 'who are you and what do you want' questions. I'm not going to tell you anything about myself so how about we both move on and stop wasting time?'

'You're a vampire, right.'

'Yes.'

'Where's Nix?'

'She's down the hall. Don't worry, she's very much alive.'

'What are you going to do to her?'

'There's no need to go into any of that, Thea. This is going to sound like empty words, but I truly am sorry you've gotten tangled up in this mess. I really didn't want to involve you, but I didn't have a choice.'

'How do you know my name?'

'We've been looking for Court for quite some time. He was careful not to have his name or details on anything that could lead us to him. Unfortunately, you rented the apartment in your name that we tracked him to. He was staying with you, Thea. From the details we can find, he probably has been staying with you since you rented it last year. Strangely, it was around the same time we lost him. So, Thea. I don't suppose you want to tell me how you know Court?'

'The best thing you can do is let us go before they come for us.'

The bastard actually has the nerve to laugh at her. 'Well, well, well. You're feisty aren't you? I presume by 'they' you mean the Blackjacks.'

'You really think they'll let you get away with taking her like this?'

'I really couldn't care less. I'm more interested in you, Thea. You see, I think you mean something to Court. I think if I were to use you to lure him back to me, he'd come running. What do you think?'

'I think you can go fuck yourself.'

Thea grunts as he suddenly wraps his hand around her throat. His silver eyes glow in the dark as he squeezes. As she looks into his eyes Thea realises this might be the wrong person to taunt. There's nothing in his eyes but a cold, calm assurance. He'd kill her and walk away without giving her a second thought.

'Keep pushing me and I will kill you and throw your body in the bottom of her cell. You need to understand that you mean nothing to me. You're human. Not worth my time. The only reason I haven't ripped your head off your shoulders is because I think I might have a use for you. Am I wrong?'

She shakes her head.

'Thought not. So, for the last time, Thea. How do you know Court?' He applies a little more pressure and his eyes glow brighter. 'My patience is running out.'

'He's my brother.' There's no way she's telling this bastard the truth, but she had to tell him something or he'd kill her.

He throws her back against the wall and leaves the room, locking the door behind him. She listens to his footsteps fade away before the lights turn on again.

Thea stares at the door and wraps her arms around her legs as a chill settles over her. Whoever that vampire was, he terrifies her. If he uses her to get to Court, she knows it will work. Even though their relationship is strained right now, Court would come for her. There isn't the slightest doubt in her mind.

She may never see Court again. Never see her father again. Never get a chance to apologise. To have him as her father. She's been an idiot the last few days. Court was right - she was acting like a spoilt brat. She buries her head in her knees and tells herself not to cry. Tears won't help her and they certainly won't help Nix. Only the Blackjacks can do that. She just hopes they find them before it's too late.

58

Court tries not to pace as Bastian gets up close and personal with any available surface he can get his hands on. He glances over her shoulder as Fallon and Davyn join him. Davyn has a bit more colour to his face and, with his wings back in his body, appears ready to fight. He nods at Court before joining Shep and Bastian.

'He good?'

Fallon shrugs. 'Beats me. He took more blood and kept it down which is a plus.'

'You noticed that?'

Fallon nods. 'He's always fed in private. Don't know what his issue is with feeding. Not going there with him. Think the fact he's Prime is the topic of the day. Back's a fucking mess, but he's strong. Pissed off too so I don't reckon the bad guys are in for a fun time. You manage to find Nix?'

'I think so. Shep gave me a quick lesson on how to track her. I'm sure she's here somewhere, but as to where exactly, I have no idea.

Then again, I haven't got a clue if I'm actually sensing her or if it's all in my mind. Guess we'll find out soon enough.'

'How's Bas getting on?'

Court shakes his head. 'Security's tight.'

'Got something.'

They hurry over to Bastian as he walks down an overgrown track leading away from the facility. He holds up his fist and points ahead. Court quietly makes his way to the front of the group. The trees thin in front of them to open out into a large clearing which leads to the edge of the mine. Dead centre of the open space he can make out the outline of a metal grate buried in the grass. 'What is it?'

Bas is already crouched with his hand on the ground. 'Old escape shaft. It's alarmed, but nothing I can't handle with a little time. There's two of them. The other is about half a mile that way.' He points across the clearing to the trees at the far side. 'This one drops about ten feet then weaves back to the main compound. It's clear right now, but as soon as I take out the alarm, they'll know we're here.'

'What are we facing?'

Bastian closes his eyes and frowns slightly. 'Hard to tell. Two dozen.'

'Nothing we can't handle.' Shep says as he rolls his shoulders. He's itching to get down there. Court can't blame him. He feels the same.

'How close do you have to be to disarm the security?' He smiles sheepishly and Court knows the answer.

'Right on top of it.'

'Yeah, thought you'd say that. Okay. We ready?' One by one, the fighters nod. Court's eyes linger a little longer on Davyn. He's still pale but his unnerving glare is back in force. He's more than ready to say hello to the bastards.

Bastian opens his eyes and looks over at him. Court nods once and Bas races across the clearing with the others. It takes him less than a minute to deal with the locks and another thirty seconds to deal with the alarm. Bas and Shep haul the heavy grate open and Court peers over the edge to the darkness below. Unlike the other facility, the air is cool and fresh.

Court drops down, landing on the concrete floor and waits while the others join him in the tunnel. Davyn lands, wincing as he slowly pushes himself upright.

'Davyn, can you pick up on Thea?'

His head tilts to the side and frowns. 'Yeah, she's that way.'

Court concentrates on doing what Shep told him to and smiles as he feels Nix nearby. He points in the same direction. 'Nix is that way too. That's something at least. Let's go.'

A few minutes down the corridor they come to a three-way intersection. Davyn frowns and shakes his head. 'I've lost Thea.'

'That just means her blood is out of his system,' Fallon says, noticing the look on Court's face. 'Can you get Nix?'

'Left tunnel.' They take a few steps forward stop when Davyn shouts at them.

'Wait!'

They turn to look at Davyn. 'What it is?'

'I don't know. I thought I heard something.' His eyes lock with Court's and glow brightly. 'Fuck!'

Court opens his mouth to ask what's wrong, but instead gets shoved backwards by Davyn as an explosion ruptures the silence.

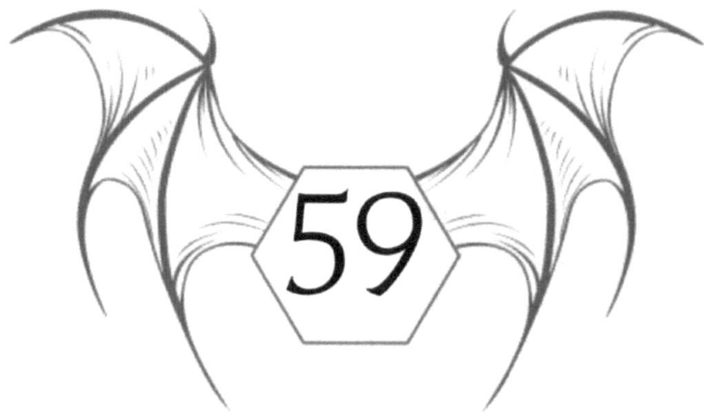

Rhain glances up as Maddox knocks on his door. 'We got trouble.' He tosses a tablet at Rhain and he looks down at the screen. The perimeter sensors have been dismantled.

'They found us?' he asks, already running through an exit plan in his head.

'Looks that way.'

'That's impossible. There's no way...' his voice trails off as he realises there may have been a way. He pushes to his feet and hurries to the girl's room. He unlocks the door and, ignoring her shouts of protest, shoves her down onto the bed. He tears her collar away from her neck and growls when he sees the faint mark of two impressive fangs. 'Who fed from you?'

She tries to extricate herself from under him, but he's not finished with her. 'Fuck you!' she shouts after her struggles get her nowhere.

'Maddox, use Phoenix to convince her to talk.'

Maddox smiles as he walks across the room and turns on the

screen. She tries to get away from him when she sees Nix on the screen. She's hanging from her wrists, unmoving with her head down. She doesn't look like she's conscious. Maddox removes a remote from his pocket and grins widely as he pushes the button. Thea stares in horror as Nix's body jolts and she screams.

'Stop!'

Rhain turns her head so she's looking up at him. 'Who did you feed?'

She shakes her head and Nix's screams intensify.

'We can keep this up all day. How long can she last for, do you think? It's been what, less than a minute? Do you really think she'd survive being electrocuted for thirty minutes? How about three hours?'

'It was one of the Blackjacks!'

'I got that bit. I'll need a name, Thea.'

'Why?'

'I need to know who's coming for you.'

She hesitates and Nix screams. 'Davyn! It was Davyn.'

Rhain gestures to Maddox and Nix's screams die away. She looks up at the screen, but Maddox switches off the feed. Rhain gets up and straightens his shirt. 'Thank you, Thea.' He leaves the room, locking the door behind him.

'You know this Davyn guy?'

Rhain glances up at Maddox before he pulls his phone out of his pocket. 'I believe so. His name is familiar for some reason. Not that it matters. The Blackjacks are here. I very much doubt this Davyn would have come alone. We need to get out of here.'

'What about the blood banks? We leaving them too?'

'Up their levels of the enhancer. Give them ten times the dose then set them free. Kill the ones in the main lab. They've given me what I need.'

'And Phoenix?'

As much as Rhain would love to take her out of the equation, he decides against it. He could do without starting an all-out war with the Blackjacks. Killing Phoenix would cause him more problems than it would solve. 'Leave her alive. Bring Thea with us though. She's the key to getting Court back.'

Rhain hurries back to his office to gather his belongings. Time to relocate the project for a second time. At least he'll have the girl with him. One step closer to getting his donor back.

~

Court coughs and groans as he pushes to his knees. His ears are ringing, and he can taste blood in his mouth. 'Anyone hear me?' There's nothing but static in his comms. 'Hello!'

'Yeah.'

He breathes a sigh of relief when he hears Shep. 'Where are you?'

'On the other side of this fucking wall. I've got Willow with me. We're both okay. I can hear Bas and Fallon in the other tunnel.'

'Davyn?'

The silence stretches on for a minute before he hears a gruff 'yeah' from Dav.

'Are you okay?'

'Yeah. Heard the timer. Sorry about the shove.'

Court gets to his feet and brushes himself off. 'Never apologise for that.' The rescue isn't quite working out how he planned, but at least they're all alive - separated, but alive. 'Shep, can you get Bas to find out where the hell we are?'

'Nix is further along your corridor, Court. Dav can get Thea. The rest of us can loop around and get to the main lab down a side tunnel. It'll take a bit longer though. You might be on your own for a bit.'

He checks his gun and finds it still in its holster. 'No problem. Keep comms open. Hopefully the corridor will clear once we get nearer the main facility. 'Stay safe.'

He wipes the blood from his mouth, takes his gun out and walks away from the team.

60

Court slows as he nears the main room at the end of the corridor. She's in there. He can feel her. He peers around the corner and finds himself looking at exactly the same set-up as the lab they found in the forest. Twelve cells are against the back wall. All of them open except for the one at the end. The one housing Nix.

He pauses as someone comes out of the other passageway and walks over to Nix. Court leaves his hiding place and quietly approaches the man. Before he realises he has company, Court snaps his neck, then lowers the man's body to the ground. Court steps over the man, his heart hammering in his chest as he nears her cell.

She's hanging by her wrists and her head is down. The air is heavy with the scent of her blood.

He's too late.

Fearing the worst, Court slowly approaches the cell, dread building with each step. One of the screens in front of the cell is displaying stats of some kind. It takes him a few seconds to realise it's Nix's vitals. He examines the data closely and smiles. She's got a heartbeat. It's weak but it's there.

'Guys. I got Nix.'

Static again.

'Fuck! Where the hell is Bas when you need him?'

He gives up on the computer screens and goes around the back of the metal cage. Like the ones they found in the old mine, this one is wired to a power source. With no other visible solution, he unhooks the thick cable from the back of the cell and climbs out from behind it. He freezes when he sees another lab technician staring at him. The man reaches for his radio, but Court is faster. He grabs the man around the neck and pulls him close. 'Open the cell.' The technician stares at him, getting locked in Court's gaze. Court can feel him relax in his grip as he continues to look up at Court.

He knows his eyes are glowing, but instead of not knowing what to do, he keeps focused on the man's eyes. Just like he did when he escaped from the lab the first time, he uses what they did to him to his advantage. 'Open her cell.'

He nods and Court releases his grip. The man does as he's told. 'Get in a cell and close the door.' Again, he does as he's told, and Court turns back to Nix. He steps inside and lifts her head. She's got a heavy metal blindfold locked around her head. He tries to push it off, but it's too tight. 'Nix. Wake up. Please.'

Nothing. She's got a pulse and is breathing but is out cold. Court unfastens her restraints and carefully lowers her to the ground. He tries his comms again and breathes a sigh of relief when he hears Fletch in his ear. 'Yeah Court?'

'I found Nix. She's alive but unconscious. I'll need help to get her out.'

'I hear you, but you're on your own for now. I can't reach Dav on comms. Bas and Fallon are making their way around to you, but have met some resistance. Shep and Willow are on their way to you from the other side. They should be with you soon. Tell me about Nix. Can you see any injuries?'

'There's two tubes in her arm. Looks like they're taking blood from her. There's another in her neck, but it's filled with a pale blue liquid.'

'Firstly, get rid of that blue stuff. I doubt it's doing her any good. Leave one of the other tubes in though. She'll probably need blood. If they've been helping themselves to hers, she's probably in haemorrhagic shock. How do her pupils look?'

'They've locked a metal blindfold on her. I'll need Bas to help get it off.'

'Helpful fuckers. Right, well she needs blood, but I don't recommend giving her any of yours, just in case it... well, kills her.'

Court looks over at the technician in the next cell. 'I have someone I can take blood from.'

'I'm not going to ask. Are there any medical supplies around you?'

With Nix on the ground he carefully eases the tube and its mysterious liquid from her neck, then goes over to the metal set of drawers at the far side of the computer screen and he pulls open the top drawer. 'Yeah. What do I need?'

'Needles and syringes. You're going to have to draw blood from your donor and give it to Nix. You can either use a syringe and inject it into the tube or link the donor directly to Nix. Whichever works best for you. Can you do that?'

'One way to find out.' He grabs a handful of needles and syringes then slides in beside Nix again. He looks over at the technician and concentrates on getting into his head. 'In here. Now.'

The man joins them in the cell and sits on the ground. Court shoves the technician's sleeve up and ties a piece of tubing around his arm.

'You okay, Court?'

'I'm trying to stick a needle in someone's arm. Give me a minute.' He finds a vein and slowly inserts the needle. He attaches the tube still attached to Nix and watches as the blood disappears in Nix's arm. 'It's working, Fletch. Now what?'

'Give it a few minutes. Keep me posted, okay.'

'Will do. Try the others. I want to know what's going on.'

As Fletch tries to raise the rest of the team on comms, Court sits on the floor of the cell watching the blood move down the tube. 'Please wake up.'

'I'm tired. Just five more minutes.'

Court smiles when he sees the faint smile on her lips. 'Nix?'

She takes a shaky breath then smiles with a little more conviction. 'Please tell me you're here to rescue me and not a prisoner yourself.'

'Yeah. We're here to get you out. How do you feel?'

'Tired. Really fucking tired. We need to get Thea.'

'It's okay. The rest of the team are looking for her.' No need to tell her Davyn is going for her alone. 'I don't suppose you know where he would have put the key to your blindfold?'

'Couldn't really see. I presume he took it with him.'

'No problem.' Big problem. It's going to be difficult enough to get out of here without having to lead a blind Nix to safety.

'Fletch? You there?'

'I'm here, Court. How is she?'

'Conscious. How long should I give her?'

'Usually I'd say a few more minutes, but you need to move. There are a lot of Fever vampires in the tunnels.'

'Got it. Any word from Davyn?'

'Not yet. I'll keep trying him.'

Court knows Dav can more than handle himself and get Thea out, but until he hears from the guy himself, he won't be happy. 'Okay, Nix. Time to get you out. Keep still while I unhook you from this guy.'

'I'm not going to ask what guy you're talking about.'

He slides the needle out of her arm and pulls her to her feet, holding her as she wobbles. 'Do you have a spare gun?'

'You can't see.'

'I can hear and I can smell. Give me a gun, Court. I need to shoot something.'

He nods, then remembers she can't see him. 'Yes, ma'am.' He puts a gun in her hand and she smiles. 'Let's go find Rhain. I think shooting him will help my mood.'

As soon as the shooting starts, Thea scrambles off the bed and hides under it. She knows it's a futile act. The vampires will be able to pick up her scent without much effort. She desperately hopes it's the Blackjacks coming to get them, but she's not going to assume anything. No doubt there are plenty of vampires with a grudge against the grey-eyed vampire and his people.

Her door bursts open, and she stifles a scream as something large and heavy is thrown across the room. It crashes into the screen on the wall then falls to the ground. She recognises the green-winged vampire's voice as he curses.

Another person steps inside, his scuffed black boots passing by her hiding spot as they launch themselves at the vampire again. She watches through her fingers as the two men scuffle, their large bodies crashing into the wall and the desk before one of them lands on the end of the bed. It collapses under the attack but she doesn't get a chance to scream as the body is lifted off the bed and thrown against the wall.

The green-winged vampire drops to the ground, blood pouring from his nose and mouth. He tries to get up, but judging by the angle of his foot, his ankle is broken.

The boots appear again and Thea watches as the other attacker kneels on the green-winged vampire's back and grabs a handful of his hair in his hand. Thea presses her hands to her mouth as a savage blade is shoved through the side of his head.

Thea tries to steady her racing heart, but she's beyond terrified. She tears her eyes from the impaled body on the floor so she can follow the scuffed black boots as they walk over to the door.

Thea holds her breath, terrified that this person will hear her breathing in the now silent room. After a few seconds she risks a quick peek between her fingers. Davyn is peering under the bed, his green eyes glowing in the dim light.

'Hey. You okay?'

'Oh my God. Davyn!'

'You coming out from under there or what?'

He helps pull her from under the bed and Thea doesn't hide the tears of relief as she wraps her arms around him. He holds her for a few seconds then gently pushes her back so he can look at her.

'Are you okay?'

'I'm fine. Really.' She looks over at the other vampire's body. 'Is he dead?'

Davyn nods. 'Knife to the brain is fairly fatal. He's not getting up again.' He goes over to the body and Thea winces as he pulls his knife out, wipes it on his leathers then slides it back in the holder on his belt. 'Your father is with the others. The bastards blew the tunnels. I was the only one who got through. Don't worry,' he adds quickly, 'they're all fine. We're still in radio contact. I'll get you out, okay. You good to walk?'

'Absolutely. Can I have a gun?'

He raises a pierced eyebrow. 'No. You can't have a gun.'

'But I've been training with Fallon.'

'Yeah, and last time I trained with her she shot me. I'll hang on to the guns. Stick close to me.' He walks back to the door and peers out. 'We're clear. C'mon.' He holds out his hand and Thea takes a firm hold. He leads her along the corridor and further into the facility. He rounds a corner and shoves her behind him as an enhanced vampire lunges at him. Davyn shoots him in the chest followed by the head when he falls to the ground.

'What's wrong with them?'

'Blood Fever. It's advanced. No way back from that.'

He pushes Thea down the tunnel ahead of him. She can hear more vampires coming after them, hear their footsteps and their ragged, gasping breaths. She can imagine their bloodshot eyes, their large fangs extended as they track their prey. Thea stumbles, but Davyn is right there, pulling her to her feet and herding her along. She hides her head under her arms as he fires two shots behind him. Something screams and he urges her forward again.

He slams the door closed at the end of the corridor and rams the butt of his gun against the control panel. Thea shouts in surprise as he grabs her by the arm and pulls her back against his chest. 'Anyone hear me?'

Thea can hear the tiny response in the comms in his ear.

'Can you get a lock on us, Bas?'

He listens for a few seconds and his trademark frown deepens. 'Don't know. We're heading north along the corridor. Got company on our tails.'

Thea doesn't hear the response from the rest of the team, but Davyn's loud, 'Fuck,' tells her everything she needs to know.

He moves more ammunition from his pocket to the belt crossing his chest. 'Bas can't find us yet. Place is like a fucking warren. Got to keep moving and hope he'll get a lock on us.' The door behind them vibrates as something hits it.

'What was that?'

Davyn glances at the door. 'Something we don't want to meet.'

62

Court takes Nix's hand as he guides her through the tunnels. Every so often, Bastian gives him directions in his ear, leading them to safety. Court shoves Nix behind him as a heavily armed vampire steps around the corner, his gun levelled at Court's head. 'Where do you think you're going?'

Court concentrates on the man in front of him and lets his unfamiliar talent have a little freedom. He holds his hand out and the man frowns then passes Court his gun. Court punches him and he drops to the ground.

'Are you okay?'

He glances over his shoulder at her. 'He gave me his gun. I think I may grow to like this part of whatever they did to me.'

'No arguments from me.'

Court takes her hand and smiles to himself as she squeezes it. 'Let's get out of here. No idea how many times I'll be able to do that.' He contacts Davyn, hoping that this time he'll get a response.

'Court.'

'Where the hell have you been, Davyn?'

'Busy.'

'Please say you have her.'

'Got her. We're on the way out, but we're not alone. Got some vamps with serious Blood Fever after us.'

'Where are you?'

'No fucking clue. Bas is trying to lead us out.'

'We'll meet you. Keep her safe, Davyn.'

'No problem.'

Court hurries along the corridor desperate to get Nix to safety so he can get to Thea.

~

Davyn points down a side corridor and looks behind him briefly. 'Middle one. Go!' Thea hurries along the corridor following closely behind Davyn who keeps stopping to check the way ahead and behind is clear. He stops and she slams against his back.

'Which way?'

She is about to answer when she realises he's talking to one of the Blackjacks.

'Got it.' He points to a small corridor branching away to the left. 'Bas said to go that way. Nix and Court are on the way.'

'Is she okay?'

Davyn nods. 'Seems to be. Go. The way is clear.' She feels her way along the side wall of the tunnel, trying to keep up the pace in the pitch black while not bumping into any unfriendly vampires. Davyn pulls a heavily rusted gate across and jams his knife between it and the stone wall to wedge it shut before following her. After a few minutes, he pulls her to a stop and points up. It takes her a few seconds to realise the roof isn't solid. A heavy metal grid is embedded in the stone. A few feet above that is another grid and above that she can see a lone star in the sky.

'We've got a few minutes tops before we have company,' Davyn says as he looks over his shoulder in the direction of the screeching. 'The others are on the way, but they've had to go another route. The tunnel is blocked and there's more of our bloodthirsty mates keeping them busy.' He examines the gate and curses. 'It's locked.' He reaches up and pushes against one of the bars, which gives way a little under the pressure. 'Rusted through here. You think you could fit if I make the hole bigger?'

Thea blinks a few times, not understanding what he's saying. Davyn turns her away from the corridor and the vampires and lifts her chin so she's looking at him. 'Just focus on me. If I break that bar, will you be able to squeeze through?'

She looks up at the bars and nods. 'I think so. But what about you?'

'You first.'

'But—'

'But nothing. I need to get you out.'

Without waiting for a response, Davyn pulls off his jacket and passes it to her along with his gun. 'Put that on, you're freezing. The gun is ready. Shoot anything that comes down that corridor.' As she slips the warm, soft leather over her shoulders, Davyn takes off his t-shirt and passes it to her. He takes a deep breath and rests his hands against the stone wall. He looks over his shoulder at her. 'Best stand back.' He arches his back and with a muffled scream to rival their pursuers, Davyn forces his wings out of his body. Thea watches in horror as blood trails from the base of his damaged wing down his back. 'Are you okay?'

He nods and rests his head against the cool stone wall for a few seconds before he stretches his undamaged wing. Davyn hooks his talon around the rusted bars and pulls down hard. The hooked claw slices through the weakened metal bar with a painful screech. As his talon digs in again, Thea hears a similar screech of metal echoing through the corridor behind them. Davyn hears it too, his head whipping around. 'Shite,' he mutters and focuses on his task again. The third draw of his talon on the metal does the trick, separating the bar from the frame. Davyn reaches up again, hooks on to the frame and pulls himself up. He hangs on with his hands and wing as he kicks the broken bar over and over again.

Thea stares down the corridor as the gate rattles against Davyn's knife holding it shut. She wants to tell him to hurry, but it wouldn't help. He's working as fast as he can.

'That's the best I can do. The rest of the frame is solid.'

'I'll get through it.'

Davyn smiles briefly and stretches his wing down to her. 'Grab on. Just avoid the talon. It'll slice your skin open.'

She takes a hold of his wing at the joint where the main talon protrudes. It feels a lot different to what she expected. Under the warm, soft, thick skin, she can feel the muscle and bone move as he pulls her up to the grid. The hole he created is actually bigger than she thought but it's still going to take a bit of manoeuvring for her to get through. Even if she can get out, there's no way he'll be able to get out.

The sound of the gate being flung open, quickly followed by footsteps convinces her to get a move on. With Davyn's help, she uses the rough stone walls as footholds as she wriggles through the hole. Davyn hangs on by his wing, firing upside-down back along the corridor as she pushes herself through the bars.

Rusted metal digs and tears at her skin, blood oozing from a deep cut on her arm as she catches it on the torn bars. Davyn looks up at her, his eyes glowing. His fangs extend as her blood drips onto the floor below them. The sounds of the crazed vampires hit her like a wave as Davyn confirms her fears.

'They can smell that. Move.' His voice sounds rough, and his eyes are solely focused on the blood on her arm. She pulls his coat sleeve down, hiding the wound.

With a roar, the vampires burst into the chamber. From his elevated position, Davyn fires again and again, but there seems to be more vampires than she originally thought. With a last panicked wriggle, she forces her hips through the gap, crying out in pain as her body is squeezed and scratched. She lifts her legs through the hole and looks back down at Davyn. He looks up at her and smiles. 'Just in time.'

She glances up and sees Court over the side, but her elation is short-lived. She looks back at Davyn and her stomach drops. Three vampires are hanging on to him, trying to pull him off the ceiling. He fights back but as more and more of them grab him, he struggles to hold on. Davyn looks at Thea as he falls to the ground. Before he hits the dirt, the vampires swarm him, pulling, kicking, tearing at him as he does the same in return. His wings slice through his attackers, tearing them open, but more keep coming from down the tunnel. Too many for him to handle alone.

'Davyn!' Thea screams, but she knows it's futile. Even as she hears the top gate opening and the rush of wind as Court lands beside her, she knows it's too late for Davyn. Court pulls at the bars, shouting in frustration when it refuses to budge for him.

'Get Thea out of here!' Davyn shouts from under the pile of bodies. Clearly sensing more trouble could be heading their way, the vampires move away from them, dragging a protesting Davyn with them.

'Help him! Do something!'

But nothing can be done. With no way of getting to him, they have no choice but to watch as he is dragged down the corridor and out of sight.

Then silence.

They stare at the ground under them. The only thing left is Davyn's gun lying in a pool of blood.

63

Court leads Nix back to the main chamber of the facility where the rest of the team have gathered. He wanted to leave her on the helicopter Ethan sent to collect them but there was no way she was sitting this one out. Besides, Bas is the only one who can take the damn blindfold off.

At least Thea had stayed with Fletch leaving them to search the facility for any signs of Davyn or anyone involved in the project. Thea only agreed to stay on the helicopter as long as Court and the others promised to bring Davyn back. Nix desperately hopes it's a promise she can keep.

Court manoeuvres her around the room. 'Okay, there's a chair behind you. Sit down and I'll get Bastian.'

She sits down and tries to hold back the growing panic threatening to consume her. The blindfold is only adding to the feeling. It's painful and claustrophobic. She resists shouting at Bastian to get over here and deal with it.

Nix barely holds back the sigh of relief when she hears two set of footsteps approaching her.

'Hey Nix.'

'Hey Bastian. Can you get it off?'

She hears him pull off his gloves and his voice comes from behind her when he speaks again. 'Not many locks I can't get through. Just hold still.'

It takes Bastian less than two minutes to deal with the padlock allowing Court to carefully remove the blindfold from Nix's face. She rubs her eyes then slowly opens them, smiling when she sees Court crouched in front of her. He looks different somehow. More like his old self.

'Are you okay?'

'I am now. Damn thing wasn't made for comfort. Any sign of Davyn?'

Court shakes his head. 'Not yet. You stay put while we have a look around. Save your strength.'

'I'm fine. I took a quick feed from Willow. After being locked in that cell I need to move around for a bit.' She pushes to her feet, accepting his support when her legs decide to contradict her.

Once she gets her balance she lets go of his arm and looks around the room. Even in a hurry to get away, Rhain had still managed to take the drives from the computers. Bastard was thorough. Unfortunately, with so many exits to cover, Rhain and his bodyguards had escaped capture.

'Have you tried Davyn's comms again?'

Bastian nods. 'There's nothing, Nix. Not even static.'

She walks over to the cell she was held in and stares at nothing in particular as she discretely wipes her face. This can't be happening again. She can't lose one of her team again. Not like this. If anyone can find Dav, Shep will. He had taken Willow with him and was tracking Davyn through the tunnels. He'll find him. Shep had to find him.

They're still no closer to figuring out exactly why Rhain wanted Court or what he was doing with the others, but she knows he's not done. There's too much expense, too many hours invested in whatever this is. If Rhain wanted to create some cure for Blood Fever he wasn't going to stop now. Would Davyn be taking Court's place?

She walks over to Bastian at the far side of the room. 'Any sign of him?'

Bastian opens his eyes and shakes his head. 'It's like he's vanished.' He repositions his hands on the wall and closes his eyes again. 'There's a maze of tunnels under the facility. No Davyn though.'

Nix holds out his blood smeared gun. 'How can this be the only trace of him. How can he just disappear? It defies logic.'

'He's a big and seriously pissed off fucker,' Fallon says. 'He'd have given them a fight. There should be bodies lining the corridors. More blood. Something to hint that a highly trained warrior was being taken against his will. The last time we trained together he broke my fucking arm. He fights. He wouldn't just...' Fallon shakes her head and turns away from Nix.

It's not like Fallon to be so emotional about anything, but Nix can swear she is holding tears back. Nix squeezes Fallon's shoulder.

As one, they turn to face the left corridor as Shep joins them with a very solemn Willow beside him. The look on his face tells her he's had no luck either. Nix lowers her weapon and hurries over to him. 'Anything?'

Shep rests his hands on his hips and shakes his head once. 'I followed his scent from where Thea got out, and down one of the side corridors, but it gets too mixed up with the scents from the other vamps. I can't track him, Boss. There are marks on the floor - fucking huge talon marks and a lot of blood along with seven more bodies. Irish git put up one hell of a fight.

'I knew he was lethal, Nix, but from what I can pick up, this was a whole new level. He could teach you a thing or two about using your wings on the ground.' He smiles but it fades as he shakes his head. 'Fuck, Nix. I've never lost a scent like this before.' Willow jumps as her brother shouts and punches the wall.

'Hey, Shep. It's okay.'

'It's far from fucking okay, Nix. I should be able to find him. But his scent just ends. I can't track him.'

Nix squeezes his arm. She can't say anything to make him feel any better.

'Nix!'

Hoping for a miracle, they hurry over to Court. But he hasn't found Davyn. He's crouching down at the last cell looking at the body of the vampire hanging inside like she was a while ago.

'He's still alive.'

Nix checks the screen on the side of his cell. The connection to his restraints was damaged. It saved his life. Dealing with this male is the least of her concerns right now, but she can't leave him. 'Bring him with us. Who knows, he might be able to give us some answers.'

Shep grunts as he examines the screen.

'Doubt it. He's fucked. They didn't manage to kill him, but his readings are barely there.'

'I said we're bringing him so get him down. Fallon, you and Shep get him back to Fletch. Make sure he's restrained though. I don't want our good deed to kill us.'

As Fallon and Shep deal with the male she knows she has to make a decision she desperately doesn't want to make. The site is secure for now but that doesn't mean it will stay that way. The True Order could be on the way with reinforcements. They have to go. She knows it, Court knows it, and the other Blackjacks know it. That doesn't mean any of them want to voice it though.

Court walks over to Nix and stands in front of her. She looks up at him, the pain of the decision in his eyes too. 'You've got to call it, Nix.'

She nods once. 'I know. The order is sticking in my throat. How the hell has this happened again? I swore I'd never give this order again.'

'If we don't move, we risk losing more than Davyn.'

She closes her eyes and curses to herself as she contacts the helicopter. 'Fletch, how are we looking?'

'Still clear, but the alarms weren't there to scare people away. Back up will be coming.'

Nix nods to herself, the decision made. 'Time to go.'

The other Blackjacks look at her, but no one argues. They all know they've run out of options.

Bastian takes the lead, one hand against the wall as he checks for any unwanted company. And for Davyn. Each of the team scans the darkness around them, senses heightened searching for any hint of their missing teammate. They emerge through the steel doors and silently move towards the landing site. Fletch brings their transport down on the top of the hill beyond the facility. The helicopter is barely on the ground for a minute before the team has boarded and Nix puts on a headset, telling Fletch to take them home. Shep straps the unconscious male to the gurney at the back of the craft then stands with his teammates at the open door as the helicopter lifts off the ground and moves away from Davyn.

Court meets Thea's eyes as she peers out of the cockpit. She looks from one Blackjack to the next before settling on Court again. After putting on a headset she asks, 'Where's Davyn?'

Court doesn't want to have this conversation with her here like this with everyone listening, but there's little option. 'We couldn't find him, Thea.'

'What do you mean you couldn't find him? He's down there. Why are we leaving?'

'We don't have a choice. We tore the place to pieces, but apart from his gun, there was no sign of him.'

Ignoring Fletch's protests, she slowly makes her way back to the rest of the team and sits beside Court. 'So you left him?'

'The True Order will have sent another team once the alarm went off. If we didn't get out now, we could have all been trapped in there,' Court explains, knowing full well she wouldn't accept that as a reason for leaving without Davyn.

'So, instead you save your own asses and leave him?'

'Hey,' Shep growls from beside Nix. 'We didn't just waltz out of there singing a happy tune. Dav is one of us. Our brother in all but blood. Don't you fucking dare say we did what we did lightly. If you had just done as you were told we wouldn't have had to come here to rescue you. This is on you, Thea. He's gone because of you!'

Nix holds up her hand and Shep clamps his mouth shut. 'Enough!' The leader is slumped on the bench running the length of the cargo hold looking completely exhausted. Court can't remember seeing her so deflated and beaten. 'We're leaving for now. That doesn't mean we're leaving him. We're also not going to help him or anyone else by throwing blame around. Every time we leave the compound, we know the risks. Davyn was no different. We stick together - all of us - or we might as well pack up his stuff and move on. Do you understand?'

Thea opens her mouth to reply but Court shoots a warning look at her and she follows Shep's example and thinks better of it.

Thea slumps back in the seat and wraps her arms around herself. Court reaches up and takes a blanket from the rack above his head and drapes it around her shoulders. She mutters a barely audible thanks and smiles at him and tucks her arms under it.

Whether she wants him to or not, Court wraps his arm around her and pulls his daughter close. He rests his chin on her head and runs his hand over her hair, smoothing the tangles.

He watches as Fallon takes a med kit from under the seat and nudges Nix's leg, startling the leader awake again. 'Give me your arm.'

'Sorry. What?'

She holds up a bag of fluids. 'Fletch wants me to give you this. Flush whatever shit they were giving you out of your system.'

'Will it work?'

She shrugs. 'It'll take time to find out what it is. For now this could help. It won't do any harm.' Nix meets Court's eyes as she offers Fallon her arm. Even with the craft moving, she easily slips the needle in and tapes it in place. Fallon hangs the bag off the rack above Nix and sits back down beside Shep.

'What did they do to you?' Thea asks as she stares at the tube attached to Nix's arm.

'Just took some blood,' Nix says as she rests her head back against the wall.

'What shit was Fallon talking about? Did they give you something to affect your memory?'

'Yeah, but Court got me out before too much went in. I'll be fine.' Nix closes her eyes and Thea lets her sleep. Court watches her for a few minutes. He desperately hopes he got there in time. He has no idea how long she was being pumped with the blue liquid. Hopefully Fletch can find out what it is from the sample Court gave him. If they find out what it is maybe Fletch or Ethan and his team can figure out how to fix his memory.

'Do you think they took Davyn too?' Thea asks as she snuggles against him.

Court would rather not think about that either. He's hoping Dav is unconscious somewhere in the tunnels and will get out when he comes too. They may not be on the best of terms, but he doesn't want any of the Blackjacks put in the same situation he was. 'I don't know. I hope not. We're not leaving him. We will find him – I promise.'

Thea nods but doesn't reply. Leaving him is exactly what they're doing. Davyn saved her by sacrificing himself. How the hell is she supposed to deal with that?

'Who's that?' she asks, nodding towards the low gurney attached to the floor.

'No idea. They killed all the vampires they had prisoner. The connection to his cell failed. We couldn't leave him there.'

'Is he okay?'

'No idea. Fletch will see to him when we get back.' Court pulls her against him. He came so close to losing her and it terrified him. 'It's you I'm worried about. Are you okay?'

'I'm fine.' She looks up at him. 'I'm fine, really. I just… I want to be relieved. I want to be glad you got me out… but Shep is right. It is my fault.'

'Thea—'

'No. I was angry and stupid and thought I knew better. If I had just stayed in the compound like I was told, this never would have happened. They wouldn't have taken Nix and Davyn wouldn't be missing. It's all my fault.'

Court holds her close as she cries. There's nothing he can say to make it better. He lies back against the bulkhead and his eyes drift across to Nix. He smiles as her eyes meet his, and she smiles back.

As much as he wants to sort things out with Nix, Thea needs him more. It's time to put all the anger and hurt aside. The truth had damaged their relationship, but it could be repaired. He's sure of that. Memories or not, Thea is his daughter and he'll do whatever he has to do to make sure she's okay. If that means walking away from Nix and the Blackjacks for a while, that's what he'll do.

65

Thea steps out of the shower and dries herself. She still feels cold. Nothing is helping to remove the chill that settled over her when she stepped into the hold and saw everyone except Davyn. She understands why they had to leave, but that doesn't ease the hand that seems to be locked around her throat, making breathing difficult.

She dresses quickly in a pair of joggers and t-shirt then towel dries her hair. The mirror is covered with condensation, so she wipes her hand across it and brushes her hair without taking much interest in styling it. She looks terrible. Her appearance matches how she feels. The strange thing is, it's got nothing to do with being taken like she was. It was her part in what happened to Nix and Davyn that's eating her up.

It's strange how circumstances can change your perception of things. When she ran away from the compound, she had been so angry. Angry at Court for lying to her about who he is and angry at the rest of the team for not listening to her about what happened with

Davyn. She had let her emotions get the better of her and it backfired.

It didn't matter that she had finally found her father, or that Court was struggling dealing with the truth either. She was dominated by anger. A completely ridiculous anger directed at someone with amnesia. He didn't remember he was a vampire. How could she blame him for forgetting who she really is? Why the hell didn't she just listen to Davyn when he told her to let it go? She acted like a spoilt child and two people were hurt as a result.

Nix may have been found, but they still don't know if she's going to be okay. They're waiting for results of a blood test to see if they can tell how much of the drug made it into her system. What if she wakes up tomorrow and she's forgotten the Blackjacks? What if she's the one responsible for Nix losing everything she knows.

All of that is difficult enough to deal with without adding Davyn to her list of epic fuck ups. She picks his jacket off the chair by the sink and buries her face in the soft leather as she cries. She's been such an idiot. She burst into this world thinking she knew everything. Instead all she did was push Court away when he needed her the most, when he was confused and hurting. Then she sticks her nose in Davyn's life and throws him to the enemy.

She wanders back into her bedroom and lays Davyn's jacket on the chair beside her bed. Exhausted doesn't begin to describe how she feels. Thea slumps on to the bed and looks around her room. She's terrified about seeing any of the Blackjacks. Shep's words to her were firmly lodged in her head, replaying over and over. Of all the Blackjacks, he was the one who seemed to accept her more than the others. To hear so much anger coming from him, and to have it directed at her, had gotten to her. His words hit her harder than a physical blow. Mainly because he was right. If he felt that way, the others must too. She's half expecting Nix to knock on the door and tell her to clear out.

Thea jumps as the expected knock sounds on her door. There's no point delaying the inevitable. 'Come in.'

Instead of Nix and a team of angry fighters, she is relieved to see Court carrying a tray of food. 'Hey. You sure you want me to come in?'

She smiles and nods. 'Of course.'

He places the tray on the end of the bed and stuffs his hands in the back pockets of his jeans. 'Gwen made you some soup and a sandwich. Try to eat something then get some rest.' He smiles and turns towards the door.

'Thanks... Dad.'

Court stops like he's run into an invisible wall. He slowly turns to look at her. 'What did you say?'

She shrugs. 'I called you dad. Is that okay? I mean I can keep calling you Court if you'd prefer. I just thought it might be nice to try it.'

The smile that hits his face is like nothing she's seen. It's not like he's never smiled before, but this is a whole different type of smile. His eyes light up - literally. It's like every part of his face is joining in.

'I'll take that as a yes.'

He runs his hand over his face and nods. 'Yeah. It's a definite yes. You sure about this? I don't want you to think you have to do the whole father-daughter thing because of what just happened. I'm good to go at your pace. If you want me to back off and give you space I will.'

Thea lifts the tray off the bed and places it on the bedside table. She pats the duvet and Court sits beside her. 'I owe you an apology. A seriously big apology. I've been a selfish—'

'Thea—'

'No. I'm saying this so please shut up.' He leans back against the headboard and nods. 'Right, what I was saying is that I've been a selfish, spoilt brat. I was so absorbed in my own issues I put everyone at risk. I thought I knew how this world worked. I thought I was the only one struggling with what was happening. I broke the rules and because of my stupidity, Nix was taken, Davyn is missing, and the rest of the team was put at risk. That's all on me and I fully understand if Nix wants me to go.'

'Hang on a sec. You think Nix wants you out?'

'I wouldn't blame her.'

'Thea, you made a mistake. She gets that, trust me. I've spoken to her and she has no intention of kicking you out.'

'And the others. Shep was—'

'I'll deal with Shep.'

'And Davyn?'

'That's not done, okay. We'll get him back. He's strong and trained better than the others put together. He'll survive.'

Thea nods, but she's not convinced. She shuffles closer to him and lifts his arm so she can lean against him. Court hesitates for a moment then holds her close. 'I'm sorry.'

'There's nothing to apologise for. I haven't handled it well either. You think finding out I've got an adult daughter was easy? For the last year I thought I was in my mid-thirties with a sister a few years younger than me. Then I find out I'm actually heading towards a century and a half and I have a daughter. It'll take both of us time to adjust to this. I'm not expecting miracles, I just want a chance to be your father. That's all I'm asking.'

She sits up and her heart breaks a little at the look on his face. He's still expecting her to push him away. 'I'd like that, Dad. Really.'

The whopper of a smile comes back. 'Thank you.'

'Just one thing though.'

The smile dies a little. 'What?'

'Probably best we stick to being siblings in public. I'm not sure anyone would believe you're old enough to be my father.'

'Yeah, you're probably right.'

'Can I ask you something?'

'Shoot.'

'You and Nix?'

His face drops a little. He doesn't want to go there with her. Tough.

He's been looking out for her since they found each other a year ago. It's about time he starts living his life again.

'There's something there, right?'

He shakes his head. 'She's my boss.'

'Don't give me that. I'm not blind. I've seen the way you look at each other.'

'Whatever is or isn't there, now isn't the time.'

'Why? Please say it's not because of me.'

The fact he can't meet her eyes is all the answer she needs. She takes his hand and squeezes it. 'I'm fine, Court— Dad. Sorry. I'm fine, really. You need this. You deserve to be happy. Nix deserves to be happy. I absolutely do not want you to miss this chance because you're worried it will get in between us or mess up our relationship. It's messed up enough, you and Nix can't make it worse.' She smiles to soften her words. 'Do you like her?'

Court takes a deep breath then shrugs. 'Fuck it. Yes. I like her.'

'Then what are you waiting for? Tell her.'

'That easy?'

'After everything you've been through the last few years, this will be a piece of cake.'

Nix slams her fists against the punching bag again and again, but it doesn't help to dispel the frustration and helplessness that's threatening to consume her. Everything is falling apart. Yet again, she let her guard down and one of her team paid the ultimate price. She beats her fists against the bag, harder and harder.

They'll take a few hours downtime then go back to the facility. There must be some clue, something to lead them to Dav. You don't take a six-and-a-half-foot, highly trained Prime male without leaving some trace, some sign of where they took him. It doesn't make sense that he just disappeared.

Nix gives up on the bag and turns to tackle the weight bench. She freezes when she sees Court leaning against the wall at the far end of the gym. 'How long have you been there?'

'Long enough to be damn grateful I'm not that bag. Has it helped?'

'What?'

'Beating the hell out of it.'

She shakes her head. 'Not really. Do you need me for something?'

He pushes off the wall and sits on the edge of the nearest treadmill. Nix tries not to look at him but it's impossible. She can smell the shower gel he always used, the familiar scent was one she deeply missed.

'I think we should talk.'

'Talk about what?'

'Don't do that, Nix!'

His shouted reply startles her. 'Do what?'

'Dismiss me like I mean nothing to you.' He scrubs his hand over his hair as he glares at the ground, hopefully reining in his temper. When he looks up again, his expression is hard. 'I remember you.'

'Remember me? What are you talking about?'

'I remember you from before I was taken. I remember getting ready to go out on rotation and you told me to be careful. I told you how I felt about you. I told you I loved you. Is that all in my head?'

'Court, I don't know—'

'Is it in my fucking head, Nix or did it happen? I need you to tell me if I'm losing my mind because that's how it feels.'

She closes her eyes, unable to look at him and see the hurt and confusion on his face. How can she explain this is for his own good?

'What are you afraid of?' he asks.

'I'm afraid now?'

'Too damn right you are. You're afraid I'll break you again.'

Nix's heart hammers in her chest. He hit the nail on the head.

'I felt it when I was in your head. There's so much pain and I didn't realise what it meant until today when Davyn went missing. You blame yourself for what happened to me. For what happened to Davyn, don't you?'

She doesn't say anything. What is there to say? If she opens up about it, she won't be able to stop. He blows out a long breath and stares at her. He's not going to let this go, and can she really blame him?

'Yes, okay! I blame myself for what happened to you and to Davyn. It's my fucking fault and I have to live with that. You have to live with that. Every single time I see you I'm reminded of what I did. Reminded that I messed up and you're suffering because of my reckless behaviour.'

Court frowns up at her as her words sink in. She didn't mean to offload like that. 'What did you do?'

Nix lowers onto the mat and tucks her legs under her. 'We were together all afternoon. In bed. When Ethan sent the report to me, I barely looked at it. I saw where we had to go and skimmed through the details, but I didn't give it the proper time it needed. I was too busy... being with you.' She licks her lips as her throat suddenly goes dry. 'We had the briefing and I sent you, Davyn, and Shep out. I didn't think it warranted sending everyone. But I was wrong. There were more Order males there than we thought. You got split up. Davyn and Shep barely got back in one piece and you didn't come back.'

'And that's your fault?'

'Of course it is! It's my job to know all the facts. I made a rash decision and got it wrong. I did the same again today. I should never have gone after Thea like that.'

'What happened to Davyn, it was just bad luck. It had nothing to do with any decision you made. And as for going after Thea, I'll always be grateful you did that.'

'Is that supposed to make me feel better? I fucked up, Court. And I'm damned if I'm going to do it again. I can't do my job right unless I keep away from—' she cuts herself off before she says the final word.

'Keep away from me?'

'If I had just spent a few more minutes looking at the details, it would have gone down differently. You wouldn't have been captured and you wouldn't have spent two years being hurt.'

'You didn't hurt me, Nix.'

She lets out an unattractive snort and angrily wipes a few stray tears from her face.

'Look at me.' It takes a few seconds to convince herself to meet his eyes. 'You didn't hurt me. Nothing you did or didn't do could have changed anything that happened three years ago. Being together didn't start the chain of events. The Order or Rhain or whoever is involved, they started that. You can't keep beating yourself up over something you had no control over. Things will go wrong from time to time. We need to pick ourselves up and deal with the shit when it comes. If we don't...' he trails off and shrugs. 'Well, I guess we should call an end to the Blackjacks.'

'If I'd just taken another few minutes—'

'Stop, Nix. If every single bad mission pushes us further apart as a team or makes you doubt what we're doing then yeah, maybe it is time to call it quits.' He joins her on the mat and crouches down in front of her. 'I know I'm new to all this, well, up here anyway,' he says, tapping the side of his head. 'But I know the Blackjacks are a hell of a lot stronger than that. You're stronger. I didn't get taken because of you. I know that. I need you to believe that too. For the team, for Davyn... and for us.'

'How can there possibly be an us after everything that's happened?'

'I'm in love with you, Phoenix. I've known since you swept into the apartment like some out of this world warrior goddess. I knew fuck all else about anything, but I knew that. Every single time I've laid eyes on you I've felt it.' He presses his hand to his chest. 'In here. Every damn time. I didn't recognise what it was until recently and it's been driving me crazy.' His pale eyes glow with an intensity that leaves Nix with goosebumps. 'I want you. I need you and I'm not just talking about sex. I'm talking about you, Nix. I need you in my life.'

She swallows deeply and pulls away from his eyes. 'I don't want you to think you have to say all this because of what happened today. Emotions are all over the place and it's easy to confuse how you truly feel. The last thing I want is for you to feel like you have to say that to me.'

'Why the hell would I tell you I love you if I don't? I'm not the one playing games, Nix. Just tell me you don't want me and I'll leave you alone.'

In that instant, she knows she's fighting a losing battle. She could never convincingly tell him or herself that she didn't want him. She may try to deny what they had between them, but she could never say she didn't want him. She always wanted him. That's why she'd been doing everything she could to avoid him since she got back.

She looks across at Court. His eyes are still glowing, but not like they do when he's about to plunge into her mind. This is the look he gets when he wants her. There's no faking that. He's pretty damn spectacular. And he's hers. All she has to do is say the words. 'I'm just scared I'll lose you again.'

'You never lost me, Nix. We just couldn't reach each other for a while. You found me and brought me home. That's all that matters.' His lips part and she sees the tips of his fangs. Goddammit. Why does he have to look the way he does? Smell the way he does. Everything about him calls to every part of her. He's the only one who has ever had this effect on her. The only one she's ever craved. His words reach her, but she doesn't want to let go of the wall around her heart. She's scared of letting go. Scared of giving her heart to him again. Scared of what will happen if things go wrong.

'I love you, Court.'

One minute Court is crouching in front of her and the next he has her underneath him in the centre of the mat. He does his heart-stopping lopsided grin, complete with one impressive fang. 'I can't tell you how amazing it is to hear that again. Thought it was all in my head.'

'I'm sorry. I—'

He silences her by kissing her. 'Not now.'

He leans over and kisses along her neck, his fangs scraping against her skin and sending spasms through her. He sucks at her earlobe as his hips move agonisingly slow against her.

'You really remember me?'

'How about I show you exactly what I remember?' His thigh shoves her legs apart and his hips drive against her. Nix gasps as his thick, hard length presses against her through his jeans. 'You feel that?' He rotates his hips, rubbing against her in tight circles, each rotation adding another layer to the delicious torture. 'Only you can do that to me. Your face. Your body. Your intoxicating smell. You, Phoenix. You drive me fucking crazy.'

His fists clench as his muscles quiver under the strain of holding back. 'I need you. I need to be inside you. I need to feel you again. I need to taste you again. Every time I see you, I want to tear your clothes off and bury myself deep inside you until you scream my name. Just you Nix. It's only ever been you. I'm in love with you.'

Nix smiles up at him. He's right. She may never fully forgive herself for sending Court out that day, but she didn't keep him locked away from everything he knew. She brought him back. That's the bit she needs to focus on. That's the bit that matters. 'Court?'

'Yeah?'

'I'd very much appreciate if you could stop messing around, tear my clothes off, and make me scream your name.'

Rhain slides into the backseat of the car and watches out the window as they pull away from the castle. The hulking form stands at the edge of a cliff on the south-west of Ireland. The intimidating stone fortress is isolated on a headland surrounded by open fields and not a lot else. It was as uninviting as a residence could be. It suited its owner to the ground.

'How did it go?'

Rhain nods at Geraint. 'Well. He accepted his gift.'

Rhain isn't sentimental or emotional. Never has been. But for some reason handing over that Blackjack isn't sitting particularly well with him. He had little choice. With the Order breathing down his neck he needed to align himself with someone who could give him the bodies he needed. The pompously self-titled Raven King was the perfect fit. He's a cruel, vile, and if stories are to be believed, downright psychotic vampire. Rhain has heard many a horror story about what he did to other vampires who betrayed him. A lot of those stories made the True Order look like saints.

'He'll keep him at another location to tame him a little before bringing him back here.'

'So it is the correct male?'

Rhain nods again. 'Yes. He's been looking for Davyn for years. Seems he got on the wrong side of him many years ago.' Rhain's father had done business with the Raven King over a century ago. Davyn had been mentioned by the King as a person of interest. He wasn't officially looking for him, but Rhain knew from his reputation alone, the vile male would not simply forgive and move on.

When Rhain's father died, he had thoroughly examined each and every document, notebook, and scrap of paper in his father's office. The King had put out a plea for information on Davyn to a small number of well-placed business contacts over a century ago – Rhain's father being one of those contacts.

When that human told him who had fed from her, the name of the fighter had immediately struck a chord with Rhain. He knew then what he had to do.

He discretely massages his side. The cut from the fighter's talon is taking time to heal. Shooting him with a tranq dart had been a coward's way to capture him, but he was out of options. He has little doubt the Blackjack would have killed him without much effort. The male probably didn't know he was still in the King's sights. It was just his bad luck to come across someone who was aware of the King's claim to him.

Rhain takes the drink offered by Geraint. He silently raises a glass to the Blackjack he just handed over. However long Davyn has left to live, Rhain has no doubts his last days will be as far from pleasant as they can be.

Nix smiles as she steps out of her bathroom. Court is sprawled out on her bed where he belongs. After three long painful years, she never thought she'd see him there again. And she loves it.

His pale eyes turn to her and glow when he sees her. 'You okay?

She climbs on the bed and he wraps his arms around her. 'Just tired. Feel like I've been run over by a few dozen busses. How's Thea?'

Court's chest rises and falls as he takes a deep breath. 'Not so good. Fletch checked her out. She's unhurt thankfully. It's everything else that's getting to her.' He runs his hand up her arm then pulls the sheet up their bodies to keep her warm. 'I don't understand how she keeps taking all this in stride. She was kidnapped and locked in a room. How is she not in bits?'

'She takes after her father.'

Court snorts. 'She's doing a hell of a lot better than me. I am worried about her though. She's blaming herself for Davyn.'

'I know how she feels. Hopefully the male we took from the facility will come round and we can question him.'

'Has Fletch examined him yet?'

Nix nods. 'According to Fletch, the odds of him surviving the next few days are slim to none let alone gaining consciousness and talking to us.'

'At least he won't die alone in that cell.'

'Yeah. That's something I guess. Ethan is going to see if he can find a match for him. He could have family looking for him. We could do with some good news. Speaking of family, how are you and Thea.'

He shrugs. 'Who the hell knows. She called me dad and it wasn't in a sarcastic way. Got to admit when she called me dad it felt incredible. I wanted her to accept me, but hearing that... I didn't realise it would sound so fucking good. I just wish I knew why I lied to her in the first place.'

Nix shuffles back from him and looks at his face. He's frowning intensely at the ceiling. She turns his head towards her and runs her fingers over his tight beard. 'We will figure out what happened to you.'

He smiles, but it doesn't reach his eyes. 'After where I've just been, I'm not so sure I want to know.' Court kisses her forehead, his breath warm on her skin. 'I'll happily open the box and let all the crap out if it means I get you.'

Nix pushes off his chest and looks up at him. 'You really love me?'

His lopsided grin instantly transforms his face. 'No. I love cheese on toast. I'm in love with you. Bit of a difference.'

Nix laughs. 'I'm glad I come above cheese on toast.'

'Only just,' he jokes. 'Seriously though. I meant what I said earlier about you. Not the toast. I need you in my life and as more than just my boss.'

'So you want to stay with the Blackjacks?'

'If I'm welcome.'

'Of course you are. This is your home. Yours and Thea's.'

'What about my memory? My blood. My damn eyes. I'm no closer to figuring out what they did to me. Are you sure I'm safe to be part of the team? Are the others sure they want me back?'

'Well, we took a vote earlier.'

His face drops at little at hearing that. 'You did? And? Should I pack my bags?'

'Unanimous yes.' She takes his hand and runs her thumb over his smooth skin. 'This isn't over. We're not going to stop looking for answers. I promise.'

'Even if we don't like the answers?'

'I know we won't like some of the answers. With everything we know so far, that's a given, but we'll deal with whatever those answers are.' She traces her fingers over the tattoo, following it across the wide expanse of his chest. 'I love you, Court.'

It wasn't a difficult thing to say to him so why the hell did it take her so long to tell him? She smiles as he grins at her, his canines on full display. 'Love me or in love with me.'

She kisses him, savouring his taste. Nix pulls away and runs her hand through his hair as she meets his glowing eyes. 'In love. I'm in love with you.'

'That's a relief. It could have been awkward otherwise.' He kisses her again then rolls out of bed and gets dressed.

'Where are you going?'

'I'm going to get us some food. After we eat, I'm tucking back in bed beside you and we are both going to sleep for a few hours. Think we deserve it. Tomorrow we start looking for Davyn.' As he gets to the door, he looks back at her. 'We'll find him, Nix.'

'I know.'

Court closes the door behind him, and Nix lies back on the pillow. How could she have been so wrong about him? Being with Court made her stronger. His support, his love is already having an effect on her. Davyn may be gone, but it's temporary. Court's right, they will find him. No matter where he is or who has him, his family will bring him home again.

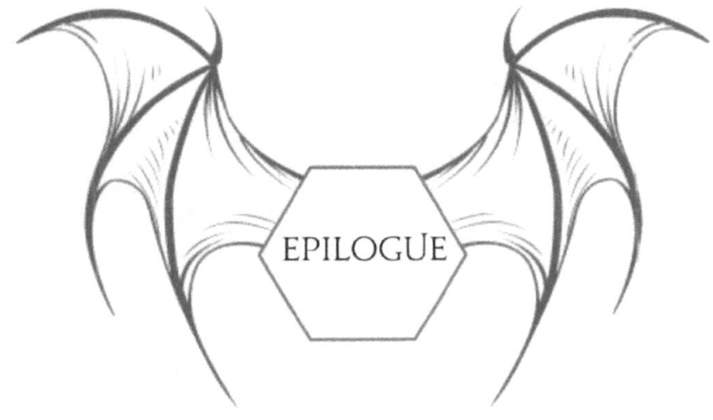

Davyn groans as the pain breaks through his drug induced sleep. His brain feels too big for his skull and every breath is agony. Definitely a broken rib or two. He tries to push himself off the cold floor, but his arms won't do what he wants them to.

With no choice, he stays where he is, willing his body to get with the fucking program so he can pick his ass off the ground and figure out what the hell is going on. He takes another breath and freezes. Why the hell can he smell salt water and seaweed? That doesn't make sense. The facility they breached was miles from the coast. There's no way even his Prime senses could pick that up.

Time to get up whether his body wants to or not. Davyn forces his eyes open and blinks as they adjust to the dim lighting. He's face down on a rough stone floor. The wall facing him is damp with green algae growing in long tendrils down the surface. Water slowly drips from the weed, pooling on the stone floor. That would explain why he's damn cold.

His jaw is fucking killing him, but he puts it down to being clocked by one of the other vampires. Or does until he swallows and realises he's got a thick metal bit in his mouth. The damn thing is digging into the corners of his mouth, tearing at his flesh.

His goddamn arms are still doing their own thing, so he uses his legs to lever himself onto his side, sucking in a painful breath as his broken ribs grate against each other. What he sees when he gets an eyeful of his arms sends his stomach on a free fall.

Both wrists are secured to a thick chain locked around his waist. He follows the line of chain trailing from his waist to his ankles, each one complete with another restraint attached to the floor. He kicks at the heavy ring embedded in the floor. The rusted metal isn't going to budge. Neither is the lock securing all the chains to the ring. He's not going anywhere.

He tests the restraints around his wrists and bites out as much of a curse as the gag will allow. Blood oozes from under the cuffs. Fuckers are lined with spikes.

Heavy leather straps are fastened around his bare chest, putting pressure on his broken ribs. He looks over his shoulder at the metal plate being held in place on his back. The contraption is fucking painful but effective. Whoever has him doesn't want him releasing his wings. How the hell the fucking things got back inside him he has no idea. Last thing he remembers they were out.

Davyn slowly manoeuvres himself onto his knees and looks around his new home. He frowns at the large gash in the thigh of his leathers. No wound underneath. He checks his bare chest and arms, but it's the same story. No injuries apart from his ribs. He knows those crazed fuckers tore him up while they were dragging him through the tunnels. He remembers them tearing at him. Remembers doing a bit of tearing himself, which only means one thing. He's been out of it for a few days. Long enough for his flesh wounds to heal.

His head spins and he crashes back to the floor, jarring his ribs. Damn bones will take days to heal unless he's fed. He needs blood.

His body is desperate to feed, the hunger is already clawing at his gut, digging its nails in. The little he took from Fallon will have worked out of his system long ago.

The cold creeps into his skin as he lies on the damp floor. He's alone in the cell. Can't hear or sense anyone nearby either. Maybe that means the rest of the Blackjacks got out. Maybe Thea got out. He closes his eyes but gives up trying to sense her after a few minutes. Her blood must have left his system.

Since he fed from her, he'd been able to feel her. Like she was with him. Like he wasn't alone anymore. Maybe if he hadn't thrown up after feeding from her he'd still be able to feel her. Once again his defective body had managed to fuck him over. He's a pathetic excuse for a vampire let alone a Prime.

He glares at the spike-lined shackles keeping his hands at his waist. He's got bigger problems than just feeling alone. As he stares at his restraints, he allows a quiet acceptance to sink in. No point trying to deny what he knew the second he got a whiff of sea air.

He has no fucking idea how, but he's back in Ireland. Back locked in a cell as a prisoner. After being free for a few decades he's landed back in a life he fought so damn hard to escape from. All the effort, the planning, the horrors he had to endure and commit while he waited for his chance to run. For what? For a few decades of a normal existence. A few decades of feeling worthwhile. A few decades of feeling safe for the first time in nearly two hundred miserable years of existence.

The bastard will make him pay for his betrayal. He'll make Davyn pay for deceiving him. For making a fool out of him. He knows that. No doubt he's already got something up his sleeve. Something to reinforce his authority. He'll want to make sure Davyn regrets stepping out of line. He didn't do himself any favours when he left, and this time he won't be escaping again.

This time the bastard will make sure Davyn dies in chains.

Thank you for reading *Breaking Phoenix*.

I hope you enjoyed meeting Nix and the rest of the Blackjacks. There's plenty more to come!

The sequel, *Reviving Davyn*, is coming in 2022.
Pre-order: https://books2read.com/davyn

Do you fancy staying updated with news about my books?

• Join my mailing list at: www.kafinn.com/

• Like me on Facebook: www.facebook.com/kafinnauthor

• Follow me on Instagram: www.instagram.com/kafinnauthor/

• Keep up to date with new releases:
https://books2read.com/ap/nE2Kdj/KA-Finn

Also, if you have a moment, I'd appreciate if you could review *Breaking Phoenix* at the store where you purchased it. The Blackjacks and I would love to know what you thought of the book.

Thanks for your support!

K.A. Finn

Coming soon...

K.A. FINN

Reviving Davyn

Blackjacks Book 2

2022

Davyn is damaged, broken physically and mentally after being raised in captivity. He joined the Blackjacks to seek revenge against those responsible, but isn't truly a part of them. He maintains distance while hiding his disfigured wing and his true heritage. His reputation as one of the deadliest is well-deserved.

When he once more finds himself back in chains, fighting for his life, he doesn't regret what led him there and accepts his fate. As long as she's safe, that's all that matters.

In the two months since he disappeared, the Blackjacks haven't given up hope, neither has Thea. Davyn sacrificed himself to save her and the guilt is consuming her. She thought she knew better and he paid the price for her arrogance.

When they finally bring him home, they can repair his body, but she might be the only one who can reach through the darkness of his mind and save him. Otherwise, he'll be lost to her forever.

Order now: **https://books2read.com/davyn**